LORDS OF

BADASSERY

REINHARDT SUAREZ

LORDS OF BADASSERY

First Printing, 2019

Interior design by Reinhardt Suarez

Cover design by Risa Rodil (www.risarodil.com)

ISBN 978-1-7337106-0-2

ISBN 978-1-7337106-1-9 (paperback)

ISBN 978-1-7337106-2-6 (ebook)

ISBN 978-1-7337106-3-3 (audiobook)

www.thereinhardtexperience.com

This is for all the unsung heroes, the couch commandoes, the MMO mavens, and the coin-op destructors with their spider rings and trinitial high scores. This is for all those who were told they weren't good enough, but were, weren't smart enough, but were, weren't tough enough, but were, and are, and will be until that final boss battle does them in.

Most of all, this is for you, the gamers who weave stories out of the pixels in your minds. May your days be filled with 1-Ups and your nights be filled with kill screens.

1

WORST. DAY. EVAR.

"This is gonna be great," said Saffron Raj, my best friend since the second grade.

Great wasn't the word I would have used. You call things "great" when they're actually great—catching a fly ball at your local sports stadium, finding a twenty dollar bill on the sidewalk, and watching *Manos: The Hands of Fate* with the *Mystery Science Theater 3000* treatment. No, a more appropriate term for this situation was *sucks low-hanging donkey gonads,* a proper descriptor for stuff like a candiru fish swimming up your penis, or being slowly eaten alive by cannibals, or watching *Manos: The Hands of Fate* without the *MST3K* crew along for the ride. Nothing I'd done up to that point could have been described as *great*.

Donkey gonads, on the other hand . . .

"Can we not do this?" I said.

"Don't be chicken shit. The fans have spoken."

Fans? Saff was talking about the 47 viewers tuning into *Culinary Distress Theater,* our weekly YouTube live stream featuring me—LeRoy Jupiter Jenkins, fat Asian nerd extraordinaire—sitting in my bedroom and eating the worst cuisine ever to come from the mind of man. This week's ritual offering to the toxic waste gods was a can of gourmet [*sic*] Thai frog meal, now with EXTRA! NATURAL! JUICES! The 47 "fans" (aka "sadists") in the chat were demanding that I commence with the festivities.

Laughin4Man: Dude, this is totally making my day.

FaztJak: I wouldn't do it. It's stupid to do it

HorizontalJustin: hes gonna do it

MaxMouse: hell yeah he'll do it

KackelDackel: He won't do it. In Germany, we call him Warmduscher.

PoltergeistRalph: You don't have to do it. Like, you're gonna do it. Just don't do it.

PoltergeistRalph was right. Despite what Saff and the rest of the chat were saying, I didn't have to do it. I had a say in the matter, right? *I'm not gonna do it,* I said to myself. Not this time. Not like last time with the canned haggis or that other time with the grass jelly. She asked me to eat pickled bull penis, and I said yes. She said, "Could you dress like Rikku for my *Final Fantasy X* review?" and on came the yellow bikini top and green mini-skirt.

No! The line must be drawn here!

"Do it for me, Jupes," said Saff, batting her eyelashes.

I was going to eat the frog, wasn't I?

OraCleXX: needs of the many, Jupes.

HorizontalJustin: I can't look

MaxMouse: your gonna miss this shit?

HorizontalJustin: I mean I can't look away

PoltergeistRalph: Be strong, hoss. Don't let the V take the lead.

Be strong. Sure, under normal circumstances, I suppose that was sound advice. But these circumstances weren't normal. It wasn't only the channel's view count that compelled me to curl my finger into the can's pull ring. When Saff was around, things like sound advice went out the window. Laws of nature ceased to be. And common sense? Yeah—fuck that. See, Saff wasn't just my best friend. She was the hottest girl in school, that one girl who came into freshman year a full-grown woman among children. She made the girls feel jealous and made the guys feel, well, the kinds of things you feel in your pants. But, she was also brilliant in that twisted, megalomaniacal, Dr. Doom kind of way—and she knew it.

So of course I was in love with her. Completely. Utterly. Madly. Wretchedly.

I opened the can. It hissed like Pandora's Box, letting out all sorts of chaotic evil amphibious spirits into the world. But was there also hope hiding inside? Oh fuck no—only a perfectly cylindrical mass of gray-brown meat product that spread rotten cat food stink throughout my bedroom. I pulled my shirt over my nose and groaned. Saff did one better. She ran out the door. A moment later, a text popped up on my phone.

MadAboutSaff

> Watching from the hallway. Still doing it, right? xoxo

I stared at myself on my computer monitor, helpless as I watched the spoon, connected to my hand, connected to my arm, connected to my obviously diseased brain, dig into the goopy ooze. I could do nothing to stop the jiggling mass of spiced frog from rising up to my mouth.

Next thing I knew, someone was screaming. That person turned out to be me.

"Jupes, that was so awesome!" said Saff, running back in. "What did it taste like?"

What do you think it tasted like? I wanted to say. But I couldn't breathe. Was I dying? I was dying! I was going to die on the floor a fat sweaty virgin, and my death throes would live forever online next to animated GIFs of sad house pets in human clothes. Why didn't I ever tell Saff how I really felt about her? We could have worked, right? I mean, when I was alive?

Interrupting my existential breakdown was Saff's insufferable ringtone (that month, it was T. Swift's "Shake It Off," a girl-power rumination on the inscrutable dualism of hatahs hatin' and playahs playin').

She answered: "Hello? Oh hi, Craig!"

Um, best friend on his deathbed here, Saff. Just sayin'.

"Tonight?" she said, getting suddenly concerned. "I forgot! Of course I'm not busy. I can meet you. Gimme an hour? Cool. See you, sweetie. Can't wait."

The breath of life shit-kicked into me, I propped myself up as far as I could go.

"Did you just make a date with someone?"

"You don't know him," she said, all innocent-like.

"Oh. Okay. 'Cause that makes it better."

I collapsed back onto the ground and stared straight upward. Saff spent a few more minutes trying on a few hollow apologies, but it didn't matter. If her looks gave her a *get-out-of-frog-smelling-shit-free* card with no expiration date, zero down, and a zero percent interest rate for forever, what use were explanations? Eventually, Saff tiptoed out the door, down the hallway, then the stairs, out the front, and back to her house, where she'd prep and primp for another guy—one of a string of other guys that weren't *this guy*.

The sweltering August heat turned the world into a sauna, helping eau de frog meal permeate every inch of my bedroom. I started contemplating stuff. Meaning-of-life stuff like: *What the fuck am I doing with all this? I'm supposed to be doing important things, things with real significance, things that would lead me from being a blob on the floor to actually being someone of measurable worth answering the great questions of the universe, such as ... Did Saff change her soap? Because she smelled more like oranges today than the other day when she smelled like strawberries.*

Fuck my life.

And that's the true way most tales begin—not with a bang, nor a whimper, but with a deflating *aw shit*. I know what you're thinking. You're thinking, *You got to hang out with the hottest girl in school doing hilarious things for the edification of a small but attentive public.*

It couldn't have been that bad.

Au contraire, my friend. Case in point: my name, LeRoy Jupiter Jenkins. It's a royal name. *LeRoy* means "king" in French, and *Jupiter* is literally king of the Roman pantheon. Not that bad, right? Until you realize that being a fat kid named after the biggest planet in the solar system isn't flattering, and is, in fact, the exact opposite.

Okay, you admit. *Perhaps I was too hasty. That is kinda sucky.* But wait! There's more! See, I'm a nerd. I like nerdy things like *Dungeons & Dragons*, maps with hex grids on them, stat sheets for my gnome barbarian sorcerer monk with a mechanical arm. A normal high school social life was out of the question. The best I could do was stay away from bully-types and shut the fuck up until the 3:00 bell. Rinse and repeat, and there you go—high school on easy street.

Except even that was an option I never had, thanks to a piddly little video on an upstart website called YouTube. We're talking notes taped to my back. We're talking freshmen giggling through the hallways after sophomores let them know that some kid named "LeRoy Jenkins" skulked the halls. We're talking members of my school's LARPing club questioning if I was cool enough to belong even though they'd let in that Chinese exchange student who thought it was simply a Mahjongg club with a weird dress code.

For those not in the know, the aforementioned video concerns *World of Warcraft*, a massive multiplayer online video game in which players controlled heroes of legend questing for fortune and glory in a war-torn fantasy realm called Azeroth. The players in this video had decided to pillage the riches kept in a location called "The Rookery," feared for its propensity to hand out total party kills (TPKs). All they had to do was carefully sidestep the ready-to-hatch dragon eggs waiting within, collect as much treasure as they could fit into their pockets, and sneak back out. Of course, this didn't happen. While the players went over their game plan, one of their number decided to break ranks and run into the main chamber, screaming his own name like a madman—*Leeeeeeeroooooooooy Jeeeeeenkiiiiins!* By the time his teammates realized what was going on, it was too late. Dragon whelps hatched, plumes of flame filled the room, and bilious megadeath ensued.

That video was one of the first huge viral hits to spiral out of YouTube and into normie-space in August of 2006. And worse, that name, *Leeroy Jenkins* (with an extra *e* tossed in), was forever etched in video game history as a synonym for epic failure. That's right. Before I could wipe my own ass, the Internet had forever doomed me to be nothing but a walking, talking, eating, crying punchline.

Except, in the wise words of Dr. Ian Malcolm, *life, uh, finds a way.* That's where this tale truly begins.

Before we get into it, I'd like to take the time for this handy PSA to set the record straight. There are no happily-ever-afters here, no extreme makeovers, no scenes in which I best the school hunk and impress the prom queen by winning a karate tournament. I start the story fat, and by the end, I am still fat. I start the story without the girl, and as the closing credits roll, it's not me riding off with her into the sunset.

Still, it wasn't all bad. Happenstance found me smack in the middle of my fifteen minutes of fame. It was a short fifteen minutes, the kind clickbait sites scarf down and shit out before moving onto the next nipple slip or insane head shaving. But during that time, in the right circles, nerdy peeps I'd never met forwarded to other nerdy peeps I'd never met links about me, my friends, and this crazy thing we'd done. One of them may even have been you.

If so, maybe you'd like to subscribe to our channel?

I stayed right at that spot for I don't know how long. I could have stayed there all night stewing in self-pity (and frog meal stench), but there was this thing called a job that I had to get to by 6:00 PM. I turned my head to look at the inert, lifeless brick of a phone next to me, hoping it would light up with a call from Saff to tell me she'd had an epiphany that we belonged together *in that way*.

And then the display lit up. I fumbled around until I swiped it open, hoping it was Saff texting to say that she'd made a horrible mistake and how could I ever forgive her for being such a shitty friend. But it wasn't Saff. In fact, it was pretty much the opposite.

PoltergeistRalph

I told you not to do it.

I know.

But you did it.

I know.

Why?

I don't know.

It's her, isn't it?

I wasn't sure what was sadder—that Polte
right, or that I'd been using a channel
PoltergeistRalph as a romantic relatio
non-existent romantic relationship.
been exchanging texts more an'

would start with an observation from her about how much of a pushover I'd been, followed by advice on how to reel in the ladies like "little baby fish" or "little baby seals" or some other kind of small-statured, larval-stage, water-dwelling vertebrate. I, for my part, did my usual spiel of inventing excuses for why I kept ignoring her words of wisdom.

And yes, Ralph was a *she*—real name Ryland.

> Not worth the pain, broham.

> She's no ordinary girl.

> And a McRib is no ordinary sandwich. Doesn't mean you eat the fucking thing.

> I'd eat it, though.

I added *love of fast food* to the mental dossier I'd been slowly building up for Ralph. Though she was generous with guidance, she wasn't very forthright about herself. Really, all I knew for sure was that her phone had a 307 area code (western Wyoming), the result of working at Yellowstone ational Park as a "conservation intern." I was also fairly e that she was a lesbian, but couldn't bring myself to ight ask. Not like it mattered—she was much more ledgeable than I was in all things girl, and I was ul for the insight.

> I am a fat, pathetic weakling.

> No man who eats frog is pathetic. Them's cajones.

> I'll try to remember that next time.

Next time, meaning *all the time*. Why couldn't relationships in real life be like the ones in video games? Take *Mass Effect*. All it took to land the space babe of your dreams was 1) giving her gifts of junk you found while blasting bad guys in the face because, apparently, she just loves space garbage that damn much, 2) being insistent on talking and flirting despite her repeated requests for you to leave her alone, and 3) agreeing with EVERYTHING she said, including fucked-up shit like "We really ought to be committing genocide. I mean, giant psychic cockroaches, am I right? Wanna screw?"

I could deal with this kind of love. It was simple, transactional: I do these things, and in exchange, I get to see some CG boobage, pocket extra XPs, and unlock a weapon upgrade that allows me to bend space-time for mega-damage.

> Just game, bro. That's your jam.

> I wish I was good at something real.

> Concentrate on the channel. That's what's important.

Yeah, the channel. Even that was Saff's doing. She was the one who first had an idea to create a YouTube channel for our particular brand of geekery. I wanted no part of it at first, preferring to stay anonymous online. But she insisted in that Saff way (with the eyes, with the hips) and got me on board. I mean, it did sound fun to do some Let's Play videos along with a few commentaries on video game news. She called the channel "Natural 11," which was both a play on *This is Spinal Tap* ("We play at 11") and *Dungeons & Dragons* (roll a natural 20 on a die for a critical hit). I tried to explain to her that the name didn't really make sense, but it's Saff. Once she got an idea, she homed in on that singular goal like a zombie at a Mensa convention.

Ralph was right. She was always right. That didn't change the fact that no amount of advice could change a shitty situation.

> I'm going to be alone forever.

> Don't lose hope. Girls will always be there. Like little baby ducks.

Just like that. Like it was so easy for her. Maybe it was easier for girls to date other girls. Maybe all the mysteries were non-issues, all the miscommunications crystal clear. Maybe her insides didn't turn to Jell-O when she saw someone she liked. Maybe, possibly, perhaps. I started typing out my reply, something about me being hopeless, when my phone started blaring the *Star Wars* imperial death march. Shit. That was the ringtone I'd given to my mother.

Cringing, I picked up and said, "Hello?"

"Lee! Lee, can you hear me? Are you at home?"

I could hear her but had to back the phone off my ear because of a roaring sound in the background.

"Where are you?"

"On the highway, in John's convertible." Grr. John Fucking Stalvern, Mom's boyfriend. "But that's not important right now. I need you to do something for me."

Let's get one thing straight. I love my mom. She's my mom, and any good person is going to love their mom as long as she's not a Nazi, a Lovecraftian Elder God, or Cersei Lannister from *Game of Thrones*. But I have to admit that she had certain ways at her disposal to get the things she wanted. Dark ways. Lawful evil ways. That being said, I wasn't exactly an impartial judge. After she and Dad divorced, I made sure to tell them that I loved them both, that I wasn't going to pick a side.

Except I kinda, sorta picked a side.

"What is it?" I said, maybe a bit too curtly.

"Is your father back from work?"

"I don't think so," I said.

"Good. I need you to go check the mail now."

"Now?" I said, leaning on my chair to stand up.

"Right now."

"What's going on? I don't understand."

"We're going into a tunnel. I'm going to lose—" The line went dead. I tried calling back but just got voicemail. Shit!

Whatever Mom was calling about, it was definitely more *donkey gonads* than *great*. There shouldn't have been any mail coming to Dad's at that point. She'd had all of her mail rerouted seven months before, ever since she permanently moved into John Fucking Stalvern's palatial Gold Coast condo. In fact, Mom and Dad didn't have much occasion to talk at all other than at custody hand-offs and awkward run-ins at Costco.

Maybe someone had sent Mom a gift using an old address? Yeah, that was probably it. Or maybe she accidentally sent something here? But what could she have possibly . . . oh.

Oh no. Oh no, oh no, oh no, oh no!

I rushed out my bedroom and thundered downstairs to the front door as fast as I could. All I had to do was step outside, *yoink* away the contents of the mailbox, and bury whatever I found there under ten tons of cement and a lead plate. That's all. Easy peasy. Unfortunately, as soon as I laid a hand on the front doorknob, I heard it. The whimpering, the sobbing, the sniffles.

Dad had already come home. He was sitting at the kitchen table, the day's mail delivery spread out in front of him.

My father was a creature of habit, a lover of routine. Thus, every day after he came home from his boring-ass job as an accounts receivable manager at Handibrush, where he balanced the books on crap-ass toothbrushes and mouthwashes containing questionable ingredients, he'd grab the mail from the mailbox outside, come in, prep a snack, and settle in for an episode of *MacGyver* on Netflix. His customary afternoon repast consisted of two chocolate-covered graham crackers with a glass of milk. On this day, he had abandoned his usual to indulge in a heinous combination I called "The Meal of Misery"—a stack of Oreo cookies with a huge honking glass of orange juice.

When I found him, he was in the middle of slinging back a giant gulp of juice straight from the carton, chasing it with two Double-Stufs. He looked up at me like a puppy sitting on a hand grenade, a freshly pulled pin dangling from his mouth.

"Hi Lee. Any thoughts on dinner?" he said, spraying juice-soaked chocolate cookie chunks in every direction. Down on the table amidst coupons for Lean Cuisine and automatic banana slicers from the *As Seen on TV* store was a glittery gold envelope.

"That's nothing," Dad said. Sure it was *nothing*, just like *Dune* was a charming morality play about the pros and cons of vermiculture. He tried to snatch the envelope away from me, but I was too fast.

For these last few months after the divorce, I'd noticed the new normal slowly settling into my dual existence. Dad, whose daily schedule had been wrecked after no longer picking up Mom from the train station and not being forced to attend the high-profile literary events she organized as literature professor down at UIC, had slowly developed a new set of routines. Most of them were unhealthy.

Mom, on the other hand, embarked on a steep life-upgrade path. Replacing board game nights with me and Dad were lavish soirées with the elite circles that her boyfriend, John Stalvern, cavorted with. So when I was staying at their place, they were mostly not home. When we did share meals, it was in a dark, overly air-conditioned dining room. In silence. Correction: she and I were silent while John engaged in endless soliloquies on how modern youth has "lost its way." When we watched movies, it was exclusively stuff from the Criterion Collection—depressing Swedish films about old, craggy-faced men having existential crises.

Only when Mom and I were alone did we talk like human beings. And even then, our conversations would always end up as lectures about exercise, good nutrition, and what extracurriculars would go best on college applications. Around a month ago, I found Mom working at her dining room table signing cards, inserting them into gold, glittery envelopes, and licking them shut. By the time she noticed me, I had seen all I needed to see, written out in her perfect, flowing script. It was that same writing on the envelope I held in my hand:

Save the Date for the Stalvenn & Martinez Wedding!

My stomach curdled with a mix of emotions and gourmet Thai frog meal. Wasn't it Einstein who said that the definition of insanity was repeating the same thing expecting a different result? Maybe I was insane when I believed that Mom would have a personal sit-down with Dad about her getting married to John. She promised me she would. Everything would be fine.

Nothing was fine. I crumpled up the card and threw it in the trash can. "Don't worry about dinner, Dad," I said. "I'll order a pizza."

Dad glanced at his watch. "What about work?"

"I can skip," I said.

"Being responsible is important."

"Being with you is important." I stacked the mail into a neat pile and slid the Oreos back into the plastic tray. "It's just a stupid job."

"It's not stupid," said Dad.

"Yes it is." I held back what I wanted to say, how I'd felt as betrayed as him and how the very thought of John Fucking Stalvern being my stepfather made me want to vomit. He'd just tell me that I was being uncharitable, that Mom was allowed to live her own life. Yeah, sure. And Dad was allowed to not take the beats like a punching bag.

"Please, Lee," he said without looking up at me. "I think I'd like some time alone."

I hated the idea of Dad sitting here by himself, stewing in the shambles of his family life—our family life. A good, proper son would have stayed with Dad and scarfed down cheap deep-dish while binging classic Tom Baker *Doctor Who*. I, being ever improperly offsprung, instead schlepped myself to work.

2

I GOT A BAD FEELING ABOUT THIS

It was 6:00 PM. The sky had darkened to a sickly green-gray, and a warm, steady drizzle had descended upon Chicagoland. The evening was young. The weather was shitty. The thoughts inside my head were even shittier—as in *how could I let this happen?* Sure, maybe Dad needed the quiet time to himself, but dammit, I failed him once in not telling him about the invitations in the first place, and then again when I didn't insist on sticking by him in his hour of existential (and gastrointestinal) need.

Ug. The *just-past-rush-hour-but-still-fucking-horrible* traffic around the intersection of Clark Street and Belmont Avenue was my karmic punishment. Back in the day, this slice of the Lakeview neighborhood was the go-to for gutter punks and goths, leather-clad badassess getting neck tattoos and piercings in places you couldn't see unless they really, really liked you. Kids would assemble at the Dunkin Donuts right at that corner—a site that once carried the nickname of "Punkin' Donuts" for people of Dad's generation, but which was now the site of yet another Super Target for neighborhood yuppies and their demon children.

No more post-concert throw downs between punk rock legends-in-training outside of Medusa's. No more rubber pakoras at the horrible Indian buffet Dad insisted was the best in town. But that didn't mean that all the rawness of the neighborhood had fallen victim to the doom engine of hipster suck. Just a little ways down Clark St. were some holdouts from the hood's halcyon days.

The Alley was still standing, hocking spiked collars and black lipstick on spinner racks to value-shopping teens blasting aggrotech through oversized headphones. A couple of storefronts down was Chicago Comics, the four-color mecca where Dad took me to find issues of his favorite 1970s superhero comic, *Brother Power the Geek*. And at the end of the block was my destination, a more recent establishment that somehow maintained the dingy vibe that the punks had long taken away with them.

This was Gamepokilips, a storefront whose windows were completely obscured by video game box art taped to the glass. Within its walls was a section for every gamer. Nintendo products sat on feature shelves along the main wall of the store. On smaller racks were stacks of Sega Genesis, TurboGrafx-16, and Atari games of all genres. Stuffed into any remaining spaces were accessories like plushies, hoodies, and a box of print magazines like *Nintendo Power*, *GamePro*, and *Electronic Gaming Monthly*, all long out of circulation. You're probably thinking, *Hey what a great place to work!* And sure, it could have been if my manager wasn't such a megadouche.

"Leeeerroooy Jeeenkiiiiinss!" called out Chuckie Dipple from behind the cash register. Chuckie was the manager and younger brother of the store's owner, Morris Dipple, who'd recently moved to California to direct pirate-themed porno movies. Unlike Morris, who was a straight-up guy, Chuckie was a rail-thin uptight fuckface who wore pink-colored skinny jeans rolled up in bicycle folds, a stupid straw fedora, and an array of ironic T-shirts ironically bought from super-ironic Old Navy. The dude didn't know anything about video games and didn't give a shit that he woefully underserved his customer base. All he cared about was lording his position over the nerdlings who innocently inquired about the copy of NES *Stadium Events* (priced at $15,000) in the counter case, and leering at gamer girls who made the mistake of thinking this was a reputable establishment.

"You're late," said Chuckie, leaning back against the glass cabinet where the real expensive shit was kept under lock and key.

"I had a hard time finding parking."

"I'll adjust the timesheet accordingly, mmm-kay?" he said with a sneer. "Anyway, we got a big shipment in. My guys brought in a couple storage lockers' worth of shit, and we need to get it on the shelves."

"Any good stuff?"

"How am I supposed to know? Bought it blind. You're supposed to tell me if there's anything good." God forbid Chuckie do anything besides being a prick.

I took my leave to the basement, my self-styled "Lair of

the Morlocks." Gamepokilips's downstairs was completely different than the world above. Gone were the colorful displays, replaced by a dank corner lit by a dim light bulb hanging from the ceiling. Welcome to my "office"—a single chair in front of a beast of an old CRT television. Spreading out like tentacles were the A/V wires connecting the TV to a slew of video game systems—everything from an old-school Atari VCS to a Playstation 4 and all the major players in between. Outside the radius of the light was my Sisyphean obstacle, two huge crates of games Chuckie had gotten that week. My job was to sift through them, make sure they worked, and mark them with stickers: blue for common, yellow for uncommon, green for rare, red for über-rare.

Usually, this was no sweat. I mean, I got to play video games for pay, albeit not very much because Chuckie paid by the game rather than by the hour. Even better, I often got to record footage for *Win at All Costs*, a show on our channel with me giving tips and tricks to beating "impossible to win" games like *Dragon's Lair* for the NES, *Target Earth* for Sega Genesis, and *Battletoads* for, well, any console those Ninja Turtle rip-offs could con their way onto. Sure, the show pulled a distant third in view count behind *Culinary Distress Theater* and Saff's fashion show, *The Starlet Letter*, but it was something that I could authentically call my own. That day, though, it was all work and no play. I lifted the lid off the first crate to find it filled to the brim with dusty old cartridges. I wouldn't have time to indulge my own interests if I wanted to make a dent in this pile. So, back to the grind.

Cart 1: *10-Yard Fight*, a crappy football game that shipped shortly after the NES was introduced to the U.S. Basically, this game is a Japanese version of an American sport with abysmal controls and hilarious interpretations of football rules. Cart worked. Blue sticker.

Cart 2: *Zillion,* a top-down exploration-based game on the Sega Master System (the NES's chief competitor). You play a secret agent rescuing fellow agents from a complex taken over by killer robots. Find your crew, locate floppy disks containing sensitive data, and blow the place straight to hell. Cart worked. Yellow sticker.

Cart 3: *Double Dragon,* the first and still best beat-em-up! Only, this particular cart was the Atari 7800 version rather than the more beloved ones on the NES and Master System. Gone was the colorful scenery, the spry enemies with advanced-for-the-day artificial intelligence. Instead, the 7800 version was a washed-out, slow-as-balls mess of blocky splotches dancing around each other until you died. Game sucked, cart worked. Green sticker, because even though it was terrible, it's hard to find complete in box.

My body settled into automatic pilot. An hour passed. Two. I became a testing, grading, pricing machine, allowing my mind to wander back to that afternoon. Saff, Mom, John Fucking Stalvern, and finally Dad sitting at the kitchen table a frothing mess.

This was all my fault. Deep down, I had to have known that Mom and John would pull that save-the-date bullshit. I should have told Dad the second I knew they were getting married. But I believed Mom—that was my undoing. Just like I was slitting my own ankles thinking that Saff would ever want to be with me. I mean, I get it—ladder theory and all that. My problem ultimately wasn't about her at all—it was me thinking that I ever had a chance.

And right there—right in those moments when you least expect—the universe flutter kicks you in the balls. I blindly reached my hand into the crate for the next game, pulled it out of the pile, and . . .

And . . .

As soon as the light glinted off the plastic case, I knew I had something out of the ordinary. Most game carts came in the same style, determined by the system. Sega Genesis games were small, black, and rectangular. NES games were almost uniformly gray and squarish with a tapered bottom. The cartridge in my hand obeyed none of the rules. It was deep red in color, and its top was shaped like a dragon, its wings unfurled and its head cocked back in mid-roar. Hmm. No label to help me out with a game name or company logo. I scoured the cart's surface for clues, only to find a single faded sticker on the back with a person's name and what looked to be a mailing address, which wasn't uncommon. Back in the day, you traded and lent your games to your friends because that was the only way to try new games. The label made sure that your game found its way back.

I tried the game on all the systems in front of me, only to find that it didn't fit into any of them. Very weird. I decided that I'd approach Chuckie with it since it was technically his problem to deal with. That was the right thing to do. I stuck the dragon cart in my back pocket while I did my final checks to the games I'd stickered up. Then I loaded today's haul up into my arms and carted them upstairs.

"Hey Chuckie," I said, putting the games onto the counter.

"LeRoy Jenkins! Just the person I wanted to talk to!" Chuckie looked in an especially good mood, which should have been my first tip that something was amiss. Two other dudes, each bearded and bow-tied, crowded around a phone. As soon as they saw me, they turned away and covered their mouths.

I ignored the weirdness and focused on the primary issue. "There's something I wanted to talk to you about."

"First, I wanna ask you something." He took the phone from his two flunkies, tapped a couple of times, and then turned it around to face me. At first, I didn't know what I was looking at. And then I did.

It was me. I was sitting on a chair in front of a camera, a dumbstruck look on my face and a can of gourmet [*sic*, again] Thai frog meal in my hand. My mouth moved, and my voice came out as words I remembered saying.

"Now, imagine my surprise when I found out that my own employee is a YouTube star."

Hardly. In the realm of YouTube stardom, our channel was double-Z list, not big enough to even be inside the barrel, let alone scrape its bottom. "I'm not a star—"

"C'mon. He's a star, right?" he said to his hipster compatriots. They kept laughing. Every muscle in my body went tense at once. The temperature in the store jumped to scalding. I actively fought the overwhelming urge to bolt and never come back.

Through gritted teeth, I started to say, "There's something I—"

"What we really want to know is, who is this?" He paused the video to a moment when Saff was briefly on camera. When I didn't answer, Chuckie tried again: "C'mon, LeRoy."

I turned to leave, but when I did, two more of his hipster minions came out of nowhere to cut me off. I tried to make the move past Chuckie's bearded crew, but they managed to stick in front of me no matter what angle I took.

"LeRoy, be a bro." There was a time in my life, maybe up until I started high school, I could have been swayed by that argument. Being a bro was more than just being one of the cool kids. It was more than being on the inside of jokes. It was a fast-track pass to being accepted. Being a bro—a brother—meant never having to say you were sorry for being so fucking repulsive, because *you're a bro*. It didn't matter how much a bro cut you down, because hey—you wouldn't want to suddenly find yourself without bros, would you?

I didn't need bros. I had Saff.

A big part of me wanted to tell Chuckie and his lackeys exactly how little I thought of them, to put together a string of four-letter words that would make the Angry Video Game Nerd blush. Because fuck Chuckie. Fuck him and his stupid posse of sycophantic shitheads. Fuck their fucking sucky-ass matching baby-blue Schwinns that they ride down to their shitty artificially ironic dive bars where they sit all day sipping craft beer and whining about how motherfucking tragic their lives are. Fuck them. Fuck all of them, fuck their moms, fuck their smug motherfucking ball sacks until they explode at the speed of light, all praise Super Mecha Death Christ.

I wanted to, but I didn't. Instead, I pushed my way out and didn't look back.

By the time I pulled up in front of my house, I'd screamed, cried, screamed again, reasoned with myself, debated going back, stopped myself from going back, screamed again, and then settled into a silent unease brought about by remembering what I'd—in my haste—carried out of the store.

I was a thief. No bones about it. I stole something that wasn't mine from my now-former employer. And you know what? I wasn't very sorry. I mean, if I was ever asked about it, of course I'd say I was sorry. But that would be a lie. Chuckie would hire some other poor sap to slap labels on games, and he'd never know what I'd done.

Breathe, LeRoy, I told myself. I could still dredge up some positive out of this shit situation. The dragon cart could at least be the focal point for one or two gaming history videos for the channel. Sure, they weren't the heavy hitters like *Culinary Distress Theater* or Saff's fashion vlog, *The Starlet Letter*. But maybe some of our viewers would find it interesting.

Lemons, meet lemonade! I even felt relieved as I walked up the path to the front door.

That didn't last very long.

A courtesy call. That's all I needed. A text, a postcard, a sign in the yard. Carrier pigeon? I didn't care as long as I had fair warning about the turd pile I was about to step into. Alas, too little, too late. The door swung open, and I found myself face to face with my mother.

Cue up the imperial death march.

"Lee!" She glided over and draped her willowy arms around me as best as she could. Dad was there sitting on Bernice, the tattered Barcalounger he refused to get rid of, no matter how much Mom had begged him to. His face was flushed of what color it held, and his hands shook as he dug his nails into the chair.

Mom herself was in full regalia—an emerald gown that hugged all her curves in the right places. She looked like a movie star on the red carpet—not exactly the normal garb of a bookish literature professor. Still, it wasn't *too* big of a stretch. At least once a day, she'd get stopped by a passerby on the street who'd mistaken her for this or that semi-exotic Hollywood maven. When I was younger, people seeing her on the street swore up and down that Sofia Vergara was shooting a film in town. Mom was that kind of hot.

"What are you doing here?" I asked her.

"Your father called," she said, glancing over at Dad.

"Hello, hello!" a voice called out, accompanied by clomping down the front staircase. Great. Not only had Mom come to ram a spike through Dad's heart, here was John Fucking Stalvern, the perfect topping for this freezer-burned shit pizza.

It's probably been bothering you for some time—that ping of recognition at the mention of John Fucking Stalvern. It might be that you recall John Fucking Stalvern from a far-off hell vortex that you had the misfortune of being stuck in. Or perhaps you're familiar with John Fucking Stalvern as the author of a mega-popular clusterfuck of a book series— the *Army of One* military espionage novels featuring lead-jawed Rambo-wannabe Carmine Stockton, wooer of personality-deficient femme fatales and vanquisher of countless stereotypes.

I mean, this is sparkling prose:

Carmine Stockton, a knife in his hand, gained the advantage over his adversary, fat with rice and drunk with excess sake. The dark-skinned Southeast Asian bandit from Manila could only let out a muffled "di di mau!" before Carmine ended his wretched existence.

I'm sure John didn't mean to offend—just like Hannibal Lecter didn't mean to eat all those nice people. After all, Mom was Filipino, and I was half Filipino. That meant that at some point, both of us could trace our lineage to the Philippines, location of the city of Manila, aka the rice-engorged, sake-swilling, bandit-filled capital of Southeast Asia. Oh, and apparently we also spoke Vietnamese straight out of *The Deer Hunter*.

"Good to see you!" His hands were clammy, still wet from the sink, but he gave me a vigorous handshake nonetheless. "Walter," he said to Dad, "your toilet could use replacing." Dad knew this, just like I'd known it. We'd both been ignoring the gurgles coming from the bathroom all week. Finding a qualified plumber-exorcist was a weekend job.

"Why are you guys dressed up?" I asked.

"We came straight from the awards ceremony." John picked up a gold trophy shaped like a hand holding a pen from the coffee table. "The Plumie for Lifetime Achievement!" he said, grinning. "I didn't even know that I was nominated! How's that for luck?"

That seemed to bust Dad into a new tier of breakdown, one in which he sunk into Bernice's cushions looking like he'd rather be anywhere in the world other than his own living room (including many of our nation's finest industrial waste sites).

"Walter," Mom began. "About the card. It was all a terrible mistake."

"Yes," said John, tag-teaming in. "I had my assistant stamp and send out the cards but forgot to tell her that you weren't supposed to get one." He waved around his award that sparkled in the light. "We had a whole plan to tell you guys!"

"We were going to take you to dinner," said Mom. "John knows the owner of this excellent sushi place."

"The best sashimi in town, Walter." Then he looked up at me. "We would have taken you too, Lee, even though you knew already."

And with that, Dad devolved into a tiny ball of primordial ooze. It's one thing to humiliate yourself on the Internet. I mean, it's done. Hundreds of people every day put up videos of themselves belly-flopping into swimming pools, falling off bicycles, and yes, eating nasty shit for a chance at viral stardom. Guilty as charged. But it was another thing to watch someone you love be completely *rekt* in real time. How much worse was it when your part in that rekkage is revealed?

That's like rolling a 1 on a 20-sided die when you're fighting the final boss of an RPG campaign. That's your controller breaking on that final stage of *Dark Souls*. That's accidentally hitting the self-destruct button on your starship while still in spacedock. It's the worst, man.

Calmly, Dad stood up and, without a single word, walked upstairs to the bathroom and shut the door.

"Dammit," said Mom. "It wasn't supposed to go like this." She sat down on Bernice and just kept shaking her head. "Please don't think we're heartless." Heartless? No. There were a lot of things that Mom loved. Books, for one. Book parties, for two. And being the smartest person in the room? That's the top ticket. She was an intellectual, someone who held a lot of esteem among her colleagues down at "the department," and don't you forget it. She loved being someone important.

Mom had a heart for a lot of things. It was just that Dad wasn't one of them. Maybe, once upon a time when the family sitch hadn't completely gone to plaid, Mom and Dad were in love. They were Gaby Martinez and Wally Jenkins, two kids who'd accidentally met each other at the senior prom after Mom's date ditched her to smoke doobies and Dad's friends abandoned him to go see The Strokes at the Double Door. Both alone, both desperate for that final rite of passage to mean something more than shitty punch and badly chosen slow dances—desperate enough to grab this last-ditch connection and make it count.

Which they did. Nine months later it *really* counted.

"It was an accident," said John, swooping down to give Mom a shoulder rub. "Walter understands, I'm sure."

Mom pushed him away. "He doesn't. I know him, John."

"We really should be home packing," John said.

"Packing?" I asked.

"Our trip to California," said Mom. "That's the other reason we wanted to stop by. We leave town tomorrow." Holy blindsides, this was news to me. Fridays were the traditional day on which I made the switch from Dad's place to Mom's or vice versa, as per the their divorce arrangement. Not that I was going to complain about not having to lug myself over to the dark cathedral that was John and Mom's condo. "We'll only be gone a week."

"I know it's last minute, but I'm sure it'll be fine for you to stay with your dad," John chimed in. "Wait till you find out why we're going! I know you're a *Star Wars* fan."

Hooookaaaay. After all the shit he'd pulled, John Fucking Stalvern dared to bring up my favorite media franchise? For what? Hadn't *Star Wars* fans been through enough? We've had to deal with Midi-chlorians, Jedi Rocks, and Vader's *NOOOOOOOOOOO!* And best not to get me started on the more recent entries into the franchise. What more did we have to endure?

John clapped his hands. "George Lucas wants to produce a movie about Carmine Stockton."

What.

"He thinks it has franchise potential."

The.

"He's meeting us at some sort of event in San Francisco. The Wrath Conference or something like that."

Fuck!!!!!!!!!

My jaw hung open. I was well aware of the "conference" John was talking about. It was a conference like I was Bruce Lee. He was talking about WrathOfCon, the newest and biggest rival to San Diego's ComiCon International. I would have given internal organs to go to the event that John Fucking Stalvern didn't even know the right name for.

That was it. As far as I was concerned, John Fucking Stalvern was the fifth horseman of the apocalypse—the one who didn't get a horse because he rode a golf cart full of baboons with a boom box blasting Vanilla Ice's greatest hits. I didn't care that Mom was going to marry him. Dude was asking for a nice thick layer of fresh Bantha fodder on his fucking face.

That's when we all heard the toilet flush, followed by a low moan and rattle that shook the entire house. Such sounds shouldn't exist in a world governed by a wise and benevolent god. But, since we'd firmly established that we did not live in such a world, I wasn't surprised to hear Dad desperately yelling, "Stop! Stop!"

"We should go, Gaby," said John.

And for once, I agreed with something he said. Mom gathered up her flowy skirt and made toward the door. "I'm sorry, Lee."

"Yeah. Me too."

"I signed you up for this new health newsletter—"

"I know."

"Okay. I love you."

Breathe, LeRoy, I told myself. Don't say something you really don't mean. I calmed down enough to mutter out the appropriate response. "I love you, too."

And, as always, John had to have the last word: "Tell your dad that I know a great guy who sells those self-cleaning toilets. He should call me."

As soon as Mom and John left, I was back at the bathroom door for damage control. It didn't take long for me to convince Dad to come out. There's nothing like a *tsewagenami* (ugh) to spur someone into action.

"Shit," was all he said before stepping out of the way. Oh my. The floor was covered with black, sludgy liquid that stank like the worst fart you ever smelled. Times twelve.

Dad and I sprang into action, scrubbing first with mops and bleach, and then with washcloths on our hands and knees. Better to keep busy than to discuss what had unfolded in the living room.

When we were done—and after long, vigorous showers to make sure no pieces of *anything* were lodged in unfortunate places—we retired back to the scene of the crime, the kitchen table, still dusted with Oreo crumbs.

Dad just sat with a glassy-eyed expression on his face.

"That was stupid," he said.

"The toilet could have exploded on anyone. Bad timing, that's all."

"I'm talking about calling your mom."

"It's my fault," I said. "I should have told you about the invitations as soon as I found out."

He smiled, shaking his head. "It's not anyone's fault. Of course she's going to marry him. Why not? He's rich, handsome, successful, and exciting."

My face started to grow hot again. "I hate him! I fucking hate him!" I pounded my fists onto the table, almost turning it over.

"Lee, let it go." Dad patted my hands, still shaking. "I have to get over it."

"Mom still loves you," I said, trying to fill the silence. "Otherwise, she wouldn't have come over."

"She loves *you*," he said. "She tolerates me. Maybe that was always the case." I didn't know what to say. I mean, sure, it was probably weird for other people seeing my dad and mom as a couple. Movies and TV reinforce the idea that only people of comparable hotness levels should ever be together, and woe to those outliers who stray from the norm. Love? What was that? You had an image to present, a culture to hold up. Think of the children.

"I'm heading to bed," he said, getting up and walking down the hall toward his bedroom—the room he used to share with Mom. "Good night, Lee."

"Dad, wait!" I called out. What was I doing? I didn't know. Dad turned and came back to the kitchen. He looked completely dry and hollow, like a papier-mâché version of himself.

"What is it?"

"I'm going to fix this," I blurted out.

"You should get some sleep, too," he said, turning back around.

I followed his advice. Only, once I was in bed, it was impossible for me to shut off my brain enough to fall sleep. Everything was going to shit. Job shit and Dad shit and plain old shit. That was like triple the shit. Shit cubed. The universe is a flat circle of shit. I lay awake until I couldn't take it anymore. Rolling off the bed, I stumbled over to my computer chair to fire up a session of *Team Fortress 2*. Nothing like working out stress by waiting for noobs to fall victim to my precision strike of jarate (a special weapon that's nothing more than a jar of piss) followed by a frying pan to the face.

After a couple of hours, my jitters had been burned away, replaced by a thick blanket of exhaustion. With a yawn, I moved to turn off my computer, only to spot the dragon cart beckoning me to pry into its secrets.

Pry. Hmm. I rifled through the junk drawer in my desk looking for the set of tiny screwdrivers I used to disassemble Saff's broken iPod to see if I could fix it. After inadvertently making sure it was broken for good (hint: pizza grease and circuit boards do not a merry mixture make), I'd sworn off tooling around in places where my big fatty hands could break things. The dragon cart proved tempting enough to override my better judgment.

First things first. I flipped the cart over and took out the four corner screws holding the back panel in place. Then I took the panel off, exposing the insides, which were decidedly less fantastical than the outer shell. Inside, like most games from the 1980s, was a green printed circuit board (PCB) with a bunch of black chips that looked like cockroaches soldered onto the surface. Using the tip of the screwdriver as a pointer, I slowly traced a trail across the PCB until I spotted a thin strip of gold-colored paint on the edge of the board. There were letters I could make out!

"A-C-H-I-L . . ." It was a name, a hero of legend I was supposed to learn about in European Lit class in sophomore year. *Supposed to* because I came down with the mumps and missed two weeks of class. Thankfully, there was *Troy*, the unintentionally hilarious fantasy epic starring Brad Pitt, to bring me up to speed. Achilles was the champion of the Greeks, son of Zeus, and terror of the Trojans.

But what did that make *Achilles Corp.* © *1983*? I did a quick Google search and pulled up a short list of hits, chief among them a stub article on Wikipedia that pegged Achilles as a kitchen appliance company located in Deadwood, South Dakota. According to this, it had gone out of business more than thirty years ago.

Next stop, YouTube, where I'd cut my teeth studying my betters in the gaming scene. For *Win at All Costs*, I didn't want to risk retreading the same old retrogame reviews that once dominated YouTube in the wake of the Angry Video Game Nerd, the great-grandpappy of all online gaming producers, as well as less well-known imitators like UrinatingTree, Armake21, and PlayItBogart that arose in his wake. Nowadays, you had a plethora of different takes on the old stuff from dudes like Norm the Gaming Historian, Metal Jesus Rocks, the Happy Console Gamer, Pat the NES Punk, and even those chodes The Game Chasers.

The one video producer I thought could have answers was PincheColada, a dude from Mexico who was scarily obsessed with collecting the most obscure video game consoles from around the world. He was a walking, talking—not to mention cursing—dervish of gaming knowledge. His house was a museum equally split between little-seen game equipment like the VM Labs Nuon, the Apple Pippin, and the Pioneer LaserActive on one side and a comprehensive collection of Luchador (Mexican wrestler) masks on the other side. I scrolled through his videos looking for any hits, and there—originally released in 2014—was a review of a console called the Mark II. I couldn't click on the thumbnail fast enough.

"Hola mis cabrónes!" greeted Pinche. "Today I have something you probably haven't seen before—the Achilles Mark II console." The long and the short of it, as explained by PincheColada, was that Achilles, indeed, was a kitchen appliance company that also dipped its toes into the 1980s video game-world, not unlike a few notable companies like Magnavox, Mattel, and Emerson. Unlike many of the others, the Mark II seemed to actually be a good system. It boasted advanced hardware specs for the day, along the lines of the ColecoVision, which is usually regarded as the most powerful console before the advent of the Nintendo Entertainment System. I watched in total bewilderment. How could something that cool get that forgotten in just a few years?

And then came the answer, or as Pinche explained, "Entonces, la mierda." There were only a handful of games released for the system, many hard to find, and the great majority of them unabashed clones of more popular games, like *Road Toad* (a rip off of *Frogger*) and *Meteors* (a rip off of *Asteroids*). He popped in those carts for a spin and, true to his word, they were basically *mierda*.

But what about the dragon game? I wondered, expecting him to cover it at some point in his review. But he never did. Huh. I did some more searching on his channel for follow-up reviews, and nothing. I scoured the rest of YouTube, and apart from a few other people mentioning the console, my search came up empty.

It was like this game didn't exist. Yet, there it was, right in front of me.

3

THE CROSSFIRE GAMBIT

"What are you doing?" That was a dumb thing to ask. The answer clearly was:

"Yoga," said Saff. "What's up?"

I was pretty sure she didn't want me to answer that question. Not that I could answer any question while Saff, dressed in a tight unitard, lay on the floor of her bedroom thrusting her hips into the air again and again and again. I know, I know. *Don't let the V take the lead*, but it was fucking leading—up and down and up and down and up and down.

"Your aura looks troubled," she said.

"My aura is fine," I said, trying to hide behind her desk chair to obscure the parts of me that were *so not fine*. I tried to think of world hunger, and the ozone layer, and anything else that could have been more earth-shatteringly vital than

Saff twirling into a sitting split. Could have been, but weren't actually.

"I'm glad *you're* fine," she said. "My date was ass. Greg spent the whole movie asking me about where this *relationship was going*. Get this—he was concerned about our 'plateau of feelings.' Where do guys get this bullshit?"

"I thought his name was Craig."

"Oh," she said. "Well, that explains some things."

"My night was *fun*. Mom and John told Dad that they're getting married."

"Why didn't you text me? You know I know that shit." On this she wasn't exaggerating. Her own parents had gone through quite the divorce when Saff was nine. One day her father, Nikhil, just up and left her mother and her to pursue his lifelong dream of being a Bollywood star back in India. According to IMDB.com, he'd found some success playing jobbers in Indian action flicks starring legends like Shah Rukh Khan and Akshay Kumar. His biggest role to date was in *Tiger Zinda Hai*, a romantic spy thriller starring Salman Khan, in which Nikhil played "Exploded Shopkeeper #5." Whenever Saff discovered a new entry in her Dad's filmography, she'd call me crying and demanding I bring her Target-brand Chips Ahoy-knock-off cookies ("the cheap shit, because it hurts more"). "Is your dad okay?"

"He's been better. Mom and John actually came over yesterday. It was bad."

"Shit, and you have to stay with them tonight?"

"At least that isn't happening," I said. "They're going out of town. And you don't want to know where."

Her nostrils flared. "Spill it."

"WrathOfCon, for a secret meeting about a Carmine Stockton movie. With George Lucas."

Saff's eyes lit up into burning red pinholes of hate. After all, I'd uttered the name of the man we thought would bring balance to the Force, not leave it in darkness.

"There goes my zen," she said. "Is this why you're here? To ruin my day?"

I pulled open my backpack and tossed the dragon cartridge onto the bed. Immediately intrigued, she picked it up and inspected it.

"What is it?"

"I don't know," I said.

"You know everything, Jupes."

"Not about this," I said. "It was made by some company called Achilles. I figured we could do a little more research, make a couple of videos. Some viewers—"

"Fans."

I glared at her. "Some *fans* might know more about it."

"Who's this?" she said, pointing to the faded sticker on the back.

"Probably a former owner," I told her. "It's not important."

"Not important? It's the most important! In fact, it's everything we need." Uh oh. I recognized that tone of voice. "If you don't know where this came from, that means that ninety-nine percent of people out there also don't know. But this guy does."

Nathan Squires
2312 Blaisdell Ave. South, Apt. 3C
Minneapolis, MN

"We should go and talk to him."

"We can't just knock on some stranger's door and shake a game cartridge in his face."

"Why not?" she said. "Besides, I already have a plan."

Oh no. In the annals of history, there are few sentences more terrifying than "I have a plan." Right before marching his army into the frozen depths of Siberia, Napoleon uttered it. When studio heads met with Nintendo executives about a prospective *Super Mario Brothers* movie in the late 1980s, the shithead in charge spoke aloud that most damning of statements. My point is that at the root of things that turn out poorly is one person with an idea and a bunch of other people who simply say, "Okay, cool."

Except the idea is never, ever *okay, cool.*

"You don't even know if this guy still lives there!" I said, trying to be reasonable.

"Good point. We can find out!"

She dove onto her laptop and started Googling search terms. I watched as her demeanor went from confident to shaky to frustrated in the course of five minutes. Saff was a pro at Internet sleuthing, always the first one pouncing on unsubstantiated celebrity rumors. She even inadvertently sparked a meme about Kanye West being an alien cyborg with a fusion reactor in his left eyeball, a fact that she denies to this day. In any case, it wasn't that she couldn't find information on Nathan Squires. It was that there was too much—about 1.89 million results. Including keywords like "Minneapolis" or "Achilles" or "Blaisdell" only reduced the hits to a still unmanageable 500,000 or so, which were filled to the brim with false positives—pages that contained all the words, but not in order and with the wrong context. We could devote years to blind-calling random phone numbers and using Google Street View to spy down on addresses with most likely nothing to show for it at the end.

"Told you," I told her.

"And I'm telling you, this is destiny. I feel it in my loins."

"We can't just do stuff because of your . . . loin feelings!"

She threw her hands up in the air. "Fine! Whatever! Let's be lame like Jupes! What's that? An epic road adventure? Long-lost treasure? An opportunity to document the whole thing and fucking own the entire Internet? We wouldn't want that! Let's stay home and be *mediocre!*"

"That's unfair," I said. But that didn't stop Saff's statement from ping-ponging inside my skull. *Let's be realistic,* I'd argue. *Let's be safe.* Not that my argument would have any play with Saff. We stood there staring each other down in silence until I couldn't take it. "Let's say, for shits and giggles, that we could actually find this guy. How would we get away with it?"

The second I saw the smile crack across her face, I knew I had lost this battle.

"My car is good to go," she began. "And you have cash from work for lunch, gas, and tolls. All we have to do is get past the 'rents, and we're home free."

"That's hardly a plan."

"It's, like, the best plan—simple and direct!"

"Except you're totally glossing over everything!"

So about Saff's plan. There were a couple of things that I had sense enough to be concerned about. First off, the transportation. Let's just say that calling Saff's car "good" in any way was being a bit too charitable. I mean, we did have a nickname for it—*Hell on Wheels*—partially because its suspension left no part of the road to the imagination and partially because the only thing that would play on the radio was a cassette stuck in the tape deck—"Rock You to Hell" by '80s heavy metal outfit Grim Reaper. Then there was the matter of the money to fund this excursion. I, like most teenagers, wasn't exactly flush with cash, especially after spending $200 on the latest and greatest screen capture tool—the BossBox, an A/V breakout box that allowed me to hook up any console, no matter how old, to my laptop for on-the-go streaming. I was sure that Chuckie would conveniently forget to send me my last paycheck, so that meant I had little more than loose change in my bank account. Finally (and most importantly), how the hell were we going to get our parents to agree to let us drive to another state, completely unsupervised?

"It's not going to happen!"

"C'mon!" she said, jumping around the room. "You can't give up this easily! We're a team! You and me together!" She took my hands and squeezed them hard. I wasn't sure if this was some kind of mind game or if she was being earnest. Whatever it was, it was working. The thought of us together—*together* together? Suddenly, *realistic* and *safe* weren't so great, and doing something dumb and exciting sounded much better than remaining *mediocre*.

I blame the loin feelings.

"Fine," I said cautiously. "Let's say I was willing to go. How do we get past the parents?"

"How about saying we were kidnapped by Bigfeet?"

"Bigfeet?"

"The plural of Bigfoot, Jupes. They're more intelligent than we think."

"Maybe something not involving mythological beings?"

"Okay, genius. How would you do it?"

Hmm. Huh. I thought about it. "Hypothetically, I'd try to play one parent against another. Like, I'd try to trick both parties into telling each other the situation while we—covered by both sides—sail on through. If my mom wasn't going out of town, we could tell her that Dad wanted me to stay with him while we could tell Dad and your mom that we were staying over with Mom and John."

"The Crossfire Gambit," she said, beaming ear to ear.

"Exactly." Saff and I shared common language almost entirely composed of YouTube memes, old TV shows we've binge-watched on Netflix, and semi-forgotten movies relegated to Saturday-morning matinees on basic cable. One of our favorites was *Cloak & Dagger*, in which a precocious ten-year-old named Davey flees Soviet superspies after discovering an Atari 5200 game cartridge containing top secret U.S. military secrets. In a pivotal scene, two gun-toting thugs chase Davy into a dead end, leaving him with only his tabletop RPG-honed wits to defend himself. Thus, the Crossfire Gambit. Basically, you hide, allowing one thug to pass you by. Before the other thug can do the same, you position yourself between your adversaries and let them know you're there. They, being stupid, let bullets (or spells or phaser fire) fly, killing each other while you stroll away no worse for the wear. "Of course, that wouldn't work in real life."

"Why not?" Once again, that glint of mischief in her eyes made my heart flutter and my stomach sink. "And your mom is even going to help us. Thoughts?"

"You do know that Mom hates you, right?" I said.

"She doesn't hate me, Jupes."

"She told me that she hates you."

"I'm sure that's not what she meant."

"She said, 'I hate that girl.'"

Saff frowned. "Whatever. C'mon!" She pulled me over to her computer, where she explained her idea. "Your mom is going to call your dad and leave a message that you and I will be staying at John's to do a school project."

"A project? It's the middle of the summer!"

"It doesn't matter," continued Saff. "School's like the magic word—they'll buy it. Anyway, he'll tell my mom about it, and she'll be quietly pissed, but still impressed that I'm taking my studies seriously. That'll give us the opening to do a run up to Minne, ask our questions, and get back before anyone knows."

"You're crazy," I said. Crazy like a fox. God, I wanted to kiss her. "Still, Mom would *never* agree to this."

"She doesn't have to. We have computers." That's when Saff explained her coup de gras masterstroke. I would call Mom and record her saying all these words in whatever order I could do that in. Then, I'd edit it all together into our message, call Dad's phone at a time when we knew he wouldn't pick up, and leave the message on his voice mail. To take care of caller ID, we'd dummy up Mom's number with a free phone app called VOIPSwagger, which, according to Saff, is "kinda like Skype, but for evil people."

Indeed, her whole plan was singularly evil in its pretense and wickedly effective in its execution. But holy shit, it could actually work. God help me—I said yes.

For the next few minutes, Saff and I wrote and rewrote what we wanted Mom to tell Dad. To say that the whole thing felt dirty would be an understatement. It felt low, underhanded, desperate. But Saff was insistent, and I was stuck on this roller coaster. We finally settled on this:

Hi Walter! Saffron is staying over tonight to work on a school project with Lee. Let Anjeli know, okay?

Short. Sweet. Jam-packed with so many lies.

By no means was I a pro at audio editing. But I'd done enough multimedia for our channel that I knew my way around the necessary software. Back in my room, I set up my studio mic and opened a fresh file for recording, naming it "everlasting_damnation.mp3."

Figuring that Mom and John took the redeye out west, by 10:30 AM, they'd have disembarked and been on their way to their accommodations. I held my cellphone in front of me with Mom's number queued up and my fingertip ready to tap *send*. I let my finger descend onto the glass and placed the speaker right next to the mic.

"Hi Lee," she said. "You're not normally up this early. Is everything okay?"

"Hi Mom!" My voice wavered, but I cleared my throat and continued. "Just calling to see how things are going. How was the flight?"

"The flight was good. I can't say the same for the food."

"Sounds good, sounds good!" Nervously, I glanced back down at the script. How was I going to dupe her into saying all this? "Uh, so, where are you staying?"

"I don't know," she said. "John's publisher took care of everything. I don't even know what hotel we're staying at."

"Any fun stuff for tonight?" Was I being too nosy? I mean, I was, but did she notice?

"Let me ask John," she said. There was a muffled sound, as if Mom had covered the phone mic. Then: "We're driving to Skyrunner Ranch. George is having us over for dinner."

"You're going to Skywalker Ranch? To his house?" *Keep it together.* Sure, that was easy to think. On the other hand there was this law of reality—every utterance of George Lucas's name annihilated something good and pure in the world. Like, a cute, innocent kitten in Ames, Iowa, just fucking exploded. "That's . . . cool," I continued, trying to change topics back to the task at hand. "So Saff and I are working on a school project."

"A project? Has school already started?"

"It's extra credit."

"I'm proud of you, Lee," she began. "Colleges like initiative. But Saffron? Are you sure she's the best partner?"

"It was her idea."

"Oh?" said Mom. "What exactly is her idea?"

Oh shit.

"Um . . . whales," I said.

"Whales?"

"Humpback whales," I began, mustering up as much bullshit as I could from my guts. "Like . . . what if whale song could be used to communicate across vast distances with, um, space probes?" Also applicable to the project: slingshots around the sun to travel through time, instant kidney pills, and nuclear wessels. "Saff's Mom showed us some articles."

My phone practically froze in my hand from the iciness in Mom's voice: "And how is Anjeli?"

"Good." A long pause followed. I felt the conversation slipping. But there were still words I needed her to say. So I had to push the big red button, the topic that shall not be named, but which I'd name because I was desperate.

"Dad's okay," I said, waiting for her to respond.

She sighed. "I know that must have been hard on you."

"Mom, you promised that you'd talk to him."

"Lee, we explained yesterday—"

"You did, but . . ." I started to say, feeling a gruff rumble emerge from the back of my throat. Flashes of Dad, his shoulders slumped, the slurry of orange juice and mashed-up cookies spraying out of his mouth. It made me mad that she was somehow responsible for that. I found myself suddenly unable to speak, because if I did, I'd say something we all would have regretted.

"I need to go," she said, her voice much weaker.

I glanced down at the page. I'd crossed off words that I needed as Mom said them. There was only one left that I needed her to say—probably the hardest of them all to get her to say out of context:

Hi Walter! ~~Saffron is staying over tonight to work on a school project with Lee. Let Anjeli know, okay?~~

"Mom, wait!"

"Yes, Lee?" She was super-distant now.

Just tell her to say Dad's name, I told myself. *She'll do it without thinking, and then you can hang up and go on your way. Nut up, compadre.* Only, I couldn't. Something felt really wrong about it, and I couldn't shake the notion.

"Tell John good luck," I said.

"Thank you," she said and hung up.

Goddamn, was I going to hell. Do not pass GO. Do not collect my thirty pieces of silver. Why was it that anything Saff thought up had to involve the infliction of pain on her best friend, and as a corollary, that best friend would always willingly step into the maw of the beast with hearts in his eyes, lust in his heart, and goings-on in his pants?

For better or worse, *Phase One: The Fellowship of the Ring(tone)* was complete. We had the payload primed and ready. All we had to do was wait for precisely the right time to deploy it (aka *Phase Three*). It was time to move onto *Phase Two: The Dastardly Dance of Death,* in which we aligned our parents to our cover story like a Voltron of deception. Saff had this one squared away. That night just so happened to be the one night a month that Anjeli attended the regular meeting of the Midwest UFO Society out in the western suburbs. And every month, she dragged Saff along to keep her company on the drive and to continue their lifelong philosophical debate on unidentified flying objects. Saff hated that drive, the meeting, and all the MUFOs that attended the meeting. And yes, they called themselves MUFOs.

Does Saff believe in aliens? you may be wondering. The answer to that was abso-frickin-lutely, but there was a fundamental difference between her and Anjeli. The MUFOs, Anjeli included, believed aliens to be benevolent beings of wisdom imparting upon humanity the great knowledge of the cosmos. Saff, on the other hand, was sure that aliens were marauding interstellar death engineers who wanted to eat us with some fava beans and a nice Chianti.

Our job that night was to convince Anjeli to take Dad to the MUFO meeting instead. Two birds, one stone. I mean, I had to hand it to her. Saff was a scarily efficient orchestrator. As for me, I still felt conflicted. On one hand, the mystery of the game was genuinely intriguing. On the other hand, the intimations about my negative karma weren't just funny ha-has. Lying to Mom was one thing. Ultimately, she had a big house, a big-time new hubby, and a shiny new life. She'd live. But Dad? He was a wreck. Lying to him was the existential equivalent of kicking an old tired dog in the nutsack while holding a T-bone steak just out of reach.

Fuck, that sounds messed up.

I was still debating my fast descent into depravity when Dad arrived home from work. I'd been sitting in the living room window waiting for him to saunter up the walkway, trudge up the front steps, fiddle with the lid to the mailbox, and then step up to the door to open it. I fired a message to Saff to tell her *Phase Two* was on:

MadAboutSaff

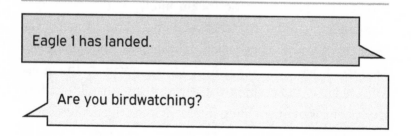

Eagle 1 has landed.

Are you birdwatching?

No. That was code.

So what does the code mean?

If I told you it would negate the need for a code!

So you are birdwatching.

Dad's here. You are literally no fun.

The key slid into the lock, its teeth clicking into the tumblers to unlatch the deadbolt. I sat up straight on the couch, picked up a magazine from the coffee table, and pretended to read it.

"Oh, hi Dad," I said with faux-nonchalance.

"Hi Lee," he droned. He headed straight to the kitchen to settle into a long night with the Meal of Misery as his BFF. No way. Not on my watch. I sat quietly as he walked in, opened the cupboards, then the fridge, and then popped his head back out. "Lee, did you see the—"

"I threw them away," I said. "You have to eat real food."

"Oreos are real. They exist in space and time and have mass. Therefore, real."

"You know what I mean," I said.

He came and sat next to me, an expression of little-kid shame on his face.

"You've been sitting here waiting for me."

"Just reading," I said. "Such an amazing story."

"I didn't know you read *Actuarial Quarterly*."

I looked down at the magazine. On the front was a dude in a suit, all smiles, holding up the XRS9000X, the newest graphic calculator on the market. *Calculate Your Way to Heaven!* read the tagline on the cover.

"I read it for the articles?"

"Lee," he began, rubbing his temples, "I know you're worried. There's no excuse for being so out of it lately."

"John Stalvern is a pretty big excuse," I said. "I'm to blame, too. I should have said something."

"No. None of this is your fault." Dad put his hand on my shoulder and shook it. That shoulder grab was the only trademark fatherly thing that Dad ever did, and I think I appreciated that about him. He always felt more like a friend than a Dad, something that I think irked Mom the wrong way.

And that's when it hit me. I couldn't do this thing. This whole Crossfire Gambit. It was wrong. It was mean. Some dude said, "The truth will set you free" (maybe it was even God), and those words never felt more appropriate. I needed to tell him everything. About the cart and the plan and everything. And just as I was about to do so, the front door opened.

"Hello!" Saff's voice rang out. "Well, what a surprise!"

Following her inside was Saff's mother, Anjeli, holding a tray of glasses filled with—oh my—freshly made mango lassis. She set it down on the coffee table and hugged me.

"LeRoy, how are you today?"

"Okay, I guess?" I was never good at answering that question, mostly because the default answer ("I'm fine") was never, ever true. It didn't matter to Anjeli, who hugged me like she was squeezing me for juice.

"You are so handsome," she said. Anjeli, like Saff, was a very loud person trapped in the body of a very small person. She must have just gotten home herself, as she was still wearing the garb of her people, the unmistakably gaudy vest of a Greenpeace organizer. Most days, she allocated teams of people to canvas neighborhoods spreading literature and soliciting donations for the environment. On that day, her skin was still hot and looked darker than normal. I'd guessed that she'd had to organize a protest downtown against this corrupt corporation or that. "We brought you some drinks."

"How's my favorite Dad?" said Saff, leaping up and taking Dad by the neck. For as much as she didn't like father figures, Saff had always had a liking for mine.

"What's all this for?" Dad asked.

Saff and Anjeli sat down at the far end of the couch.

"I know about Gaby," said Anjeli.

Dad looked at me, and then at Saff, and then down to his fingers, which were fiddling with his cuff buttons.

"It's okay," he said.

"No, it's not," said Saff. "So Mom and I have a plan."

"A plan?" I said.

"Yes," said Anjeli. "I'm going to a meeting tonight, and you should come. It'll be fun."

"Fun like an anal probe," Saff muttered in my ear.

"I appreciate what you're trying to do, but—"

"But nothing, Walter," said Anjeli. "When Nikhil left us, you and Gaby supported me and Saffron. Now I want to give that to you."

"I don't think—"

"Don't think," said Saff. "Mom's right."

Dad turned to me, then shook his head. "I can't. I have to drop Lee off at his mother's."

"Saffron said that she'd drop him off," said Anjeli. "They have to do some sort of school project anyway."

"Yeah. We should get to the library soon," said Saff. "To do all the studying. For the project."

Okay, time to nip this in the bud. Before Saff and Anjeli barged in, I'd already made up my mind to abort this mission. No time like right fucking now.

"Dad, about that . . ."

"Okay," Dad blurted out. "I think I'd like to go."

Everyone stared at him for a moment, surprised that it had been that easy to convince him.

"I should meet new people."

"Really?" I said.

"Yeah. I think I've been cooped up in here too long." To Anjeli: "What time is the meeting?"

"I leave in a half an hour," said Anjeli.

"I'll meet you outside, then."

And then, for the first time in seven months, Dad smiled. Really. That left me frozen, my mouth hanging open. This was the part when I was supposed to embrace the truth. Sure, it would have eradicated the only bit of happiness I'd seen him have in almost a year, but being honest was more important, right?

No. No it wasn't. If hanging out with Anjeli and some crazy alien worshippers would give Dad even a shred of feeling like a normal person again, I'd lie my fucking ass off till the end of time. So I shut the fuck up and let what happened happen. And it happened. Saff, Dad, and Anjeli engaged in a little more small talk while I sat and sucked my lassi in silence. Then Saff and her Mom took their leave, and Dad went upstairs to get ready.

The coast was clear once Dad and Anjeli pulled out of the driveway. It was go time.

4

SHOULD HAVE MAILED IT TO THE MARX BROTHERS

Saff and I did our parts to get on the road. Saff made sure her makeup was right to be seen in public. Me? I played pack mule, fetching Saff's luggage (she precisely specified her black rolling bag) and Tetrising our stuff into the back compartment of the van. Eventually, we made it onto the highway, and even had some good luck in narrowly avoiding the clutches of Friday afternoon rush-hour gridlock.

The only thing left was *Phase Three: The Call de Grâce*, in which we strategically placed a call to Dad's phone with our perfectly crafted fake message. Saff slated 7:00 PM sharp for such a call. The MUFOs meeting would have just begun, and Dad's phone would be on silent or off altogether.

"Why do you look like that?" asked Saff, out of the blue.

"Like what?"

"Like you have to take a shit, but you can't take a shit."

The dashboard clock ticked up to 6:45. "I don't get it."

"The human excretory system?"

"Seven months. Seven months of feeling sorry for himself, and suddenly he's happy?"

"You should just be glad for him."

"Maybe he's snapped. He'll climb the Hancock Building yelling that he's Spiderman."

"Or maybe he's made the turn. You know. Acceptance."

"Dad still hasn't accepted that Deckard's a replicant."

She gave me the side eye and frowned. "You were gonna squeal, weren't you?"

"I was not!"

"I can hear it in your voice! Remember when I stole Mr. Tarmin's toupee in seventh grade and ran it up the flagpole? I'm pretty sure you told the principal."

"I definitely didn't tell anyone."

"Who else knew about it, then?"

"How about the kid you stole the fishing pole from?"

"I didn't steal anything from Aaron Bliss," she said. "It was a trade! He let me use the fishing pole, and I let him touch my sports bra."

"You *what*?"

"I wasn't wearing it!"

"Well, it wasn't me. I swear."

She settled back into the driver's seat. "That doesn't change that you were gonna screw me over today."

"I don't like lying to Dad, okay?" Did my voice always jump two octaves when I was upset?

"You get used to it. Parents expect it."

"You didn't see how bad it was last night."

"No, but I did see how happy he was about going to that dumb meeting." She shook her head. "The Reptilian agenda is real, Jupes. Stupid MUFOs."

We cruised along the highway in *Hell on Wheels*, its unrelenting jank rattling us toward our destination—not that I'd ever call it names in her presence. That van was Saff's baby, a trophy to her iron will and craftiness. Bernard, a former fling and lead guitarist of local thrash metal band SpleenHammer, gave it to her in exchange for a second date (boys rarely got past the first). True to her word, Saff made nice with Bernard until the end of the night, when she dumped him and drove off in her sweet new ride. Insult its rusty rims, its ineffective muffler, or the decal on the side of a spleen being squashed at your peril.

Steve Grimmet's gravelly vocals eased us into 7:00 PM. Pulling out my laptop, I brought up the program I'd used to edit the message together, held the phone next to the speaker, and tapped the VOIPSwagger app. I punched in Dad's number, and on the fourth ring, it picked up: "This is Walter Jenkins's phone. You can leave a message if you like. But don't if you don't, because then I'd feel bad that my phone made you do something you didn't want to do. Then again, if it's really importa—BEEP!"

One mouse click, and Mom's voice was pouring out my computer speaker. I'd modulated the tones up and down so that it wouldn't sound so unnatural and added a staticky background to cover up the obvious splices. It still sounded less like Mom and more like a Cylon (one of the old silver robot versions), but it was probably fine over the phone.

There. It was done. Saff was happy, and I was guilty as sin. I sat back and closed my eyes. They felt like they needed to stay closed for a little bit.

Halfway to Minneapolis—around ten o'clock or so—Saff woke me up, and we did the switcheroo. I yanked back the driver's seat to squeeze my fat ass in, and Saff retired to the back. She zonked out within minutes, subjecting me to the scourge that was her snoring.

Yes, Saff snored. She denied it no matter how much I told her that she did. And I'm not merely talking about loud breathing here. It sounded more like someone strangling a cat. Every few minutes, I reached back and nudged her, which would cause her to roll and stop snoring for approximately seven and a half minutes.

Still, I would have given anything to wake up to that sound and think: *This is us. This is how it will be.* God, that's depressing. And when I got down, I retreated to the one source of comfort that never failed to satisfy. Spotting an exit with a gas station in the next two miles, I made the decision to stop to grab some snacks. At the station, I left Saff to slumber in the car while I went inside to inspect the goods. I was in my element, surrounded by extra-large bags of Cool Ranch Doritos and Mountain Dew Black Cherry Kickstart with extra caffeine. Fuck yeah. Then I figured that I should be nice and look for something for Saff to eat—not an easy feat. We didn't exactly share the same palette. She was more into "healthy" snacks, meaning food so heinous that even I couldn't stomach the notion of eating it. We're talking shit like kale chips, tempeh jerky, and kombucha tea that tasted like armpits. I settled on a prepackaged salad, water, and a banana for her.

I paid, and on my way out the door, my phone buzzed. I froze. A dozen scenarios played out in my head, all of them bad. Did Mom call Dad, or Mom call Anjeli, or John call Dad? I dared to check my phone, and *phew!* It was Ralph:

PoltergeistRalph

> What's up my homie? No stream tonight? Eugene's got me dusting shelves.

Eugene was Ralph's manager at the Yellowstone National Park Gift and Souvenir Shoppe. From what she was able to tell me, Eugene gave Chuckie competition for the shittiest manager ever award. That past July 4, Eugene decided that the store not only needed to be open, but had to be open extended hours. Never mind that its staff wasn't paid overtime—it wasn't paid at all. It was officially made up of "interns" compensated with room and board.

> Yeah. Sorry about that.

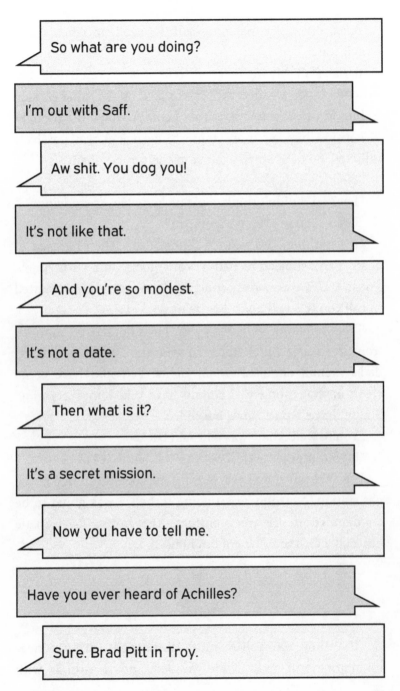

So what are you doing?

I'm out with Saff.

Aw shit. You dog you!

It's not like that.

And you're so modest.

It's not a date.

Then what is it?

It's a secret mission.

Now you have to tell me.

Have you ever heard of Achilles?

Sure. Brad Pitt in Troy.

Buzz, buzz. An incoming call. I seized up when I saw who it was.

It was Dad. My instinct was to let it go to voice mail, but my conscience pleaded with me to pick up. I'd done enough to him in the past two days that I couldn't take the thought of causing him anymore anguish, even if it was passively inflicted. So I answered against my better judgment.

"Hello?"

"Lee? Hi! I didn't think you'd pick up. How's studying?"

"Um . . . good? What's going on?"

"It's nothing," he said. "A dumb idea." Then he tried to change the subject: "I had a really good time with Anjeli. Those MUFOs are pretty cool people. Anyway, I just wanted to call you to say thanks. For being a good son."

Twist the knife, why don't you? I was not a good son—far from it. I was a duplicitous liar who took advantage of my dad's mental anguish. By all rights, I should have come clean in that moment. I should have told him everything. Should have, would have, but didn't.

"You're welcome?" was all I said back.

"If your mother asks about me, tell her that I'm okay."

We said our goodbyes, leaving me teetering outside the gas station. Not only was I going to hell, I was going to be condemned to the very bottom—the frozen layer made especially for the prince of lies himself.

By the time we rolled into Minneapolis, it was near midnight. Saff was wide awake and bristling with excitement. We followed the directions presented to us by Google Maps and eventually eased into a parking spot in front of an apartment complex.

"We're here," I said, looking at the building. I didn't see anyone around. No lights were on inside. "Looks like everyone's asleep."

"What are we waiting for?" She opened the door and hopped out.

"It's late, Saff. We can't just go up and ring the doorbell."

"You keep saying that."

"Saying what?"

"That you can't just do stuff."

She shook her head and closed the door. Dammit. I jumped out the driver's side and caught up to Saff, who was tapping on her phone in front of the door into the complex.

"Let's just leave a note," I said.

"Or let's get our answers now." The LED light on her phone turned on, and she held it up to my face. I shielded my eyes from the light. "Hello, my lovely fans. It's Saff here with Jupes, who's being chicken shit again. Say hi, Jupes."

"What are you doing?"

"Streaming."

"Live? We're gonna blow our cover!"

"Yeah, like the 'rents watch our shit." To the camera: "Remember I promised something special for our loyal fans? Well, get a load of this. Yesterday, Jupes found this mysterious game cartridge, and in pursuit of the truth, we've tracked down the former owner to here." She swung her phone to face the apartment complex, then back to her. "Gimme the cart, Jupes."

Begrudgingly, I handed over the game. Once Saff got it in

her head to do something, nothing short of a steamroller, thermonuclear bomb, or planetary collision could stop her. Best to let her do her thing and get out of there ASAP.

As she was bantering back and forth with the chat—mostly fielding questions on how her eyeliner was sooooo perfect—I traced my finger along the sides of the names next to the apartment buzzers. I first checked apartment 3C. Unsurprisingly, the name beside it was not Nathan Squires. In fact, Nathan Squires didn't live in any of the apartments. I looked back at Saff just in time to see another shape step up behind her.

"Who are you?" boomed out a voice, spooking Saff into my arms. It was a man, in his late fifties or so, with a scowl on his face and a long heavy flashlight in his hand. "Are you trying to break into my building?"

"We're looking for someone who lives here," said Saff. "Nathan Squires?"

The man stepped closer to us, casting the bottom of his face into the light, but leaving the top half masked in darkness. "Squires. I remember him. Who are you?"

"We're his, uh, niece and nephew," said Saff, elbowing me. "Right JohnRalphio?"

"Uh, yeah. That's right, Pixie-Murgatroyd."

"Your uncle should have given you his current address, then," said the man. "He hasn't lived here in five years."

"Do you have his address now?"

"Follow me to the office. I'll see if I can find it."

With trepidation, we followed the man into the building. Indeed, he seemed to be, if not the landlord, the super of the building making his nightly rounds. We waited outside a cluttered office while he rifled through his file cabinets.

"Here it is," said the man. Now, under the fluorescent overhead lights, he looked decidedly less threatening. He walked with a slight stoop, and the few rust-colored hairs on his head swayed and danced when he moved. He passed us the paper.

Nathan Squires
c/o Lowry Grove RV Park
2501 Lowry Ave. NE
Minneapolis, MN 55418

"Tell him Serge says hi," the man said as he ushered us out. "We talked sometimes. Nice man."

"What did he talk about?" I asked, hoping to squeeze a few more clues out of the man.

"The weather. That's what lonely people talk about."

We took our leave and were back on the road. I typed our destination into my phone and directed Saff where to go—an RV park north of downtown Minneapolis. Saff set up her phone on the dashboard to stream out our minute-to-minute progress on this crazy chase. It hadn't taken long for viewers to congregate in the chat:

RobbinsBaskin361: over under on them getting arrested tonight?

HorizontalJustin: $40 says Jupes ends tonight with no pants

FaztJak: $80 says Saff ends up with no shirt

PoltergeistRalph: I for one would take that bet and gladly lose it

"In your dreams," said Saff, flicking the camera off. I was

too preoccupied to enjoy the company of our online friends. There was too much going on, too much to keep track of, too much to worry about. This was all fun and games for Saff, but what if, for some strange reason, Dad or Anjeli did tune into the channel? I mean, it was a possibility.

It was like this all the way to the RV park. We pulled in and made the rounds up and down the rows of trailers. Eventually, I hopped out and walked along the side of the road, reading the names on the mailboxes while Saff crept *Hell on Wheels* forward. A few folks leered at us from their windows as we passed.

After half an hour, we found a mailbox marked with the *Squires* name. Saff parked in front of the trailer—a brushed-steel Airstream—and together we approached the front door.

"It's dark inside," I said. "Maybe we should wait."

"I disagree." She rapped on the door and stepped back. I listened for movement inside—footsteps, locks unlatching. Silence. Saff knocked again, harder and faster. And again, nothing.

"What now?" I asked.

Saff spun on her heel and made straight for the mailbox.

"What are you doing?"

"Nothing," which was funny, because she was absolutely doing *something*. She yanked out all the envelopes and flipped through them one by one.

"Stealing mail is a federal crime!" I yelled.

"No it's not," she said, tucking the whole pile under her arm. "Besides, this isn't stealing."

Right. In Saffland, we were just taking the mail into our possession without permission. No stealing around here!

"Jupes, all we're doing is taking this mail to its owner." She fished out what looked like a check from the pile and dangled it in front of my face. "Paycheck. And right there—" She pointed to an address printed at the top left of the page. "Place of business. We'll find our guy there."

"I'm terrified that you know how to do all this."

A wicked smirk appeared on her face. "You should be."

We parked across the street from the bright red neon sign of Mon Woo's Chow Mein Palace, where Mr. Squires worked. I called him "Mr. Squires" because while the name of the person we'd been hunting was *Nathan* Squires, the name on the paycheck was *Austin* Squires. Whatever. I was more interested in the prospect of actual food. A person could only eat so many preservatives.

So about Mon Woo's. The façade of the building was painted brick, and once we got close enough, it was apparent that the "windows" of the place were painted on as well. That meant that no matter what time of the day, the only sunlight that came into the restaurant was through the small window cut into the front door.

"This place is . . . *nice*?" I said once we were inside.

"Sure," said Saff. "And Lo Pan totally *doesn't* live in the basement with Raiden from *Mortal Kombat* and that dude who gets so mad he explodes."

She wasn't exaggerating. Mon Woo's had been ripped straight from the madcap ending to *Big Trouble in Little China*. This place wasn't so much a fine dining establishment as it was a thinly veiled fighting pit. Oh, there were "booths" and "tables" and "chairs" and "waitstaff." That didn't stop people from shouting threats across the dining room, nor did it prevent said ornery patrons from slinging handfuls of food at each other. In the far corner was a jukebox with a giant pink sign taped to it that read, "No Refunds. Play at Your Own Risk."

A waitress covered in tattoos sidled up to us.

"Uh, table for two?" I said.

"Straight up! Follow me." The waitress led us through a crowd of Chinese grandmas playing mahjongg for pennies sitting next to a group of terrified-looking frat dudes quietly sipping from goblets of red liquid. Any time one of the frat guys leaned too far into the mahjongg space, a grandma would slap him. Saw it happen twice in the span of one minute.

The waitress sat us in the corner, dropped two menus in front of us, and skipped away.

"How are we going to find this Squires dude?" I asked.

"Relax, Jupes," said Saff, opening the menu. "I can't imagine their bok choy is locally sourced."

"Relax? There's a man and a woman both dressed like sea otters staring at us across the aisle." Indeed, a pair of furries was out on a first date. "It's like a *furst* date! Get it?"

"Jesus, Jupes," she said, folding her menu back up. "You know that feeling when you're out on a date at Enrico's, and you look up and see like three other guys you've been on dates with, and they're staring at you like *why are you with that guy and not me?*"

"It's been a while," I said with an eyeroll. "Remind me."

"The game cart was obviously a call for help. I think this

guy purposefully sold it, hoping that someone would come looking for his story. He'll be looking for us."

"That makes no sense."

"I know shit, Jupes." Saff, ladies and gentlemen, single-handedly nullifying scientific inquiry.

"Fine. We'll try it your way. I have to pee."

I got up and took my place at the back of the line for the single, unisex bathroom.

"Hey," grunted the guy one spot ahead of me. I craned my neck up to look at him—and I'm not a small guy. He was stacked, with pythons to rival Hulk Hogan's and legs the width of Saff's entire body. His choice of dress was post-apocalyptic chic—a dusty black leather jacket with cut-off sleeves, spiked bracelets, and bright yellow boots made of what looked to be alligator skin. He smiled down at me with nicotine-stained teeth showing through his untamed beard.

The man stepped aside. "I'm in no hurry."

"Thanks." No eye contact, no unnecessary banter. In other words, my usual awkward M.O.

"The small courtesies," he said, slipping a cigar out from his back pocket. He lit it up, puffed once, and then breathed out a plume of smoke. "What's your name?"

"LeRoy," I said, throwing all my stranger-danger training from second grade out the window. "I don't think you're supposed to smoke in here."

"You can call me The Sheriff," he said, ignoring my comment (and the NO SMOKING sign). He sucked in on his cigar again, its end glowing red like the menacing eye of Sauron. He placed his hands on his hips and stretched his neck, which cracked with a loud snap. "You're not a regular here, are you?"

Nothing in Mon Woo's—including The Sheriff—could be described as *regular*. "I'm on a date," I said.

"Sure," he said, giving me a look-over. Could this get any weirder? He didn't know me at all! I have it on good authority—which consists of several reputable online surveys—that my personality is somewhat above average and would be compatible with individuals in the food service or housekeeping industries. "But what the hell would I know? I ain't one to judge. Enough about me—what do you do?"

Up until a day ago, I would have given my stock answer: *I work at a shitty game store and otherwise live out my pathetic existence.* Chuckie had made that null and void. But where there was pain, there was also opportunity. This moment was my chance to make a statement on my own future—not *what I do*, but *what I want to be*. Maybe all I needed was a single tiny white lie that would eventually turn into truth: "Producer. Web content."

"That sounds important," he said. "How old are you?"

"Twenty-three," I said, stroking my sad, sad chin pubes. "I run a YouTube channel called *Natural 11*."

"YouTube."

"We have lots of programming about nerd-type stuff."

"Nerd stuff."

"Yeah, like comics, movies, and video games." At that last item in the list, his eyes focused directly on me like twin jackhammers.

"Video games," he said. "Interesting. You heard of one called *Forever Throne*?"

"I don't think so," I said. There was something about this guy that made him seem suddenly dangerous. And then it hit me. It was the necklace he was wearing. It took me a couple of minutes to come to the fucking terrifying realization that the jangly bits on it were HUMAN TOES with the nails painted in an array of bright colors.

The bathroom door opened right then to save me. Quicker than I had ever moved before, I slid into the tiny single-serve lavatory.

He's just some weirdo in a restaurant full of weirdos, I told myself. *There's nothing to be afraid of.* I came back out the door hoping to just duck past him and return to the table. No such luck. The Sheriff stopped me with his beefy arm stretched to the wall.

"I don't gotta light a match, do I?" he said.

"You're good."

"Good." He lowered his arm. "See you around, LeRoy."

I tried to look casual until I rounded the corner. Then I broke into a sprint back over to where I'd left Saff. Unfortunately, nature had taken its course, and as soon as other male patrons noticed her by herself, they had come a-flocking. In related news, the world is round, the sun sets in the west, and oops, Princess Peach has just been kidnapped by King Koopa.

"Hey, baby," said one guy, a college-aged kid with a goatee and a backward Cincinnati Reds cap on his head. "Like, what's your name?"

"Gonorrhea," said Saff. "Sorry, did you ask for my *name*?"

"Oh," said the dude, making way for his fellow frat *bruh* to try his moves.

"New in town?" said second guy—he of the black shirt with a single button fastened. "This is my hood. I can show you around."

"Really? I'm so glad! 'Cause I need a pap smear right now. Like *really right now*."

Another one down. Another one up.

"A lady like you shouldn't be eating alone," said a suave guy in a tight muscle tee. Of all of them, he fit the Saff boy-toy mold the best, with his wavy blond hair and granite jaw. "Wanna join our table?"

"Oh my god, I thought you'd never ask! Can my spirit guide come along, too?" She leaned over to the empty chair across from her. "C'mon, Travis. Their souls will provide more than adequate sustenance for the ritual." She looked them all over. "Of course no one will miss them, silly!"

Man, that was like seeing a bunch of four-year-olds watch *Eraserhead*. You know it's so wrong, yet you can't help but derive a sadistic satisfaction from it. The *bruhs* shuffled away in defeat, never to be heard from again. Normally, I'd savor the sight, but there was no time to celebrate karmic justice—we needed to make progress. Stat.

"Any luck?" I said, taking my seat.

"No," she said. "This menu is like an invitation to the E. coli family Christmas."

"I mean have you figured out who we're supposed to talk to here?"

She shook her head. Fuck. I sat back and took in the surroundings. Mental gears bit into other gears and churned, processing the data into nothing but a bunch of dead ends. This was hopeless! There couldn't be anyone notable in a room full of notable people! We couldn't just sit here and wait for someone we've never met to come to us. We needed to be proactive, to think of a plan—one involving grappling hooks and ninja strike teams, and—

"Who are you, and what are you doing with that?" I looked up to see the busboy giving us the third degree. He pointed to the piece of paper Saff had laid out on the table—the paycheck she'd swiped from the mailbox back at the RV park.

No way. The guy we were looking for had to be a lot older. In fact, the dude standing in front of us didn't tick any of the boxes I'd expected. He was tall, black, and handsome—someone who looked more like a star athlete than a retrogamer. And even more strange, he didn't look much older than Saff or me. "Mr. Squires, I presume?" said Saff, giving me an *I-told-you-so* look.

The busboy lunged for his paycheck, but slid the paper from under his fingertips, stuffed it into her shirt, and glanced back up with her most obnoxious smile. "How about you sit?"

The busboy slung his dishtray onto the neighboring table and pulled up a chair. "You're gonna tell me exactly what you're doing with my shit. I demand—"

"You are in a position to demand nothing." Saff was enjoying this. "I, on the other hand, am in a position to grant your wildest dreams."

He turned to me. "Is this, like, a pimp thing?"

"What? No! I'm talking about this." Saff pulled out the cartridge from my backpack and placed it onto the table.

"What the hell?" said the busboy.

"You mean, you don't know what it is?" I interrupted.

"It's some shitty game that I sold to a pawn shop a couple months ago. That's what it is. Now give me my paycheck, or I'm calling the cops. I'm not fucking joking."

Saff looked at me again, this time with concern. Slowly,

she reached back into her shirt and pulled the check out. The busboy swiped it, this time with astonishing speed, and tucked it into his pocket.

"I suggest you get out of here while you can, because I'm calling the cops anyway. Stealing mail is a federal crime." The busboy left us, taking his dish tray, but not bothering to refill our water glasses. Just as well. It was time to leave.

Outside, Saff was suddenly not in the mood to talk. Once in the car, I expected her to put it into gear and get going back home. But she didn't. She just sat there, fuming.

"He knows something, Jupes. And we're gonna see exactly what."

5

OIL UP AND HIT THE GYM WITH ME

For two whole hours, we stayed put, listening to Grim Reaper's never-ending stream of songs with *Hell* in the title. Around 2:30 AM, Saff shook me awake.

"There he is."

The busboy was unchaining a bike from around a parking meter in front of the restaurant. We gave him a quarter of a block lead and then started in pursuit, following as he wound about the streets in the direction of the RV park. Saff stayed slow and steady on the accelerator, keeping him barely in sight. By the time we arrived back at the RV park, he was barely a single blinking tail light in the darkness. Whatever. We knew where he was going. But when we pulled up to his place, there was no sign of him.

"He couldn't have gotten past us!" said Saff.

She was right. He hadn't gotten past us. The passenger

door swung open, and a hand grabbed me and pulled me out and onto the ground.

"Who are you?" I rolled onto my back and saw the busboy hovering over me with his hands balled into fists. "Answer me!"

"Please!" I whimpered. "I told you! It's about the game!"

"And I told you that I don't know a fucking thing!"

"Hey!" Saff called out. "Can we just talk for a fucking minute here?"

"You're the one that stole my mail and showed up to my work. What do you want from me?"

"Achilles," I said, shielding my face from any incoming blows.

"What did you say?"

"Achilles Corporation," I said. "That's who made the game. Do you know anything?"

His scowl softened into a confused stare. Then he pulled me back up to my feet. We stood eye to eye, not something I was used to. I'm 6'2", which is tall for most high schoolers and really, really tall for an Asian dude.

"What do you know?" he said.

"So you have heard the name?" said Saff.

"I want you to leave. Now."

I stepped in front of him. "You know something."

"Go away!" he said, storming past me and back into his trailer.

Saff came over and brushed gravel dust off of my knees and elbows. The lights over in the trailer remained off—a loud and clear signal that we were not welcome.

"What do we do?" I asked Saff.

"I'm thinking."

Just then, the trailer door swung open.

"Fine! You wanna talk? Let's talk."

"My name's Austin," said our tentative host. Saff and I sat across from him at the trailer's tiny dinette table. People of my height and girth were kind of an afterthought in the minds of the Airstream engineering team. I squeezed in, hoping against any wayward sneezes that would blow the house down. "Nathan was my father. If you're looking for him, you're a couple of months late."

"He left?"

"He's dead," said Austin. "A neighbor found him right there, where you're sitting."

Saff went pale (pale for Saff, anyway).

"I'm sorry about your dad," I said.

"Don't be. I didn't know him very well. Just ask your questions."

"Fine," said Saff. "So where'd you get the game?"

"Here, along with a whole load of other crap," he replied. "This place was a wreck when I got here. I sold off everything I could as fast as possible." If Austin had been on constant clean-up duty, I couldn't imagine that place before he got there. Despite his efforts, it still looked like a hoarder had been given free rein to collect to his heart's content. Shoe boxes full of papers were precariously propped up floor to ceiling against the wall opposite us. Down by the rear of the trailer were piles of clothes, books, and various pieces of electronic equipment.

"So he lived here," Saff continued. "By himself?"

"That's what the cops said when they called me. I guess I was listed next of kin. I didn't have much going on where I was, so I came up here."

"Achilles," I said. "You recognize the name."

Austin paused before getting up, opening a cabinet above the sink, and pulling out what looked like a small wooden music box. In fact, that's what it was—a music box with a tumbler and pin mechanism that would play a tune when you opened the lid. Only, whatever switch caused the music to play was broken.

"I found this a week after I got here. I thought it was junk like all the rest of this shit—until I dropped it on the floor, and it split apart." Austin lifted the box by its sides, exposing its understructure. "This was inside." In a small compartment, there was a bundle of what looked like small metal chain links. Austin tipped the music box and the chain tumbled out onto the table. Turns out it was much more than a chain—it was a gold medallion studded with red, green, blue, and white stones. Etched on the back were these words:

First Place
Forever Throne Tournament
Achilles Corporation

"Holy shitballs," said Saff. "Is that real?"

"Seems real," said Austin. "But I have no idea what it is."

They may have been bewildered, but the dots were starting to connect for me. Not only did the medallion feature the name of the game company, it had something far more important (and far more frightening): *Forever*

Throne—the same game The Sheriff mentioned to me earlier that same night!

"Who else has seen this?" I asked.

"Are you crazy? I shouldn't have shown you."

"Jupes, what is it?" Dammit. I couldn't hide my concern from Saff.

"That name—*Forever Throne*. I heard it earlier tonight. Some strange guy mentioned it."

"At the restaurant?" asked Austin. He sat back in his seat, his jaw clenched. "What did he look like?"

"Scary—like Harry from *Harry and the Hendersons* if Harry *ate* the Hendersons."

"Did he have a beard and tattoos?"

"Yeah."

"I knew that guy was bad news," Austin said. "He started coming in a week ago, and he'd always sit in the corner booth for hours ordering drink after drink. Every time I passed by, I could feel him staring. I tried to ignore it."

"Maybe it was a good thing," I said, then turned my attention back to the medallion. "What do you know about this tournament?"

"A little bit." He motioned toward that leaning tower of shoeboxes. "My dad's papers are all in there. I haven't had a chance to really go through them, but I thought I saw something about a tournament in there."

Six hands were better than two. We divvied up the stack and got to work plowing through old bills, expired coupons, folded-up articles from newspapers, and most notably a bunch of yellow legal pads covered in messy cursive notes.

"Here!" Saff and I stumbled over the trash heap we'd created to see what Austin had found. It was a ratty old copy of *Electronic Fun with Computers & Games* magazine from November of 1983. Austin flipped it open to the ad in the centerfold.

At the top of the spread were the words *Forever Throne* etched into a gleaming broadsword. Below that was a full-color fantasy painting with a knight in blue armor bashing a ball and chain into a surprised-looking ogre. If that didn't get the juices of twelve-year-old boys pumping, the very bottom of the ad would have—photographs of three great treasures: a medallion on a chain, studded with gemstones, a jeweled cup made of gold and platinum, and a sword with a silver blade and jewel-encrusted hilt.

And below that:

> *The land of Rendon needs heroes! Work with a friend to unravel the riddles of Isak the Death Enchanter and his dungeon of horrors. Your prize? Revenge for your family and the thanks of the people of your kingdom! And best of all, the chance to win $150,000 worth of REAL LIFE treasure! Play all three Forever Throne games and enter the tournaments to become the ultimate video game hero!*

I was speechless. A few years later, in 1990, Nintendo would pull off its own tournament—the Nintendo World Championships. A video-game-laden caravan barnstormed through twenty-nine cities across America, letting hundreds of gamers compete for a chance to become the official NES world champion. There were ultimately three winners in three age categories, with Thor Ackerlund taking tops in the most competitive 12–17-year-old bracket. The prize? A $10,000 U.S. savings bond, a Geo Metro, a 40" rear-projection TV, and a gold-painted Mario trophy. Damn, son. That was quite the prize.

It was nothing compared to real treasure. Gold, jewels, and glory. So how the hell had this thing fallen into the memory hole? Well, maybe the same way a lot of other shit winds up there. There's always so much new shit to keep track of that the old stuff sort of fades away. Achilles and its games came and went long before anyone could talk about it online, unlike Nintendo, which populated hordes of dinky fan pages in the '90s and now has several thousand YouTubers hanging on every peep coming out of its Japan HQ.

Still, the *Forever Throne* tournament was too insane to have been forgotten so easily. How, then, was it? I studied every inch of that advert, trying to commit the whole image to memory. Down at the bottom was the name of the company itself, Achilles Corporation, next to its official logo of a black night standing with his tower shield up and ready.

I reached into my backpack and pulled out my laptop. "You got Wi-Fi here?"

Austin hooked me up with the login creds, and I commenced with what I did moderately better than a significant portion of the population—namely, look shit up online. I typed *Achilles + "Forever Throne"* into Google and waited for the results. I didn't even notice Saff and Austin head outside to give me some space. I was in the zone, tasted blood in the water, and I wouldn't stop until I'd cornered my prey.

The name of the game was the secret sauce. It led me straight to Barbarian-Bros.com, a website that made my eyes bleed. It had frames. It had spinning GIFs. It had an epic-sounding MIDI that looped without any way to stop it. It was the epitome of an Internet 1.0 site in form and function—and in content. See, back in the day, websites weren't these sleek commercial affairs. Most of the big sites in the mid-to-late 90s were fan sites. These passion projects often celebrated obscure movies, TV shows, and the actors who brought them to life. This one was a shrine to a pair of late-1980s action movie hunks—twin brother bodybuilders named David and Peter Paul, stars of, well, nothing very good. But who could ever resist all the grunting, all the gags involving meat products, all the twin switcheroo shenanigans?

Anyway, the central feature to sites like these were the message boards, where diehards could find other people out there who shared their obsessions. A lot of sites like these were scrapped after hosting services like GeoCities and Tripod were shut down. Luckily some were mirrored onto random active servers to exist as windows into the not-so-distant past.

And here, served to me on a platter by Google, were the messages that filled in the gaps:

Post by: Dave (Kuchuk&Gore)
Date: 9/7/2000
Location: Atlanta
Subject: Need some help IDing a game

Found a weird cart in my uncle's attic. It's a red-colored cartridge. It looked like it could fit in an Intellivision slot. But when I tried it, it didn't. Any clue on what this is?

Post by: Shane (KadarIsMyWitness)
Date: 9/9/2000
Location: Jersey City
Subject: RE: Need some help IDing a game

Have you tried opening it up?

Post by: Dave (Kuchuk&Gore)
Date: 9/10/2000
Location: Atlanta
Subject: RE: Need some help IDing a game

I took your suggestion and unscrewed the back. There wasn't much to go on. I did find a company name. Achilles. Ring any bells?

Post by: DeShawn (Hey_Ibar126)
Date: 9/10/2000
Location: Salt Lake City
Subject: RE: Need some help IDing a game

My dad used to work for a company called Achilles back in the 1970s. He made microwaves. They're located in South Dakota, I think. Maybe you could give them a call?

Post by: Dave (Kuchuk&Gore)
Date: 9/10/2000
Location: Atlanta
Subject: RE: Need some help IDing a game

Thanks! I will.

Post by: Bryan (RubyDawn775)
Date: 12/23/2008
Location: The Nexus of Sominus
Subject: RE: Need some help IDing a game

I know this thread is 8 years old, but I just came across it today. I'm the programmer of that game. It's called Forever Throne. If you're still around, I'd be happy to answer any of your questions. You can send me a PM.

I clicked on RubyDawn775's username, but the link gave me a 404 error. I tried using the Internet Wayback Machine to access an archived version, but the page was way too obscure, way too old for the Wayback Machine to have captured it.

Dammit. Nothing about any tournaments. Nothing about the prizes. But I knew that info was somewhere out in the digital ether. I searched for another hour, but I only managed to find a few more choice scraps before a wave of tiredness made me want to rest my head on the table. *Okay,* I thought. *A short rest, and then I'll pick back up again.*

Just a few minutes. That's all I needed.

The accumulated hours of driving and stress were a sweet, sweet lullaby that quickly beckoned sleep. I began to dream.

It was pitch black, a low, droning foghorn faintly audible from all directions. Then, color slowly crept into view— bright oranges, blues, magentas—and I found myself standing inside Gamepokilips in front of a magazine rack full of brand-spanking-new issues of *Electronic Gaming Monthly*, *GamePro*, *Nintendo Power*, *Tips and Tricks*, *Video Games and Computer Entertainment*, and others.

Huh? I thought. *Did all these magazines decide to start back up again?* My confusion turned to horror when I started reading article headlines on the covers:

LeRoy Jenkins is a Failure

Jenkins Deceives Loved Ones, Spreads Pain

Area Man Eats Frog, Children Cry

Saffron Raj Ditches Dead Weight, Attains Superstardom

And the Award for Best Picture Goes to . . . John Stalvern!

The grinning faces of once-upon-a-time video game friends like Mario, Sonic, and Crash Bandicoot took on a threatening pallor, and I heard a familiar cackling from the end of the aisle. Looking up, I saw Chuckie standing with his mutton-chopped goons.

"LeRoy, you are just stupid as hell!"

That was all I could take. I turned tail and ran the other way down the aisle, intending to bust out onto Belmont Avenue and find someone, anyone, who could help me. But no matter what I did, I couldn't find the way out. The aisle just kept going, going, going. I ran until I had to stop and catch my breath. Leaning over with my hands on my knees, I saw a pair of battered, worn-out loafers enter my peripheral vision.

"Hi, Lee," said Dad, smiling for the first time in what seemed like forever. "I've figured everything out—the secret to happiness!"

"What is it?"

"I don't need a son around who betrays me."

"I didn't—"

"Of course you didn't. You never do anything."

I turned and ran, but the Gamepokilips aisle stretched into infinity. No matter how far I ran, Dad and Chuckie were mere steps behind. Knowing that I couldn't outrun them, I tried a more unorthodox tactic—I closed my eyes and launched myself right into one of the game shelves, expecting the impact of the shelf on my shoulder. Instead, I rammed nothing but air and stumbled onto the hard, cold ground. A low fog settled in while I lay there, and for a second, I thought I was safe.

Until I wasn't. The vague background drone suddenly exploded into a brutal rumble, like a buzzsaw on the inside of my skull. I stood up to see that I'd been transported onto a stretch of highway with an inky black void on either side. Instinctively, I started to run away from that sound, glancing over my shoulder to catch a glimpse of my pursuer. I was blinded by a single high beam beating down on me. It was him, The Sheriff, riding upon a hellish motorcycle made of bone and fire. I pushed myself harder, willed myself to run faster.

For this was no man on my heels. He was a harbinger of doom cloaked in black and smelling of tar and leather and death. This wolf, this animal, this force of nature. The tires of his motorcycle bit into the asphalt, gaining on me no matter how hard I ran. His shadow grew bigger and darker over me. The heat from the bike warmed my legs, my back.

It was over. No hope. Only blissful, blissful oblivion.

My eyes shot open. Damn, that was one hell of a dream. Only, the rumbling of motorcycles had somehow accompanied me into the waking world. I sat up to find myself still seated at the dinette table. Out the window, I watched a fleet of motorcycles zoom by the trailer.

Which was moving. On the highway. Really fast.

My first thought was that I was caught between the dream and reality. I uncrusted my eyes, hoping that the scene would return to what it should have been—the trailer park in Minneapolis. But it didn't. Instead, I had to confront the horrible notion that everything was epically wrong.

Holy shit. The motorcycles outside the window were real.

Holy shit. Those were fucking mountains outside.

I'd lived in the Midwest all my life. It was the flattest place on Earth. So topographical features of any kind meant that we were far, far, far away from home. Fuck my life! And Saff—where was she? Shit! I looked around for her, but she wasn't anywhere. Shit, shit, shit! Dammit, I knew we couldn't trust Austin! *If he did anything to her . . .*

MadAboutSaff

Where are you?

> Please tell me you're okay.

> If anyone hurt you, I'm gonna freak.

No answer. My heart was doing triple time. Austin must have tricked Saff into getting control of *Hell on Wheels*, maybe even threatened her or something even worse! With me zonked out, who the hell knows? What was I going to tell Anjeli? How could I live with myself knowing that I'd gotten the girl that I love hurt?

C'mon, LeRoy, think! What would Nathan Drake or Solid Snake do in this situation? Nah, those guys were infinitely more capable than I was. What would Guybrush Threepwood from the *Monkey Island* games do? His level of (in)competence was close to mine.

"Probably wait for Elaine to save him." Wait a minute. That's exactly what I needed to do—get a girl to save me! Please, please be awake:

PoltergeistRalph

> Help! Saff and I are in trouble!

> Whoa, dude. What's going on?

Some guy kidnapped us.

Does this have anything to do with the update video?

You mean the stream from last night?

The one Saff is on this morning. The one about hunting for treasure.

Also, you're in S. Dakota? You're just a state away! Come to my crib!

A slow howl of pain escaped from my mouth. *This is not happening! This is NOT happening!* I switched the phone to GPS to get a read on where we were.

"Sturgis, South Dakota?" I screamed. Swiping the map away, I opened the YouTube app and went straight to our channel. Yup. Posted fresh and frosty that morning was a video only thirty-six seconds long. I could feel my stomach churn and gurgle as I tapped PLAY. The video started as a dash cam focused on Saff in the passenger seat. You couldn't see who was driving, but I didn't have to. It was fucking Austin.

"Hi, my adoring, wonderful fans! For those of you who missed the stream yesterday, fear not! The one today is gonna be amazeballs. Right now, we're in South Dakota! If you want to be in on this action—" Naturally, Saff pointed the camera at her cleavage. "—then you'll like, subscribe, and follow this channel. Or are you lame? Don't be lame."

She blew a kiss to the camera and the video ended.

I texted furiously to Saff demanding to know what the hell was happening. Still no answer. Shit! I threw the phone across the trailer and slumped across the dinette table in defeat. In retrospect, I shouldn't have been so surprised at the turn of events, because what did Saff say? *An epic road adventure, long-lost treasure, an opportunity to document the whole thing and fucking own the entire Internet.* She'd Crossfire Gambited me! She had no intention of just toe-dipping and then going back home.

I heard the buzz of a new text message from my phone, which was in the pile of boxes and papers on the floor. Somewhere. I got down on my hands and knees, rustling about for it. I imagined all the things I wanted to say to Saff, and I couldn't separate the positive from the negative. I hated how she'd unilaterally fucked our whole plan. But at the same time, that flair and spontaneity was exactly what I loved about her. Now where was my phone? There? Or maybe there?

Something caught my eye. Peeking out from underneath a pile of old game magazines was a slip of paper with the black-knight sigil of Achilles Corp at the top. I pulled out a time-yellowed piece of stationary with a handwritten note:

Nate,

I'm sad to tell you that Achilles is going out of business. But I didn't think it was right that our champion not get a chance to play the next game. So here it is. Don't tell anyone. They might fire me if they found out.

Bryan

Holy shit. What did this even mean? I didn't know for sure, but it sure felt important enough to keep around. I folded the note, stuck it in my back pocket, and continued the search for my phone. When I finally found it, there was a new text message.

MadAboutSaff

Sup.

Sup? SUP? The last shreds of concern melted away, leaving only a radioactive nugget of densely compacted hate. I had just been double-butt-fucked over by my best friend.

What the hell is going on?

I'm up with Austin.

I KNOW THAT. WHAT IS HAPPENING?

Saff stuck her hand out the passenger side of *Hell on Wheels* and waved. Rage! I screamed as loud as I could, not that anyone could hear me.

> Austin said not to use the bathroom. We'll be there soon. So hold it.

We'll be *where* soon? I texted her more messages furiously in all caps with no punctuation and with angry emojis. But none of it mattered, because I knew exactly what our destination was.

Deadwood, home of Achilles Corporation. God fucking help us.

6

FORTUNE AND GLORY, KID

Hell on Wheels—and the trailer it dragged—eventually pulled into the parking lot of the Starlite Diner and Truckstop on the outskirts of Deadwood, South Dakota. I didn't know why we'd stopped there specifically, and I really didn't care. We were six hundred miles farther from home than we should have been, effectively killing our cover story. Not that Saff cared. She'd been broadcasting our real locations on YouTube all morning, giving our parents license to ground us forever.

FOR. EH. VER. FOR. EH. VER.

As soon as the van stopped moving, I busted out the trailer door, ready to take down anyone in my way. Well, anyone but the one person actually in my way.

"Jupes!" she said, checking her complexion in *Hell on Wheels*' side-view mirror. She whimpered at the sight of a pimple next to her nose. "There probably isn't a Sephora within a hundred miles of here," she sighed.

"I can't fucking believe you!"

"It was for your own good," she said, still preoccupied with her pimple.

"Hitler said the same thing!"

"Godwin's Law, Jupes. Your argument is invalid."

I heard a sound from behind me and whipped around to see Austin dragging along Saff's luggage. My face twisted into a scowl, and my mind filled with so many four-letter words that the only thing I could actually say was:

"You . . ."

"Let's talk," Austin began.

"You fucking piece of fucking shit!" I screamed, accessing a secret reserve of testicular fortitude that my body had been saving to wrestle grizzly bears. "I even thought you were halfway cool!"

"You did?" He looked almost amused. What's with the nonchalance? This had to be a Jedi mind trick. How are you supposed to tear the shit out of someone who's not fighting back with equal and opposite force? "Look, Saffron and I talked it over, and both of us agreed that the best thing to do with that Sheriff guy out there is leave town."

"Yeah, but we went in the wrong direction!"

"I beg to differ," said Austin. "This is exactly where we should be."

"We kinda sorta read over your research," said Saff.

"You hacked into my laptop?"

Saff smiled. "We didn't hack into anything," she said. "I know all your passwords!"

"Let's talk about it inside," said Austin.

"Why the hell should I go anywhere with you?"

"Suit yourself." He handed off the luggage to Saff and started walking toward the diner. Fuck him if he thought I was going to follow. He could sit in there and eat until he passed out. I was going to convince Saff that she'd made several horrible mistakes, unhitch the trailer from our ride, and then head back home.

"Gimme the keys," I said. "I'll drive."

"We're not going anywhere, Jupes." Saff applied concealer to the pimple, which quickly disappeared into her otherwise flawless skin.

"If we start now, we can tell Dad—"

She closed her compact. "Did you hear me?"

"What about the plan?"

"It's a stupid plan."

"It's *your* plan!"

She glared at me. Between the both of us, I was the one more likely to complain, more likely to walk away from a conversation feeling that I'd been tricked into agreeing to my own demise. But on this, I wouldn't—couldn't—back down. That being said, butting heads with Saff was only going to result in serious skull fractures. I had to try a different angle.

"You didn't even wake me up before leaving. I thought we were a team."

Saff shook her head. "You know how you get."

"How exactly do I 'get'?"

"Remember in eighth grade when you slept through our *Texas Chainsaw Massacre* marathon? It took me an hour to wake you up, and in case it slipped your mind, those are movies about FUCKING CHAINSAWS."

She had me on that. I wasn't exactly the most chipper morning person.

"C'mon," said Saff. "This is bigger than just you and me. And definitely bigger than our parents. This is Old Testament shit. Fire and brimstone coming down from the skies. Rivers and seas boiling! Usurping Pewdiepie from the throne of YouTube! This is our destiny. Now let's go get some breakfast." My stomach gurgled at the very mention of food. Greasy food sounded just about perfect right then. But no, I couldn't.

"I came along because I thought no one would find out," I explained. "We wouldn't get in trouble, and no one would get hurt. What am I supposed to tell Dad? That I lied to his face *again*, this time with feeling?"

"I'm actually hurt that you doubt me, Jupes." Saff handed me her phone and pointed to the conversation on screen:

> Anjeli, darling. This is LeRoy's mother. The kids are doing splendidly. Their project is going to rock the house when they turn it in. I predict a major award in their future! But they'll need a few more days here. Saffron is such a delight to have around! Ta!

> As long as she's no trouble to you and John. Please have Saffron call me when she is able.

"Mom has never uttered the phrase, 'rock the house,'" I said.

Saff rolled her eyes. "It worked, didn't it? Can we stop freaking out and eat?"

I silently had to admit that Saff had addressed my immediate concerns. That text would at least buy us time to sort out what we were going to do from there. That was enough for me to stand down from our impasse. I'd have to figure out a way to finesse our direction back toward home. Right then, my hunger was mounting, and my resolve was bottoming out. Saff sensed me relenting and, taking my hand, dragged me into the diner.

Austin was sitting at a booth in the back, past tables of leather-clad biker dudes and their spiky-collared biker chicks. Chowing down at the counter were truckers wearing T-shirts celebrating the three sacred pillars of Middle-'Murica—fishing, beer, and blowing shit up. Right next to Austin's booth was an old friend I hadn't expected to see—a venerable arcade cabinet of *Street Fighter II: The World Warrior*. I took my seat across the table while Saff sidled up next to him. Curious.

"I'm glad you decided to stay with us," said Austin.

"I didn't say I'd do anything," I said.

"We're your friends, Jupes." Saff reached across the table, but I pulled my hand away.

"Friends don't kidnap friends."

"You were hardly kidnapped!" she exclaimed. "We just took you from one place to another without you knowing and probably against your will."

"Let's focus," Austin began. "We're here in Deadwood now. It should be a simple thing to find someone who knows about Achilles."

"Quite the plan there, Sherlock."

"How come you're making this so hard?" Austin asked.

The waitress came over and took our meal orders: a lumberjack plate for me, a spinach and feta omelette for Austin, and a fruit cup for Saff, who grumbled that it probably wasn't organic.

"And three showers," added Austin. "Breakfast's on me."

After the waitress left, a cold war descended onto the table, our glances traded like sword blows. Our standoff lasted until the food arrived. Oh man. Heavenly grease, how I had missed you. Sausage, hash browns, eggs fried perfectly so that the yolks were exactly fifty percent solid, fifty percent liquid. I kind of wanted to cry.

"Shower's ready, number six," the waitress said.

"Ooh!" Saff squealed. She popped up out of her seat and skipped over to the door to the showers, towing her little rolling luggage bag behind her. That left Austin and me to talk. Man to man. He took a long drink of water and crunched ice between his teeth. I flapped sugar packets like a rattlesnake shook its tail.

"Why are we at each other's throats?" he said.

"You started this."

"All I was doing was working. You traveled hundreds of miles for a YouTube channel. Seems like *you* started this."

"And now I'm trying to end it."

Austin sighed. "It doesn't have to be like this. We're after the same thing."

"Which is?"

"Answers," he said. "You want to know about the game, and I could stand to learn about this medallion before I pawn it off. Up that value a bit. Deadwood helps us both."

Again with the Jedi mind tricks. Yes, the whole point of

this was to find out about the game. And yes, Saff and I were hoping that making content about it would result in 7,500 views.

Wait a second.

I refreshed the YouTube app to make sure that number was legit, and it seemed so. Most of the videos we posted took around a week to get anywhere near that view count. That morning's stream had garnered it in less than an hour! Did Saff know?

"Look, if you want me say I'm sorry—" he began, but I didn't let him finish.

"You're not *that* sorry."

"No, I'm not. An opportunity presented itself. I took it."

Once again, it was a battle of stares waged across a tabletop. Austin, to his credit, understood this, too. He took stock of the room around us, casting his gaze from right to left and back like a lighthouse searchlight. Finally, he nodded his chin over to the corner. "There."

I looked over to where he motioned. "*Street Fighter II?*"

He put his fork down and slid his butt across the booth and out. "We play a match. If you win, I drop everything and we head back right now. If you don't, you come with me. Willingly."

"You're joking." Not to be an arrogant prick, but I was no slouch in the video game realm. Speed run NES *DuckTales* in twelve minutes flat without the moon glitch? Yeah. Routinely submit myself to classic bullet-hell shmups like *Ikaruga?* Abso-fucking-lutely. Fly through endless rings in *Superman 64?* Unfortu-fucking-nately. The proof's all online. While I couldn't say I was a grandmaster of Street Fighting, I wasn't about to go home and be a family man.

"I used to play *Street Fighter* when my grandmother took me to the laundromat."

Alrighty then. We assumed our positions in front of the arcade cabinet with me at the Player 2 position and him at Player 1. The cab definitely showed its age (*Street Fighter II* came out in 1991), with peeling decals all around the screen, joysticks that were lazy and loose, and buttons that had lost most of their spring. But it was the real deal. My fingers effortlessly found the right place to be. A quarter dropped into the coin slot, and we ready to select our fighters.

You can tell a lot about a *Street Fighter* player from the character he picks. Most people interested in dishing out crushing punishment pick either Ken or Ryu. And why not? Their move sets are solid, fairly speedy, and have a good range. They are also my favorite characters to play against because they always fell into familiar patterns: dragon fireball, followed by dragon punch, and then a hurricane kick thrown in for shits and giggles. Repeat until the opponent is dead. Predictable, which Austin clearly wasn't.

"Honda's my guy," he said.

Huh. E. Honda isn't exactly a tier 1 choice. He's far from the easiest fighter to maneuver (being a sumo wrestler and all). His lack of speed often puts him at a disadvantage against characters who could fire projectiles like Sagat with his tiger fireballs or Dhalsim and his yoga fire. What Honda does do well is pack some heat behind his hits. If he can corner you, it's a quick end to the fight.

Good thing that my guy Guile, the flat-topped dude in military fatigues, was basically custom built to deal with the E. Hondas of this world. He's similar to Ken and Ryu in basic fighting style but enjoys a slightly longer reach and more unorthodox set of special moves like the flash kick and sonic boom. That makes it easier to catch opponents in bad situations and set them up for devastating combos.

Round One! Fight!

Austin maneuvered E. Honda back and forth on the left side of the screen while I started my steady volley of sonic booms to keep the pressure on. Then, in a veteran move, he stepped back, buying enough time to unleash a sumo torpedo, which I had no choice but to block. While I took little damage from the hit, the net result was that Austin had closed the gap between the fighters, priming him to unleash some serious damage on my ass.

First blood. A good start. I started by jabbing at Honda, pushing him back and creating enough space for me to flash kick his ass to the ground. Then, as soon as he got back up, I pulled off a spinning back knuckle, knocking Honda to the ground again. When he stood up, he stumbled and saw stars, giving me enough time to execute a killer combo— low jab, low jab, low strong punch, flash kick into a K.O.

"Damn. Saffron said you were pretty good," he said.

Round Two! Fight!

Austin started off with a strong jump kick, which I was a half-second too late to block. With Guile reeling and unable to flip backward, E. Honda easily closed in and unleashed a devastating hundred hand slap, knocking Guile to the ground. Honda was now in close quarters, which was right where he was most dangerous. I righted Guile up only to fall once again to a sumo drop, a belly-flop move that took off a fourth of my life bar. My only chance to salvage this bout was to try and jump out of the corner that Austin had pinned me in.

I hit a sonic boom as soon as Guile got up from the ground (again), and this time, I caught him off guard. I maneuvered Guile to jump over and behind Honda and prepared to hit him with a back knuckle. Unfortunately for me, he saw this coming, swiveled, and grabbed me in a throw, reducing my life bar to zero.

It was one to one now, and I was pissed.

"Looks like we got sudden death," said Austin.

"Yeah. Sure." I flexed my fingers in preparation.

Round Three! Fight!

Austin once again got the step on me and knocked me solid with a sumo torpedo. Only five seconds into the match, and I was already on the ropes. But this time, I knew enough to block his hundred hand slap and counter with a medium and fierce kick combo that sent him reeling. I retreated and spammed sonic booms across the screen.

"Fucking deal with that," I said under my breath. He did, with perfectly timed leaps across the screen. Jump one—he cleared that sonic boom. I let another one loose, and again he jumped it perfectly. One more good leap, and he'd be within range to get me with Honda's hard-hitting special attacks.

I wasn't about to let him do that. Getting my fingers ready, I planned to meet him up in the air on his final jump, grab him, and throw him to the ground—another of Guile's unconventional, yet immensely useful moves. From there, I'd get a flash kick in, and it would be over.

He jumped over my sonic boom one more time, and I leapt up to meet him in mid-air. Oh, it was going to be glorious! Except somehow, he knew. He knew, and he did the one thing that he needed to do to derail my plan. He swiped with light punch, hitting me back and allowing him to land unscathed right next to me. Then he followed up with a couple of nasty leg sweeps and an uppercut, knocking me down.

Fuck! He had managed to corner me. One more monster move, and the best-of-three would be his. Fuck no was I going to let that happen!

"I'll at least let you get back up," he said, laughing. "Don't say I'm not gracious in victory."

Fuck this guy. That was the fucking last straw. I was forced to admit that he was a better player than I was—that much was clear. But I'd be damned if he won.

Not if I could help it. And I could help it.

In the one second Austin gave me, I pulled off a fierce throw, which he easily blocked. However, in the middle of the animation, I hit the button combo for a flash kick. This time, he wasn't ready for what happened.

The screen went black.

"What the hell?" he said, tapping buttons.

"I don't know," I said. But that was a lie. While pretty well known by scholars of the game, even some expert players aren't all that familiar with some of the quirks of *World Warrior* since it was the first iteration of *Street Fighter II* to hit the arcades. By the time the game got really big, newer versions, like *Champion Edition*, had taken the limelight. Most of the plain vanilla *STII* cabs were quietly retired—but not before some enterprising players found out

how to use the Guile character to glitch the game out—
including an at-will hard reset.

Yes, I cheated.

"Hey, your machine ate our quarter!" Austin called out to
no one in particular. None of the waitstaff seemed to care,
nor did the bikers take notice. They were too busy dealing
with something—or someone—else.

Behind us, the din of the restaurant suddenly hushed in a
way that meant either the rapture had happened, or Elvis
had entered the building. Neither was true. It was Saff
dressed in skin-tight leather hot pants and a half-shirt crop-
top with black suspenders and long leather gloves up to her
elbows. And to top it off all, she looked just a teensy,
weensy bit angry.

"Um, Saff?" I said.

No answer.

"Why are you dressed like Tifa Lockhart?"

"How about you tell me something, Jupes?" she hissed.
"What color is this bag?" She shook her piece of luggage.
Hmm. This had to be some sort of trick question. That was
the *black* bag she had packed for this trip, the very *black* bag
she had instructed me to lug to the car. Of course, the fact
that she asked me meant that *black* was the wrong answer.

"Black?" I asked, taking a step backward.

"Austin? What color?"

He glanced over at me, puzzled. "It looks black to me."

"IT IS NOT BLACK! IT'S EBONY!" Saff screamed. All eyes
were on our little corner of the diner. The bikers up front
were clearly agitated that their relaxing breakfast had
turned into a shouting session about the difference between
two colors. I imagined brass knuckles under tabletops

sliding onto fingertips, looks exchanged over English muffins and home fries. Someone was gonna get their ass kicked for ruining a perfectly relaxing morning. And since no one was going to hit a "delicate flower" like Saff, it fell upon Austin and me to absorb the blows.

"Aren't those the same thing?" said Austin.

Saff stomped her red boots on the ground. "Has the whole world GONE CRAZY? AM I THE ONLY ONE AROUND HERE WHO GIVES A SHIT ABOUT HUE, TINT, SHADE, AND PIGMENT?!"

Exchanging a look with me, Austin dropped a twenty on the table, and we took our leave.

7

IT'S DANGEROUS TO GO ALONE!
TAKE THIS!

The thrill of my *SFII* "victory" was short-lived. Even though I'd prevented Austin from beating me, I also didn't win—which meant that, technically, I was on the hook to go along with his and Saff's crazy idea of marching up to the former Achilles headquarters and demanding an audience with *someone who exactly*?

"Someone who knows something" said Austin, who'd managed to snag shotgun with Saff at the wheel. She slammed on the horn in a serious case of road rage. Yes, I fully admit that I'd made a mistake. I'd grabbed the wrong bag from her room, the one containing a bunch of her still-unfinished costumes. In an attempt to fix the situation, I bought her a temporary wardrobe from the diner's gift shop.

It wasn't high fashion—a pair of basketball shorts and an XL T-shirt with a picture of a semi-truck and the words *Big Haulin'* emblazoned on the front.

Still, it was the thought that counted, right?

We drove into Deadwood proper, following GPS to the location where Achilles once existed. That was one of the interesting factoids I'd dug up the previous night. The former Achilles headquarters had quite the history, all the way to the 1800s, when it went by the much-to-be-desired name of the Homestake Slime Plant.

Slime plant? you may be thinking. No, it wasn't where the Ghostbusters processed all that ectoplasm they collected on their spook runs. Deadwood became a central hub for the gold rush that brought people out West with a shovel and a dream. Miners and prospectors dug out gravel from creek beds and then took it to Deadwood, to the processing plant at the top of the hill. The gold would be sorted out, leaving water and rock and muck—the slime. After the rush ended, the plant closed shop and stood abandoned until Achilles Appliance Corporation moved in to make electronic kitchen amenities for the modern age.

Since that semi-lawless slime time, Deadwood had progressed from mining town to cowboy-themed family resort, complete with go karts, mini golf, and frozen custard. Like most of middle America, Deadwood's central strip was "Main Street," where you could find most of the major businesses. And by businesses, I mean casinos. Holy shit, were there casinos. Some were much grander than others, with the smaller ones down the strip looking more like pawn shops than places to see Elvis impersonators while grabbing a brunch buffet.

"Son of a bitch!" screamed Saff when a sleek, red sports car cut her off. She wasn't exactly an expert at handling stress, much less road rage. The clogged streets in downtown Deadwood were giving her conniptions. "I swear, if that mini-van cuts us off one more time, I'm going to go out there and murder everyone inside!"

"You mean the church van?" I asked. "The one with all the nuns?"

"If they love God so much, I'D BE HAPPY TO HELP THEM GO MEET HIM!"

"Why don't we just walk?" said Austin, trying to keep things calm. I couldn't help but be a bit amused at the whole scene. This amazing plan of theirs was off to a rocky start. But a promise was a promise. I wasn't going to complain or say a thing. I'd follow, and when all leads dried up, I'd then insist we go home.

We parked on a side street and waded into the stream of tourists—perfect families on Wild West vacations, bleary-eyed moms and dads trailing teen girls in belly tees and hip huggers, teen boys in ten-gallons ogling all the other families' teen girls.

Austin led the way with his phone's GPS directing us to the Achilles building. We passed umpteen souvenir shops, a dozen leather stores, a cigar store, a frozen yogurt shoppe, a barbecue pit with a cartoon pig mascot cannibalistically hocking the entrails of his brethren. Eventually, the throngs thinned out, and we were climbing uphill toward our goal: the Golden Gulch Casino and Resort. After Achilles went under, the building lay unused for a decade until the casino renaissance took hold of any available space in town.

Of course, the old Homestake/Achilles stomping grounds

made for a killer resort. Everything about it screamed richness—but in a movie set kind of way. From far off, it was bright and fancy, lit up by carefully tested mood lighting that oozed romance and history. Up close, though, you could see the paint spots. You could see where the chalky caulk along the windows had split and succumbed to the elements.

Two refrigerator-shaped security guards side-eyed us as we walked into the building. Inside, I was surprised to find the lobby austere—quiet even. The style of the place could have been described as "upscale Paul Bunyan." The exposed wood décor made you feel less like you were gonna lose all your money at the flip of a card and more like you were gonna go chopping wood and roasting large animal portions on spits out back.

A hostess approached us right away.

"May I help you?" she said with a confused expression. High rollers we were not, and we sure didn't look the part.

"We'd like to talk to somebody," said Austin.

"I can help you with accommodations, restaurants—"

"Can we speak to the person in charge?" he continued, his voice edgy and breaking. He tried to move past her, but she stepped in front of him.

"Excuse me! I want you to leave now."

"All you have to do is make a call!"

"C'mon, man! Chill!" I reached out to take his arm, but he jerked it away.

From behind us, the pair of burly door guards came stomping over.

"Guys," I said, "We should do like she says."

"Why can't you be reasonable?" Austin protested.

"We're done, man," I said, trying to grab his wrist. Once again, he twisted away, and for a second, I thought he was going to wind up and hit me. Instead, he took a look at the toughs bearing down on us, frowned, and backed down from the scene.

Outside, the walk back downhill was silent and awkward. Austin was clearly upset, but how'd he expect that to go? A bunch of kids weren't going to have an audience with the casino president. I wasn't sure what his ultimate aim was with that show. In any case, it seemed that I'd gotten my wish. After that shitshow, there wasn't much else to do but go home.

"Hey," said Saff, walking backward in front of him. "That kinda sucked."

"You don't have to tell me that."

"I know," said Saff. She reached out and touched his forearm. Unlike with me, he didn't recoil. "We should figure out what to do now."

"We're leaving," I said. "If we hurry—"

"Yeah," said Austin. "You'll make it. Your parents won't know you've been gone, and you'll live happily ever after."

"What's your problem?"

He stopped and looked right at me. "Maybe I'm tired of you saying the same shit."

"What did you think was going to happen, huh?" I said. "You can't just demand your way into getting what you want. It's like you're playing *Zelda* and you think you take on Ganon without even getting the wooden sword."

"I don't even know what the hell you're talking about!" Austin shouted back. People on the street stood and stared.

"Jupes is right," said Saff.

"Then what was I supposed to do?" he said. "Just leave and give up?"

"Retreat and fight another day," I said. "Or better yet, find an alternate way around, a different path to the goal."

This line of thinking seemed to intrigue him. "Such as?"

"First thing's first. You gotta talk to the man in the cave."

"What does that mean?"

"Jupes is saying that you have to know what you're dealing with, get the lay of the land."

I smiled at Saff. We'd conquered every RPG we'd ever played together. There were sleepless nights when she and I would try and figure out the puzzles in *Chrono Trigger* or try not to cry when (spoiler warning) Aerith meets her untimely end at the hands of Sephiroth in *Final Fantasy VII*. She knew just as much as I did what it took to win despite long odds.

"Like a tourist office or something," I said. "A museum."

"That makes sense," Austin muttered. Swiping and poking at his phone, he searched up any museums in the area, finding something called the Deadwood Historical Society on the other side of downtown. "I'm going. You coming with?"

I was still bound by the *Street Fighter* agreement. And Saff was already on board. Together, we took our time going around the busy Main Street instead of through it. Outside of the ritzified center of town, with Golden Gulch as its nerve center, Deadwood was more dust-covered, run-down, authentic. There were still some original building façades, crumbling warehouses with cracked windows.

We tracked the museum to one of these buildings, which looked like a house rickety enough to topple over in a strong breeze. Taped to the door was a handmade sign with *Deadwood Community Historical Society* written in Sharpie. Then, in smaller lettering underneath:

Just leave the pizza here. Charge my tab at Tony's.

The click of a deadbolt startled us backward. The door opened, and an older woman—gray-haired and built like a mean old snapping turtle—gave us the long-stare look over.

"Hmph. No pizza."

"Were you expecting one?" I asked.

"No, but I was hoping I ordered one and forgot," she said. "Y'all just gonna stand there?"

"Is this the Deadwood Historical Society?" I asked.

"That's what the sign says."

"We need to talk to you," said Austin. "About Achilles."

She cocked her head. "There's something I haven't heard in a while." She locked the door behind her with a ring of keys attached to her belt. "You'll have to come back later. I gotta be somewhere right now."

"Can we walk and talk?" Austin asked. "We don't have a lot of time."

"You have more than me," she said, smirking. "But sure. Name's Edwina. Call me Ed."

We walked with Ed back downtown, plunging back into the crowds of tourists.

"We're looking for info about Achilles—specifically a game called *Forever Throne*."

"One thing at a time, kid." Ed pointed to her head. "This old brain can only handle so much, and right now, I gotta be on point."

We weren't sure what she meant until we turned a

corner and were greeted by a densely packed group gathered around a table and chairs in the center of the street. A sign on the sidewalk denoted the purpose of the gathering: *1:00 PM—Free Show, Courtesy of the Deadwood Community Historical Society.* Ed fought her way to the front of the crowd. She took a bow, to a round of applause.

"Howdy, folks!" she yelled. "I hope you're having a good time in our fair town today. It's a sunny Sunday, and you're in the right place if you want to learn a little bit of local history." Faster than I could blink, Ed quick-drew a gun tucked into her pants. Damn, I never would have known! The crowd erupted into hoots and applause at the display. "We got this here show for you, courtesy of the Deadwood Community Historical Society. But before we do that, we have to ask you a big favor. Please stay clear of this area." She pointed to the center of the street where the table and chairs sat. "This is a real gun. Now, back in the old Hollywood days, actors used real guns on set, just like this one. This is an 1858 Remington cap and ball revolver, 36 caliber. And it ain't loaded with bullets. Instead, it's jammed with cream of wheat, powder, and half a can of Crisco." From one of her pockets, Ed produced a small apple, which she placed onto the table. "Packs quite the punch." Ed took aim at the apple and squeezed the trigger, exploding the apple into sauce. The crowd whooped and applauded.

"Now, our troupe of esteemed actors is going to reenact the story of Turkey Creek Jack Johnson, Wyatt Earp's trusted right hand and a formidable figure in his own right. Enjoy the show." From out of the crowd walked a bunch of men, dressed in dingy cowboy garb. Ed took her leave and joined us back in the crowd.

"Now," she began, "Why are kids like you asking about shit that don't matter no more?"

"Because it matters," said Austin.

"Hmph. Yeah, I know Achilles. Worked there until it closed down."

"So, you remember the tournament, *Forever Throne*—"

"Hold your horses, kid. That was a long time ago, and if it didn't happen in packing and shipping, I wasn't really a part of it."

"Remember anything about the games?" I asked.

"I remember at the very end that it was a lot of freakin' games, not a lot of toasters. And not a lot of money. Old man Meadows went all in on the games, and that was the end."

"A lot of companies fell apart back then," I said.

Before we get too far, let's pause and talk history. Let's talk video game history. Today, as I'm sure you're aware, video games debut into a world that treats them like Hollywood movies. There are press conferences, interviews, trailers, hoopla. Live actors don motion-capture outfits so that their actual performances are digitized and put straight into the game. We praise the games that "break the rules" at the same time that we pay sixty bucks a copy for the same old *Call of Duty* clone with shiny new map packs and new skins to make our characters look like the Predator.

That's why when we talk about gaming from years gone by, it's important to understand that "the industry" wasn't always like this. When video games began, it was a niche thing centered on arcades where games were paid for quarter by quarter. Compared to the ultra-corporatization of your Xboxes and your Playstations, games back then were a new frontier—you couldn't "break the rules" because there were no rules to break.

The main demarcation point we need to note is the year 1983—as in "The Great Video Game Crash of 1983." If you're not familiar, here's the Cliff's Notes version: before Sony and Microsoft, you had a single generalissimo at the head of video-game-dom—Atari. The best anyone else could achieve was second banana. But that didn't stop pretenders from hopping on board and trying to huff some fumes off Atari's successes.

You had the main competitors of the day in Intellivision and the ColecoVision. You had distant thirds with big dreams like the Vectrex and the APF Imagination Machine. You had large manufacturers vying to gain control of the cash prize with consoles like the Fairchild Channel F and the Emerson Arcadia and the Magnavox Odyssey^2. There was money to be made, and everyone wanted some.

Come 1983, the scene was crowded. Too crowded. As the market ballooned, bottom-feeding companies who had no business in the video game space smelled easy pickings. Rinky-dink outfits shoveled out barely-slapped-together turds like *Chase the Chuckwagon* (made by Purina, *a dog food company*) for the Atari 2600.

Gamers got sick of shit, so they stopped playing. More importantly, they stopped *buying*. Entire collections were mothballed. Swap meets teemed with unwanted games and systems. Dumpsters ate them up like Pac-Man ate power pellets. *To hell with video games,* said everybody. In the course of a few months, the bottom fell out of what was a multi-billion-dollar industry.

The Great Video Game Crash of 1983 ushered in a dark age that would not end until the Japanese-produced Nintendo Entertainment System made its North American release in 1985. That's two years in which video games were literally buried in a nuclear desert under a concrete cap—a great wall of mystery two years thick, a solid fog that made learning about stuff before the Nintendo renaissance scattershot at best.

Anyway, on with the show.

Ed took us back to the Deadwood Community Historical Society (which turned out to just be her house). Showing us in, she led us to a breezy enclosed back porch, which doubled as the nerve center for Deadwood's most precious historical archives. The room was big enough for a small desk, some folding chairs, and two overflowing file cabinets.

"Don't eat the donuts," she said, meaning the contents of the Dunkin' Donuts box on top of her desk. A thick layer of grimy dust coated the outside, which made me not want to see anything on the inside. Ed leafed through some of the drawers in the cabinets and pulled out a couple of manila folders. "A lot of young folks worked at Achilles—mostly packing jobs with me in the warehouse. Gimme a name."

"Nathan Squires," said Austin. "He was the winner of the *Forever Throne* tournament."

"Excuse me, but what are those?" Saff pointed to a glass container spanning the top of the file cabinets. At first, I'd thought it was a terrarium for mosses and other small plants, but then I noticed that there was something moving inside it. I thought it best to ignore and carry on, but you know Saff—she was concerned that they were parasitic brain worms that wrapped themselves around the cerebral cortex, rendering the victim susceptible to suggestion, then inducing madness, finally causing death. You know, that common worry.

"Sun beetles. Want to see one up close?"

"No!" she said, vehemently. "Um, no thank you."

Ed looked back at Austin. "Nathan . . ."

"Squires," Austin repeated.

She bit her lip in thought, then shook her head. "Doesn't ring a bell. Sorry."

"Not your fault," said Austin, visibly disappointed.

"I do remember *Forever Throne*, though," Ed continued. "His 'grand slam,' Alvin called it. More like a strikeout. Hedging the bank on those games was a bad, bad move."

"Alvin?" I asked.

"President of the company. Most of us were hired by his daddy, so we had a soft spot for him. But it was pretty clear that he didn't really want to be in charge." Ed opened up one of the folders and pulled out a photo. "Here." The black-and-white image showed several dozen people lined up in front of the Achilles building. Instead of the words *Resort Casino* hung the name *Achilles* in dark, solid letters. Posing at the very front of the photo was a thin man with thin lips squinting through his glasses. "That's Alvin there. And those two kids next to him—they made the games."

Standing with the president were two young men, one with dark, short cropped hair, and the other with blond floppy hair that went into his eyes. And by young, I really mean young. They looked like eighth-graders compared to all the other workers around them. Kids among adults.

"I didn't know that one at all," she said, pointing to the dark-haired kid. "But this one—a bunch of the guys in the back and I had this bowling league every Wednesday. And this kid, he liked to have lunch with us sometimes, especially when Harold and Stu were bringing in homemade chili to see which one was better. So he got wind of our bowling league and begged to be put on the team. So we did it, but he never showed up. His name was Bob, I think. Or Brendon. Or—"

"Bryan?" I asked, repeating the name on the note I found in Austin's trailer.

"Yes! Nice guess!" said Ed. "Bryan! Only, we called him Mr. Average 'cause we had to pencil in an average score every single week."

"Wait a second, did you say Mr. Average?" Saff grabbed her phone and started tapping and scrolling until she stopped and stared at the screen. "Jupes, you have to see this."

The YouTube app was open to Saff's latest upload, the video from earlier that morning. Saff had scrolled into the comments area, to a particular comment that simply read, "You should contact me." The author: **MrAverage5427**.

It couldn't be the same guy, right? That sort of kismet moment doesn't happen in real life. But *what if it was?* What were the odds? I mean, we were a microscopic channel, not even a blip on the YouTube radar. We had a small bunch of dedicated subs and knew their handles on sight: HorizontalJustin, KackelDackel, PoltergeistRalph. For lack of a better term, these were my friends (albeit sadistic ones). MrAverage5427 was not one of the regulars.

"It's probably a coincidence," I said.

"No way," said Saff. "It's fate."

"There's only one way to find out," said Austin. He took Saff's phone and typed a PM back to MrAverage5427 with the following cryptic note:

We're with Ed. You have info to prove who you are?

Edwina insisted on us watching her feed wood pulp and leaves to her beetles—something that fascinated Austin and me, but which forced Saff to go outside and binge on shopping-haul videos. Before leaving her office, I asked her where we could get a working Mark II console.

"Try checking in your time machine," she said. "We were sitting on a crapload of returned product right at the end. It all went out with the trash. Couldn't tell you where you could find one now."

By the time we got back to the car, it was late afternoon careening into the evening. There'd be no point in getting on the road no matter which direction we were headed. Our focus became finding a place for the night (preferably somewhere that wouldn't hit ye olde debit card too hard). I rode in back while Saff and Austin excitedly talked about the MrAverage5427 message.

Do you think he'll write back?

Absolutely—otherwise why write in the first place?

I wanna make a stream about it.

No, not until we know more.

I was (in)conspicuously silent on all counts. Not that the quest for *Forever Throne* didn't interest me. But at that moment, video game glory took a back seat to good old-fashioned jealousy. Not noticing Saff and Austin's fast-developing rapport would be like not noticing a baby arm growing from my forehead. The little touches they traded, the looks that lasted a second too long to not mean *something*. I tried to distract myself by continuing Achilles research on my phone, but I couldn't concentrate. Even getting home under the 'rents' noses couldn't compare to my urge to throw him out of a fast-moving vehicle.

"Let's hit up the Super-Walmart," Austin suggested. "We'll get supplies and we can stay overnight for free in the parking lot." This was a sensible suggestion. Walmart is your best friend when traveling through Bumblefuck U.S.A. You could buy value-priced, moderately functional electronics as well as a selection of processed, packaged food products all under one roof *and* park your RV out in the parking lot for free road rests. Not too shabby.

Too bad Austin suggested it. So I had to hate it.

Grumble, grumble.

"Jupes, relax," said Saff. "We're home fucking free."

We are neither of those things, I thought.

The Walmart at the end of town turned out to be a mega-sized Super-Walmart—only your godfather, fairy godmother, and genie in a bottle rolled into a single mega box store. Great. Just in case I needed to buy a baby stroller and a rope to hang myself with. Upon entering the store, we all went our separate ways. While Saff and Austin went off to do their things, I went off to do my thing—which was eat.

So there I sat, in the front snack bar stirring cheese dip with a tortilla chip. The endless spiral in the neon orange cheese of my Bonzai Chicken Nachos Supreme was engrossing, hypnotizing. In Japan, this is called *uzumaki*, a vortex or whirlpool signifying the perpetual dance, the infinite cycle of creation and destruction. How fitting. I thought about Achilles and the ultimate fate of the Mark II consoles that didn't get sold. Back to the slag heap, just like Atari's ill-fated *E.T.* cartridges at the height of the '83 crash. I continued to swirl the cheese, the spiral seeming to wrap around me, enveloping shoppers ogling Cuisinarts and XBones and Spongebob-printed socks into an unnaturally orange explosion of time and space.

I wish.

Look, I know I should have been excited. Something special was brewing with *Forever Throne*, and we were slowly assembling the pieces to this crazy puzzle. But *Real life*™. Mom and John. Dad alone. Now Saff and Austin. At least I had nachos, but they were cold and lifeless—not at all the promise of juicy ecstasy like on the wall-sized menu. Whatever. I inhaled a chip loaded with jalapeno slices, olives from a can, and little red flecks that I believed were supposed to be bacon bits.

"That's not real cheese."

I looked up, and there was Saff. She'd slung a bunch of clothes over her shoulder. The outfits looked like they'd been plucked from Walmart's Young Miss *Mortal Kombat* section—skimpy unitards, belly tees, and shiny vinyl vests.

She slid into the other side of the bench. "Don't eat that."

"Too late."

"Your arteries—"

"Are fucking happy," I said, crunching another chip.

She tapped her fingertip on my forehead. "What's going on in there?" Dammit. This was Saff at her most charming—in those intimate moments when it was just her and me. Change the scenery, and we could have been in Dad's kitchen having the same conversation. "I'm worried about you. You're being weird."

"I'm not being weird."

"You are, too," she said. "Talk to me."

"Just thinking." I reached for another chip, and she pulled the tray away and shoved my shoulder.

"You're still worried that we're going to get caught," she said. "Don't be. Our cover is bullet-proof! We just have to wait for the dude to get back to us, and we are so winning."

"Those sound like famous last words," I said, my voice cracking. Call it a moment of weakness, because that's probably what it was. "But I guess we've already gone this far. We should see things to the end, right?"

"Right, Jupes!" she exclaimed. "It's nine-hundred fifty miles to Chicago, we got like a quarter tank of gas, it's getting dark, and I'm going commando. We're on a mission from God."

"You're going commando?"

"Not important," she said, popping up from her seat. "What is important is that we're a team, like always. Now if you'll excuse me, I'm off to the dressing rooms."

Oh yeah. Her wardrobe. My bad. "Sorry. I didn't mean to grab the wrong bag. At least you can get new clothes."

"These?" She flipped the tags to show the disembodied head of Miley Cyrus on them. "I wouldn't be caught dead wearing this shit out in public. You really think I'd dress like her?"

"That's a trick question, right?"

"For your information, I'm making a video for *The Starlet Letter*. Anyway, could you go find Austin? He's getting some food. I just wanted to make sure that he's buying the right stuff. You know what I like."

"Ugh. Yeah. I do."

"Don't even. You love Tempeh Crisps."

"Sure. *Love.* That's the right word."

Saff gave me the stink-eye but wasn't up for arguing. If anything, my emotions were in more of a shambles than they were before. Because talking with her reminded me of everything I loved about her. Underneath that hard exterior, the fake eyelashes, the gauzy blouses, and the skirts that could double as handkerchiefs, she was a real person. A true friend. Or maybe that's what she wanted me to believe.

Enough with sad-sack nachos. I left the orange vortex of doom and headed into the store to find Austin. Aisle after aisle in the grocery section was filled with delectable pre-packaged snacks, from Chicago's own *Matt's Cookies* to all the dazzling colors of *eXtreme Doritos*. But Austin was in none of them.

Eventually, I found him in the sporting goods department taking shots at a basketball hoop set up in the back corner of the store. I watched as he drained shot after shot. Fifteen footers, twenty footers. Short bunnies, hook shots. He hit them all with a fluid grace I couldn't develop no matter how hard I practiced. Capping the display was an alley-oop dunk off the backboard. The ball bounced right to where I was standing.

"How long have you been there?" he asked.

"Long enough." Put athletic prowess on the heap of Austin's virtues, along with good looks, self-confidence, and a tough spirit. Basically all the things that I wasn't. In gym class, I was obligated to play whatever sports the gym teacher, Mr. Rodgers (no, I won't be your neighbor, you creepy bald man with a pornostash), wanted to subject us to. That meant whole weeks of badminton and floor hockey, as well as the usual unholy trio of basketball, baseball, and flag football. Didn't matter. I was singularly bad at all of them.

"You have the ball," he said. "It's your shot."

"Me?" I was standing about fifteen feet away from the basket—free throw distance. I gripped the ball and wound my hands up over my right shoulder and then heaved the ball up like a shotput. The ball spun like a knuckleball, slammed into the backboard and then careened back at my face. Austin caught the ball with an extended hand.

"Your form is *interesting*." He shot a couple more shots that went down without even grazing the rim.

"Damn, you're really good."

"Sure," he said sarcastically. "*Black Kid Good at Basketball* reads most stereotypical headline ever." He tossed me the ball, but my stone hands bumbled the catch, launching the ball back upward right into my nose. Ow.

"Not a sports guy."

"I can see that." He picked up the ball and aimed himself at the basket. "Has Mr. Average written back yet?"

I checked my phone. "Not yet."

Swish.

"I guess we were going to have to talk about this sooner or later," he said. Talk about a hard swerve in the conversation. He and Saff was about the last thing I wanted to talk about—maybe second to genital warts (but it was close). He corralled the basketball and put it into my hands. "Look, I get how you feel."

"You do?"

"Yeah. You're scared that you're going to get in trouble. Believe me, my grandma whupped me good if I came home after ten."

"Is that who raised you?"

"Yeah. Just me and her most of the time, until she died three years ago."

"What about your mom?"

"Mom didn't want me around, and the feeling was mutual. When she wasn't strung out on something, she was hanging around shitty dudes who hated me. Grandma would always say, 'Austin, don't you fuck up like my baby did.' So when she died, I shuffled around friends' houses rather than see my mom. When I wore out my welcome, I was out on the streets."

"Shit, dude."

"Don't worry about it."

"I didn't know."

"Don't. Fucking. Worry." He took another shot, angled off the backboard, straight into the net. "I didn't tell you all that so you can feel sorry for me. I don't have a job, don't have any friends, don't have anyone in the world who gives a flying fuck about what happens to me. I just wanted you to see that this game thing is all I got. So I'm going to take it as far as it goes. I'd like for you to be with me, since this is your world."

"Could have fooled me. I'm just as lost as you are."

"Then it's nice not to be alone in that." He tapped the ball. "Your shot."

"I suck at this." I put the ball on the floor and stepped back. "Let's just get out of here, okay?"

8

WHAT A HORRIBLE NIGHT TO HAVE A CURSE

Austin and I filled up a cart with Saff-approved foods, a much harder task than we'd thought. Walmart was a store geared toward the masses, and the dearth of soy-based snacks on the shelves reflected the tender, paunchy, and frankly much tastier center of the country. So our dinner consisted of granola bars, active-culture yogurt, designer melon water, and a bag of "all-natural" white cheddar Cheetos.

After eating, we all decided to call it a night. Saff and Austin, being dead tired after being up all night and all day, got to crash in the comfort of the trailer while I sat in *Hell on Wheels* nursing my insomnia by watching *DuckTales* speedruns on YouTube.

Brr. It was cold that night. According to my phone, the temperature dipped into the lower forties—a record low by all accounts. In other circumstances, I would have run the heat, but we had places to go and barely enough moolah for gas as it was. So I huddled up with the ratty blanket Saff kept under the front seat, trying not to wonder how long it had been since it had last been washed.

I checked back to the YouTube app to see if any new messages had arrived. Still nothing. How long would we have to wait? Surely if MrAverage5427 was legit, he'd have gotten in contact by then. I was antsy, and it wasn't all about the looming arrival of a PM that may or may not ever come. It was about Saff. And Austin. And me. And about how we all fit together.

I needed a consultation. I texted Ralph.

PoltergeistRalph

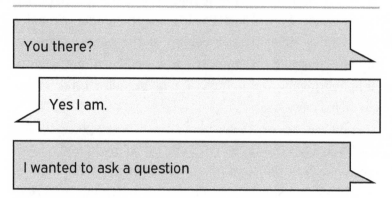

You there?

Yes I am.

I wanted to ask a question

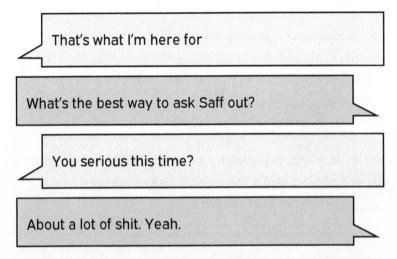

That's what I'm here for

What's the best way to ask Saff out?

You serious this time?

About a lot of shit. Yeah.

Talking to Austin earlier hit me pretty hard. It made me put all the shit—the channel, school, the future—into perspective. Unlike him, I did have parents who cared about me, even if Dad could hardly take care of himself, even if Mom was currently busy overseeing handshake deals with the Galactic Empire. They still loved me and let me live a pretty comfortable life, all things considered.

I needed to grow the fuck up.

I needed to get the fuck in shape.

I needed to take my future into my fucking hands.

I needed to tell Saff how I really fucking felt.

I needed to, I needed to, I needed to.

It pained me to think it, but maybe Mom was right. About everything. I mean, putting together the channel is fun, but where exactly was that going? Was I prepared to be doing that for the next however many years? Maybe I had to step away. Maybe it was time for me just to be LeRoy Jupiter Jenkins, human being.

Grab her and take her.

You fucking serious?

Just kidding. Dude, just be straight with her. Tell her that she's the bee's knees and take her out. What's her favorite food?

Horrible vegan bullshit.

Okay, skip dinner. What movies does she like?

Anything with Jean Claude Van Damme.

So do a night in with Bloodsport and see where things fall.

You think that'll work?

Fuck yeah! Kumite! Kumite!

Okay. Okay! I was going to do it! As soon as I woke up the next day, I'd take Saff aside and tell her exactly how I felt

about her, come what may. I was excited, energized, and
still awake. A short walk was exactly what I needed to calm
my nerves. Before jumping out the car, I checked the
YouTube inbox one last time.

This time it wasn't empty. A new message was there,
fresh from MrAverage5427:

> **Tell Edwina that I haven't forgotten the league fees
> I owe her. If you want to know more about Forever
> Throne, come visit:**
>
> **La: 39.972127, Lo: -112.126570**
>
> **bjs**
>
> **This login will self-destruct in 5 . . . 4 . . . 3 . . . 2 . . .**

Oh my god, this was happening. Like, this was all real—
every part of it. I read and reread the message, eventually
figuring out that "Lo" and "La" stood for longitude and
latitude. Those were map coordinates! I pulled up Google
Maps and plugged the numbers in, which fetched up a
location in Eureka, Utah, a town just to the south of Salt
Lake City.

Further west? My heart sank. No way, no how, no
number of fake texts would give us enough time to make it
to Utah. As soon as Saff saw the message, though, she'd drag
us and half the world to get this scoop on our channel.

Unless she never found out. Unless I deleted the message
while she slept. She'd never know. My fingertip hovered
above the screen. And I couldn't do it. How would I ever be
truthful to Saff if I had to start out with a lie? I couldn't do
that to her. I couldn't do that to me. And, frankly, with the

shitty hand he'd been dealt, I couldn't do that to Austin. He deserved his answers—about the medallion, about his father. He'd just have to go get them by himself.

I was going to tell them right then about Bryan's message. That way, everything would be out in the open in front of all of us. No lies. Nothing to hide. I hopped out of the car, walked to the trailer door, and opened it.

There come those times when your mind disconnects from your body—some call it an out-of-body experience. The more scientific among us classify it as sudden-onset dissociation. Shellshock? PTSD? Whatever it was, it was happening to me. Right there, right in front of me on the bench opposite the door sat Austin. Sitting on his lap was Saff, and they were kissing. Making out. Snogging. However you say it, they were doing it.

I had to leave. I stepped out of the trailer, suddenly aware of how dry and cracked my lips were, how tingly my tongue felt. Stumbling back out into the frigid night, my head swam with the brightness of parking lot lamps, the blaring fluorescents pouring out the Walmart windows. That's where I had to get—inside and away. Those two words directed me forward, the spark of resolve from talking with Ralph all but extinguished.

I stumbled past the glass doors of Super Walmart and made for the snack bar. Another set of nachos was in my immediate future, followed by chicken tenders, double chili fries, and a chocolate milkshake—the biggest they had. And then something caught my eye, right at the edge of my peripheral vision. At first, I thought I was seeing things. My eyes were still cloudy from the lights in the parking lot. Standing at a spinner rack of shitty DVDs (you always put your shittiest stuff by the door for those impulse buys) was the monster I thought we'd left behind back in Minneapolis.

The Sheriff.

Under the department store lights, he looked even more out of place. Two leather sashes criss-crossed over his huge, barrel chest. Both were worn and crumbling, but still held strong over his frame. His legs were like iron pillars, the fragile flaps of leather on his worn boots kept together by a weave of rusted chain. The hair around his face looked feathered, as if he'd just walked through a wind tunnel or, more likely, just stepped off his doomsday ride.

Fight-or-flight took over, and it was all motherfucking *OR FLIGHT*. I ran as fast as I could back to the trailer, which couldn't ever be fast enough. I could feel him just over my shoulder like a specter lapping up my fear.

As I closed in on *Hell on Wheels*, a pair of figures stepped out of the darkness. It was Saff and Austin walking toward me. What were they doing? I waved my arms and screamed for them to go back to the car until my lungs felt like they were full of shattered glass.

"Jupes!" Saff called out. "We can explain."

"Get the fuck in the car!" I wheezed, just before I collided with both of them, landing all three of us on the blacktop. "He's . . . he's . . ."

"What the hell?" said Saff.

"Sheriff!" I stammered out. Of course, by then it was too late. A Harley-Davidson roar ripped through the night like the bellow of a demon singing its stygian song of destruction. A second later, a single high beam lit up the world in searing light.

Fuck explanations. I grabbed both of their hands and

dragged them behind me all the way to the van. The Sheriff gave chase, and the race was on.

"Give me the keys," Austin yelled.

"What? Why?"

"Just do it!" he ordered. To Saff: "You and LeRoy get all our stuff out and run to the highway." He pointed into the darkness opposite the gleaming oasis that was Walmart.

"What are you going to do?" I asked.

"Distract him," he said, nabbing the keys from me.

"Austin, that's insane," Saff said.

"Trust me." The Sheriff's hell-beacon was looming close.

I froze in place, my insides a mess of exhaustion crossed with overly angry teen boy overload, and watched as Austin climbed into *Hell on Wheels*, turned the engine on, and cranked the Grim Reaper as loud as it could go. Meanwhile, Saff and I dove inside and grabbed our bags along with anything that looked remotely interesting—including Austin's music box.

"Hurry the fuck up!" yelled Austin. We jumped with our stuff and started running toward the highway, away from the vile, yellow light of the Sheriff's cyclopean high beam.

As soon as we were clear, *Hell on Wheels* came to life with a lurch. Austin hammered the gas, pushing the car and trailer into the way of the headlight and casting us back into darkness. Saff and I ran, carried by fear and adrenaline. So many things were running through my head that I couldn't sort them out. I wanted to stop Saff and ask her what the ever-loving fuck I'd just seen her and Austin doing. I also wanted to not be squashed into a human pancake by The Sheriff. One of those was a teeny, tiny bit more pressing.

I kept running. Saff and I reached the hill at the end of

the parking lot next to the highway. I pushed her ahead of me while heaving up all of our combined baggage. Just as we made it to the top of the hill, the sound of a collision—of plastic snapping and metal twisting into metal—filled the air. I looked back over my shoulder to the parking lot. There, smashed into one of the light poles illuminating the parking lot, was *Hell on Wheels*.

"Jupes . . ." said Saff. Her voice quivered.

"C'mon, man," I whispered, keeping my eyes trained for any sign of motion, no matter the source. I didn't see any trace of The Sheriff or his motorcycle, not did I see Austin. After a moment, I saw something moving in the darkness, a shape taking form. Was it friend or foe?

"Keep going!" Austin screamed as he charged past us.

Back down by the trailer, the hulking shoulders of The Sheriff lurched out from behind it. His steps were unsure, and he seemed to be holding his head as he walked out of the radius of the overhead lamp into the darkness. Whatever happened down there between him and Austin wasn't fucking Disneyland.

Clutching my backpack, I ran to catch up to Saff and Austin, who were already trying to flag down passing cars, jumping and hooting at the sets of headlights passing by. One set of headlights passed. Then another. I allowed myself to relax a bit—we'd made it to the road. No sign of The Sheriff. Maybe he'd gone back to his charnel pit to lick his wounds. And wouldn't you know it, a second later, the headlight of his motorcycle lit up, a spirit of vengeance sniffing for the blood of those who had crossed its master.

And eventually it would find us.

I joined Saff and Austin in our desperate attempt to get

someone, anyone, to stop and save us. The next pair of headlights came careening around the bend, a creaky silver station wagon. When its high beams hit us, we jumped back to the very edge of the road, expecting it to speed past. But it didn't! The car slowed and pulled over with the driver's side window rolled down.

"What's going on?" said an older, rosy-cheeked man with a thick Brooklyn accent.

"There's a crazy guy after us," said Saff. "Can you help us get out of here?"

As we waited for an answer, I detected some movement from the rear compartment of the wagon behind the back seats. Was it my crazed imagination animating the shadows, or was there something really there?

"All right," said the driver. "Get in."

I know, I know. This is how horror movies begin. But if our choices were between living out the plot of *Maniac Cop* or *The Hitcher*, the latter was preferable. *The Hitcher* was just a serial killer (though one played by Roy Batty). *Maniac Cop*, on the other hand, was a fully undead juggernaut of destruction played by the almighty chin himself, Robert Z'Dar. Shitty choices both, but there we were.

It turned out that we needn't have worried. Our rescuer was neither a zombie law enforcement officer nor a roving psychopath. He was a wolf person, which is not the same as a werewolf. Thank fucking God.

"I'm Benny," he said. "And that's Maude back there."

Maude the wolfdog. Upon hearing her name, the huge shape rose up and out, extending into the cabin between Saff and Austin, who had gotten into the back seats. Then she decided on the appropriate action—licking Saff's face.

"She's a sweetheart," said Benny. "Don't be scared."

"Not scared," said Saff. "But she's ruining my makeup."

"Maude, let's not get too friendly."

Maude whined and retreated back into her space. I turned back to Benny, who looked ready to ask a whole host of questions which, considering his position, he was within reason to ask.

"So, wanna tell me what that was all about?"

"It's complicated, sir," said Austin.

"Hmph," Benny grunted. "So where am I taking you?"

"Our car's back at Walmart," said Saff.

"We can't go back," said Austin. He was correct on that score. We couldn't take the chance that The Sheriff would be there, hoping that we'd make the mistake of coming back. It's what an alpha predator would do—why use more energy hunting his prey when he knew where we would inevitably be? "Where are you headed?" he asked Benny.

"West to Idaho Falls. How about you?"

"Utah," I blurted out. "Eureka, Utah?"

"Utah?" asked Saff between yawns.

"The message came in." That's all I needed to say.

"Can't say that I'm heading that far south," said Benny. "But at least I'm going west. If you're okay with going to Idaho, you can ride with me all the way."

I called up the map app on my phone. I pinched and pulled to get our current location and Idaho Falls on the same screen. Goddamn. Between us and Benny's destination was the entire state of Wyoming. Ya don't say.

Fuck it. I was desperate. Quitting out of the app, I fired up a text.

PoltergeistRalph

Are you still awake?

My jimmy-leg was in overdrive. I could have pumped out some serious church organ tunes or spun a quilt to cover all of Cleveland, Ohio.

Sure as shit. What's going on?

I have a weird question. Don't freak out.

It's not weird. And let me say that I'm touched that you came to me.

Of course I'll tell you how to go down on a girl. I gots diagrams, yo.

That's not what I was talking about.

Then what is it?

> Can you help us?

In a series of frantic texts, I explained to Ralph what was going on, hoping that it made any sort of sense. Meanwhile, the back seat remained quiet and still. I glanced up to the rear-view mirror and saw that Austin and Saff had fallen asleep, their heads nestled into each other.

C'mon, LeRoy. Concentrate.

> You'll need a new car, then? I think I might be able to help.

> Serious?

> As a heart attack. Come find me at Grant General Store.

> Also, to double-check, you don't need those diagrams, do you?

"Can you drop us off at Yellowstone?" I asked Benny.

"I was planning on stopping there anyway, so sure."

I sat back, a wave of relief washing over me, followed closely by another rush of worry and doubt. Just because we were momentarily safe didn't mean that we weren't suddenly without a car, woefully underfunded, and terminally out of time and excuses.

I wanted to go to sleep and wake up back at home. But I dared not even rest my eyes. Benny seemed like a nice guy, but we'd just met him. He could have been an authentic good Samaritan, or he could have been a nefarious bat creature who sucked out your brains through your feet.

"I've learned not to pry," he began, "but should I be worried about something?" Benny looked over to me in case I didn't get what he was suggesting. Believe me, I did.

"I don't think so," I answered, trying to summarize the last twenty-four hours without sounding completely nuts. I eventually gave up and just came out with it: "There's a guy after us. He wants something we have." I reached into my backpack and rummaged around until my fingertips found the smooth plastic of the dragon cart. "This," I said, holding it up.

"What is that?"

"A video game." I almost laughed at how absurd this had to have sounded. We were running away from someone who was after us for a video game. A fucking game. The Sheriff didn't even have the decency to explain what he wanted with it. I mean, it was a *game*. Not only that—it wasn't like the game was one of a kind. Rare, sure. But how much was it really worth?

He smiled. "Maybe I'm slow, but that don't make sense."

I shared his grim sense of glee. "Nothing makes sense." Snatches of time seemed to flicker in front of my eyes with every set of headlights going in the opposite direction. "All the same, thanks for picking us up. It's the first real stroke of luck I've had in a long time."

"You too, eh?" he said.

"Not sure I follow."

"Guys like us. Losers."

"I'm not a loser." A bit too defensive?

"Yes you are," he insisted. "Hey, trust me. I know, and I can tell. I used to be a professional boxer. And I've been on the losing end pretty much every time out."

"What's your record?"

"One and two hundred seventeen."

"Two hundred seventeen losses?"

"Yeah. And the one win was by forfeit. The guy I was supposed to fight got lost on the Jersey Turnpike."

"You sound almost sad about that."

"Would have had a perfect record," said Benny. "Didn't really matter in the long run, though. I still got a plaque up at the Bronx Boxing Federation HQ. Benny 'The Bronx Bomber' Carone they called me. I thought that it was because they thought I was as tough as Alex Ramos, who had the name before me. Really, it was because as soon as I stepped into the ring, I'd bomb out." That may have sounded depressing, but you wouldn't have been able to tell from how happy Benny looked. It was like he was proud of being possibly the worst boxer to ever lace up the shorts and slide on the gloves. "You don't believe me."

"I believe you," I said. "It's just that I don't get how easy it is for you to say that you're a loser. I mean, maybe you can say you're a winner because you never stopped trying."

"Nah. I'm a loser. No bones about that."

"Well, I'm not one, okay?"

"Hold on. I think you misunderstand me." He raked his fingernails through his chin scruff. "You eat turkey on Thanksgiving? Like, where's your family from?"

"I'm Filipino—well, half. My mom's Filipino. But both of

us grew up in the U.S., so we have turkey and all that other stuff. That and eggrolls."

"Oh! Those tiny ones with the pork and green onions?"

"Yeah. Those things are like crack."

"You don't happen to have a recipe, do you?"

"No, and even if I did, I couldn't tell you. The Lola Mafia would come after me."

"Lola Mafia?"

"It's a quasi-legal ring of old Filipino women who run small food stores out of their houses. Best egg rolls you'll ever taste at twenty bucks a tray. But you have to know a guy who knows a guy who has a grandma."

"Heh. My parents were both from Sicily, so I get the whole in-between feeling. We had turkey, but only because my ma insisted on inviting *medigán*, as my father called them—Americans that she worked with at the shoe shop. Anyway, my point—one Thanksgiving when I was twelve, my pops wanted me to say the prayer before we ate. This was a big deal in my house. So I started saying 'God bless Mama and Papa,' and then I named everyone at the table and a bunch of people not at the table. And lastly, I said, 'And God bless the turkey.' Well, my father just burst out laughing at that. 'Don't be a *mameluke*,' he said. Then he explained to me that the turkey was probably raised on a farm and was happy as a clam getting fed every day. He probably didn't even notice when his friends and family would start disappearing, one by one. And then one day, the people who fed him would lead him out to a yard, and then, well, you know."

"He'd get killed," I said.

"Yup. For us to 'win' and have a Happy Thanksgiving, one

particular turkey had to lose. Really, all turkeys are losers. They're the fowls of destiny."

"That's kind of depressing."

"Maybe. But you gotta think about it like this. For every person that wins anything, there's got to be someone who loses. For every Rocky, there's a Spider Rico."

"For every Mario, there's a King Koopa."

"I'll take your word for it," he said, shrugging. "It's an important role. You gotta just embrace it." Benny glanced up at the rear-view mirror. "Case in point—look at them. A couple of good-looking young people in love. That means that there's some guy out there and some girl out there that's lost out. No shame in that. In fact, all those losers out there made it possible for them two to get together."

"See, that's where you're wrong—"

"Kid, you live fifty-seven years on this mudball, you see things. You meet people. You get to know how things work and how things feel. There's something between them."

That something was hormones. I mean, they've known each other for, what—a couple of days? Teens had needs. But that? It wasn't love, right? Attention-seeking. Loin feelings.

"They're not in love, okay? They just met."

"Aw, kid, I'm sorry. I didn't mean to—"

"Sorry for what?" I let out a shaky laugh. "They're just not in love, okay?" I looked at them again. Austin and Saff had curled into each other, a yin and yang. I wanted to pull them apart, wake them up so that they'd help me prove that I was right and Benny was wrong. Instead, I turned back around and stared straight out into the endless expanse of night. "You don't even know us."

"Understood," he said. "Why don't we change the subject? We got a long drive ahead, and I need you to help me stay awake."

During the course of the night, Benny and I talked—thankfully about stuff other than Saff and Austin—and occasionally stopped to let Maude have a short walk and bathroom break. And all through that time, my friends caught up on sleep. Eventually, I did too. Somewhere shortly past Billings, I must have dozed off, because I remember seeing the sign and noting that we'd made good time. The sun wasn't even up yet, and we were less than three hours away from Yellowstone.

The next thing I knew, Benny was shaking me awake. I opened my eyes and was instantly blinded by the sunlight coming through the window. When my vision cleared, I sat up and looked outside. We were parked in a lot next to a long wooden building. And around the lot were dense forests full of tall trees that seemed to go on and on into infinity. Fuck, we'd made it. We were at Yellowstone National Park.

"How ya feeling?" he asked.

"Um, okay." I turned around to find the back seat empty. "Where are Austin and Saff?"

He pointed off to them walking around the building. "They were a little confused about waking up here."

"I should explain to them—"

"You'll have time. One last walk with Maude?"

"Sure." I got out, went to the back, and let Maude out the hatch. It was surreal to see this huge wolf nearly the size of me wander out dopily and then sit still while Benny affixed her leash onto her. Benny had explained to me during our drive that she looked the part of a wolf, but was ninety-nine percent dog. The look, however, was enough to scare most prospective owners. He, on the other hand, loved hard-luck cases. They were made for each other.

Benny, Maude, and I walked into the forest a ways until we couldn't see the building—or Saff and Austin—any longer. Maude sniffed the ground and then scratched a couple of times at an old, gray tree that looked about ready to fall over.

"That's right," Benny said to Maude. "Not long now. You can tell." To me: "Maude has a knack for finding the dying trees. I think she's obsessed."

"Is that a dog thing?"

"It's a Maude thing. You know, she was really sick when I adopted her. Worms, fleas, the whole shebang. She got a sniff of the old Grim Reaper and it stuck."

"Well, you've taken good care of her. She looks great."

"We take care of each other," said Benny, his eyes dropping. "See how she's patting the tree with her paw? It's nearly done. A good, strong wind, and *timber*!"

"You should make a video of her. People go nuts for animals on YouTube."

"Nah. I don't need any of that. We're going to Idaho Falls to have some peace. Do some good work helping other dogs like Maude." Benny looked straight at me. "Y'know, I'm dying, too."

"Benny," I said, my breath suddenly hard to catch. "I'm so sorry. What is it?"

"Brain cancer. The big C. Heh, my father would have said that it was impossible. I don't have enough brains for them to be sick." He knelt down and placed his hand on Maude.

"She knew way before the doctors. That's my girl." Maude twisted, placing her front paws on Benny's shoulders and licking his face. He laughed a good, genuine laugh. "Thanks for keeping me company on the trip."

"I hope you win this one, Benny."

"Don't be a *mameluke*," he said, smiling. "My record speaks for itself."

How could he be so calm about this? I mean, he was talking about being fucking dead. That's not something to take lightly. It's something to fight, to stay angry about, to claw and scream and will yourself to victory over it. And if that doesn't work, you look into out-and-out cheating just for a chance at sticking around. But here he was, accepting it. Accepting loss. I couldn't ever do that. Gamers are programmed to win, and that's what we did—at all costs.

"Sorry if I hit a sore spot last night. About your friends."

"It's cool," I said. "You don't know them, that's all."

"Ah, well. It'll play out how it'll play out. That's not meant to be comforting. But that's fate for you." Fate. I've never been comfortable with that word. I didn't believe in fate—or more precisely, I didn't like to believe in fate, unlike Saff. *There is a fate*, she'd say. I'd rebut by saying that she was agreeing with the central premise of *Terminator 3*, and we both knew what a pile of shit that was. People die meaningless deaths every day, and fate says that they're *supposed* to go out that way? Was it fate that Benny was going to die? Was it fate that would leave Maude without her friend? Was it fate that had taken us farther and farther away from home no matter how much I tried to defy it?

Fuck that.

"We better go," said Benny.

"Thanks again. You really saved us back there."

"You never told me your name."

Fuck me. Here we go. "LeRoy. LeRoy Jenkins."

And nothing. It didn't seem to register with him at all.

"Good to meet you, LeRoy." Benny shook my hand and then came in for a hug. I gave him one right back.

9

YOU CAN'T PISS ON HOSPITALITY

After seeing Benny off, I cased Grant General Store for Austin and Saff, hoping to find them safe and sound and hoping not to find them safe and sound *and making out*. Not finding any trace of them, I ventured inside to see if they were there.

Sweet Jesus. Talk about an explosion of merch. There were the requisite kitschy keychain/bottle openers and fuzzy, bear-shaped slippers, and along the wall opposite the door was an old-style soda fountain counter, complete with red spinning diner seats. Toward the back was a fairly well-stocked grocery where campers could restock their provisions (at premium prices, of course).

Saff was by herself, eyeing the rack of face creams.

"Crème de la Mer or Golden Glow?" she asked, holding up two tins of face cream.

She wasn't going to talk about it. This was so like her to conveniently ignore the giant wooly mammoth in the room, even if it was taking a massive dump on the floor.

"So, why are we here again?" she said, applying a generous dollop of Crème de la Mer from the sample container.

"I had to make a decision on the fly," I told her. "My friend can help us."

"Which friend?" Saff looked at me suspiciously.

"PoltergeistRalph. You know, from the streams?"

"Wait a second," she gasped, her eyes widening with realization. "Are you going to be on *How to Catch a Predator*?"

"What? No! That's not—"

"Because Golden Glow is better for the cameras."

"We're not here for an illegal booty call!" I suddenly regretted how loud I said that.

"Then why?" It was Austin, surprising us from behind. "Not that I mind. Let's meet your friend."

I led the way, doing my best to ignore how couple-y Saff and Austin were acting. I wanted to turn around and ask Saff what the actual fuck. And then I wanted to punch Austin in the balls. But this wasn't the time for a scene. Passing shelves of Yellowstone-branded sweatshirts and pewter statuettes that resembled silver splooges locked up mid-projection, I led the way to the cash register manned by a tall, sandy-haired surfer-looking guy organizing individually wrapped postcards.

"I'm looking for Ryland," I said.

"In the back, dude," he said, pointing to a door marked "Private" by the restrooms. Our little caravan set forth toward the back when we heard a voice shout, "I'm about to layeth the smacketh down on you would-be rulers of Catan!"

I peered through the slightly ajar door. Five people were seated around a table, a full-on gridlocked game of Settlers of Catan in progress. One of the players, a girl with pale blonde hair streaked with a dash of purple at the front, stood over the others.

"So for my turn," she began, "I'd like to discuss terms of surrender. Hand over your resources, and I'll graciously spare your lives."

"This isn't how the game works," said a dude in a Michigan State sweatshirt.

"Au contraire," said the blonde girl. "This is a game of crushing your enemies, seeing them driven before you, and hearing the lamentations of their women! Now what's your answer?"

"Stop wasting time, Ryland," said another guy, a straight-laced, fratty-looking guy with chiseled abs showing through his too-tight T-shirt.

"Ain't no time being wasted here. Surrender or die!"

"No!" said the last girl, a red-haired cheerleader, all-American type. "You can't threaten us."

"Well then, I'll start by invading *your* territory—with my bloodthirsty army!" The blonde girl laid down her entire hand of cards, all showing illustrations of sheep. Normally in Catan, you gathered and traded commodities to construct settlements and control economic thoroughfares. A diversified portfolio was best—a nice combination of brick, lumber, sheep, grain, and ore would allow the savvy player to take over the game board with mercantile prowess.

Ryland had a different plan. Cornering the sheep market for imperial conquest was a novel approach, certainly worth a commendation for original thinking at the very least.

"First, they'll eat all your wheat. Then they'll shit in your bricks." Ryland took two sheep cards and dangled them around each other like they were humping. "And then they'll fuck like crazy so that your mines are stuffed full of wittle baby lambs."

Everyone else at the table slammed their cards down with a groan and walked out.

"Double-J!" she said, once she saw me. "You are officially the best YouTuber any fangirl could ask for." She practically leaped into my arms and hugged my neck tight enough to make me lightheaded.

"Ahem," said Saff, coldly. "Introductions, Jupes?"

"Well, hello, hello," Ryland cooed, taking Saff's hand. "Je m'appelle Ryland. Enchanté, ma chérie." Then she turned to Austin. "Buenas dias! I'm Ryland. I hope you like my park."

They shook hands. "Your park?" asked Austin with an eyebrow raised.

"Right. It's mine. You like fudge?" She led us out into the store, grabbed a box of chocolate from a shelf, and opened it right up. "Don't be shy."

He smiled politely. "It's a bit early."

Ryland popped some fudge into her mouth. "So, I-way ear-hay ou-yay eed-nay a-way ar-cay."

"A car," I said. "You can get one?"

"It depends. Where are we going?"

"*We* are not going anywhere," said Saff.

"If you want wheels, we're a package deal. Comprende?"

"You can't just invite yourself to things," said Saff.

"You're so cute when you do that."

"Do what?"

"That! Besides, this is a take-it-or-leave-it thing."

"Welcome aboard," I said. Shots across the bow.

A throat clear from outside our circle of trust broke us apart. We turned and standing there was a gourd-shaped man—his body overly inflated but his head a tiny, tiny Ping-Pong ball on top of his neck. Eugene, I presumed. He pointed a stubby finger right into Ryland's face and said, "Ryland Taggart! Do you know why I'm upset?"

"If it's about the vibrator, I can explain," said Ryland. "I use it to masturbate. Like all the time."

"This is not the place for such coarse language!" said Eugene, seemingly out of breath. "How many times have I told you to clear all the Etch A Sketches out?"

"You want a specific number, or . . . ?"

"Just go do it! This is a family establishment, and we don't need those *things* on display." He grunted as he stomped away to another corner of the store.

Ryland shrugged and led us over to a section of the shop gussied up for the younger set. Board games like Hide the Pic-a-Nic Basket and the National Parks edition of Monopoly (in which you buy and sell our nation's precious natural treasures for power and profit) lined the shelves.

A whole wall was devoted to Etch A Sketch tablets of various sizes, from your full-size in traditional red, to smaller, baby blue models for the artistically inclined toddler. Except on this day, every single Etch A Sketch pad had been decorated by a drawing of a penis. Some were more detailed than others—detailed as in more anatomically correct, with even tufts of hair in creative places. Others were more Picasso-esque in their jagged representations of the penile ideal.

"Welcome to my job," said Ryland, clearing out the pads. "Most girls get paid a lot more for shaking dicks around."

"That's disgusting," said Saff with disdain.

"Oh? Maybe later, you and I can have a private sit-down about how much we don't like penises. Interested?"

"Uh, you mentioned the car situation," Austin said, bringing the conversation back to sanity.

"Can't discuss it here." Ryland slipped a keychain off her belt, took a long brass key off the ring, and set it in my palm. "Go straight down that road out front and take the first path to the right. Then you wanna go to the big building all the way at the west side of the parking lot. Room 201. Store your shit, take a shower, and I'll meet back up with you. It shouldn't be long."

"Taggart!" Eugene screamed. Ryland rolled her eyes.

"Duty calls," she said.

We followed Ryland's directions to her room, which she apparently shared with a troop of angry and possibly rabid baboons. Around the room were piles of clothes that had no discernable organizing strategy, and in the center were two double-sized mattresses pushed together into some kind of mega-bed.

The distinct stench of B.O. and pot lingered in the air. I didn't care. A place where we could put down our stuff and actually rest was sorely needed. Saff didn't quite agree.

"I need a bath just to cope with this." She promptly shut herself in the bathroom, and a second later, she cried out, "Ever hear of cleaning out the drain? Ugh!"

Once again, that left me and Austin to talk—like with words and shit. We sat for twenty more minutes until one of us, Austin, broke the silence.

"Saffron said you have my music box."

"Yeah," I said, digging out the box from my backpack. I tossed it to him, quietly hoping to catch him off guard. I didn't, of course. Austin caught it like a pro, opened it, and took out the *Forever Throne* medallion. He draped it around his neck and placed it inside his shirt. "About last night—"

Barging through the door to the room came Ryland bearing gifts—a smorgasbord of fudge, rock candy, fruit leather, and locally made deer jerky nabbed from her place of work. Just in the nick of time. God forbid we dudes converse about deep shit.

"Hola, mis amigos," she said. "Where's the chick?"

"Saffron's in the shower," said Austin.

Ryland smiled. "Let me dwell on that image." She tossed her offerings onto the mega-bed, along with a bunch of green T-shirts like the ones store staff wore. Just then, the bathroom door swung open and a newly fresh and so clean-clean Saff emerged through the steam like a goddess descended from heaven.

"Oh. It's you," she said upon seeing Ryland. "What are those?"

"Work clothes."

"Work?" asked Saff, with suspicious eyes. "For who?"

It turned out that we'd arrived in Yellowstone at an auspicious time. A large percentage of the summer staff had been ravaged by a bad flu. To take up the slack, reserves from facilities park-wide were continually shuffled back and forth. Ryland eagerly volunteered for these bouts of extra work, if only to spare herself Eugene's constant berating. She'd nominated us to join the ranks of the unfairly unpaid as well. That day, there was a gig to volunteer at Old Faithful Inn, the high-end lodge where choice travelers could spend a shit-ton of money to experience Yellowstone's most beloved natural offerings—y'know, like buffets, room service, and plumbing. More importantly, it was where our contact for the car would meet us. So, naturally, we went—though not altogether willingly.

"I want to officially say that I'm doing this under protest," Saff stated when she jumped out of the van and into the parking lot. "I'm not built for menial labor."

Ryland pounced on that opening: "Maybe you just need someone to test your stamina."

"Have I mentioned that I hate you?"

"In other words, you're falling for me."

"Jupes, she's so annoying!"

Ryland further explicated our task for that day. The hotel's restaurant needed some extra support for a large business meeting that afternoon. That meant two things. One, there was probably a free meal in it, a full-on, real-ass dinner instead of mixed nuts and pudding cups. And two, we'd be able to talk to Melvin, the dude with the car.

Walking into the lobby was like walking into the rustic hunting retreat of a medieval king. Through a pair of oversized red doors was a lobby featuring a seven-story stone chimney extending from floor to ceiling. Spiraling around this central spine were wooden terraces winding upward like an ornately carved ribcage. This place was a *Game of Thrones* set that would also double as a backdrop to a Harry Potter LARPing session. Our handy-dandy (or, according to Saff, ugly-as-sin) shirts enabled us to waltz past security and into the corner office (read: broom closet) where Melvin held court.

Melvin, a springy-curled dude with sleepy eyes and droopy lip, looked up from his desk, where he was eagerly perusing that week's JC Penny circular, laughing as he turned the pages. He looked surprised to see us.

"Whoa, Ry-dogg. Way to announce your entrance."

"Catching up on lingerie sales, Melvin?"

"No, man. These things are hilarious! That kid looks like a tool!" He pointed to a young boy wearing a denim vest and a backpack, smiling just like the photographer must have told him to. "So you're my lapdogs today?"

"Eugene's fault. Fucking guy's all up in my junk about showing Yellowstone spirit."

"Do you have to keep talking about your crotch?" Saff cried.

"Yes. Yes I do."

"Let's jet, foolios." Melvin led the way upstairs, pulling out a crumpled piece of paper from his back pocket and reading tasks off it. In the second-floor lounge, a smattering of early-afternoon drinkers was already getting the booze on. It was *vay-cay*, I guess. "It looks like we have to prep the second floor deck. The Federation of Astrological Enlightenment is having a shindig tonight."

"A con-artist convention," said Saff. "Fucking great."

"I think that stuff's kind of neat," Ryland said.

"You would."

"You're such a Scorpio."

"I just need to stop talking to you."

The second-story deck was as choice a spot as you could get to Old Faithful without jumping the fence and being tackled by park rangers. You were close enough to feel the hot spray raining down if the wind was blowing the right way. Melvin directed us to split into two-man teams (me with Ryland and Saff with Austin) and conducted our movements: "Like, that table goes there, man. Oh, and that chair . . . Yeah. Like that. Or maybe not? I don't know." Luckily, arranging tables was pretty easy to figure out. Eventually, Melvin just took a seat and scrolled through his phone while we literally did all the heavy lifting.

I snuck looks at Austin and Saff talking, lifting, laughing. I lifted and heaved my sorrows away, helping Ryland to finish rearranging and tableclothing our section before Saff and Austin polished off their section. They weren't even half done, all that *having fun* getting in the way.

"Picking a scab doesn't make it better," said Ryland. She gave me this look that I'd seen Mom sport on many occasions, the *we-both-know-you're-full-of-bullshit* look that she'd get when I tried to nod away her suggestions for taking up yoga or the new fad diet her fellow professors *just happened* to tell her about.

"I can't help it," I said. "It's like watching the Large Marge scene in *Pee-Wee's Big Adventure*."

"I get it. You know it's coming, you don't want to watch it, but you *have* to watch it." She took my hand and pulled me up to my feet. "So let's go help them."

"But what about the whole scab thing?"

"Better to rip it off all at once."

She pulled me over to where Saff and Austin were working in time to catch Saff at the tail end of a story: "So his Mom said, 'well, why don't you have the lobster, then?' He was so pissed that he picked up one of those cheddar biscuits and crushed it in his hand like this." And then she cupped her hand like Thanos clutching the Infinity Gauntlet. "But that wasn't enough."

Wait a second. I knew this story.

"Saff!" I shrieked.

Saff, suddenly sheepish: "Oh hey, Jupes."

"What are you talking about?"

"Nothing."

"It didn't sound like nothing. It sounded like . . . *The Lobster Incident*."

"Um, what if it was . . . *The Lobster Incident*?"

"We're not supposed to talk about . . . *The Lobster Incident*."

Saff looked at Austin, then looked at Ryland, and finally looked back at me. "Okay."

"No way," said Austin. "We have to know what this is."

"It's highly inappropriate!" I insisted. Because it was. Because everyone does shit when they're really little that they regret, stuff that at the time made sense in your half-formed mind, but in retrospect only got more and more embarrassing as time went on. For me (I can't believe I'm confessing this), it was the time when my family went out with Saff's family, way back when Nikhil was still around and when our moms didn't think that the other was a secret demoness ushering in the end times. We'd gone to, of all places, Red Lobster to have a nice dinner. Only, I didn't want to go to Red Lobster. Because I hate fish. I hate shellfish. I hate any food that once swam in the ocean. I know this is heresy for a Filipino, but I'm only half—that's my excuse. If it swims in the sea, I want no part of it. That didn't stop Mom from insisting that I eat it, citing omega-3 fatty acids and muscle-building protein.

That day, she only managed to convince me to go by promising that I could order the macaroni and cheese, which I did. But when it came, there were clearly bits of ground-up crustacean in the cheese sauce. Mom had betrayed me! This would not stand! And to prove my point, I stood up on my chair, unzipped my pants, and . . .

They say that you can't piss on hospitality. But that day, I proved that you sure as fuck could do just that on the chive-and-cheddar biscuits. Mom grounded me from all video games for a month and made me write a letter of apology to the head of Red Lobster. Not the manager of the particular restaurant, mind you, but the CEO of Darden Restaurants, Inc., who owned the whole fucking chain. A few weeks later, I got a reply that consisted of a lobster bib and a fifty-percent-off coupon for Red Lobster's all-you-can-eat shrimp festival.

"Amigos!" exclaimed Melvin, holding a tall glass of blue liquid and chomping on a turkey club sandwich. He took a sip from the straw and said, "Grub's inside, buddies! You know what they say—ya snooze, ya don't get free shit."

With all four of us on the job, setting up the remaining tables only took fifteen more minutes. And then our reward: our pick of any dish on the menu, including dessert. We ate out on the patio along with Melvin, who'd drunk his way through one of those lethal-looking drinks and had started on another.

"Good job, dudes. I couldn't have done it without you."

"You could have," said Ryland. "But you wouldn't have."

Melvin sipped his drink. "So true."

"About the car," began Austin.

"I know you know the dudes at the service station," Ryland said to Melvin. "They got that van in the back that's been covered in a sheet for weeks."

"That thing?" said Melvin. "Tad says it needs a new alternator, but his boss won't sign for it. Too expensive."

It took a moment for the reality to sink in. She wanted us to *steal* a car.

"*Borrow*," Ryland explained. "No one will know it's gone."

"Except Tad," said Melvin. "And he won't be sad."

"I don't have a problem with it," said Saff.

Ryland gently placed her hand on Saff's. "Thank you."

"You're touching me."

Ryland went back to scheming. "The way I see it, we get access to the garage, fix the car, and drive it away. I have a guy with an alternator. No probs."

"You've got some connected friends," Austin remarked.

"Sure. Friends." Ryland pulled a folded-up piece of paper from her pocket—one of those souvenir maps of the park with all the prominent tourist attractions labeled—and spread it out on the table. "My room—where you guys were earlier today—is right here." She pointed to a spot on the western side of Yellowstone Lake. "And right here . . ." She moved her finger over to the left—". . . is the lot for all the official Yellowstone cars." Her finger moved again, over to a red gas pump icon. "That's the service station."

"So we know where everything is," said Austin.

Ryland nodded. "And knowing is half the battle. But the

other half . . ." She pointed to Melvin. ". . . is execution. We need you to help us clear the way, Mel."

Sluuuuuurp. "Sure. Um, how?"

"Steal the garage key from Tad."

"Dude, I can't do that," said Melvin. "Tad's my boy. He's one of my most valued customers." We all stared at him for a second to clarify: "Christmas trees. My family owns a farm in Iowa. He buys from us every year."

"Oh," I said, "I thought you were going to say—"

"Dude also buys a shit-ton of pot from my garden."

Yeah. That. I hoped that negative karma didn't stack like penalties in D&D (though they probably did because apparently fate was a merciless, merciless dungeon master). I'd already earned enough bad mojo from stealing the dragon cart from Chuckie. What more a whole car?

While I deliberated on the eternal stains my continued descent into depravity was searing onto my soul, Saff was quietly studying Ryland's map. And, as we know by now, bad things happened when Saff was quiet. To be fair, bad things also happened when she wasn't quiet—horrible, nasty things like:

"I have a plan!"

Sparks singed the air when Saff said that, like mini bolts of insight from a cold, cruel universe.

10

RAMPANT NINJA RELATED CRIMES THESE DAYS...

After finishing our food, our tasks shifted from dinner prep to dinner serving. Ryland and Austin—the two of us with food-service experience—waited on people while Saff and I did cleanup duty as buspersons. We'd originally pegged Saff as a perfect waitress, as pretty people often got bigger tips. We found quickly that this only applied to pretty people who didn't irritatingly insist that astrology was, in fact, an extraterrestrial mind virus meant to make our skulls suitable for alien infestation.

By 9:00 PM, we'd served our last plate of bacon-wrapped dates, swept the deck free of crumbs and stray cocktail straws, and tossed all the tablecloths and napkins in the laundry bin. As a bonus, Austin and Saff had gathered up

$166 in Washingtons and the occasional Lincoln. We actually felt pretty accomplished for this and for getting the inside track on a ride to carry on with our quest. The good feeling stopped abruptly back in the parking lot.

We were walking back to the Yellowstone van when Saff stopped dead in her tracks. She'd been scanning her phone for our latest YouTube metrics when she screamed bloody murder.

"*Jupes! Les jeux sont faits.*"

"*Quelle surprise, ma chérie,*" said Ryland. "I didn't know you spoke French."

"She doesn't," I informed her. *Les jeux sont faits* was the code phrase Saff and I used to convey the deepest, darkest, most foul depths of shit we could find ourselves in. The last time either of said it was when Saff went on her date with the son of a Transylvanian baron who wanted to give her a personal tour of his authentic Moldavian torture implements collection. I showed up just in time to save her from being cut up and stored in a meat locker (probably).

This situation was far worse.

"It's my mom," said Saff. "Jupes, she knows."

Shit. "Let's not panic," I said, entirely meaning it. And then I felt my own phone vibrate—a message from Dad. That no panicking line went straight out the window. *Les jeux sont faits.* Translation: *The game is up. Your ass is mine!* A waterfall of swears poured out my mouth.

Saff started losing it. "They're going to triangulate on our signals right now! I bet the department of parental control at Google is pinpointing our phones! We're fucked!"

"It's okay," said Austin.

"It is NOT okay!" wailed Saff.

"I think we have to call them back," I said. We were in damage control mode, and the best we could do at this juncture was enter negotiations for a grounding that concluded sometime before *the end of the universe*. I tapped Dad's image in my contacts list and got prepared.

"Hello?" said Dad. Funny, he didn't sound distraught. "Sorry if I'm interrupting anything."

"Um, that's okay."

"Good. One question—are you and Saffron in South Dakota right now? Because Anjeli really thinks that Saffron is in South Dakota, and last we knew, she was with you."

"We're not in South Dakota," I said. "We're in Wyoming."

"Sure, sure. Those are different states," he said, nonchalantly. "Another question?"

"Go ahead."

"Why are you in Wyoming?" At that, the background noise became filled with shouting, and a second later, Anjeli's voice came blaring out my phone.

"Lee, put Saffron on now." Shit. I dangled my phone out to Saff like it was made of plutonium.

"Hi," she said weakly. And then it was on. A torrent of non-English followed as Saff battled her Mom in her first language—the Portuguese-speckled Konkani language native to the Goa region of India. This put Saff at a disadvantage, which Anjeli was well aware of. This is a particular thing that plagued first-generation Asians all across America. Mom used to tell me about how her own parents would do that all the time to her, how they'd code switch into Ilonggo. She hated it because they were obviously talking about her, but she couldn't penetrate the conversation. *I'm mad that I can't do it to you*, she'd tease.

She was joking. Mostly.

"I know what I'm doing!" shouted Saff. "Hello? Hello? She hung up on me!" Before we could reassess the situation, the phone lit up again with a call from my dad. I took the phone and answered.

"Anjeli's a little upset," he said with a weary voice.

"How did you find out?"

"South Dakota state police," he said. "They found Saffron's car abandoned in a parking lot. We thought that it had to be a mistake, but they knew the license plate and everything. Then they described the car's condition."

"Condition?"

"They said it looked like . . . how did they say it . . . oh, like 'Godzilla did it in the butt.' We were worried, Lee. Really worried."

Why did I feel like Dad was setting me up for the punchline of a very, very bad joke?

"So we called your mom."

FUUUUUUUUUUUUUUUUUUUUUUUCK!

"She didn't answer, so I left a message."

Okay, good. Crisis temporarily averted.

"But then she called back a couple minutes later."

No! Crisis unaverted!

"And then Anjeli asked her where you were."

This is the most unfunny joke in the history of man.

"And then your mom got upset."

In other news, air is good, water is wet, fire is hot!

"And then she made me promise to find you."

With the power of the DARK SIDE!

"And that when I did, I should tell you to expect her call."

No. Fucking. Way.

"Are you in a safe place?"

"We're safe," I told him, which was true, save for my imminent and long-delayed *hara-kiri*. Just then, my phone buzzed, and up popped Mom's image on my phone.

"There's a call on the other line," I told Dad.

"Who is it?"

"Who do you think?"

BUZZZZZZZZZZZ!

"Why does she hate me?"

"She doesn't hate you, Lee."

"It feels like it! I'm just a constant failure to her!"

"You really should answer," said Dad, as politely as he would ask me to pass the salt. Answering was the last thing I ever wanted to do on this goddamn Earth, just after leaping off a cliff into a ravine full of rusty needles and lemon juice. But fuck me, I did it. Didn't even say hello.

"LeRoy Jupiter Jenkins, you will tell me right now what in the world is going on!"

"Well," I started. "Me and Saff—"

"I knew it! How many times have I told you that she's not good? Where are you right now?"

"Yellowstone National Park."

"This is outrageous, Lee! What were you thinking?"

"I don't know," I mumbled.

"Well, we'll have to get you out of there," she said, followed by muffled talking. "According to John, there's some kind of . . . He'll tell you."

The characteristic rustle of a phone exchanging hands followed, and then I was suddenly talking to, of all people, John Fucking Stalvern. It's true what they say—when it rains, it pours malicious, flesh-eating space parasites.

"Lee," said John, rather calmly. "Your mother is rather upset."

"She made that pretty clear."

"I think the best thing to do is sit tight. I'm going to reserve a room for you at the Old Faithful Inn. It's a grand place. You'll love it."

"I've been there. It's okay."

"Tomorrow, George will send his plane to pick you up at the Yellowstone airport and drop you back off in Chicago."

"George?"

"George Lucas." Muffled: "What time, George?" Then to me: "Be at the field at eleven o'clock. Lee, are you there?"

I didn't know. Was I there? John was telling me that we were going to ride George Lucas's private jet back home? What was I supposed to say to that? I mean, here was the man responsible for one of the greatest sci-fi franchises ever created and simultaneously the man arguably responsible for its downfall. And he was offering his pimpin' ride to a bunch of kids who'd never met him but judged the fuck out of him because it was fun to do on the Internet. My brain short-circuited from these conflicting realities—one very real, the other an electronic fantasy that I was a little ashamed to be a part of at that moment.

"I'm here."

"I'll call your father with the details," he said. "Also, be sure to eat at the inn's bistro. The pork osso buco—*c'est magnifique!*" What the actual fuck was going on? Why was John Stalvern suddenly sounding like a human being? "Will you be okay, Lee?"

"Uh, yeah. I think so."

"Good. Stay safe. We'll see you soon."

"I will."

I hung up.

"What is it?" Saff pleaded.

"John's arranging for a plane to pick us up tomorrow at Yellowstone Airport."

"John has a private jet?"

"It's not his," I said. "It's George Lucas's."

"THE FUCK YOU SAY WHAT?"

"It doesn't matter," said Austin. "We stay the course."

No. Fuck this guy. "In case you didn't notice, our fucking lives are imploding!" I said.

"Boo fucking hoo!" he shot back. "I don't have a home to go back to, so I'm going forward."

"Why do we have to come with you?"

"Jupes!" yelled Saff, her jaw tense. "I'm not going back, either."

"But your mom—"

"What if fucking Indiana Jones was like, *too many Nazis*?" she said. "What if the Voltron Force was like, *four out of five lions ain't that bad*? What if the Ghostbusters were like, *well, actually, bustin' doesn't make me feel good after all*? This is our fucking destiny, Jupes. Yours, mine, and Austin's."

"What about me?" said Ryland.

"Did you hear something? Anyway, my point is that as long as we're out here, we have a chance to do something amazing. Our parents, they want the best for us. Right now, they're doing what's best for them. But here? Right now? It's our time, and we gotta get shit done. Who's with me?"

"Me," said Austin, placing a hand on her shoulder.

"You are like so hot right now," said Ryland. "I'm in."

All eyes were on me. Man, you ever get that weird feeling that you stand at a crossroads in your life? Choose one way, and your life spirals out in a particular direction. Choose the other way and you end up in a place at the opposite side of the universe no matter how slight the difference at the start. There was the responsible way: going home, taking my lumps, and then trodding down a well-defined path laid out by my parents. Then there was the other way. The void. The unknown. That scared me shitless, completely sans feces.

"I'm not going to convince you otherwise," I said to Saff. I meant it as a question, but it came out as a firm declaration of truth.

"No," she said. "Going forward is the right thing to do."

The right thing, the non-mediocre thing.

"Fuck it," I spat out.

"Fuck it *good*, or fuck it *bad*?" asked Ryland.

"I'm going. Just promise me that as soon as we find our answers, we'll go straight home."

"That's the plan, LeRoy," said Austin.

"Also," I noted, "I'm pretty sure Saff ripped off her speech from *The Goonies*."

"It's a good speech, Jupes."

Back in Ryland's room, we binged on the snack smorgasbord she'd brought earlier. The sugar and salt took the edge off the anxiety high of talking to Dad. Saff coped with the situation by going over the plan again and again, searching for potential flaws. With the map in front of her, she traced her finger from location to location while dictating the optimal course of events:

1. Melvin calls Tad to arrange a meeting. It doesn't matter over what, and it would probably be better if we didn't know. In any case, they are to meet at the service station, where Melvin is supposed to leave the back door unlocked.
    a. This is the riskiest part of the plan.
        i. We don't know if Melvin will be able to do what we want him to do.
        ii. We don't have a better option for gaining entrance into the garage.
        iii. We're pretty sure Melvin is constantly stoned.
2. Ryland calls her contact to arrange a rendezvous.
3. Melvin texts Ryland when the way is clear.
4. We move out, making the journey on foot to the main access road between Grant General and the service station, where Ryland's contact will meet us.
5. We get inside the station, Ryland's contact makes the switcheroo with alternators, and we all get out of there.

We chilled until it became dark and waited an extra hour to give the employees of the store and service station time to clear out. With that, we ventured out into the humid evening with Ryland manning point with a flashlight. Bringing up the rear was Austin to make sure that no hyper-inquisitive fellow conservation interns were following us. Saff and I were in the middle, walking side by side. She'd changed into uniform for this mission, a little cosplay into the tight black leather bodysuit of the Baroness from *G.I. Joe*. Predictably, this was quite popular with the people watching her stream an impromptu (and ill-timed) video update on her phone.

"Saff and Jupes here," she whispered into the camera. "You might be wondering what's been going on with the channel. I won't lie—there have been a few snags. Right now, we're in Yellowstone National Park. But shh. Keep it on the DL. Our lives have never been more in danger."

"You're being a bit dramatic," I said.

"Jupes here is trying to be strong for you, but seriously, this is life and death. No matter what, we're proceeding with the ultra-secret mission. And by ultra-secret, that means we can't tell you."

"Then why are you telling them?"

"Because we have a responsibility to our fans."

Ryland stopped and shot an angry look back at us. "You obviously haven't seen enough heist movies. First rule of doing something quasi-illegal is to shut the fuck up!"

"That's superfan PoltergeistRalph as our special guest tonight. Leave a comment and tell us if you want to be on the show, and what you're willing to do to make it happen!"

Ryland rolled her eyes. "Your face looks puffy."

"That's a lie! Take it back!"

"And let's not talk about the muffin top."

Saff sighed. "This is the last time PoltergeistRalph will be on the show, so enjoy it while it lasts. Later, my dears!"

"How's it back there?" Ryland called back to Austin. "Everything clear?"

"I think so," he said. "I hear noises, but it's probably squirrels or chipmunks."

"Or shadow people," Saff muttered.

We journeyed westward on a forest trail that crossed a

couple of paved roads en route to Grant General Store. Once we stepped out from the treeline, the sky shone brighter than full-on street lamps. Of course, we needed to stay hidden. If we could see things, things could see us. Just then, a light turned on inside the store, so we ducked back into the brush.

"It's been closed for an hour!" said Ryland.

Passing by the window was Ryland's manager, Eugene, drinking from what looked like a carton of milk.

"Please don't let this be a messed-up fetish," Ryland pleaded. "I gotta work with that shithead."

"What if he's, like, a secret drug lord?" said Saff. "Eugene, Emperor of Meth?"

"No way. He's an idiot."

"Maybe that's exactly what he wants you to think."

"He's coming out," Austin said.

The front door to the store swung open and out stepped Eugene, thankfully with pants (we'd been expecting the worst). He leaned down and placed a small bowl on the ground, and then poured milk into it. Like bees to honey, or, well, kittens to a bowl of milk, a bunch of cats walked in from the surrounding brush to come lap up some of that dairy fat. Eugene knelt and scratched each one on the head.

"I think my ovaries just exploded," said Ryland.

Waiting a minute longer, we made our move along the tree line once Eugene was clear. We ducked in and out of cover like we were LARPing *Gears of War*, all the while keeping the store in sight until we came to the edge of another parking lot.

"There's good news and bad news," said Ryland.

"Good news first," Saff insisted.

"We haven't been caught yet."

"That's barely neutral news."

"All right fine. There is no good news."

"What's the bad news, then?" asked Austin.

"From here, it's a sprint to the next group of trees. The problem is that light." She pointed to a lamp mounted on a pole in the middle of the lot. "We'll be exposed and in the open. If we're not fast, we'll get caught."

"You mean I'll get caught," I said. Saff and Ryland were small targets and would be hard to spot. Austin was tall, but could lope like a werewolf to cover ground quickly. That left me—slow, clumsy, jelly-rolled me. The tree trunks had shielded my girth so far, but that wouldn't be the case out in the open.

"It's not about speed," said Austin. "It's about timing."

"If only we could shoot out that light," Ryland commented. "My kingdom for a sniper rifle."

"Saff could climb and knock the bulb out," I said.

"Thanks for volunteering me, Jupes."

"You used to climb up to the clubhouse all the time."

"Sure, when I was ten."

"That was only six years ago."

"But I'll be seen!"

"You're dressed as a ninja!"

"A sexy ninja," Ryland blurted out. "Um, carry on."

"Fine. But if I fall, I'm kicking her ass."

"What did I do?" said Ryland.

Saff skipped through shadows until she reached the iron rungs of the ladder. Her all-black Baroness costume more or less cloaked her in ninja magic, allowing her to ascend unseen until she reached the top of the pole twenty feet up.

With a gloved hand, she took hold of the light bulb and gave it one, two, three twists, casting the area into darkness.

"Gun it!" Ryland said. We ran for the other side of the lot. Immediately she and Austin were ahead of me—in one blink, ten feet ahead, and in two, twenty. I barely made it to the pole when I completely lost sight of them.

"Hey! I can't see!" I heard someone call out. In the starlight, I made out the vague outline of Saff making her way down the rungs.

"I'm here!"

"Jupes? Where's everyone else?"

"They're ahead of us. C'mon." I helped her down from the pole and then dragged her along with me as I ran where I'd last seen Ryland and Austin heading. Sure, the lack of light gave us cover, but it made it nearly impossible to be sure where we were going. Eventually, we reached a bunch of trees on the other side of the lot. But where were the others?

"Where are they?" Saff dug out her cell phone and turned on the LED. "Austin? Where are you?" We heard what sounded like footsteps on the other side of the trees, so Saff and I walked in that general direction hoping to find our friends. Instead, we found ourselves face to face with a burly security guard brandishing a flashlight.

"What are you doing here?" he said, startled.

Saff and I froze in shock.

"Uh . . ." I started to say. "We're lost?"

"No one's supposed to be in the park."

I tapped the bullshit spigot hoping that enough would come out to cover our escape: "We're with a special program—the Night Rangers."

"Night Rangers?"

"Yeah!" said Saff, piggybacking off me. "You know how there are animals that are only active at night-time like the Chupacabra."

We were fucked, weren't we?

"How come no one's told me about this?"

"It's brand new." Ryland emerged from the brush from behind the guard, startling him into entangling himself in some low-lying branches. "There you are!" Ryland's face had a wide smile on it—too wide, from where I stood. "I'm sorry, officer. I told them not to wander off, but you know these young lovebirds. All hormones and no sense."

"I should call this in."

"You really shouldn't," said Ryland, helping the guard out of the brush. "I don't want to get your superiors in trouble for not informing you about the program. Lord knows that they'll just pin the blame on you, and then you'll be fired."

"On me?"

Ryland put on her best patronizing mother face. "Yup. I'd feel so terrible. And the kids would, too. Wouldn't you?"

Oh yeah. Uh huh. Sure thing.

The guard's fingers inched closer to the radio on his belt.

"Look at those faces," said Ryland. "They're so in love! Take young Hildegard right here. Just a couple months ago, she survived by jumping little kids before school, stealing their lunch money, and then using it to buy candy bars, which she would sell to diabetic mobsters at above-market prices." Then she pointed to me. "And that's 'Silkworm.' He had his tongue ripped out while fighting in the battle-pits of Indochina. Dude's only fifteen, and he's a living weapon, but you wouldn't know it with how much he loves butterflies!"

"But I heard him talking just a minute ago."

"They've come so far!" Ryland faux-sobbed.

"Just move on and go home, okay?"

"Will do, officer." To us: "Mosses and lichens will have to wait." We followed her away from the scene and didn't look back until we reached a two-lane road. There was Austin, standing next to another person—a black-haired woman straddling a motorcycle.

"Found them," said Ryland as we all approached. Austin ran straight for Saff.

"I thought you were right behind me."

"Who is that?" said Saff, looking past Austin toward the mysterious woman. This was the person we were supposed to meet? She looked like Wonder Woman—tall and dark with broad shoulders and arms like knotted ropes. She just stared at us without saying anything.

"Double-J, Saffron—this is Vera."

The woman hit the motorcycle's kickstand with her boot and let it rest.

"Faith," she said, tossing her helmet back to Ryland, who caught it. "Only my mother calls me Vera, and I hate my mother." She had a distinct Eastern European or Russian accent, something I hadn't expected to hear out here. "Where is this car?"

"Back that way," Ryland said.

"Push my bike," said Vera—er, Faith—looking at me. "Break it, I do the same to you, пизда."

"Jesus Christ, Vera!"

"Call me that one more time, and I fucking leave."

"Fine. *Faith*. Don't shit on my friends."

"Your *friend* better not trip."

I wheeled Faith's bike along slowly, measuring my steps to not lose my grip and let it crash to the ground. I mean, Faith was only a little taller than Saff and not much thicker. Yet, I completely believed she could break me like she threatened.

The service station showed no signs of life. Ryland had a look around to the back door, which easily opened with a twist of the knob and a click of the latch. Score one for Melvin. We snaked through the office and through the door that led to the garage proper, which stunk like grease, gasoline, and sub sandwiches.

"There she is," said Ryland, channeling her innermost Khan Noonien Singh. "Not so wounded as we were led to believe. So much the better!" Ryland may have seen the jewel in that junky car, but I sure didn't. If any vehicle could possibly look like a bigger piece of shit than *Hell on Wheels*, it was that sorry jalopy. Maybe once it was a serviceable vehicle, one of many identical vans used by Yellowstone staff to get around the park. Now it was a puke-green piece of shit with the arrowhead-shaped symbol of the National Park Service peeling off the side.

"Shit, this thing is locked," said Saff, trying the driver's-side door. In fact, all the doors were locked. Ryland and I went back into the office and scrounged around for keys, knocking a pile of washers and sparkplugs onto the floor. Of all the things we'd thought about, how did we forget about the car keys?

"Got it!" yelled Austin, wrenching me from my thoughts. Ryland and I went back out to see what the commotion was about. Austin had taken off his shoelace, tied it into a loop, and slid it into the car window, which was open a crack.

After a few tries, he'd snagged the door lock and pulled it open.

"How'd you know how to do that?" I asked.

"You learn things when you need to," he said, pulling open the door and sliding underneath the seat. "Go find a hammer, a screwdriver, wire-cutters, some heavy rubber gloves, and electrical tape."

"Are you performing surgery or something?"

"There's only one way we'll get this thing to run without the keys."

He was going to hotwire the car. And dammit, if you could have seen Saff swoon over Austin's gesture of gallant illicitness, you also would have seen my face twist into a mask of absolute disgust. Before I could say anything, Ryland clutched my arm and dragged me back into the office.

"What are you doing?" I said, wresting my hand away.

"Saving you from your shitty mouth. Now help me find those tools."

"This isn't about me!" But of course it was. Ryland was perceptive enough to know what my deal was. Every time Austin did something terrible, like interstate kidnapping, property damage, and now carjacking, Saff was all over him like syrup on a waffle. When I did stuff like stay behind and help her down that light pole (ostensibly lawful good things), I got jack. Nothing. No thanks and no praise and definitely no kissing.

While I stewed, Ryland quickly checked off all the items on Austin's shopping list. She ran and delivered them back to Saff, who was holding a light for Austin to see by. While they were occupied with that, Faith was busy under the hood of the car. I continued to absent-mindedly look around the office, trying to distract myself from my own pissy mood. Pulling open a drawer, I spotted the sizable candy stash of one of the mechanics—probably Tad's private reserve after enjoying some of Melvin's Christmas bounty.

"Now we're talking!" said Ryland, coming back into the room. "They even got Zagnut!"

"I'm not hungry," I said, which was a lie. That Kit Kat bar was calling to me.

"You have a problem."

"Don't you think I know that? You think that seeing them *together* makes me feel all tingly inside? Because it doesn't!"

"That's not the problem I was talking about," she said, tossing a Three Musketeers bar at my face. "Your problem is you're too fucking worried about what other people are doing. You're worried about your dad. You're worried about your mom. You're worried that Saff's gonna start boning Walker Texas Ranger out there and leave you high and dry."

"You don't understand—"

"Believe me, I do," said Ryland. "Your parents sound real messed up, but at least they care. My dad's a fucking corporate lawyer who helps shady fucks get away with murder, probably literally. That, and he hates my fucking guts. I'm not going to waste my time worrying about him. And you shouldn't worry about what your parents are doing. That's their jam, not yours. And as far as Saff goes? Sorry, dude. She's her own person. You can't will someone to want the naked shimmy with you."

I maybe wouldn't have said it that way, but the truth was

the truth. Everything—Saff and Austin, Dad and Anjeli, Mom and John Fucking Stalvern—was more than any amount of whining would soothe. My life had detonated hardcore, and I didn't know how to handle it.

"As your emergency big sister, I hereby offer myself as your designated decision-maker," said Ryland, her mouth full of Butterfinger bar. "First decision—stop dwelling on shit you can't control."

Too late, I thought, as the engine coughed and sputtered to life.

11

THIS IS WHAT HAPPENS WHEN YOU FIND A STRANGER IN THE ALPS

D espite its looks, our new ride ran like a dream, thanks to its brand-new alternator. We cruised right out of Yellowstone—we four in the van and Faith leading on her bike—without anyone trying to stop us. For over an hour, all you could see was the wall of darkness on the left formed by the dense brush, the same on the right, and the strip of nighttime sky between that extended from horizon to horizon. In the last third of the journey, the trees parted and the skies opened up, giving way to scrubland backdropped by shadowy mountains.

Saff was struggling to get Spotify to work on her phone.

"The one time I actually want to hear Grim Reaper!" she exclaimed.

"So about where we're going," said Ryland, who was at the wheel. "It's Faith's bar. The place is a little rough."

"Why are we going there again?" whined Saff.

"Because after all the shit we've been through, I think we all need some down time."

"Exactly how rough is it?" asked Austin.

"Ever seen *The Warriors*?"

Onward we went into Jackson, Wyoming, a resort-type getaway for the über-rich and/or über-famous to lay low and pretend that their expensive ski lodges and high-end outdoor facilities gave them a taste of "normie" life. Downtown Jackson was a bastion of neons and incandescents, rumbling motors of antique muscle cars on joyrides, rowdy bluegrass karaoke nights spilling onto the sidewalks. Three Starbucks cafes within a mile of each other? Check. Two cowboy-hat stores on opposite corners of the same intersection? Double-check.

Eventually, the lights dimmed and the ritzy storefronts started to thin out. We were entering an older, shadier, somewhat truer part of town—one not propped up by corporate coffee hounds and an infinity of artisan sandwich shops hocking meat wheels. Our destination was a grungy wooden building ready to fall from either age or termite infestation. A faded red neon sign displaying the bar's name flickered in the window: *Bourneau's Tap*.

"Who's Bourneau?" I asked.

"The guy who used to own this place," said Ryland. "Faith won the bar in a card game."

"Must be a card shark," I said.

"Nah, she took down an illegal gambling ring that the old owner had set up. Wore a wire and everything. The state seized the property, and she bought it at auction for cheap."

"How old is she, exactly?" asked Austin.

"Old enough to kill you if she heard your question."

We entered Bourneau's on Faith's heels, and holy Mon Woo's flashbacks. Bourneau's had the same danger-filled verve that we'd encountered back in Minneapolis, with one notable difference. There were no men in sight save for the lone tatted-up Mohawk dude serving up booze at the bar. Other than him, it was all chicks as far as the eye could see.

"Did I mention that this was a dyke bar?" said Ryland.

Faith was standing at the bar giving orders to Mohawk dude. "Alexei, four Cokes!" She flicked her chin over to our little outfit standing inside the doorway and then waved us over. "Here," she said, spreading out the drinks on the bar. "Drink." Mohawk dude also pulled down some bags of pork rinds from an adhesive strip on the wall for us to eat. High times here.

"Oh, I can't," said Saff. "Do you have—"

"No," said Faith. "Now sit down and don't make trouble." Then she sidled right up to Ryland. Close. Uncomfortably close. "We are even now, yes?"

"I guess," said Ryland.

Anger flared in Faith's eyes, followed by a steely coolness.

"You always were a fucking bitch, Ryland."

"Takes one, Vera."

"Give me your phone."

"Gladly." Ryland tossed her phone to Faith, who caught it easily. She accessed Ryland's contact list, sifted through the names until she found her own, and deleted her entry. Then she pressed the phone back into Ryland's hand and held it there, pushing her whole body against Ryland.

"Don't ever contact me after tonight."

"I won't."

"Good."

"Awesome."

"Perfect."

And then they started making out like they were trying to swallow each other whole. It was uncomfortable. I retreated to my glass of Coke. Austin and Saff did the same. We sat there not saying a peep until Ryland turned to us and said, "I'll be back." She and Faith ran to the back door and exited together.

"I think I need another shower," said Saff.

Austin swiveled his bar stool and sat back against the countertop. "We're so close, LeRoy," he said. "I can taste it."

"All I can taste is high fructose corn syrup," said Saff.

"What do you think we'll find in Utah?"

"How about destiny?"

That word again. Destiny. Fate. It had hung around the fringes of our trip the entire time, enticing us with potential greatness. Maybe I was letting my pessimism get the better of me, but all I could think about when I heard the word *destiny* was the string of shitty things that had happened to me ever since that damn *WoW* video made its way onto YouTube. That's what it was to me—shitty thing after shitty thing, one after the other.

"Check, check," said a woman into the microphone on the stage at the back of the room. Great, we'd come just in time for karaoke to begin.

"Let's dance!" said Saff, leaping off her chair and walking

over to the tiny square of dance floor underneath a spinning disco ball. "Austin! C'mon!" He looked at me with a curious smile and a shrug as he hopped off the bar stool. I grabbed his arm and pulled him back. All conflicts with him aside, I couldn't let him make this fatal mistake.

The fate of the universe depended on it.

"For the love of god, don't do it," I said.

"What are you talking about?"

"Don't. Let. Her. Dance. The things that I've seen . . ."

"You're acting crazy, LeRoy."

"Crazy? I'm not crazy!" Actually, I was kind of crazy, but it was for a good reason. See, the only dance I'd ever been to in my entire school career was the seventh-grade mixer at Aida Ward Junior High, in what could be construed as my first and only "date" with Saff. She'd been hyped to show off her dance moves, which she'd painstakingly constructed by locking herself in her room and watching hours of Britney Spears, Christina Aguilera, and Beyoncé videos. Come the night of, we walked into the school gym, and I have to admit that I felt some kind of pride. At all of twelve years old, I'd started feeling other things for Saff besides the usual frenemy feelings. Loin feelings. And why not? I was the guy who brought the hottie to the dance. I had the trophy on my arm, the apple of all the other guys' eyes. I was the fucking man.

Until she got out on the floor and started dancing to Lady Gaga's "Born This Way." People cleared out the dance floor, creating a circle around her. She took this to mean that she was the star of the show, that she was John Travolta and this was her personal *Saturday Night Fever*. In actuality, she was a walking, dancing Umbrella Corporation unleashing a hellish t-Virus of moves closer to a demonic worship ritual to Shub-Niggurath than *Step Up 2: The Streets*.

In short, that shit was wrong.

"It'll be fine," he said, and he walked off to join Saff in front of the jukebox, which had started playing—gasp—a groovy *slow-dance* song. I could only watch in terror as she wound up her arms and started thrashing the air in an inexplicable mutant abomination of off-time gyrations, spastic arm movements, and inexplicable little kicks.

Sweet fancy Moses. It was happening.

That's when Austin surprised me again. He gently took Saff's hands in his, and with a smile, got her to move to his rhythm. No words were exchanged. None were needed. She ceased to be jerky. The kicks stopped. No more flaying of fists in random directions. It was just him and her moving gracefully in their own world.

Fuck. That was the moment that I knew I'd lost her for real. No conjecture, none of this *still-in-the-realm-of-possibility* bullshit that I'd been feeding myself all these years. The dream was done. Over. Dead. What Benny saw— I couldn't deny seeing it any longer. Maybe it started on that night between Minneapolis and Deadwood, and it grew behind my back, under my nose. However it came about, that connection between Austin and Saff was undeniable, no matter how determined I was to deny it.

Even so, I couldn't sit and watch it. I left the bar and jumped back into the van, where I could have a moment to myself—a moment I finally allowed myself to cry. What started as a whimper quickly burst into a wave of burning heat in my stomach like a gravy-soaked Portillo's Italian beef sandwich with extra peppers. Soon, snot was running out my nose. Tears scarred my cheeks like alien blood.

Suddenly, I heard a noise from the rear of the van. I turned around to see what it was, only for Ryland to rise up from the back, her shoulders bare and her hair mussed up. A moment later, Faith sat up next to her holding her shirt shut.

"This is awkward," said Ryland.

"You," Faith ordered. "Get out of here."

"Sorry, I—"

"Double-J, it's cool." To Faith: "Can you give us a few minutes?"

Faith scrunched up her face. "We were doing something."

"I know . . . it's just . . . c'mon."

With a scowl, Faith pushed her way past Ryland and leapt out the side door. "Take as long as you want. I don't care." She slammed the door and stormed into the bar. Ryland slid back down into the seat, and a pants zip later, she made her way up to the passenger seat.

"You have impeccable timing," she said.

"Sorry."

"Don't be. It's complicated, like thermodynamics."

"Sorry again."

"Stop apologizing for other people's shit."

"Sorry. I mean, sorry I said that I said *sorry*."

She placed her hand on mine. "Where are the lovebirds?"

"Still inside," I said. "I was kind of a third wheel. Or fourth or fifth wheel." She gave me that *I thought we talked about this shit* look. "I'm trying! I can't just fucking turn my feelings off!"

"Let me level with you, Double-J," she said. "I'm horny

like twenty-four seven. Like seriously, I just want to fuck ALL. THE. TIME. And you'd figure that I'm not a virgin, and that all the illusions about sex have been broken. But no— it's as good as advertised. Better, even."

"What happened to not following the V?"

"Do as I say, Double-J. Not as I do."

"That's the thing!" I said. "It's not even about sex. We like the same things, watch the same movies and TV shows, even finish each other's sentences. There's no one else in the world that knows me like she does."

"Sounds like a good friend."

"But I don't want to be her friend!" I rested my forehead on the steering wheel. "I'm going to be alone my entire life. I mean, who the fuck would want to be with me, right?"

"Double-J, stop."

"Fat rolls as far as the eye can see. And that's not even counting how I'm singularly untalented."

"Seriously, you need to shut the fuck up."

"Like really? What do I do?" I stared at the ceiling of the van, as if the answer to my question would peel back the roof and descend from on high. "Mom was right. I've amounted to nothing in my life, and now that I'm actually accountable for it, what do I have? I suck. I suck! No one's ever going to be with me. I'm never going to have sex. I'm never going to be kissed!"

"Why do I have to do everything myself?" she said. And then taking my face with both her hands, she leaned in and kissed me. Hard. On the mouth. With tongue. Lots of tongue. Then she threw me backward into my seat and sat back with her arms crossed. "There. Now knock it off."

"You . . . I . . . but I thought . . ."

"It's nothing, Double-J. Kisses are just kisses."

No, it wasn't just a kiss. It was my *first* kiss. And it was not what I expected—the fireworks, the beauty, the rush of feeling that I'd always thought would accompany my lips locking with someone else's wasn't there. That's not to say that I didn't think Ryland was pretty or that she was bad at kissing (not that I had any frame of reference). It's just that I hadn't expected it to be so wet and slimy, didn't think it would taste like deep-fried pig skin.

I mean, it's absurd, right? Jamming faces together shouldn't be something we want. But I did want it. Experiencing it firsthand only let me know exactly what I was missing. I imagined that Ryland's tongue was Saff's, that her hair was falling into my face, and that when I pulled away, she'd be there smiling at me. None of that was true.

"I think I feel worse now," I said.

"Yeah, it was a stupid idea." She curled up her legs in the seat, pulling her knees into her chest. "If it was that easy to stop loving someone, everyone would be doing it." She punched the ceiling, shaking dust bunnies loose. "Fuck love."

"But aren't you and Faith together?"

She gave me this look—I'd seen Saff do it plenty of times—that *please don't make me have to tell you look*, that *I'm 'bout to shut you down* look, that clenched-jawed, twitchy-eyebrowed, *gonna get REKT, son* look. "How am I gonna . . ." she muttered to herself. "Ah! Okay." She sat up in her seat and cleared her throat. "Darmok and Jalad at Tanagra."

"Wait a minute," I said. "Are you speaking Tamarian?"

"Don't interrupt." Ryland held out both her hands in

front of her, her palms up. "Darmok on the ocean," she said, curling her left hand into a fist. She *was* speaking Tamarian, one of the many made-up languages of the *Star Trek* universe. Only, it wasn't a straight-up language at all, like Vulcan or Klingon. It was more a set of allegories meant to stand in for certain situations. Jesus, it had been forever since I'd seen that one episode of *TNG*, but I'd managed to lock down enough of it to meander through her meaning. *Darmok* is a name that represents a person, probably Ryland herself. And being "on the ocean" means being alone, feeling alone.

"Jalad on the ocean." And in came the other fist. Jalad represented an outsider, someone else who came to where she was. Someone equally lonely. Did she mean Faith? "The beast on the ocean." And here, she formed a circle with her thumb and index finger on the left and moved her right index finger back and forth through it—the universal gesture for "doing it."

"Darmok and Jalad at Tanagra," she continued. Then she pointed to herself and made a gesture like she was being whisked away into the wind. "Mirab, with sails unfurled." I was pretty sure that meant that she'd left the relationship, if not physically, then at least emotionally. "Zinda, his face black, his eyes red! Kiteo, his eyes closed!" She shook her left fist vigorously. Someone was mad, and that same someone refused to listen. That, I could plainly see, meant Faith. "But the beast . . ." Again with the finger through the hole. *Do as I say*, she'd said before. And now I could understand why. No matter what her brain told her about the world, no matter what truth she'd uncovered about people and relationships and love, all that got trumped by what she felt when she was with Faith. Like a drug. A beast that was always hungry.

"Shaka, when the walls fell," I said.

"Sokath, his eyes opened!"

"You could have just told me all that normally."

"No, I couldn't have. Besides, I needed to test your nerd cred. You passed. Barely. F+."

"Then why? Why do we want something so fucked up?"

"I don't know. Some people think that you have to fill your heart with something, and that biology makes it easy to think that it's that one perfect person. *Romeo and Juliet* shit. Think about it—maybe we only want 'love' because it's force-fed to us by books and movies and everything else. Buy this box of chocolates! An expensive bouquet of flowers for your honey! A butt plug shaped like former Panamanian dictator Manual Noriega!"

"A what now?"

"TMI. My point is that maybe we should fill our hearts with that toxic waste shit at the end of *Robocop*. So when someone breaks your heart, they'll be really fucking sorry— and possibly a radioactive mutant that explodes into goo when you run them over with your car."

Ryland and I sat there letting everything soak down into our pores. Both of us were a little broken, a little leathered and weathered.

"Fuck this place," said Ryland, jumping out of the van. "Let's get the barf-worthy duo and jet."

I nodded. I'd had as much of the barf-worthy duo as I could stomach. Moreover, it was soon going to be apparent to the 'rents (and to George Lucas) that their rescue plan was a no-go. And then fuck-all was going to happen. Best to be as far along as possible before the biggest pile of shit ever hit the rickety-est fan ever made.

We ventured back into Bourneau's with a mission. It was like the jazz-club scene from *Spider-Man 3* in there (the Tobey Maguire version). Everyone had gotten up from their seats and stood watching Saff and Austin cutting a rug on the dance floor. Ryland and I marched up to the edge of the crowd but were stopped by Faith.

"What are you doing back here?" she said to Ryland.

"Getting our friends and leaving, *Vera*."

"Good. That saves me the trouble of kicking them out."

"Glad to do you a favor, then."

"Leaving was the best thing you ever did for me."

"Second best," Ryland quipped back, putting two fingers on her lips.

"I hate you."

"Hate you first."

Oh God, please don't start making out again. Please.

"Fine," said Faith. "Then this is goodbye. For real."

For the slightest split second, Ryland's mask of confidence broke. The tips of her mouth struggled to decide between flat affect and frown. Her breathing got faster. In this contest of who would lose her cool first, was she the one who would falter?

"Then goodbye," Ryland said, turning away. I moved to follow, but Faith slid in front of me.

"She is running with you, now?"

"Yeah. I guess."

"Then let me ask you this." She pounded the bar with her hand, and like clockwork, Alexei poured her a glass of clear liquid from an unlabeled bottle. One whiff of that shit was enough to make my eyes feel like they'd bathed in onion juice. Faith slung the whole glass back and asked for another. "You think she is strong?"

"Yes?" I said, not sure what she was getting at.

"Wrong. She is a scared child like the rest of you. You think she is wise about the world, but she is not. And when you need her the most, she will not be there."

"She's my friend."

"Which is less than what she was to me."

"Why don't you tell her that?"

"Because this place is not for her."

"So you *do* care about her."

Alexei poured another glass of paint thinner. Faith downed it like she did the first.

"If she gets hurt, if anything bad happens to her, I will find you and kill you."

"I don't think that's necessa—"

"It will be painful," she said, her hair shrouding her face.

Ryland returned with Saff and Austin in tow. Faith stepped out of the way and turned back toward the bar. Back out in the humid night, we all climbed back into our stolen ride.

Onward, to Utah, to uncover the secrets of *Forever Throne*. And none too soon.

12

Press F to Pay Respects

The night carried on into day, with us taking turns on driving duties so that we could each enjoy a few hours of sleep. My turn was the shift after Austin, from 3:00 to 4:30 AM or so. The mountains and the rivers decorating the landscape were entirely lost in the nighttime, allowing my imagination to fill in the blackness. My thoughts meandered until they settled on the conversation Ryland and I had at Faith's bar. What was I supposed to do with Austin and Saff? Was I supposed to do anything?

Shaka, when the walls fell.

I didn't arrive at an answer. At 4:30 AM, I handed over driving duties to Ryland and promptly fell asleep in shotgun. I woke up to Saff at the wheel, not-so-quietly singing along with Sisqó's "Thong Song" on the radio. How the others managed to stay asleep I had no idea.

Where are we?" I asked, squinting from the sunlight.

"Almost there," she said, tossing her phone onto my lap. The programmer's coordinates were keyed into her GPS. We were a little blue dot on the screen moving steadily closer to the red pin that was our destination. Fifteen minutes out from the town of Eureka, Utah.

"How you feeling?" she asked.

"Crusty."

"That's disgusting, but I don't care. You know why?" Uh oh. Saff sounded happy. That meant something was wrong. "How many views do you think last night's video got?"

I pulled out my phone and *oh shit*.

"It's over nine thousand!" she squealed.

That was a lowball. Our view count as of that moment was 17,844 for a span of around eight hours. For a low-quality two-minute video? Understandably, for YouTube juggernauts like Jenna Marbles and Boogie2988, this was dinky potatoes. They could reach that number in twenty minutes. But for us? This was big.

"We're doing it, Jupes. You and me. Like we said."

Sure. Saff and me, whatever that had become.

My phone started to vibrate. Shit, I'd missed three calls from the previous night—two from Dad and one from Mom's cell. No way in hell I was going to listen to the voice mails they left, because I could pretty much predict that they'd just be additional exhibits in the case against me being a human being of measurable worth. There was also a text from a phone number with a 775 area code—Reno, Nevada? Weird.

Or not so weird.

(775) 287-9183

> Lee, this is John. I wanted to make sure you're okay and see how you liked the hotel! Your mother had a rough night, so best to call me directly at this number. We also want to make sure that you're at the airfield on time. Call me before 9:00 this morning. After that, I'll be in press events all day.

"I need to call him," I said.

"You certainly do not!" Saff said, swiping at my phone.

"He was trying to help us. The least we could do—"

"Is what we've done," she said. "Jupes, we're nearly there. Don't mess this up."

"He put himself on the line for us."

She shook her head and smirked knowingly. "Oldest trick in the book. Gain their trust, and then shove them into a nuclear accelerator."

"Not everyone thinks like you," I grumbled. "Can I at least text him?"

Her glare game was strong that morning. "Do whatever you want. I mean, who wants to listen to me? It's not like the Loch Ness Monster totally isn't a conspiracy by the Rand Corporation to secretly harvest dinosaur DNA for military use!"

> I got your text. There was a change of plans, so we won't need the plane. We're still heading west. Will call later. Hope Mom feels better.

> Also, tell George thanks.

After another minute, John shot me one last text:

> Your mom won't be pleased. But I suppose that can't be helped at this point. Please let me know if you run into trouble. If you can't reach me, call my agent. She's located in Reno. I'll send you her number.

"Good now?" Saff asked.

"Not really."

Our drive toward the coordinates took us right through the heart of the town of Eureka, Utah. While not technically a ghost town—the houses and cars parked out on the outskirts proved that non-undead people lived there—it was still a stabbed-in-the-gut-and-bleeding-out kind of place. Its humble downtown, with its mining museum and unassuming City Hall, was deserted. No people, no chipmunks, no birds—nothing but a few cheeseburger wrappers as proof of life.

We were all alone.

The west side of town was in the roughest shape. Instead of being merely empty, it was littered with buildings that were actively falling apart. You ever see photos of River

Country, the water park by Disney World that was abandoned when new and better ones opened nearby? West Eureka had that same eerie sense that you're being watched, just behind a corner or through a broken-out window. Adding to the spookiness was a distant rumble of thunder, followed a split-second later by a fork of lightning cracking the sky.

"Storm's coming," I murmured.

After a few more minutes, we'd cleared the town completely. The few traces of humanity quickly thinned out, leaving us with only hilly scrubland north and west of town. Tiny droplets of rain started pelting the roof of the van. I hoped that we didn't have very far to go. We followed GPS to where the map showed a small road jutting out from the interstate and headed into a location called Cole Canyon.

"I don't like this," Saff muttered.

Agreed. This was straight up getting creepy. "You sure you typed in the right coordinates?"

"Positive," said Saff. "But right now, I think it's more important to talk about the cannibals."

"Cannibals?"

"They'll want you the most. I mean, you do offer the best meat-to-bone ratio."

"I can't believe you've thought this through!"

"Negotiations have to start somewhere, Jupes!"

Truth be told, I wasn't scared of man-eating mutant psychopaths. I was more scared that my dream from a couple days before was coming true. A grease-stained man. A beard billowing in the wind like flame. Huge arms brandishing twin sawed-offs. And he called himself *The Sheriff*. Every second that passed, I feared seeing his gorilla-like silhouette rise up from the asphalt with shotguns akimbo and a cigar in his mouth billowing plumes of black smoke.

"You have arrived at your destination," the phone blared out. Our little blue dot was sitting right on top of the red pin. Saff stopped the car and stared out the windshield at a lot of nothing. I mean, that's not altogether true. There were bushes. And a small lizard darted from rock to rock, trying to get a good look at us. *Oh shit*, I thought. *Was this some kind of trap?* I shot a look over my shoulder, slightly expecting to see The Sheriff there. What I saw instead was, thankfully, not that. But not nothing, either.

"Saff. Get out of the car."

"Why? What is it?"

"Just get out of the car and turn around."

Both of us hopped out and met back up behind the van. Built into the side of a hill facing away from the highway was some kind of dwelling place. It would have been a stretch to call it a "house." There was no "roof," no "porch," no "chimney" in any conventional sense. Just a gouge made of concrete and sliding glass doors.

"I'll wake up the others," said Saff. "You send a PM to the programmer guy."

Understood. I sent a quick PM to *bjs* and waited for a response. The thunder had grown deeper since we'd left town, and I could feel the ping of tiny water drops on my nose. This wasn't going to be a light drizzle—more like a fireball-spitting, laser-sword-swinging, bazooka-toting beast and feast from the days of yore. We needed to get indoors real soon.

By the time Austin and Ryland were up, the drops had

grown heavy and fat. Still no word from the programmer, but we couldn't just stand there. We approached the doors to the place, hoping the lack of an answer was because of a phone on mute or a dead computer.

Austin rapped his knuckles on the front door. "Hello? Anyone home?" Ryland didn't wait for a response and just tried the door. It slid open with ease.

"This feels like a trap," said Saff. "Watch out for laser tripwires."

"Settle down, Bourne Identity," Ryland said.

We stepped inside. No alarms, no killbots programmed to search and destroy, which was a little surprising because of the serious moolah splooged all over the place. The décor inside was the crossbreed baby between Apple store sleekness and Tomorrowland retro-eccentricity, but with a weird artificial tint. The appliances in the kitchen—which we passed through first—all looked like *Star Wars* droids. A fruit basket on the counter was still wrapped in plastic, even after the apples and oranges inside had shriveled and rotted.

"Let's get out of here," Saff said.

"Hello!" Austin called out.

"That's the opposite of what I just said!"

"We're here," I said. "We might as well see this through." I couldn't believe I was saying that, and I really couldn't believe that I was on a side with Austin versus Saff. I mean, she was right to be afraid. The owner was in his rights to repel intruders with deadly force if necessary. I took note of the knife set next to the toaster oven just in case.

Heading into a living room, we encountered the same feeling that this was all for show, like a house staged to sell. We'd reached the last of the ground-level rooms. The only way left to go was down, via a staircase that spiraled into a basement area.

"That's where the C.H.U.D.s are hiding," Saff said.

"C'mon," said Austin, leading the way down. "We're wasting time."

"You're brave," said Ryland.

"Impatient," he said. "Besides, if anything happens, don't I die first?" That is the movie rule—that and never, *ever* go back for the cat.

Slowly we descended until we reached some kind of den or lounge space. No expense was spared for this man cave. Built into the far wall was a giant widescreen TV, something like a hundred inches, with a big subwoofer on the floor. And around the ceiling were surround sound speakers perfect for playing survival horror games like *Alien Isolation* or *Dead Space*. While all good, none of these caught our attention more than the apparently dead body of a naked man in the center of the room.

"Oh my god," Saff gasped. "Is he . . ."

"I don't think so," said Austin, putting his ear to the man's mouth. "He's breathing."

"We should call the police," I said.

"No!" said Saff, knocking the phone from my hand. "We're sunk if the narcs get involved."

"Saff, this isn't *The Wire*!"

"He's going to need some water," said Ryland, who joined Austin's side. "Find him some clothes," she told me and Saff. "Me and Austin will get him upstairs onto the couch."

Done and done. Saff and I started scrounging around the room, finding, among other things, a bong, old burrito wrappers, and several empty bottles of whiskey. In an adjoining bathroom, we scoured the cabinets and drawers filled with the usual toiletries, but still nothing we could use. Then we both glanced down at the dirty clothes hamper.

"Fuck no, Jupes. I have a line."

"They're just used clothes."

"Of a crusty dude with saggy man-butt. No fucking way."

Fine. I stuck my hand into the pile, feeling around until I snagged a pair of jogging pants. I fished them out along with an AC/DC T-shirt with a greenish-brownish stain on the front. Best not to think about it, I thought. I turned to go back upstairs when Saff stopped me.

"I'm getting really weird vibes from you and Ryland."

"I don't know what you're talking about."

"You disappeared with her last night." Why did she even care? It was clear that she was more than occupied with whatever was happening between her and Austin. I was vying on her priority list with chopped liver, and the liver was winning.

"Saff, she likes girls."

"That's the perfect cover. You're always *leaning* into her. Like that one tower in Italy."

"The Leaning Tower?"

"That's the one."

"Some help?" Austin yelled. "This guy's heavier than he looks!" Saff begrudgingly let me through, and I rushed over to catch his leg when it slipped out of Ryland's grasp. Together, we carried the unconscious man up the stairs, laid him on the couch, and slid the clothes on over his limp arms and legs.

"You're sure he's not dead?" Ryland asked Austin.

"He made some sounds."

"Yeah," said Saff. "Braaaaaaaaains."

I crouched down to look at the guy closer. He was breathing, but shallowly.

"I have an idea," said Ryland. She bolted into the kitchen and started noisily rummaging through the refrigerator, cupboards, and drawers. Then she moved onto the rest of the ground floor. A couple of minutes afterward, she brought back an armload of miscellaneous supplies scavenged from around the house and spread them on the coffee table. "All he needs is a little pick-me-up."

She started by slamming her fist into a packet of children's Tylenol until it became powder, and then poured it all into an oversized coffee mug that read "Damn, I'm Good" on the side. Next came a couple of antacid tablets, then two heaping spoonfuls of instant coffee crystals.

"What are you making?" I asked.

"One of Faith's inventions," said Ryland, pouring half a bottle of flat Pepsi into her concoction. It fizzed minimally at first, but then frothed up thanks to the antacid tablets. In a few seconds, the mug was overflowing with dense brown liquid that resembled melted chocolate ice cream, but which smelled like a dead rat stuffed into a dead skunk shoved into an old gym sock.

"Jupes, I'm pretty convinced that she's crazy."

"Miracle hangover cure," Ryland said, putting the cup to the unconscious man's mouth. Some liquid made it into his mouth, but an equal or greater amount spilled onto his cheeks, down his neck, and then onto the couch and carpet. We watched over him for a minute, hoping for a sign of life. Then, all of a sudden, his eyes shot wide open as if he was in pain. He rolled right off the couch and onto the ground, gagging on the horrible stuff Ryland had given him. "It just *hurts* a little going down."

Rolling over again, the man breathed hard and looked around at each of us in turn. He focused his eyes on me. "You're those kids from YouTube," he said, weakly. "What are you doing here?"

"Um, you invited us?" said Saff. She pulled up the PM on her phone and showed him. "You're Bryan, right?"

He took her phone and read the message, furrowing his brow as he did so. "Oh, shit." He pulled himself up into a sitting position against the couch. "I don't remember sending this."

"So was it someone else?" I asked.

"No," he said. "It's only me here, so I must have sent it." He frowned and massaged his forehead. "Now that you're here, what do you want with me?"

"Answers," said Austin. "About *Forever Throne*."

"Do you have it? Do you have the game?"

We took out the dragon cart and the medallion for him to handle and look at.

"I haven't seen these in more than thirty years," he said. Looking up, he focused his gaze on Austin. "Nate was your father?"

"Yes."

"What did he tell you?"

Austin paused before speaking. "He died. A couple months ago."

"Oh God." His face went even more pale than it already was. "I'm so sorry."

"It's fine," said Austin. "We just want to know more."

"Help me up." Austin and I pulled the man up and steadied him until he could stand on his own. Then he beckoned us to follow him back downstairs into the TV room. "Nowadays, I design missile guidance systems for the army. Strict hush-hush stuff. But back in those days, I was nineteen years old, poor as shit, and didn't know anything. Best time in my life. Now where is that thing?"

Bryan started feeling up the wall behind the TV. He didn't say what he was looking for, only that everything would make sense once we saw. Did he intend to show us a video? A catalogue of photographs of his phone? Secret microfilm? No to all of those. There was a click, and a second later, the entire wall slid back and then receded, revealing a pitch-black passage with a whoosh of cool air.

"I apologize for the dust," said Bryan. He hit a light switch on the other side of the door, and one by one, overhead lamps turned on with a crackle and a buzz. "It's been a while since I've been in here." *Here*, like he was talking about a charming attic where he stored his rock collection. No, this was just the opposite.

"Holy fucking shit," I said under my breath. Because really, *holy fucking shit.*

Before us was a ramp leading down to a long, long room with arches and columns on either side. In the middle of the room were rows and rows of pristine arcade cabinets. Along with the lights, the cabinets bleeped and blooped to life, washing the room in vibrant neon colors and the unmistakable symphony of old-school chiptunes.

"It's a personal collection," Bryan remarked as he led the way. I scanned the names of the games as we walked past them. Of course there were classics like *Tempest, Asteroids,*

Breakout, and *Pac-Man* in minty mint shape. Between those were more obscure titles like *Black Widow* (some kind of *Tempest* clone), *Devastator* (sort of like an over-the-wing POV space shooter à la *Space Harrier*), *Inferno* (an isometric run-and-gun), and *Thayer's Quest* (a full-motion Laserdisc game like *Dragon's Lair*).

"I think the joystick on *Mad Planets* is sticky. Gotta remember to get that fixed."

Bryan continued to lead, and we continued to follow, right through a door at the end of the room, which fed right into another room—this one smaller, its walls made of wood and glass. Upon closer inspection, the glass panels along the walls were windows with some kind of wallpaper on the other side to make it look like it was outside on a bright summer day.

And that didn't even take into account the room's contents. Instead of arcade cabinets, the room was filled with glass cases, each containing some piece of video game memorabilia. Some featured symbols and names that were instantly familiar.

"Jupes!" yelled Saff as she ran up to a life-size statue of Samus Aran, the hero(ine) of the classic Nintendo game *Metroid.* She stood there in battle pose, her helmet on and her arm cannon raised and firing. "This thing is awesome!"

"That stood in the foyer to Yamauchi-san's office at Nintendo headquarters for many years," said Bryan. "It took a lot of convincing to get it over here. And a lot of money."

"What is all this?" asked Ryland.

"This is my hall of fame," he explained. "All these things I've collected over the years—even the room itself. It was an Elcon Industries Model 1 trolley. A mobile arcade."

This was all too much. Chuckie had nothing on this dude. This wasn't only a collection. This was a museum of the highest order. I couldn't help but think what a shame it was that all this stuff was buried underneath the ground in the middle of nowhere—away from people who would love to learn more about it.

Bryan didn't let us linger very long. He continued to lead us further, deeper into his lair. I mean, what else could he possibly show us that wouldn't top what we'd already seen? The ground had been sloping downward the entire time, but after leaving the wooden room, the incline of our path increased enough to slow our pace to a crawl.

"Just through here," said Bryan once we reached a metal submarine door with old-school wheel lock. "One last stop."

On the other side of that door was a dark, circular room. The only light source came from lines of light shining through the floor panels leading from the center of the room, up the walls, and meeting back up on the ceiling. It would have made for a pretty epic Laser Tag arena. In the dead center of the room was a black pillar of some kind that loomed large and ominous. It turned out to be some kind of hexagonal kiosk with a television screen built into each side.

"You know what this is?" he asked us, only to receive blank stares in return. "This thing was called the Atari Theater. One of these—I'm not sure if it's this exact unit— stood in Powell Street Station in San Francisco in the 1970s. Imagine—six games running at the same time, up to ten people playing simultaneously." From the looks of it, each side featured a different game—one was a car-racing game with a steering wheel (*LeMans*), another side had dual joysticks for *Tank*, another had a rotary paddle for *Pong*. "I bought it off someone who found it in a junkyard, rusted and rotting. Restoring it was a nice project to pass the time. I ended up replacing one motherboard with an Achilles Mark II console." Bryan held up the dragon cart. "How about we take this for a spin?"

Bryan disappeared behind a small door at the base of the kiosk, and within moments, it lit up, casting the entire room in a bluish glow. Every side of the kiosk was now live and spry, showing pixels of vintage arcade goodness. One of the screens above all caught our attention. Though the marquee above the monitor read *Jet Fighter*, the game on screen was a different one altogether:

Forever Throne II: The Chalice of Malice

I did a triple take. Not only was this actually happening, but then there was the double surprise. Our game cartridge wasn't an uber-rare copy of *Forever Throne*.

"Wait," I said, dumbfounded. "*Forever Throne II*? I thought the sequels never came out."

"It looks like I have some explaining to do," he said, emerging from the cramped space inside the kiosk. "But first things first. I'd say that by reaching here, you have proven yourselves worthy."

"Worthy?" I asked. "Of what?"

Bryan directed us to look above our heads while he flicked a switch on the wall. A platform slowly lowered from the ceiling. Sure, that was neat and unexpected and all, but it was the thing sitting on that platform that caused us all to gasp: a golden chalice gleaming with emeralds, sapphires, and rubies—the same one pictured in the advertisement for the *Forever Throne* games.

"The second *Forever Throne* tournament—that's why you're here, isn't it? To right the wrongs of the past, to finish a quest that was started thirty years ago."

13

THE ASHES OF DYING DREAMS

To *right the wrongs of the past.* In the movies or on TV, something bad usually happens right after someone says that. Think *Back to the Future.* Think *Timecop.* (Actually, don't think *Timecop.* You'll get a migraine.) It's basically an unwritten rule that to right wrongs in general, you have to undergo a not insubstantial amount of pain.

Bryan was hell-bent on holding the tournament that night, promptly at six P.M. We'd been through too much shit to say no. He offered up his ground-floor guest rooms to rest, freshen up, and get our heads in the game. And boy, did we need it. I mean, this was surreal. We went from a fact-hunting mission to a quest for a literal grail. I needed to lie down and allow my brain to process all this shit before I could be a functional person again. Bryan's sweet digs made it pretty easy to do that. The rooms—one for each of us—

were outfitted with a private bathroom and great big California king bed that gave me that little bit of extra space to spread out and cogitate.

Bryan had made it clear what the tournament entailed. "Choose your champion," he'd said. We had to choose one player among us to brave playing *Forever Throne II*. By a nearly unanimous vote (with me abstaining because I'm a chump), I was nominated for this honor—the honor to choke when the chips were on the line. Unlike with *Win at All Costs*, I had no time to master the game, no time to discover its Easter eggs and perfect my technique. I'd never played *Forever Throne I*, not to mention its sequel. I was going in blind.

I suppose that's why Bryan insisted that I take the guest room with the giant wooden console TV straight out of the 1970s. There, on top, sat a vaguely toaster-shaped Achilles Mark II console all hooked up and ready to play. He placed two dragon cartridges in my hand before he left to get himself washed up—one was the game we'd brought with us, and the other was an original edition *Forever Throne I* cart.

"I'm sure this is all a bit confusing, but it'll make sense in due time," he said. "For now, you should practice. You'll need it."

"How am I supposed to get good at a game that I've never played?"

"You'll get the swing of it real fast," he insisted before leaving me.

Guess I had work to do. After taking a quick shower, I dove headfirst into it, starting with *Forever Throne I*. I picked up the controller connected to the console, which greatly resembled the Sears Tele-Games version of an Atari 7800 controller with a single knob-topped joystick and two fire buttons on either side. I jammed the cart into the top-loading port and pushed the power button. When the title screen loaded, I hit the fire button on the controller.

Let me, if you will, indulge in a short aside about a little old game you may have heard about called *Gauntlet*. You know *Gauntlet*, right? Among retrogamers, its status is legendary. You played one of four adventurers who has been tasked with fighting monsters and gathering treasure in a 100-room labyrinth. The goal is one of survival and point gathering. Pretty basic so far. In truth, it was *Gauntlet*'s execution that made it one of the most revolutionary games ever produced by Atari. Everything about it screamed ballsy, from its concentration on co-op play, to the differences between each playable character, to the digitized voice taunting players with "Wizard needs food badly!" and "I've not seen such bravery!" *Gauntlet* was the juggernaut of the arcades, a giant four-player quarter magnet that made other games around it cry home to mama.

Gauntlet was released to arcades in 1985, a full two years *after Forever Throne I* was released. So how come I was looking at *Gauntlet* in front of me? Were we looking at proof that Atari stole one of the most influential video games of all time from a poor upstart with no clout in the industry?

Not quite.

The more I played, the more I could pick out differences between the games. Though both games had players wandering down twisty corridors, *Forever Throne*'s dungeons didn't have that zany random quality that made

Gauntlet feel like an exercise in masochism. For lack of a better way to say it, *Forever Throne made sense.* Strongholds with soldier enemies were laid out like maps of barracks you'd find on a modern RPG with more realistic design sensibilities.

Not only that, but there was an actual story attached to this game as well. While games with actual narratives were pretty easy to find by the time I was jamming discs into Playstations, back in the day, you had to settle for games with premises like, "You're a plumber, and you have to save the princess of the Mushroom Kingdom. Go get 'em, tiger!" Games in the Atari age fared even worse, doing away with stories altogether in favor of *you = ship, other things = destroy!*

Forever Throne actually had an on-screen crawl:

For nearly a century, Isak the Death Enchanter has ruled the land of Rendon from his fortress deep under Mount Death. None know how he has extended his life so long, nor do they know how he has managed to raise armies of terrifying creatures.

Ultimately, the task of descending into Isak's lair and stopping his tyrannical rule comes to you, fair knight.

You say goodbye to your wife and daughter, and then ride off for the mountain.

For the day, this was fucking Tolkien.

Now for gameplay. *Forever Throne*'s control scheme was as basic as *Gauntlet*'s—you controlled your little character with the joystick, and either fire button launched his ball and chain out in front of him. You didn't have much of a range—maybe two lengths of the knight's body—but you made up for that with the power. One hit was enough to dispatch most enemies, and you could swing it fast enough to keep both flanks defended while still moving forward.

Maybe I could actually do this.

That feeling kept up until I reached around level seven. I seemed to hit a brick wall—or, more accurately, a wall of lava-spewing demons. Up until then, all I had to do was stay one step ahead of the enemies rushing at me. Now, I was dodging fireballs trying to get close enough to dispatch the demons because of my lack of range. They could just sit there and lob their projectiles at me with impunity. I started to die—die and die and die and die enough that the death animation, a smiling angel sprite sailing upward, got burned onto my retinas. When I finally croaked for real, I wouldn't be surprised if the last thing I saw flashing before my eyes was that fucking angel sprite sailing away into video game Valhalla.

I'd cut my teeth on *Forever Throne I*. But the tournament that evening was on its sequel, *Forever Throne II*. Setting aside the fact that this game wasn't supposed to exist, I popped the cart into the console and fired it up.

Knock, knock.

"Jupes?" Saff cracked open the door and stepped in dressed in nothing but a towel. "So I had this great idea!"

Idea? That's what brains have! You know, brains—those things that are melting inside my skull! I tried to look anywhere but where my eyes wanted to look, which was at the insane amount of boobage and leg Saff was currently showing off. But that only resulted in me acting like I'd just gotten up from a hard blow to the head. I opened my mouth, but nothing came out.

"Okay, if you're gonna be weird, I'll just go—"

"We weren't having a moment! Not at all!"

"You're being weird," she said.

"*You're* being weird."

She looked over at the TV screen and her eyes bugged out. "Is that it? The game?"

"Yeah."

"You nervous about tonight?"

"It's only like actual gold and jewels on the line. Nothing to be nervous about."

"You got this," she said.

I nodded. Yeah. I'd beaten some pretty hard shit. *Dark Souls* several times over, not to mention legendarily unfair games like *Ninja Gaiden* (pretty sure everlasting damnation included playing level 6-2 over and over). "Yeah. I feel good." I laughed. "At least it'll just be you guys there."

"Right! Us, and all our fans on stream!"

Aw fuck no!

"This is it, Jupes! Our time!"

"Our time?"

"You and me, just like it should be." She stepped closer and looked up at me with her soft brown eyes. God, she wasn't wearing any makeup at all, but in that moment, she'd never looked more beautiful. And in that moment, I didn't know what I was thinking. Actually, that's a fucking lie. I know exactly what I was thinking in that moment. I was thinking, *This is it*. If I'd ever had a chance in my entire life with her, it was that moment to take it.

I opened my mouth just the smallest amount, and a force pressed me forward toward her, like the hand of God pressing on the back of my head. A kiss. No words would need to be said. My eyes closed and a warm feeling enveloped me.

"Jupes!" Saff said. "What are you doing?"

I opened my eyes to see Saff several steps farther back. The horror of the situation set in then, ratcheting up the steam works in my armpits. My face felt like it was on fire. I wanted to be anywhere but there. It was like a spell had taken over my legs. All I could do was run past her out of the room toward anywhere else.

Next thing I knew, I was among the cabinets in Bryan's hidden museum, listening to the electronic sounds of an antique arcade. But even those normally soothing sounds didn't comfort me. I couldn't stop hyperventilating. No, I needed to find somewhere quiet where I could catch my breath and collect my thoughts. I retreated into his memorabilia museum, where I found Ryland pensively staring at one of the exhibits.

I really needed a friendly face right then.

"Hey," I said, my throat on fire.

"Are you okay?"

I shook my head. "I tried to kiss Saff."

I could tell she was genuinely upset at me. I mean, I was upset at me. What could have possessed me to think that going in for a kiss was a good idea? In what universe did that even make sense? It was clear as fucking day that Saff was into Austin and vice versa.

Ryland didn't shoot back with a quip or a platitude. She crossed her arms and looked back over at the exhibit that had caught her eye. "You heard of this lady?" She pointed to a small plaque next to a glass case containing a tiny T-shirt with the word *Hustle* printed on the front. Was that something important, something notable? Next to the plaque was a grainy black-and-white picture of a tall, lean woman with shoulder-length hair and an expression of supreme confidence. She was wearing that same T-shirt that Bryan now had behind glass.

I read the short statement on the plaque:

In 1977, Lynn Reid and Sabrina Osment (pictured), the first professional gamers, toured multiple cities to promote Gremlin's new arcade game, Hustle. *Final win-loss record: 1,233 wins, 7 losses.*

"That's one hell of a record," said Ryland. "And she's scorching hot to boot."

I mean, I'd heard of professional gamers, guys like Billy Mitchell, notable for being the all-time high scorer in *Donkey Kong*, a title he would repeatedly reclaim as challengers lined up to usurp his throne. He's also reportedly the first person to achieve the *Pac-Man* kill screen, reaching level 256, which was where the game would literally disintegrate in front of your eyes. But he wasn't alone. You also had dudes like Todd Rogers, the first professional gamer hired by game companies to hock their wares; Johnathan "Fatality" Wendel, the lord of esports; Steve Juraszek, *Time* magazine's "*Defender* Champion of the World"; Thor Aackerlund, first Nintendo World Champion; Isaiah "TriForce" Johnson, master of the Power Glove.

I'd never heard of either Reid or Osment.

We walked around looking at the other exhibits. A poster advertising the 1981 Atari World Championships, along with a photograph of the champion at *Centipede*, a Korean woman named Ok-Soo Han. A ticket for the *TRON* video game tournament in 1982 signed by Sterling Ouchi, who still held two top-ten arcade records thirty years after his untimely death. This wasn't just a museum. It was a shrine to the forgotten, those who loved games like I loved them, but who didn't have the Internet to share that love with others all over the world.

"It's spooky in here," said Ryland. "Like I'm surrounded by ghosts."

"You believe in ghosts?"

"No. But I wouldn't be surprised to be wrong." Ryland reached out and touched the glass case containing the *Hustle* T-shirt.

"What do you think happened to them?" I asked Ryland.

"In my dreams?" she said. "They shacked up together for a week eating ice cream off each other. But in reality, they probably had families. White picket fences. Their kids never knowing about the amazing shit they'd done when they were young."

Slowly, my reality set back in. "I fucked everything up, didn't I?"

"Yup."

"How do I fix it?"

"Tonight? You don't. You just kick ass and win this tournament thing. Then we'll figure out how much you've screwed the pooch." She got on her tiptoes and kissed me on the cheek. "Now I have to go."

"Where?"

"Girl business. In the bathroom. You know, with the tampons and blood. From the look on your face, maybe you don't. I'll shut up now."

"I don't know if I can do this."

"You can," she said, and then she was gone, leaving me alone with phantoms. I continued to wander the aisles after Ryland left, looking at each person Bryan had singled out. Bryan had gathered tiny bits of each of their lives—some as momentous as prototype consoles and circuit boards, others handwritten letters and signed cardboard punch cards, and still others as innocuous as napkins exchanged at hotel bars. Case after case. Name after name. Faces lost to time. Eventually, I wandered into the back room with the kiosk only to spot Bryan and Austin inside, deep in conversation. I ducked back behind the heavy metal door so I wouldn't disturb them:

"I confronted Alvin and demanded to know what was going on," Bryan began. "He said the company had been sold, that it was the end. I'm not very good at accepting things. I just thought if they'd just release the other two games, it could turn the company around."

"Why did he sell?"

"Look, Alvin was more than a boss to me. He took care of me, of all of us. Looking back, I wish I wasn't so angry with him. He was in a hard position, what with the company in such a bad way. But I was barely nineteen and thought I was hot shit. So I did what any stupid kid would do—I rebelled. I flashed a *Forever Throne I* cartridge with the code for the sequel and sent it out to your father. If anyone deserved to play it, he did. By the time I told Alvin, it was too late."

"Why'd you tell him?"

"Because no matter what, I respected the man. He gave me a chance to live out a dream—that's something special, you know, even if the dream isn't exactly what you thought it would be. When I look back after everything that came after—working for the government, programming systems for things that I can't even tell you about—that time was still the best of my life, the most exciting."

"Do you remember my father's address?"

"Nah. Somewhere in Indiana, I think? Ring any bells?"

"No."

"I'm sorry I can't tell you more," said Bryan. "I wish Nate could have told me what he thought. You know, programming stuff—you get tunnel vision, forget about the people on the other side of it all. It was nice to know that I did something joyful for someone once."

Austin nodded and started walking toward the door. I jumped back, not wanting him to know that I'd been listening that whole time. I made my way back into the museum area and pretended to be engrossed in the exhibits—like this one:

"Jack Palevich, designer of *Dandy Dungeon*." As with all the other names in this room, there was a black-and-white photo of the person, a bright-eyed guy with short dark hair going gray at the temples leaning over what looked like a small R2-D2-like robot made out of a trash can.

"Old Jack," a voice said behind me. I looked over, and there was Bryan. He'd shaved his five-o'clock shadow, making him look years younger—almost like the image we'd seen in Edwina's office. "If there was any justice in the world, Jack Palevich's name wouldn't be stuck down here."

"Did you know him?"

"For a short time. I went to school with him at MIT. He let me test-drive *Dandy* before it even had a name. Back then, it was his "Thesis of Terror"—a school project. I can't describe what it felt like to play that game for the first time. It changed everything." He laughed. "That's why I borrowed his idea when I made *Forever Throne*."

"I can't help but notice that it looks like—"

"*Gauntlet*, right? Well, *Dandy* was an underground hit on the Atari 800. It inspired a lot of people, like Ed Logg, who created *Gauntlet*."

"If that happened today, there'd be a hundred videos calling him out for theft."

"Theft? You know what was theft? Swiping the chalice, hiding it in the second-floor bathroom, and waiting until everyone left on the last day to walk out the door with it."

"You stole it?"

"Sometimes you have to take what is rightfully yours, even if it breaks a few little rules," he said. "Anyway, you have to understand that games were the Wild West back then. Most of the time, we were just trying to prove that we could make something that wouldn't break. If I saw that someone modeled their game after mine? That was an honor—as long as you shared the credit. I was inspired by *Dandy*. It made me feel that there were infinite possibilities. We had big dreams."

"Like what?"

"Online multiplayer!" he said. "I mean, not truly online like you have now. But we wanted to wire up consoles with modems so that you could call your neighbor and play remotely. We even had prototypes hooked up with each other. Three, four, or even five player! Team versus team! That would have been amazing in the early '80s."

I could only imagine. There were a couple of attempts like GameLine for the Atari 2600 and PlayCable for the Intellivision that at least allowed games to be downloaded through a modem. These were fraught with issues, including limited availability, a small game selection, and sky-high prices. What Bryan described was a full-on multiplayer system to match the capabilities of thousand-dollar computers of the day. It would have been amazing if they'd pulled it off.

Bryan leaned back against the wall and surveyed the room, staring at faces frozen in grainy snapshots alongside his exhibits—faces of people like Willie Crowther, who programmed a game called *Colossal Cave Adventure*, later expanded into the first great text adventure game, *Zork*; Danielle Bunten Berry, who pioneered real-time strategy games with *M.U.L.E.*, paving the way for later hits like *Warcraft* and *StarCraft*; Rob Hubbard, musical maestro of the Commodore 64's beloved SID sound chip. "You heard about any of the names in here?"

"Not many. Did you know them all?"

"I knew some," he said. "Some I met once, and some I consider friends."

"Why not open this place up? People need to know—"

"People know, LeRoy," he said. "All the bits and pieces of our history are out there on the Internet in plain sight." He looked down at his toes. "It's that no one cares. I think it's part of getting old. You make it into the history books, or you don't."

"I don't think it's that way anymore."

He smirked. "You know, for someone so miserable in his videos, you have an optimistic outlook." That's the first time I'd ever been described as *optimistic*. *Sensible*—that's what Dad would say. And Mom? She considered me *short-sighted*. And Saff? Who the fuck knew what she thought about me at that point. "Don't look so shocked. I was the one you found with his face in a pool of vomit. I'm not exactly the most hopeful person myself."

"I didn't think you wanted to talk about that."

"You know, it was my birthday, two days ago—first time in five years that I wasn't on a job or wasn't in some board meeting with suits that I wanted to strangle. So I sat and thought about what I wanted to do, and I didn't know. I couldn't call anyone, couldn't talk to anyone. So I decided to celebrate by myself."

"Most people just get a big cake," I said.

"I like bourbon more than cake."

"Why are you telling me this?"

He chuckled. "There's no reason not to. Besides, there's far more that I'll share once the tournament is over."

"What if I lose?"

"I've watched *Win at All Costs*. You have what it takes." He looked one last time into his personal hall of fame. "Just like all of them. Now, they're just forgotten, lost in time."

"Like tears in rain."

"No, like the ashes of dying dreams. That's something that Alvin told me once."

"Sounds like you were close with him."

"He was like a father to a lot of us. We even called him 'old man.' Funny, forty-three years old seemed like such a crazy age back then—*don't forget your walker, old man! Did*

223

you take your fiber today? Now I'm older than that, and watch out if I don't take my meds."

"I guess time flies."

"Oh, it does."

Fifteen years hence, your father, Voltan, the famed Azure Knight, disappeared on a quest to rid the land of the tyrant, Isak. As his only child, you were convinced that Isak had captured him and held him captive all these years. You took up the arcane arts with the hope of one day seeking out Isak, completing your father's quest, and hopefully reuniting your family.

After talking with Bryan, I mustered up enough courage to venture back upstairs. As I got closer to my room, I concurrently got closer to Saff's. I wavered between trying to explain my epic mistake and fleeing into my room and taking cover in the shower stall. Turned out that I didn't have a choice in the matter. Her door, opposite mine, was closed, and voices were coming from it. I couldn't make out the words they were saying (good job on the thick walls, Bryan), but I could tell that it was her and Austin having a discussion.

Fuck my life.

I passed the rest of the time practicing my *Forever Throne* skills until the appointed time—six-o'clock on the dot. That's when I descended back down into the dark room beyond the metal door. I walked as fast as I could down there, not stopping for a second. If I did, I'd have just enough time to actually think about what I was about to do and probably have a panic attack.

When I stepped into the room, a bunch of lights shined on me like I was a star arriving for a red carpet premiere. These were staging lights, and behind a camera that cost more than God stood Saff making sure everything was running smoothly.

Don't think, don't think, don't think.

Ryland was the first to speak. "How you feeling?"

How was I feeling? In a word, unprepared. I wasn't used to being on the spot without dozens of hours of practice. I'd had a couple of hours at best with both games and felt woefully short of expert level. *Forever Throne II* differed from its predecessor in a couple of key ways. First, you no longer controlled a knight with a short-range attack. Instead, the main character was a sorceress who fired bolts of energy that stunned enemies, but did not kill them. If you hit both fire buttons on the controller at the same time, that activated some kind of telekinetic power the sorceress had to pull stone blocks toward herself. Then, if you hit the buttons again, she could fire blocks away. This was her main way of dispatching the various baddies in the dungeon.

This new ability proved much more useful than the old ball and chain. Not only did it provide extra range, but it fundamentally changed the nature of the game. *Forever Throne II* was much more of a puzzler, shifting blocks around the room to open up new passages and trap enemies, akin to *Boxxle*, *Daedalian Opus*, *Lode Runner*, and *Adventures of Lolo*. Those types of games weren't my strong point. They required patience when I had very little. I found it much easier just to gut out a level in *Silver Surfer*, trusting my reflexes rather than actually thinking stuff out several moves in advance.

"I'm not ready," I told Ryland.

"Did you yank one out? Totally helps the nerves."

That's when Saff would have chimed in with a *That's disgusting!* or *So gross!* Instead, she stayed quiet, busying herself by turning knobs, checking sound levels, and adjusting lights. The camera was wired into a souped-up laptop—one of those deals with a shiny, cherry-red finish and a sports car logo stamped on the back panel. She touched her fingers to the trackpad, guiding the cursor until she tapped the mouse button.

"We're live."

Bryan tugged down at the jacket of his scarlet-colored leisure suit. He was either competing for the hokiest game-show host competition or getting ready for a heated night at the disco. "Good. Welcome, everyone." He paused awkwardly, as if waiting for an audience response.

"Just keep talking," said Saff.

"Oh. Okay, then. I'd like to thank LeRoy and Saffron for letting me use their YouTube channel for this special occasion. My name is not important. What is important is what you're about to see. Thirty or so years ago, video games were a lot different. I was a programmer who worked for a company called Achilles. You probably don't remember it. Few people do. The best of the games that got released was called *Forever Throne*—the first of three. I was excited when it came out, but by that time, things were getting bad. No one was buying games, and even a contest to give away thousands of dollars in prizes was too little, too late. I thought that maybe there wasn't hope for those games to see the light of day. I like being wrong."

Bryan brought out a remote control from his pocket and hit a button on it, powering up the kiosk. All six screens lit up simultaneously, casing the entire room in the phosphorescent glow of ancient CRTs blasting radiation in all directions. On screen was the title of the game—*Forever Throne II: Tournament Edition.*

"We managed to award the first of three treasures before lights went out on the company. Today, one person gets to try to win the second treasure—the Chalice of Malice." The camera panned across the room to the window in the wall where the chalice was visible behind bulletproof glass. "So without further ado, LeRoy."

"Holy shit, the chat is going ballistic!" Ryland yelled out. Her voice seemed so far away, so distant from where my head was. This was really happening. I approached the console on one of the sides of the kiosk, laying out my fingers across the buttons.

"You can do this," said Austin, from behind the camera.

"Yeah, Double-J," said Ryland. "Kick 'em in the balls!"

Kick 'em in the balls. I hoped I knew the button combo for that special move. I looked back at Saff, who glanced up for a millisecond before pointing her eyes back down at the laptop screen. I turned back to the TV screen with a tiny pain in the center of my chest.

"You have one life," Bryan began. "One chance. There are no power-ups. There are no shortcuts. Your life meter goes from full to empty. You have to get from level one to fifty. In ten minutes."

What? Every level of a *Forever Throne* game was a grindfest of epic proportions. That was challenge enough. But in ten minutes, with one life? Was there some code I was supposed to enter? A Game Genie I could use to turn on God mode?

It was too late to complain. I reset my stance, leaning ever so slightly forward so that my lower back wouldn't start feeling my weight in ten minutes' time. Once, I went three hours undefeated in an arcade down by Chinatown, defeating all comers in some old-school *Killer Instinct* fighting action. I had to recapture some of that magic.

Bryan reached up and pressed the START button, dropping me into the action. Angry goblin-looking enemies barreled down a hallway at me, hurling knives that I deftly sidestepped. Grabbing a couple of blocks from the walls, I tossed them at my enemies, vanquishing them easily. I entered the doorway to room two and thought, *Maybe this won't be too bad.*

Still, I had forty-nine more levels to traverse, and the second room had a big spike in difficulty. The doorway out was barred by several blocks that I had to shift out of the way. Stopping me were snake creatures that kamikazed their way into me when I got close. *What if I could just wall them in by carefully rearranging the blocks?* I thought.

It took some time, but I managed to slide along the walls, grabbing blocks and hurling them into place to create a barrier between me and the snakes. At the same time, I slowly worked my way closer and closer to the exit. Anytime that a snake came close, I tossed a stun bolt at it, freezing it in place long enough to move another block in the way.

End result: I reached the exit to the room, my health

meter stayed almost at full, and the timer said that three minutes had elapsed. Pretty good, but way too slow. At this rate, I'd get through four rooms total.

Think, McFly. Think! My head buzzed with the possibilities. I'd taken light damage, barely a scratch. It was obvious that the challenge here wasn't the fighting. Every room was a puzzle. The entire dungeon was a puzzle. The whole contest was a puzzle. A Lament Configuration. It was pretty apparent that I couldn't attack this challenge conventionally. Normally, I would have doubled down, leaned in, and picked each room apart more expertly, dispatched enemies more decisively. But doing that was exactly the wrong thing to do. Every incremental victory was a distraction from my true nemesis—time.

Eyes on the prize, LeRoy. Instead of accepting the surface level of the game, I had to figure out a way to leap forward, warp-zone style. And to do that, I had to see more of the game. Thus, I got sloppier, wasting no time or effort on efficient tactics or precise movements. I did whatever it took to get past each room's obstacles, only shifting around blocks I absolutely had to and not caring whether or not enemies hit me. As long as I lived, I had a chance.

It took me five more minutes, but I managed to reach a portal in the seventh room that a pair of warthog dudes was zealously guarding. They were bigger sprites than other enemies I'd dealt with previously. The fireballs they spat from their mouths fired in rhythm, inviting me to figure out the correct timing to avoid them. But I didn't—there wasn't any time. Rather, I barreled my way right into them, hoping to squeeze into the door with a shred of life left.

I made it through. More importantly, I made it through

with more than half of my life bar intact. Wait a second. I was on the brink of dying just a minute before, and now, I'd just polished off those enemies, which were clearly mini-bosses. In video-game logic, they hit much harder than normal enemies. Taking a barrage of fireballs and then getting double shoulder-tackled between them, I should have been done for.

No time to think! Keep moving! Next level. More path clearing. More hits to the face. And at the end of it all, I had exactly one minute to go, thirty-eight levels yet to clear— and a full life bar. I had to stop and put my controller down to realize what was happening.

I was regenerating health. The question was *why?* I was playing as recklessly as possible, barreling down the hallways like a lunatic. Had the game been nerfed for the tournament? That didn't make any sense. If anything, enemies should have taken off more damage with every hit. Why would it be *easier?* I looked over to Bryan, who stood with his arms folded. He wasn't smiling at all. Instead, he was completely focused on the screen. Ryland, Austin, and Saff were on the other side of me, watching quietly without saying a word.

Everything moved in slow motion with the exception of the timer in the corner of the screen, now counting down from fifty seconds. I had one gut instinct that was so out of the box, so wildly against everything I was as a gamer, that I could feel my fingers rebelling against the mere thought. But what else could I do?

I had one shot, one chance.

So I did what I always did when I wasn't sure of myself. I looked back at Saff for something, anything. At first, she, like Bryan, was transfixed on the screen in front of me. But then she noticed that I was looking over at her. Our eyes met, and she went pale. She rolled her lips and furrowed her brow in an expression of confusion. She looked away.

Fuck it. I had nothing to lose. I needed to double-down.

Calling forth blocks from across the screen, I built a small enclosed space around a spiny, bullet-spewing turtle monster in the corner of the screen. There was space enough for it and me, and nothing else. I held my breath as I rushed right into that space and held my ground. I was taking constant damage from the turtle, causing my life to slowly drain away.

"What are you doing?" Ryland yelled.

Every gaming instinct I had was on red alert. How was I supposed to win the tournament when I was dead? Yet, it was the one last avenue I had to try. As the counter ticked down to zero, so too did the last few traces of the life bar. Once it ran down to zero, the timer stopped with three seconds to spare. The same death animation appeared from *Forever Throne I*—my character becoming an angel sprite rising to the top of the screen. But unlike the first game, there was no reset, no return to the title screen.

The angel kept rising, past level thirty. Then forty. And then finally to the small room on the fiftieth level. There, another tiny figure clad in purple pixels raised a staff to the heavens. Twin lightning bolts struck the staff, and then the whole scene slowly faded to black.

GAME OVER

The room was silent. Did I do the right thing? I mean, technically, I'd reached level fifty in the allotted time.

Stone-faced and with his arms crossed, Bryan walked over to me and placed his hand on my shoulder. The seconds hit like atom bombs until he opened his mouth.

"Congratulations."

"I won?" I turned back to the GAME OVER screen. It sure didn't feel like I had.

"You won the tournament," explained Bryan, "but Sorscha the Sorceress did not. In challenging the dread lord of the land, she discovered that Isak the Death Enchanter had long been dead. In his place ruled a warrior of bone and darkness, one who wore faded blue armor. In the battle—a battle she fought for the soul of her father—she made the discovery that it was the throne itself that emanated evil. Seeking to destroy it with her magic, she instead created a time rift, thrusting her into limbo itself. She lost. That's how *Forever Throne II* was supposed to end."

"What happens next?"

"You'll have to play the sequel." Bryan's smile faded. "I think our show's done for the night."

Eureka, Utah, wasn't exactly the *haute cuisine* capital of the world. But it did have its share of surprising culinary options, such as my new favorite Vietnamese restaurant on the planet, Pho King Klassy Vietnamese Eatery.

"Naturally, not a lot of places deliver to my door," said Bryan, placing two large bags full of amazing-smelling food on the dining room table. "Then again, I do pay extra for them to deliver from Spanish Fork. It's worth it though—all locally sourced, organic." He nodded to Saff. "And very authentic. So enjoy. You've earned it—all of you."

All four of us tore into the first real food we'd had since Saff and I embarked on this crazy odyssey. I tried not to stare at her across the table. A couple of times, Ryland caught me holding my gaze a bit too long and nudged me on the ankle with her heel. Things were different—anyone could tell. She was quieter, more somber, even though she tried to hide it with effusive comments about the food.

"I wanted to thank you," Bryan continued. "For helping me when you got here. Frankly, I'm embarrassed you found me like that."

"I get it," Austin said. "Sometimes you slow down enough to see how alone you are."

Ryland nodded in agreement. "Shit, I think all of us feel that way at one time or another."

Did we though? Did Saff have any concept of what it felt like to be alone? How could she? Everyone wanted to either be with her or be her. There wouldn't be one day in the school hallways when I wouldn't overhear a conversation about her. If boys, it was mostly lewd—*man, what I'd do to her! I just want to see those tits! I'd pay so much money for that ass!* If girls, it was mostly cruel, unusually cruel—*that slut fucked Joey Ugin last summer. If I was as skanky as her, I'd fucking shoot myself. If she didn't suck dick, no one would pay attention to her.*

Maybe being alone was better than dealing with that.

"Change of subject," said Bryan after slurping up some soup. "What are your plans now?"

We all looked at each other. This was the big thing—making it to Bryan's, revealing the secret of the mysterious dragon cartridge. The rest of it—I looked over at the chalice sitting in the middle of the table—was gravy, I suppose. Man, that thing sparkled like miniature fireworks were exploding all around it. That was, of course, a trick of the light. The fake grail from *Indiana Jones and the Last Crusade* looked all glittery, too. That didn't stop it from turning you into a walking corpse if you drank from it.

"Good. Because I have a proposition. There was a third game in the series. I was hard at work on it when Achilles was sold. They took it all away—both the full and tournament versions." He wiped his mouth and then put both his palms onto the table in the universal sign of *shit-coming-down-like-RIGHT-NOW*. "Do you know anything about contracts?"

"Only that they're for suckers," said Saff.

"Basically, that's right. If you sign a contract, you're bound by what it says, even if you don't like it. Even if you don't know it." He paused, perhaps hoping to see a glimmer of inspiration, a sign that any of us had connected the dots that only he could see. "What I'm trying to say—and obviously failing to say—is that the *Forever Throne* contest never ended. That's why you being here and doing what you did was so important."

"But Achilles is long gone," I said.

"In name, yes. But legally, the buyer of the company assumed all responsibilities. You see, for the deal to go through, Mr. Meadows—Alvin—had to sign on that dotted line. He ultimately did, but not before adding a few provisions of his own to the final deal. First, he got himself a nice payout—a golden parachute that let him retire early. And second, the purchasing company was required to honor all of Achilles's agreements with its customers, including holding the second and third *Forever Throne* tournaments."

"How do you know?" said Saff.

"Because he told me," Bryan said with a smirk. "The sad part is that Alvin basically disappeared after that."

"Why didn't you say something?" asked Austin.

Bryan shook his head. "Who would have believed some nineteen-year-old punk? Besides, I didn't think anyone cared anymore. I'd given up hope." Then Bryan leaned forward. "But if you went and demanded the final tournament, holding that medallion and that chalice, they'd have to put it on."

Austin then asked the key question: "Who is *they*?"

Bryan sat back into his seat. "SunnTech Software."

Whoa. You might as well have told us that God himself and his host of angels were holding *Forever Throne III* hostage. Back in the '80s, SunnTech was a publisher of boring-ass programs like word processors that weren't as good as *Microsoft Word* and photo-editing suites that weren't as feature-rich as the early renditions of *Adobe Photoshop*. However, in the early 90s, they came out with the first game in their smash-hit fantasy RPG series, *The Ancient Tablets*. That put them on the map, and from there, the SunnTech empire flourished. Today, they hold a position with Electronic Arts, Ubisoft, and Nintendo as producers of games people save money to buy.

"We can't just march into SunnTech headquarters and demand an audience," I said.

"Why not?" said Austin. "Bryan said we have the law on our side. Why not go all the way?"

"I know it might be asking a lot," said Bryan. "But I think

this is destiny. For the good of gamers everywhere, the third tournament must be held. The Sword of Ultimate Truth must be awarded. The plan was to bring back the winners of the first two competitions and have them compete to see who was the one true gamer. One sword to rule them all."

"Us?" I said, pointing at Austin.

"You representing your father, and LeRoy as the champion of *Forever Throne II*. It's all right there, ready for you to take."

Austin backed up from the table, making the same face that Charlie Bucket did when he found out about Alberto Minoleta's fake golden ticket shenanigans.

"We're doing it," he said.

"Go to SunnTech and get your answers." Then Bryan turned to me. "Remind them of their obligations. Then find the son of a bitch who sold me out—the other half of the video game division. His uncle was a bigwig business guy—I think he even worked for SunnTech itself. I have no doubt they brokered a hush-hush deal behind all our backs."

This was all too conspiratorial for Saff to resist. "What's his name?" she asked.

"Harry Leeds."

"No way," I said. "*The* Harry Leeds?" Really? For the love of fuck, why did everything have to be ice-skating uphill? It was one thing to take on SunnTech. It was only a faceless, soulless corporation that no one really had sympathy for. Harry Leeds, SunnTech's VP of Operations, on the other hand, was a gamer through and through. He had his own weekly streams on Twitch and was a role model for many, many other game creators. Dude was as handsome as George Clooney and as charming. He was the closest thing to a movie star that the current game industry had. He could talk the nerd talk *and* walk the star walk.

"My *best friend*," he said with a poisoned edge. "That fucker sold out every single person who worked for Achilles by organizing that deal. And me? He stabbed me right in the gut."

"So what exactly are you suggesting?" I asked.

"WrathOfCon in San Francisco," he said. "It's too big of a stage for SunnTech to miss. So Harry will be there. Go and make a spectacle. Post it online. He'll have no choice."

"You're serious about this?" I asked. Someone had to. Maybe for practice we could have taken on a more realistic figurehead first.

Like the Pope.

Or Abraham Lincoln.

Or the Easter Bunny.

Or Goku at max power.

"I am," said Bryan. "Oh, I know what he is today—he's a great ambassador to the industry. An icon. But I also know who he really is. He was fucking lucky to be in the right place at the right time. He's a rat who cares about no one but himself. Think he cares about gamers? Nope. Only money and his ego. It's time the whole world knows that."

"So this is about revenge," said Ryland.

"I want you to set everything the way it should have been," he said, pointing at me and Saff. "And I want you to find out who Nathan truly was." Straight to Austin's heart. "And I want to make Harry Leeds pay." He paused when he said that. "Okay, fine," he had to admit. "Maybe it's about revenge."

Despite the comfy bed, I didn't sleep well that night. I tossed and turned, trying not to think of what we'd agreed to do. I mean, I didn't agree to it specifically. No, but I just ate my damn food while the rest of the gang schemed up ways to get in front of Harry Leeds like a ninja hit squad armed with sleep darts (because that's how ninjas roll).

I lay in my bed staring at the ceiling—a position that I found myself in a lot lately—wrestling with my insomnia. So I was wide awake when my phone started to bounce and churn on the nightstand. Hmm. An email.

Hi Lee.

It was Dad.

> Wherever you are, I hope that you're okay. John assures me that you and Saffron are well, and I guess he's not one to lie about that sort of thing.

Dad's never written me anything. Not an email, not a letter, not even when Mom convinced him to send me to fat camp for a month in Northern Wisconsin. In my experience, he's never been much for disclosure about his inner workings. Just when you thought he'd be okay, you come home and find him scarfing Oreos and OJ. So this had to be big:

> I'm writing you because the thought of calling you on the phone to talk makes me want to vomit. In some ways, this feels worse, because it's about your mother. But it's the best I can do.

You know what I said about picking sides in the split? Fuck it. I was tired of putting up pretenses, making nice just so feelings wouldn't get hurt. If Mom was getting her jollies from kicking the shit out of Dad, then she could take John and her perfect life and shove it.

I don't know why you've gone and left, and I hope one day you'll tell me. But for now, I want to make sure that you know everything—including all the things I've been keeping from you.

You see, it felt good to have you with me. I don't have much in this life, and to have you is the greatest thing I could ever hope for. But for a little while, a long time ago, I didn't want to be a father. I didn't want a family. I didn't want you to exist.

What the . . . ?

You never knew your grandpa and grandma. That's because by the time I was born, they'd figured out that they didn't want to be together. Two years—that's all it took. Dad moved away and started another family. I stayed with Mom, but one day she left, too. Just said she'd go out for juice and never came back. I stayed with your Aunt Violet until your mom and me happened.

I freaked out when I found out your mother was pregnant. I told her that she didn't have to go through with it. I talked to her parents. They agreed with me. She wasn't showing. No one had to know. She was cheerleader captain and valedictorian and had such a future ahead of her.

She wouldn't have it. When no one else in the world was willing to, Gaby fought harder for you than anyone has ever fought for anything. She cut out her own parents to protect you. She would have cut me out too, if I didn't relent.

She loves you, Lee. She always has. More than anything in this world, she loves you. Maybe she shows it in strange ways, but she does.

I love you, Lee. And for what it's worth, I'm proud that you had the guts to do what you believe in. Whatever it is you're doing.

And like that, my house of cards fell apart. What Dad had revealed filled in so many gaps about my childhood. Why Dad never talked about his own parents. Why my mom's parents—Lolo and Lola—moved to Florida right around when I was born. Why I'd only met them twice: once when they came to visit when I was four years old, and then again three years later when we went to Disney World and stopped by their place. I never heard from them otherwise.

It also answered why Dad worked the same miserable job for as long as I knew him. Why Mom was away all day working at a bookstore and then taking night classes for years when I was little. They were on two separate tracks, lived two separate lives, even though they lived under the same roof. They play-acted the happy household routine for around sixteen years before they admitted that this whole thing had been a mistake.

Because I was a mistake.

I needed to talk to Saff. These were the times when I leaned on her, because she'd always been stronger than me, always been able to cope with whatever shit came her way with enough mettle left over to spare for me. Only, she wasn't going to be there for me this time. I'd fucked that right up.

Mistakes beget mistakes.

14

TOTAL PROTONIC REVERSAL

ryan saw us off the next morning with little fanfare, save for him pulling Austin and me aside before we climbed back into *Ol' Yeller* (what Ryland had begun to call our ill-gotten ride). He smiled and then pulled a small envelope out from his back pocket.

"Here," he said, pressing it into Austin's hand. Austin, confused, opened the envelope. The insides were green with numbers and presidents, specifically the number fifty over and over, and the face of legendary Union general Ulysses S. Grant staring at us like an army of bearded clone troopers. "I should have tried harder to help your father."

Austin shook his head. "You didn't know."

"Not an excuse. Anyway, you're gonna need that where you're going. First things first, get some fresh clothes." His stuff long abandoned with *Hell on Wheels* and the airstream trailer, Austin managed to nab some extra T-shirts and a pair of grease-stained work pants from the service station back at Yellowstone. "People in San Fran are snooty." He turned to me. "You'll also need this." Bryan lifted up a grocery bag holding the Achilles Mark II console and the twin dragon cartridges. "They'll help prepare you for playing the third game."

"You really think that we have a shot?" I said.

"At convincing Harry to let this happen? Without a doubt. He's got too much reputation on the line. But beating my game? That'll take some work."

The honk of the van horn interrupted our moment. Ryland, ensconced in the driver's seat, leaned out the window and yelled, "Let's go, ladies! Lots of road to cover!"

With that we said our goodbyes and shoved off.

Our route would take us through the last bit of Utah and into Nevada via U.S. Route 50, aka "The Loneliest Road in America." And fuck, them Great American nicknamers weren't kidding. As soon as we crossed the state border, it was like an EMP had gone off. GPS was offline. Cell phone reception was at zero bars. Shields would be useless. There was nothing—and I really mean nothing—around us except for a crumbling road and desert, no order to the universe other than a fading yellow line keeping the driving lanes in place.

Morning gave way to afternoon. Ryland and Austin switched driving duties while Saff sat in the back strangely silent. I sat in the middle seat wondering how to fix my broken world. The quiet was maddening. Saff's coldness from yesterday had gone all liquid nitrogen.

"We have a problem," Austin called out suddenly. I

looked out the front windshield, then out the back. I didn't see anything amiss. Then I looked at the dashboard. It didn't take me much time to spot the issue. Though we'd filled the gas tank at what ended up being the last shred of civilization we'd seen (the tiny hamlet of Austin, Nevada), that was almost four hours and several gallons of gas ago. The needle on the meter hovered precariously over E, and the car was starting to sputter.

"You've got to be shitting me," I said. Frantically, I slid open my phone, hoping to catch enough of a signal to fire up a map of where we were. Lag was a supreme bitch out in those boonies, but I managed to pinch and zoom the sputtering app enough to locate a nearby town: Dayton, Nevada. Of course, nearby was a relative term—in this case a terribly relative *fifteen* miles away. With how the engine was bumping and clanging, we wouldn't make it.

It didn't take long for us to reach a complete stop well short of the goal.

I slumped my shoulders and leaned back into my seat, then looked back at Saff in the rear-view mirror. It was so unlike her to not be part of a conversation happening anywhere near her. One peep, one snarky remark would have made me feel more at ease, like the world was at least somewhat on its same axis.

"I guess we get out and walk," said Austin.

"Right," I said, sarcastically. "It would take us roughly five hours to walk there. Then we pump a gallon of gas and carry it all the way back here. That's five more hours."

"Oh? You have a better idea?"

No. No I didn't. I mean, we could have sat there and waited for someone else to drive by, but how long would that be? A day if we were lucky. More likely a few days. On the hierarchy of plans, that was firmly underneath Austin's and slotted just above digging a hole to China. I knew that fifteen miles in that heat with little water and no shade could have been the death of us—literally.

"Let's call 911," Ryland suggested. "If this doesn't count as an emergency, what does?"

"Maybe you forgot that you had us steal a fucking car," Saff snapped from the back. Her first quip in hours, and it wasn't one of biting snark. There was rage in those words.

Ryland wasn't one to back down from a challenge. "Maybe if you planned better, we wouldn't be in this shit!"

"Hey!" Austin shot back. "That's enough!"

"She's not fucking helping!" said Ryland, to which Saff replied with a nearly imperceptible low growl. If we didn't figure out something, we weren't going to die of thirst, hunger, or heatstroke. We'd tear each other apart before then. *Think, LeRoy.* Maybe Ryland's suggestion wasn't too far off. Saff was right—the police were the total last alternative to consider. I tried to Google up numbers for tow services, but that blip of a signal I rode earlier was nowhere to be seen.

Who else to call? I wondered. I thought at first that I'd have to break down and call Mom or John. But then I had another thought. I fumbled about trying to pull up my latest text messages. And there, in John's last message, was the number of his literary agent. *Call her in an emergency,* he wrote, and this totally qualified.

I typed in the number and prayed for my ping to be answered C'mon, c'mon, c'mon. And *connected.*

"We are so not in Kansas, Toto," said Ryland, elbowing me in the ribs. But I couldn't feel the elbow. I couldn't feel anything. That's because all life as I knew it had stopped instantaneously, and every molecule in my body was exploding at the speed of light. That's what happens, I think, when you've had one too many shocks to the system in too a short time.

Total protonic reversal.

We stood in the dining room of a giant house—or mini-mansion, if you wanted to get precise about things. We were safely away from being marooned in the middle of the Nevada desert, thanks to that phone number John Stalvern had passed along.

John Fucking Stalvern. His awards sat on the fireplace mantel next to a complete collection of hardcover first editions of all his books. This was no surprise, as we were in his house, not the fake condo full of higher-end Ikea furniture that he shared with Mom. No, this was where he had actually lived until certain events happened, where he'd been married, the home where he'd raised his family.

That's right—his family. His *two-grown-kids-that-he-conveniently-forgot-to-mention* family, his *oh-did-I-forget-to-tell-you-my-literary-agent-is-my-ex-wife* family.

"I'm trying not to shit my pants," I said.

Ryland leaned back and eyed my backside.

"You did have that extra cup of coffee this morning."

"What am I supposed to do?"

"Hold it, I guess?"

"About this situation! About everything!"

"Double-J, you gotta relax." She kept on telling me that, but I increasingly didn't know what that meant. I mean, I couldn't relax waiting for some mysterious woman's voice on the phone to come pick us up from where we'd broken down. Imagine my surprise when a tall, blonde, long-legged woman in a black dress stepped out of the car. My first thought was, *That's his agent? She's so young!* And then she introduced herself.

"Cassidy Stalvern. I'm John's daughter."

With that hesitation, I understood that she was feeling exactly as awkward as I know I looked. She'd had the advantage of knowing about me the whole ride up there. That way, she could imagine all the ways that this moment would play out. Would I storm away pissed off? Would I hug her and tell her that I always knew? Would I stand there like a drooling idiot?

That last one—yeah.

Fast-forward to now, with us staring at snapshots of John's first life—that of a husband to a glamorous-looking wife who looked like she'd stepped off a Miss America runway back in her day and father to two glamorous-looking children—Cassidy and her brother, Otto. The kids definitely shared a resemblance to their father—the same long, angular features, the broad shoulders. The height, for sure. The slightly auburn blonde hair. The perfect family.

Austin and Saff came through the front door toting all our bags, just in time for a redhead in a bikini to barge in from another room, followed by a hippie bearded dude in a blue dashiki.

"Give it to me!" she squealed, reaching for a cell phone that the dude held away from her.

Cassidy came in behind Saff and Austin, engrossed in some business call she spent most of the car ride on. Upon seeing bikini girl and hippie dude, she politely said, "Could you hold for a second?" tapped the mute button, and proceeded to layeth the smacketh down.

"Who the hell are you?" she said, snatching the phone away from the dude.

Sheepishly, the dude spoke up. "I'm Randy."

"That's obvious," muttered Ryland.

"What is going on here?"

"A pool party?" offered bikini girl.

Indeed. That would explain all the cars parked out front—some crookedly hugging the street curb, others parked right on the lawn. It would also explain the little (read: very large) backyard shindig visible through the sliding glass door in the living room. Dozens of barely twenty-somethings were strutting and drinking and grinding against each other.

"You're Otto's friends," Cassidy said coldly.

"Yeah," said Randy, casting his eyes on us. "What's with Teen Girl Squad?"

"Get out. Now."

Randy and bikini girl scurried away out the front, obviously spooked by Cassidy's ice queen routine. Clearly, all this was quite the surprise—and not the good kind with cake and ice cream. It was the bad kind—the one that usually left you crying in the shower.

"I want to lie down," Saff said to Cassidy.

"I'm sorry, sure." Taking up our bags, we all followed

Cassidy upstairs to the second level. "You can rest in any of these rooms," she said about the six doors in the hallway. Without missing a beat, Saff chose a door at random, and dragging her luggage behind her, went inside and closed the door. Saff had never maintained a mad-on for this long. Fuck, I'd actually done it this time—I'd irrevocably destroyed our friendship. What did our channel matter at that point? Cassidy, meanwhile, got back on her phone and disappeared behind another door at the end of the hallway.

"What's wrong with Sundance, Butch?" Ryland asked, motioning toward Saff's room.

Austin shot a telling look at me. All at once, I knew that my suspicions about her hating me were correct. "She's not feeling well."

"I could see that. But why?"

"It's not my place to say."

"So she told you about it?"

He nodded. Did he hate me too? Want to kick my ass?

"Hey . . ." I stammered. "Look, I know things are weird—"

"It'll be okay," he said. "She's just taking it really hard."

Ryland took my arm. "Why don't we let Hubba Bubba over here console his special lady friend while you and I chill, huh?" She started dragging me down to another bedroom door. But I didn't want to go yet! I needed to know—needed Austin to tell me—if Saff hated me, or if I needed to apologize, or what. He took the opening to head on into her room and close the door behind him. Shit. Double shit. Three shits on a stick, even. Ryland managed to wrestle me into a room and onto the bed. "I can't keep saving you like that," she said.

"Saving me from what?"

"Yourself. Again. Let Saff be alone."

"She's not alone," I said. "Austin is in there."

"Let them be alone, then."

But I was her best friend. I was supposed to be the one in there trying to cheer her up. *Was*—the operative word. I fell backward onto the bed and lay there for a moment, basking in my own uselessness. It was over. Everything was over. The channel, our friendship—everything. Worse, I'd been replaced with a better model of friend, one with pecs and abs and cheekbones. One with benefits. Once more, I stared at the ceiling of a room, my life unspooling out of control, and all I could do was fucking let it.

"Nice legs," said Ryland, picking up a framed photograph of Cassidy in a volleyball uniform. She did have nice legs, which she showed off in a wide array of sports including swimming, basketball, and cross country. There were posters on the walls of the Phoenix Mercury WNBA team, of several past Olympic volleyball teams. Over on the shelf were rows and rows of sports trophies and marathon medals. Most Valuable Player awards. High recognition.

She was John's daughter, all right. Cassidy Lynn Stalvern, overachiever.

"We need to leave here soon," I said.

"Oh no. This is exactly where we need to be, Double-J. It's party time."

"That is the absolute last thing I want to do."

"Which is why you have to do it."

"Aren't you supposed to be giving me *good* advice?"

Ryland didn't respond. Instead, she started rifling through Cassidy's things.

"What are you looking for?"

"I kind of smell like a hobo's ass crack right now," she said. "Ah!" She plucked out a small spray bottle from a makeup case and sniffed the top. "This'll do. Eau de hot girl." She pumped out a few puffs of fragrance onto herself. "I could use a wingman, compadre."

"I'll pass."

"Then is it okay if I ask your sister?"

"Cassidy is not my sister."

"She will be, right? You know, if she and I got together, that would make you and me—"

I stopped her right there. "Not one more word." As it turned out, no words were needed. Knocking on the door was Cassidy, as if on cue. I sat up on the bed trying not to look like a little brother investigating his older sister's things, but Ryland's words were branded into my mind. Cassidy was going to be family—at least on paper. What was I supposed to think about that?

"Sorry to interrupt," Cassidy began.

"I didn't know this was your room," I stammered. "We can move."

"Don't worry. It hasn't been mine for a few years. I don't really care."

"I think that's my cue to skedaddle," said Ryland, walking over to the door. "I'll be downstairs, Double-J. I strongly suggest you find me, okay?" She slid out the door, leaving me face to face with Cassidy by myself.

"I'm sorry we had to meet like this," Cassidy said.

"There's no way this wasn't going to be weird."

"Yeah." She sat down on the bed right next to me but stared straight ahead while she talked. God, this must have been as awkward for her as it was for me. This morning neither of us knew we existed. Now, we had no choice but to recognize it.

"I'm having a hard time reaching Dad. He's not answering his phone."

"He told me that he'll be doing promo events all day."

"Of course," she said. "That makes sense."

"That's where we're headed, you know—WrathOfCon."

Cassidy raised her eyebrow suspiciously, but didn't press. "There's an evening train that heads there every night through Sacramento," she said. "I could take you down to the station later on."

"That would be perfect."

"Sure. Perfect. I can order tickets ahead of time."

"How much would they be?" I asked, cringing ahead of a big number with too many zeroes.

"Don't worry about it," said Cassidy. She got up and walked to the door. "I'll do that now." A momentary smile appeared on her face, but just as fast, it blinked out of sight. As soon as she was gone, I fell back onto the bed, a pile of jelly slowly spreading out and surrendering to gravity. Slowly, silence gave way to a soft bass *thump, thump, thump* that grew louder over time, the sound version of Chinese water torture. Out the window, in the back yard, a veritable throng of half-naked twenty-somethings surrounded a crystal-blue, peanut-shaped pool. They all grooved and grinded to the musical stylings of a turntable-armed DJ while holding up bottles of their alcoholic beverages of choice.

PoltergeistRalph

> Come to the par-tay!

Say it with me: *AAAAAAARRRRRRRGGGGGGGGHHHHHH!*
The last thing I wanted to do was wade into that pit of
attractive humanity as the lone troglodyte. Which was why I
needed to do this. It was either that or despair here by
myself (pathetic) or pace wildly in the hallway trying to
figure out how much Saff hated me (more pathetic).

So I ventured down and out to the back yard, which was
even more expansive at ground level than it seemed from
above. A sea of barely covered college students roiled and
surged in time with the beats pouring out of the sound
system. I'd seen parties like this in movies, on TV, in videos
posted on YouTube by people with too much money and
not enough practical ways to spend it. The first thing I
noticed right away was the free flow of alcohol. Most people
standing or dancing had some kind of drink in their hands.

How was I going to find them in all this? Wandering
around, I found myself on the other side of the pool
slammed against a long table lined with coolers of different
colors. Peering inside each cooler, there seemed to be a
color code thing going on. The left-most cooler was red and
filled with clear bottles of amber liquid—all manner of beers
with names you see plastered on TV on Sundays during

football season. The second cooler (blue) had been stuffed full of canned beverages. The last cooler at the edge of the table had the heads of wine bottles sticking out of it like a spike-trapped treasure chest.

"Dave, right?" asked the guy behind the table refilling the coolers with more bottles.

"LeRoy," I told him.

"Who'd you come with?"

"Cassidy."

A skeptical smirk appeared on his face. "I didn't know my sister had so many friends."

Oh shit. "Otto?"

"Hey, she even told you about me. Maybe she's softening up." He picked out a particular bottle of beer—one made of dark-brown-almost-black glass with no label—and handed it to me. "Good shit." I accepted it like I knew what the heck "good shit" actually meant. "So you're with her." He pointed behind me to Ryland sitting by the pool making small talk with another girl. "How do you all know Cassidy, anyway?"

It was clear that this had shifted from a friendly conversation to more of an interrogation. Red fucking alert, LeRoy. Batten down the hatches. I'd already hopped aboard the deception train, and now it was full speed ahead.

"She helped me out of a jam once."

"So she tutored you in nuclear physics? Wrote your philosophy papers? Covered the spread when you bet on UNLV women's basketball?" He twisted off the cap on a fresh beer and took a big gulp from it. "Whatever. It's cool. Where you from?"

At least I didn't have to lie about that. "I'm in from Chicago. On my way to San Francisco."

"I love the bay, man. I have a few friends there in a band. You heard of Paper Jam?"

"Do they sing about inopportune tech support issues?"

"All sorts of shit. They even wrote a song for me." Another big swig. "It's called 'Fucking Pieces of Shit.' It's dedicated to Mom and Dad. You know how that goes." Otto raised his bottle and clinked it with mine. To be polite, I took a sip of my bottle's contents. Good god. I'm no prude, but I was unprepared for how much the beer tasted like how I imagined roadkill skunk would taste. Was it haggis bad or Korean pickled vegetable bad or Chinese thousand-year egg bad? No. But it wasn't good. I took another swig for looks and tried not to pinch my face too hard.

A mob of fratty dudes descended onto the coolers, taking Otto's focus away from me long enough to break free. After wandering around for a bit, I spotted Ryland sitting by the pool spreading lotion on the shoulders of an Asian girl in a green bikini.

"Double-J!" she called out when I got close. "This is Tomiko. We're moving in together and adopting a cat. A big fat cat with no tail. We'll name him Horace, and he'll have an eating disorder, but we'll love him anyway."

The girl blushed. "Hi," she said, quietly.

"Hi." Awkward.

Ryland tucked down her glasses. "Liquid courage, I see."

I put the bottle down with the full intention of leaving it there. "Cassidy's dropping us off at the train station tonight," I explained. "We'll get into San Francisco tomorrow morning."

"That's good. So now you can relax, right?"

"I don't think so," I said, beginning to suspect that the

genetic sequence that enabled humans to relax had somehow skipped me over. "I should go upstairs and talk to Saff."

"That would be a waste of time, considering she and Tall Sexy Dude™ came down a few minutes before I saw you. I thought you were together." I stood back up and tried to look over the crowd to see if I could spot Saff. While I had a height advantage over most people there, Saff was a pretty small target to look for. I peered through conversations and around impromptu games of beer pong, trying to spot a hint of Saff or even Austin, as he'd be easier to pick out of the crowd. "You know, you could just hang with us."

No. No I couldn't. This pall had been hanging over our entire crew for two days now, and it was driving me bananas. If Saff wanted to end things between us, I wanted to hear her actually say it—rip that scab right off. In the long run, that would hurt less than letting her recede further and further into the distance until one day, I'd look around, and she'd be gone. Making more rounds, I finally spotted her sitting on a swing hanging from a branch of a weeping willow at the far back of the yard.

Unfortunately, she wasn't alone. There were a bunch of people there alongside her—most of them dude-bro-looking guys. This is mostly why Saff never went to high school parties, even though she was always invited to them. Guys routinely fawned over her, ignoring all the other girls around. Inevitably certain words would be whispered, *slut* and *cunt* chief among them.

I made my way over, catching a few snippets of conversation as I got close.

"I'm getting my own place next year," said a jacked, beefy

dude in a half-tee and tight football shorts. "We should hang out."

Saff was silent. The snark was still.

"She's shy, Kev," another guy said, laughing. "Lay off her."

"That's why I'm pulling out the welcome wagon," said the dude bro. "So what's your name?"

"Saffron," she said.

"Wow. My favorite name."

"Saff," I called out. At once, Saff looked up, saw me, jumped off the swing, and ran into my arms. Fuck, she was shaking. Her nails dug into the skin on my arms. Something had rocked her deeper than anything I'd ever seen before.

"Wanna go inside?" I whispered. She nodded yes.

"Hey!" I heard behind me a split-second before an oversized mitt grabbed by shoulder and swung me around. It was dude bro. Kev. "I was talking to her."

"Whatever, man." I turned to leave, but once more, he stiff-armed me.

"Who the fuck are you, you fucking fat-ass?"

"Look, I don't want any trouble—"

Kev broke out in a wide smile. The other dudes around him stood up and assembled. Man, they were all jacked to the nines. Two things struck me right then. One, I suddenly got the same feeling I felt when cornered by Chuckie and his henchmen in Gamepokilips—this feeling that troops were being rallied against me. Two, the troops in this case were roided-up carbon copies of one another, almost like they were a team. That's because they were. I'd unwittingly pissed off the captain of UNV-Reno's football team. Because of course I did. Because of the Iron Law of LeRoy Jenkins, which states that *the maximum amount of suckage in any*

257

given situation is inversely proportional to the distance you currently hold from LeRoy Jupiter Jenkins. Me, being at zero distance at all times, was subject to the inverse of that number—namely, infinity.

It was then that a third thing struck me—a big old solid fist to the face.

This was new. I'd largely managed to stay away from physical altercations with bully types because my height tended to discourage them and because I made sure not to pull aggro when I could help it. None of this helped me with Kev. He was as big as I was, only with muscles instead of flab, and I'd basically unloaded a special attack in his face, in front of his posse.

All I could do was raise my arms to try and deflect the blows he was raining on me. I could hear people shouting all around me—mostly the other football dudes, but also some girls' shrieks in there for flavor. It didn't matter. Nothing did except preventing my skull from being caved in by this Ivan Drago clone.

All of a sudden, the noise crescendoed, and Kev was off of me—or he was knocked off of me. I rolled onto my stomach and looked around for where he went. And there—a few feet away was Kev on the ground wrestling with someone. Holy shit, it was Austin. A second after, three of Kev's friends joined the struggle, burying Austin in a sea of biceps. I couldn't let him get pummeled, not after him coming to my rescue. Not after everything.

So I dove back in, more trying to reach Austin and pull him out than trying to get a few more shots in at Kev and his cronies. The rush and noise enveloped me again. I felt elbows and knuckles collide with parts of my body, but I managed to stay focused on reaching my friend. I tasted copper in my mouth, felt warmth ooze out my nose. A distinct ringing came in through both ears. Just a little closer.

"ALL RIGHT EVERYONE GET THE FUCK OUT OF HERE!"

In a Pavlovian response, everyone in the scrum stopped struggling and pulled apart. We all turned to see Cassidy, her face bright red, every muscle in her body clenched and tensed to the point of exploding. The party quickly dissipated after that, with angry comments sent our way by Kev and the rest of the musclebound mooks. Man, Austin looked the way I felt—broken and battered. We leaned against each other as we walked back to the house.

15

. . . AND MY AXE

"You have to be kidding me!" Otto's voice echoed throughout the house. No *thump, thump* to drown it out. No cannonballs into the pool as a distraction. Once Cassidy told him exactly who we were and exactly why we were there, he was none too pleased.

Saff, Austin, Ryland, and I sat close together in the designated boys' room. I pressed a towel to my lip to stauch the bleeding. My black eye was tender to the touch. Austin was worse off. Scratches criss-crossed his arms and a big welt on the side of his face was dark and swollen. We listened behind a closed door to the siblings arguing back and forth.

Otto: "I want them out!"

Cassidy: "Now you care about what happens around here?"

Otto: "I can't believe you're taking their side. His side!"

Cassidy: "You're being a fucking shit."

Otto: "Because you're so perfect, right?"

There was the sound of a door slamming shut followed by stomping footsteps through the hall and down the stairs.

"We're leaving in a little while, anyway," said Austin. "Just let them be."

"I'm siding with Austin," said Ryland. "Bad ju-ju in the air. Best not to get involved."

I mean, they were right, technically. It was best for us to get on with the show and avoid all trouble. But I didn't want to run away from this—if I really could. The more I thought about that phrase, "my sister," the more it sank in. For better or worse, and not because of anything we did or deserved, we were going to have to deal with each other. Because we were family. Besides, I was tired of running from things, always feeling scared that I'd stepped on a toe. Truth was that I was always out there, all the time, always toe-stomping.

"You hungry?" said Ryland. She grabbed Austin's arm, making him wince. "C'mon, let's go raid the fridge. A ham and cheese sandwich will help heal those cuts. You cool?"

Austin got the hint. "Sure. I could use a bite."

They made their not very subtle exit, leaving me and Saff to finally have the talk that we should have had a day before.

"Jupes . . ."

"Before you go on, can I say something?" I took her silence as a yes. "How long?"

"How long . . . what?"

"How long have you known about how I feel about you?"

"Does it matter?"

"Yes."

"A couple years. Since freshman year, probably."

I groaned into my hands. All that time, I thought I'd worked up a pretty good poker face. I thought if I rode it out, I'd feel differently, that it would fade. Or she'd meet someone else that stuck around for more than a couple nights. But it never worked out that way.

"Why didn't you say something?"

"Because it would have changed everything—you and me, the way it's always been."

"And how exactly has it always been?" The words seemed to tumble out of my mouth, and even worse, they kept coming. "Has it always been me feeling like a bag of dogshit and you ignoring the fact that you can tell? Or how about you going out with guy after guy while I just stand aside and smile?" I let her go and stepped away from her.

"How about best friends?" she said. "Why is that so bad? I need that right now. You know, yesterday Mom sent me an email." Saff got an email, too? *Oh shit.* "And she tells me that for years, my dad's been trying to contact me. Letters, phone calls, everything. She hid it all." She grabbed my arm. "Nothing but lies for fucking *years!*"

I felt like I'd been in a boxing match and just got clobbered by a right hook followed by a left haymaker. I didn't know what to feel. Saff had raised grudge-holding to a high art in her hatred of her father. I'd been there, trying to convince her that it wasn't healthy to buy cheap DVDs of Nikhil's movies off eBay, only to throw them against the wall after watching them for twenty minutes. When you harbor that amount of anger for so long, it becomes comfortable, I think. You get used to always having it close by. But what if you find out that your carefully sewn garden of loathing had been a fiction all along? Could I build that for myself, a fortress of solitude made of frozen hatred for my once best friend?

No, I couldn't. I reached out and hugged Saff. Sure, maybe that made me a wuss. Maybe it made me weak. But she was right. She was my best friend. She'd always been there in those times when I truly needed her. She stuck up for me, always told me to stand up for myself. And maybe being her best friend was about doing just that.

"I fucking hate her," Saff sobbed into my arm. I let her cry as long as she needed to get all those years of pent up resentment out.

"Dad sent me an email, too."

"He did? What did he say?"

"He told me that he wanted Mom to have an abortion when she was pregnant with me," I blurted out, my words *thunking* on the ground like lead blocks. "That he didn't want me."

"That's sick, Jupes."

"I fucked everything up," I said, every single incident in my life suddenly making perfect sense. "Even before I was born, I was a fuckup. That's my destiny."

"Don't say that."

"But it's true, right? I mean, they had me and weren't able to go and have exciting lives because they were too busy wiping my shit and feeding me formula. And once I'm finally able to take care of myself, I go and do something like this and wreck them again." I couldn't even look at her. "And then I screw up you and me, too."

"Jupes . . ."

"Don't, okay? You don't have to be nice to me."

She pounded my arms with her fists. "You're such a fucking asshole sometimes! You think it would have been easy to say, 'Hi Jupes, let's stream, and bee-tee-dubs, can I crush your heart until it dies'?"

"It was easy to tell Craig."

"You think I care about some stupid guy more than you?"

"Don't you?"

"Ooh! I'm going to fucking punch you in the neck!"

"What about Austin?"

She stayed quiet.

"You're going to tell me he's different. He's not like other guys."

"Is that so hard to believe? It doesn't change the way I feel about you."

Now that everything was in the open between us, the entire room felt uneasy, like it was on one of those wave machines going up and down and up and down. I sort of felt like I was going to throw up, but funnily it was a good throw-up feeling, like some dank blockage had finally gotten cleared. But it still stung. It all stung. It was going to sting for some time.

"I'll always be your friend," I said. "But things can't stay how they were. It hurt too much."

"I never wanted you to feel bad," she said.

"I know," I said. "But after all this is over maybe we should take a break from the channel. Not forever, but for a while. Just so we can figure all this out."

Saff inhaled the way she would when she was about to mount an argument but stopped short of making a sound.

Instead, she pressed her lips together and nestled her head against my chest, holding me tight. We stood there for I don't know how long—at least until there was a knock at the door, followed by it opening a crack and a hand sliding in a plate with a couple of BLT sandwiches and a bowl of sliced pineapple.

Saff and I ate and composed ourselves, and afterward came downstairs to where Ryland and Austin were talking with Cassidy.

"We can help clean," said Ryland. "Wouldn't be the first time this trip."

"It's Otto's responsibility," said Cassidy. She crossed her arms and stared out the window to the back yard. There Otto was, gathering cans and bottles into a black garbage bag. Dude looked pissed as hell. "LeRoy, hey."

"Hey," I said. "I'm sorry for all this shit. I'm sure you didn't need us popping up."

She walked over into the kitchen, opened a drawer, and pulled something out. "Mom booked her illustrious vacation in Tahiti the same day this came in the mail. Cruise, resorts, mountain hikes where there's no cell coverage." Well, fuck. Let's just say that I'd already seen the kind of damage a sparkly gold envelope could wreak upon a perfectly functioning dysfunctional household. Not pretty the first time, not pretty any time. "That leaves me trying to help Dad finalize a three-picture deal."

"So it's official?"

"As of yesterday," said Cassidy. "They're starting with *Fist of the Iron Wolf*." Ah yes. That was book number six in the Carmine Stockton saga, in which a syndicate of ruthless industrialists attempts to extort the restaurateurs of the world by patenting the concept of brunch. Not kidding about that. "I'm not even supposed to be here today. A friend of mine rented us a cabin at Yellowstone. I should be there right now."

"Trust me," said Ryland. "That place is overrated."

She crumpled up the invitation and dropped it in the kitchen trash. "Look, I'm not mad at you. I understand. Otto, though? He blames Dad for everything that's gone wrong with him, even though most of it is his own fault. And since it was your mom and our dad . . . I mean, what they did . . ."

"Cheat." There. I said it, that poisonous word. Dad had asked me never to use that term around the house, even if I was referring to cheat codes in games. I guess he figured that if he exiled that word from his life, maybe Mom couldn't be guilty of it. She was lonely. She wanted something else from life. She didn't get what she needed. All those euphemisms to dance around a single word.

I wish we'd met under different circumstances. Cassidy's last words to us before we boarded the train stuck with me, because I wished the same. She'd gone out of her way to help us, and the best way to help her back was get out of her hair. So we parted ways, with the gang boarding a train destined for Sacramento. From there, we'd transfer to another train to Richmond, and then to San Francisco, where we'd hop the BART to take us into the city proper.

The hot, dry afternoon congealed into a sticky night

before cooling off toward the end portion of the journey. All the while, I kept my head leaned against the train window in an attempt to rock myself to sleep. No dice at all. My mind raced, thinking of the tasks ahead of us. On my phone, I scrolled through page after page on SunnTech. Wikipedia, various fan sites, the company's own About page. Achilles was never mentioned, which didn't surprise me. It was a name at the edge of the abyss, a tiny footnote in a larger tapestry of the Great Video Game Crash. But there were real people involved—people like Bryan, Harry, and the mysterious Alvin. Even Edwina and all the folks back in Deadwood who earned hourly summer wages. All of them, once upon a time, called Achilles home.

Once we arrived in San Francisco, we had to figure out how to get from a train platform at 2:00 AM to an audience with one of the most powerful executives in all of video games. Sure! All we had to do was navigate a city that none of us had ever been to, figure out how to weasel ourselves into an office probably crawling with buff security guards trained in Krav Maga, and spit out the right configuration of words to convince said executive to hold a series of impromptu game tournaments for a video game that no one had ever heard of.

All in a day's work, eh? Thankfully, that first challenge was taken care of before we got out of our seats.

Clancy was a short, stocky Scotsman who was overly excited about, well, everything. We ended up sitting next to him on the train from Sactown. Dude immediately stuck out among the other passengers because he was decked out in the stereotypical garb of an American tourist—brightly colored Hawaiian shirt with a palm tree and hula girl pattern, big sunglasses, an old film camera around his neck, and a goofy smile that screamed *Steal my wallet, please!*

I liked him immediately.

"I tell you what, boyos. You're gonna love it! Clam chowder at six in the morning! Soul food for brunch! A burrito and then some Ghirardelli chocolates for dessert!"

"How come all you talk about is food?" asked Saff.

"Shut up," Ryland replied. "If you scare him away, how am I going to capture him and keep him in my basement?"

"I love it when girls fight over me! Except, of course, when they're actually fighting me—like this one girl who liked to punch me in the face."

By the time midnight rolled around and the train eased into Richmond Station, Clancy thought enough of us to invite us over to crash at his place: "It's spacious, gets a lot of sun, fresh fookin' air in the morning. Don't stay at a hotel. Live as the natives live—and that's with me."

Seeing that it was the dead of night and we didn't have much else going on, we decided to say yes. Clancy walked us to the BART train, which would take us into the city proper. On the way, he gave us the rundown of the city and of his neighborhood, which was called "the Tenderloin."

"It's got character," he told us.

That should have been my first warning. Any time someone describes anything as "having character," that's a nice way to say that it sucks. And while it may be unfair to simply say that The Tenderloin sucks, it wasn't exactly Beverly Hills. You could tell that something was in the air when the drunk yuppies and cheerful vagrants slowly emptied out for a more-hardened bunch who didn't seem to have places to go, people to see.

When we got out at Civic Center station, San Francisco's City Hall was lit in rainbow-colored lights. But the streets were eerily deserted. Clancy, being his ever-cheery self, led us northward into the heart of the neighborhood he called home. Soon, we found out where the people were. Huddled shapes shivered inside the doorways to empty retail spaces and should-be-condemned old warehouses, their hands often holding paper bags hiding bottles of hooch or worse. The gold glint of the lights on the drizzle-slicked streets shone off long, greasy tendrils of hair on the heads of old men digging through trash cans. At a stoplight, I made out a teenage girl sitting in a doorway to a shoe shop, stretching her log legs onto the sidewalk. I did my best not to let my gaze linger on anyone for longer than a couple of seconds. It didn't feel respectful, even if they couldn't see me stare.

Eventually, we rounded the corner of a building with a large mural of humpback whales painted on the side, stopping at the front door of the drab gray building next door. Hmm. I wondered if the barred windows and the small pile of broken bottles out front were cause to worry. We helped Clancy heave open the door, weighed down by heavy iron slats—"Great security," he mused—and he led us up a staircase and down a long, dusty hallway. We stopped at a door at the end of the hall—ominously numbered 237 like the dreaded room in *The Shining*—and Clancy rapped his knuckles on it.

"Hola! Oy!" Clancy announced.

A moment later, the door cracked open and an older man with graying hair and a righteous moustache stuck his head out. "Quién es—ah! Clancy?"

"Carmelo! I'm back!"

The man pushed open the door to let us in. The smell was what hit us first—this heavenly salty sweetness of sautéing onions. Gathered around a low table topped by a hot plate were two more older Mexican dudes heaping carnitas onto tortillas. All three of them were dressed identically, in off-white pants and jackets with solid black shirts. They were using guitar cases for tray tables as they gobbled up their food. Won't lie—the unmistakable scent of sizzling meat in a frying pan activated all my latent Filipino-ness. All that was needed was some garlic, rice, a dab of soy sauce, and some fried eggs, and you had a real Filipino feast.

Apart from that initial thrill, the rest of the apartment was, well, less than stellar. Clancy had painted his place to be an opulent loft space like you see in those airplane magazines. The reality was that Clancy lived in what was more or less a giant warehouse room (more than less), with a series of folding screens dividing what was flat, empty space into sections.

"These are my mates," said Clancy with his characteristic enthusiasm. "That's Arturo, Carmelo, and Juan. Guys, these are some new friends. They're staying the night here."

"Mucho gusto," greeted Ryland, shaking each of the confused men's hands. "Me llamo Ryland. Ustedes son mariachis?"

"Sí," said Carmelo. He took a paper plate off the stack on the table, quickly made up a taco, and extended it out for one of us to take. "Comida."

"Gracias!" said Ryland, eagerly taking the offering.

Clancy gave us the nickel tour of the "apartment" while explaining his situation. "Not sure how much you know about San Francisco, but it's expensive as fook to live here.

Me and the boys, we're pretty handy, though. Arturo's a carpenter. Carmelo's a plumber. Juan's a crack with masonry and tile. And me? I learned a thing or two about electrical work at my father's factory. The landlord lets us stay here for cheap in exchange for fixing up the place."

Indeed, this place looked like a work in progress. Off in one corner, a rigged-up hose hung from the rafters, extending down to a bucket attached to a contraption that turned out to be a water heater used for camping. And right smack dab in the center, blocked from view by a pair of well-positioned folding screens, was a single toilet. Why someone would build a toilet in the middle of the room was beyond me, but there it was, in all its porcelain glory.

"You expect me to pee there?" Saff asked.

"Don't worry," Clancy reassured her. "If you need privacy, that's what the screens are for."

"That makes me feel *so much better*." Sarcasm mode engaged.

"C'mon, it's like camping!" said Ryland. "I'll tell you what. You let me know when you have to go, and I'll gladly be your human shield. What are friends for?"

"I hate you."

We all sat with the three mariachis, who had just come home a few minutes before from a run in the Mission District, famous apparently for the string of high-end Mexican restaurants. This late-night meal was a celebration of sorts—Carmelo's daughter back in Guanajuato, Mexico, was celebrating her fifteenth birthday. In both Mexican and Filipino traditions, girls celebrated coming of age with elaborate parties (Mexico had quinceañera at fifteen, and the Philippines observed a girl's "debut" at age eighteen). If

I'd been a girl, I bet Mom would have wanted to throw me an awkward-ass party celebrating my flowering woman-hood. At least I dodged that bullet.

I could tell that Saff wasn't very thrilled with our digs, but we weren't about to find any place better at this time of night. After we ate, Clancy furnished us with a couple of spare blankets and pillows, and we had ourselves a safe, dry place to stay. After we helped Carmelo, Arturo, and Juan clean up our late-night dinner table, we replaced paper plates and plastic forks with battle plans.

"Gentlemen," began Saff.

"Lady here," Ryland piped up.

"Gentlemen," she repeated. "What I am going to propose to you is highly lucrative, yet highly dangerous. If you prefer not to be part of this, you can leave now. Except for you, Jupes. You have to stay."

I've said before how frightening a prospect it was for Saff to have a plan. What I didn't mention, but which must be fairly clear by now, is that her plans have a knack of *actually working, despite being painful*. First things first. We needed to know where Harry Leeds was going to be the next day. Luckily for us, we knew generally where he'd be. Unluckily, it's also where several thousand other people would be. That meant our usual MO of sneaking (more or less) would be out.

Austin was already on his phone doing recon. "According to the convention homepage, there are a couple of events that have to do with SunnTech. There's a panel called 'Gaming in the Future' and a special press event."

"About what?" I asked.

"Something about ancient tablets."

"He'll be *there*," said Saff.

We crowded around Austin's phone. Along with dozens of pictures showing the convention halls full of gamers and superfans was a full map of the Moscone Center, where the convention was taking place. The convention center was a labyrinth subdivided into a North, South, and West building. There were sections both above ground and below ground. Our central focus was on Hall H on the main exhibit level. That's where the SunnTech event was going to take place—the very next day at 5:00 PM.

"The plan is simple," Saff began. "We get into Hall H before five, get backstage, find Harry Leeds, confront him on live stream, *question mark, question mark*, profit."

"Except that it's a press event," Ryland pointed out. "That means no plebs." In plain terms, the event was closed to the public. We'd have to not only sneak our way into a completely sold-out convention, we'd have to do it again to get into the event itself. Damn. Perhaps there was a way to scout out the area and pinpoint a weakness in security to slip into the convention. But that press event? Lockdown for sure. Without the right credentials, we'd never get in.

"Maybe we could steal some press passes?" said Ryland.

"Or maybe we can just walk right the fuck in," said Saff. She took out her own phone and started tapping like mad. "These aren't clear enough." I leaned over to look at her phone's screen. She'd pulled up an image search of WrathOfCon press pictures. Not only did it show various shots of expert cosplayers, crowds gutting up the entrances, and thousands of people crowding the exhibition hall, it showed many press members getting interviews with game developers, comics creators, and movie stars. "There." She

273

dropped her phone on the table, a photo on the screen of an IGN reporter interviewing a developer. On her shirt, prominently pinned, was a purple and orange press pass. "All we need is Photoshop and the address of the nearest FedEx/Kinko's."

"We make our own passes," said Austin. "Genius."

"Not we—you and Jupes. It shouldn't be hard for him to scan this thing in and make passes for each of us." That was true, but I didn't like where she was headed. "Meanwhile, me and Ryland will go and find appropriate things to wear. Because I'm not wearing *Big Haulin'* one more fucking day."

"Wait a second—you and me?" asked Ryland.

Saff sighed. "I didn't say this was a perfect plan."

"This is how it starts, y'know. This is how the magic happens between us."

"Also, we have to keep an eye out for a piano."

"For what?" asked Austin.

"So we can DROP IT ON HER HEAD!"

When you watch as many questionable '80s movies as Saff and I have, you learn a few things about getting stuff done. In fact, you learn exactly three main things over and over that you absolutely must not do if you want to live to the end credits:

1. Don't assume the killer is dead.
2. Don't cross the streams.
3. For the love of God, don't split up.

That last point scratched the inside of my skull. Even the words "split up" suggested a machete-wielding maniac standing just off camera waiting for us wander into the woods at night or venture into the wrong side of town. Still, Saff was right. If we were going to get shit done, we had to be in multiple places at once.

Luckily, we had a little bit of help. Clancy and the mariachis rested quietly while we discussed these plans, and at the end, one of the musicians—Arturo—informed us that his nephew ran a theater company in the city, one with "costumbres locos." That was good enough for Saff to work with. And Clancy was willing to lend his wheels to the cause because, well, hanging out with two hot girls was better than hanging out with a bunch of sleeping mariachis or a pair of smelly teen boys. Couldn't blame the guy.

Come the morning, we woke up bright and early. We took turns showering under the cold, cold water spraying out the hose, and then ate bananas and oranges fetched for us from an early-morning market by Clancy. Then it was go time. Before leaving, Clancy took us downstairs to show off his "fookin' great wheels." As it turned out, his "pimpin' ride" wasn't an Aston Martin or Truckasaurus. He was talking about his shiny yellow bike taxi in the foyer.

"Are you serious?" said Saff.

"Why wouldn't I be? This beauty is my day job."

"San Francisco has hills. No one in their right mind would operate a bike taxi in this city!"

"That kind of thinking is how I cornered the market."

"*That* kind of thinking means you're insane!"

"Ach, don't be like that. You haven't seen me behind the wheel."

"That bike has handlebars, ergo no wheel!"

"I love it," said Ryland, hopping in the back. "Oh, nice cushions."

"Thank you, love."

"I hate you all," muttered Saff. But she got in, and together, they went one way while Austin and I went the other. We located the nearest print shop, Willy's Print-O-Rama, and camped out in the café next door to get work done. While I madly clicked my mouse in a futile attempt to rub out all traces of aliasing, Austin was on his phone learning as much as he could about SunnTech games.

"Did you know that *Ancient Tablets* is supposed to be a ten-game series?" said Austin.

"Yup."

"And that it's earned a hundred million dollars?"

"That's just for the last game."

"That's crazy. I can't even imagine what I would do with that amount of money."

"I can. I'd buy my own chicken wing bar, invest in transporter technology—stuff like that."

"The things I really want I can't buy."

"World peace—that kind of shit?"

"Nah," he said. "I promised my grandma that I'd get her a brand-new house, far away from where we lived. I wanted people to cook and clean for her for a change."

"You can still get that house."

"But not for her."

"Quick," I said, ready for the finishing touches on the passes. "Where do we work?"

"The *New York Times*?"

"Nah. Something less well known."

"How about the *Alamo Post-Gazette*?"

"Never heard of it, but it sounds perfect."

"That's because I made it up."

"Double perfect." I altered the base image to read "Alamo Post-Gazette" in orange letters underneath where the person's name would go. Then I made four copies, one for each of us, to go with the four fictitious names and job titles I'd come up with. All that I had left to do was place photos of us into the right spots and *blammo*—instant all-access pass. Pics of Saff and me were easy. My phone was chock full of them (more of Saff than of my pokey old self). Ryland sent one over of her doing her best Miley Cyrus tongue action after a quick text. That left Austin.

"You got any pictures of yourself online?" I asked.

Austin shook his head. "Not big on selfies."

"Well, I need an image." Firing up the camera app on my phone, I raised it to snap a quick pic of Austin to slide into the last pass. Man, even impromptu pictures of him looked good, his deep brown eyes and those fucking cheekbones. Standard GQ cover-boy looks.

I had to stop. Focus on the mission. There was no use in me dwelling on this shit anymore. I shut my laptop and hopped off my seat.

"I think we're ready."

More horn-tooting: these passes were the shit. I compared them with the zoomed image of actual passes on my phone and couldn't pick out any details that were dead giveaways for fakery. Good news was that they were dead ringers as long as we were careful to keep moving and not let anyone get a long, extended perusal.

Armed with our passes, Austin and I went to our rendezvous point at the sidewalk sandwich shop right outside the Children's Creativity Museum located kitty-corner from the Moscone Center. Austin and I arrived at 11:30 or so expecting the others to be there waiting. Instead, we had to kill forty-five more minutes sipping hot-into-cold coffees and watching fanboys and fangirls of all ages go in and out of the convention. As was my usual habit, I obsessed about everything that could go wrong. Maybe the passes wouldn't pass muster. Or what if there was a schedule change? I sat on the patio outside the sandwich shop, nudging an organic curried chicken crepe.

When they finally arrived, Saff was all smiles. In between her and Ryland in the taxi's back seat were two black garbage bags. As I'd hoped, the bags contained the costumes that they'd set out to get. And even better, they turned out to be *Star Wars*-themed duds, making them perfect for where we were going.

Once we were all sitting at the same table, Saff started doling out the goods to each one of the crew: Han Solo's iconic smuggler's duds for Austin; Luke Skywalker's beige padawan outfit with belt, binoculars, and lightsaber for Ryland; and for herself, classic cinnamon-bun-haired Princess Leia with her white toga and blaster rifle. These weren't cheap knockoffs, either. Each looked very high-end.

"What about me?" I asked.

Saff looked at the not-quite-empty garbage bag with a frown. "There was only one in your size, Jupes."

What? What could be so bad? I mean, it was *Star Wars*! How awesome would it have been to wander around WrathOfCon as Chewbacca or even fucking Darth Vader! I mean, sure there'd be a dozen more dudes in those costumes, but fuck all, it would be glorious! I reached into the bag, felt around, and pulled out a long, red, neck-to-foot frock along with a diamond-patterned wrap that almost looked like one of Anjeli's saris. Reaching deeper, I felt some kind of rubbery prosthetic and pulled it out, and—oh no. No. No, no, no.

NOOOOOOOOOOOOOOOOOOOO!

"Jar Jar fucking Binks?! You couldn't find anything else?"

"Most actors are really short," Saff said, sheepishly.

Abort! Abort! screamed my brain, but it was too late. We used the restaurant's bathrooms to change into our final forms, crossed the street, and approached the doors. As we walked up, people from the crowds outside asked us for photos, and we obliged. Yes, even me. Because far be it for me to rip away a kid's dream of posing in a photo with the worst fucking character in *Star Wars* history.

Be chill, I repeated to myself. *You did good. Your passes are perfect. It'll be fine.*

We got in line for the doors. Everything became about getting to the other side. While crowded, the front entrance wasn't as mobbed as it could have been. After the morning rush to get in, foot traffic had decreased to be more manageable for security, making it worse for us. Purple-shirted volunteers flanked every way in, stopping each person to make sure they had a valid badge to get inside. So far, so good. Maybe this plan would actually work.

Of course, whenever I even had an inkling that things

would go well, they turn out not to. With only two people in front of me, there was a personnel change. New purple-shirts got swapped out for old, and the jolly-looking bearded fellow that I was sure would let me in no problem got replaced by a tiny, blonde, brace-faced-wannabe-totalitarian dictator:

"Okay everyone!" she yelled. "Make sure your badges are out where I can see them! And don't think you can hide them under your clothes. Because I'll find them. I'll find them all!"

Why? Was I Genghis Khan in another life? Attila the Hun? One of the other dictators that Cobra combined into Serpentor? Ryland looked nervously over her shoulder for a nod of confidence. All I could do was wince as we stepped closer to the chopping block.

Austin was the first among us to come under scrutiny. Man, this girl really gave off some major *Omen* vibes. I'm talking *daughter-of-the-devil, gonna-make-way-for-the-end-times* kind of mojo that would make you recite Hail Marys until your throat went raw. She glanced at him and at his Han Solo get-up, and simply waved him in. Next came Saff, and again, no problem. I let out a breath. Oh man, we were going to get through this. Ryland strutted up with her chest puffed out, exuding all sorts of confidence. Our would-be adversary glowered down upon her with squinty eyes.

"How do I pronounce your name?" said the volunteer.

"Shailene Explosion," said Ryland, echoing the name on her pass. Maybe I had a little too much fun coming up with pseudonyms. "It's Chilean. *Explosión.*"

After way too long of a moment, the volunteer let her pass as well.

280

Then it was my turn. I wasn't sure why I felt so nervous about this—maybe because anything that seemed so relatively easy probably seemed that way because I was overlooking something important. Or because I was paranoid. Or both.

Probably both.

I walked forward holding my breath, hoping that I could just stride right on through. Unfortunately, the she-beast stepped right in front of me with her hand stretched out in the universal symbol for "hold the fuck up."

"Now I recognize you!"

"Me?" I said, stepping backward right into a lady dressed like Harry Potter.

"All of you!" The volunteer's mouth curled into a terrifying smile made not of teeth, but of a steel cage of razor wire inside that mouth—braces that reminded me of that awful scene at the end of *Superman III* when one of the bad-guy ladies gets sucked into the evil supercomputer and is converted into a psycho robot.

Gulp. "You do?"

"How could I forget!" And then she started singing and dancing. I shit you not:

Mister Skywalker, sir
What will your pleasure be?
Let meesa save
Good Qui-Gon Jinn
You ain't never had a friend like mee(sa)

As it turned out, we'd rolled into town just as the theater company was wrapping up a run of their hit musical, a mash-up of *Star Wars* and *Aladdin* featuring timeless classics such as "Alderaanian Nights," "Vader's Hour," "One Lightspeed Jump Ahead," and, of course, the title song, "A Whole New Hope":

A whole new hooooooooooope
We are the Jedi knights of lore
We've got to stay the course
We'll use the force
Oh, and these aren't the droids you're looking for

"I went to your show like six times!" said the girl. She was jumping up and down.

"That's great?" What else was I supposed to say?

"Can I get a picture with you?"

"Sure." She huddled close, her arm around my back while I leaned into the shot. Fuck, it was hot under that mask, but this seemed to be my in. When opportunity knocks—or when it breaks out into the softshoe—you gotta take it. "Just wait until you see the sequel," I said after she snapped the photo.

"Oh my god. What is it going to be called?"

Fuck. "Uh . . . *Let It Flow*. It's a mash-up between—"

"*Dune* and *Frozen*?"

"Riiiiiiight." I took a step forward, and then another, and pretty soon, I'd cleared security to join the rest of the crew in the lobby.

"Have a fun day today!" the volunteer yelled out to us.

16

YOU'RE ENTERING A WORLD OF PAIN

Yes, we were well aware that by the time we made it into the main hall of the convention, we had maybe an hour and a half to get into that press event and prepare for the final confrontation. This one was for all the nuts, the final fight we were hoarding all our potions and sushi for.

But c'mon. We were in nerd-vana. We were absolutely going to do some looking around. If you've never been to a game convention of epic proportions, imagine that time when your parents first took you into a toy store. There's that sense that the universe is suddenly a bigger place than you thought before, that possibilities were fuzzy and vague, that dozens of worlds lay beyond the confines of your home. Then multiply that by approximately eight quintillion.

That was WrathOfCon for you—in a word, *overpowering*. Swarms of people jammed into tight aisles between booths in the main expo hall. Around every corner were elaborate displays set up by game companies hocking their newest and best. Streaming on huge TVs were brightly colored games you'd argued about on Reddit with other try-hards and die-hards, projects that had mostly existed in the world of conjecture until this moment, when they intruded into meatspace. No matter how important our business was here, a significant piece of me wanted to get lost, get my hands on a controller, and sink into game after game.

Video games not your scene? Don't think that they were the end of things. Oh no. You had a whole section of the con devoted to tabletop games like *Dungeons & Dragons*, *BattleTech*, and *Warhammer 40K*. Not interested? Maybe card games like *Magic: The Gathering* are your cuppa? And for those who are more on the hunt for celebrity sightings, might I suggest a visit to autograph alley, where a bunch of TV stars were up on the docket: Lou Ferrigno, of *Incredible Hulk* fame, former wrestler Mick Foley, Jeri Ryan, who played Seven of Nine on *Star Trek Voyager*, and others.

"They're real, and they're spectacular," Ryland whispered to me. I didn't know what she was talking about, but she seemed pretty happy about it. Meanwhile, Saff and Austin walked arm in arm in front of us, giggling to each other and pointing out things I couldn't pinpoint. I felt myself slide back into that pit of jealousy and pessimism but caught myself swilling in those thoughts and pushed them aside. It's not like I could just let these fucking feelings go like a lead weight—that's not how shit works in real life. But at the very least, I could delay the impact by staying focused.

It had taken us more than a half an hour of shoulder-to-shoulder gridlock just to get to the other side of the main hall. According to the map of the convention in the handy-dandy guide given to us after entering the hall, we were still a whole building and level away from Hall H, where the SunnTech press event was going to happen. At the rate we were going, we'd be cutting it close to the five o'clock start time of the event. Better to speed things along. Standing tall, I took deliberate steps forward, dodging people going the opposite way in order to gain a step past others in the aisle. I was so concerned about making forward progress that I almost tripped on someone plowing right into me. Stopping short, I looked down and saw that it was Saff, white as a sheet.

"Jupes! *Les jeux sont faits*! *Les jeux sont faits*!" Saff pointed to a table about fifty feet ahead of us. There sat a name tag of the person giving autographs to his adoring fans—John Stalvern, author of the *Army of One* series. Son of a fuck. Austin and Ryland joined us from opposite directions, and we pow-wowed right there and then, causing a substantial blockage in the flow of foot traffic. Whatever—this was kind of an emergency.

"What do we do?" said Ryland.

"I'll put on this Jar-Jar mask, and they won't recognize me. We can walk right past."

"What about me?" asked Saff. "I'm so fucking beautiful!"

"And humble," said Ryland. "Lest we forget."

"Right! Jupes, your mom will spot me for sure."

I looked up and around, and despite my hopes and dreams, my mother *was* there, seated right next to John, making sure his water glass was full and looking sort of bewildered at the chaos around her. This was definitely not her element. She was more about hobnobbing with stuffy professors and making sure her grad students knew who was boss. Ignoring stares from an endless stream of passing geek dudes was not something she could have possibly prepared herself for.

"That's your mom?" said Ryland, biting her knuckle. "Wow."

"Don't do that!"

"I got this," said Austin. "As soon as they're occupied, make your move to the far exit." He pointed to the stairway down to the tunnel connecting this hall to the building next door. "I'll meet you." Then he spun on his heel and queued up in line, advancing one person at a time while we loitered a few booths away, waiting for the coast to be clear.

He stepped up to John, flashed a million-dollar smile, shook his hand and engaged in conversation. Austin had never met the dude before, and still, he looked more comfortable with John than I'd ever felt. Again, that twinge of discomfort hit—not jealousy per se, but the notion that in the casting call for the movie of my life, I'd at best get the understudy role with Austin in the lead.

"C'mon!" Saff said, pushing me forward. I slid the Jar-Jar mask back on and shuffled past John's table, careful to make sure that I stayed between Mom and Saff at all times.

The plan worked. Me and the girls reached the stairway down, and a minute later, Austin walked up holding an autographed photo of the dude who was going to be my stepfather. As soon as he cleared the crowds, Saff jumped into his arms and peppered him with kisses, making the photo drop from his hands. I picked it up.

The image was one I recognized: it was the pic of John from around ten years before—his mid-thirties. His hair was still on the red side of auburn and not the blond-to-white that it had become. The wrinkles around his nose and bags under his eyes weren't as prominent as they would become. You could really see the resemblance between him and his children.

Scrawled at the bottom of the photo was a note: *Austin, always thrilled to meet a younger fan. Yours, John Stalvern.* I folded it and stuck it into my backpack, and away we went, down into the bowels of the earth and back up into Moscone North, the location of Hall H, which was another name for a portioned-off section of the grand Gateway Ballroom.

I couldn't help it. I had to know: "What did you say to him?"

"I told him I liked *Dawn of the Vanguards.*"

"Good deal," I said. "Get him talking about his books. Perfect distraction."

Austin shook his head. "Actually, I'm a fan. Seriously."

"Isn't *Dawn of the Vanguards* the one in which Carmine Stockton stops Russian terrorists from replacing all the mascots in Disneyland with murder robots?"

"You're thinking of *Elegy of the Nomad.*"

"The one about Kali cultists trying to hold the world's pineapple supply for ransom?"

"No," said Austin, seemingly bothered by my needling. "That's *Sanctum of Vileness.*"

"Oh, then it's the one where Stockton literally fights against an expertly trained band of monkeys, right?"

"Chimpanzees are very smart and very strong. And

they're not monkeys. Maybe you should read the books more closely before making fun of them." Geez, hit a nerve? Then again, Austin was right. I'd based my impressions of John's books on snarky web reviews without thinking about whether they were accurate or not. I didn't much care. The caricatures of John and his work were what I wanted, what I looked for, and what I found. Turns out I was wrong on the man. Was I wrong about his books? At the very least, I owed it to him to give them a chance.

We slowly pushed forward through the throngs until we reached the entrance to Hall H. Thankfully, it was far enough away from all the mobs frothing at the mouth to try the newest Naughty Dog game that we didn't have to worry about being overrun. That was the lone piece of good news about our situation there.

The bad news?

Beep. "Thank you. Next!" *Beep.* And repeat.

So it turned out that while I may have replicated the front of our press passes to near perfection, we'd neglected to see the all-important bar codes on the back side. As journalists filed into the room, they one by one took off their badges, flipped them over, and let one of the purple-shirted volunteers pass over it with a handheld scanner.

I threw my Jar-Jar head onto the ground in frustration. Our meager amount of luck had taken us right up to the pearly gates, but stopped just short of getting us to the other side. That's when I heard it:

"Jupes!" Only it wasn't Saff shouting it across the way. We all turned to see a girl in a purple volunteer shirt flared to the nines with patches and pins. I was positive that I'd never seen her before—not at the con and not ever anywhere else. She was short and stocky, with red hair and freckles all over her face and arms. "Oh my god, you didn't say you were coming here!"

Nope, no clue. "Hi?" I said. Okay, this felt weird. She obviously wasn't here to kick me out of the con. In fact, she seemed actually happy to see us.

"I'm Ophelia," she continued.

"I'm sorry. I don't—"

"FaztJak!" That name I did recall from the hundreds of times it appeared on our livestream chats. I'd always assumed that FaztJak was a guy, but if this trip had taught me anything, it was that I didn't know what the fuck. I couldn't help but break out into a smile and relax my shoulders. It was like meeting a person for the first time, knowing that she'd be a longtime friend. "All of us have been wondering where the hell you guys were!"

All of our *fans*. Like she's read my mind, Saff punched me right in the arm. Old times.

"Wait a second. Why are you here?" Ophelia continued. She turned around and looked at the entrance to Hall H. "Is this still about *Forever Throne*?"

We all huddled close in with her. "Yes," I told her. "Is there any way you can get us in there?"

"You need a press pass to get in," she said. "I'm working the room, making sure people get to their assigned seats." It took a second, but Ophelia connected the dots. "Wait, I can get you in!"

"How?" asked Austin.

"Can one of you meet me by the bathroom in ten minutes?" she scurried off back into the crowd, leaving us with ten minutes to kill before we either succeeded beyond our wildest dreams or crashed back to painful, jagged-edged reality. Nothing like living, eh? Ryland and Austin went off to meet Ophelia while Saff and I sat on the floor against a nearby wall, monitoring the hall door. As the crowd of reporters slowly shrunk, the level of anxiety slowly rose. Whatever Ophelia had planned, it needed to happen fast. I figured that once those doors closed, they'd stay closed, and we'd lose our only opportunity to catch Harry Leeds with his pants down (metaphorically, of course).

Saff nudged me. I turned my head and was staring straight into her phone.

"The break comes after we get back, right Jupes?" Saff was back to being Saff, holding court like only Princess Leia could. "I think it's time to let the cat out of the bag, my adoring, adoring fans," she said. "But of course, we're going to do it in style."

The chat lit up.

MaxMouse: five dollars says she robs a bank

HorizontalJustin: she's a riddle wrapped in an enigma

OraCleXX: sum shit gonna go dooooooown

KackelDackel: its 2am where I am I WILL STAY UP!

"All of you have to watch the SunnTech feed this afternoon. That'll answer all your questions. Tell your friends, tell your enemies."

"You're enjoying this too much," I told her.

"And you're not enjoying it enough." She placed her head on my shoulder and pursed her lips at the camera. "This is gonna be off the chain."

"Hey!" said Austin, emerging from the crowd. He and Ryland were decked out in decidedly un-chic purple T-shirts, two more in hand ready for me and Saff. It was the classic *mug-a-guard-and-take-his-uniform* trick, only there was no mugging needed. Instead, we relied on the dedication and generous heart of one of our . . . *fans*. There, I admitted it. I shed my Jar-Jar robes and pulled the shirt over my head. Never thought a tacky volunteer tee would feel so good. While that was happening, Austin went to hand Saff her shirt, and at the last second, snuck in for a kiss on the lips. Chat, of course, responded.

HorizontalJustin: the dream is dead

OraCleXX: I don't know that guy but I hate him

MaxMouse: hey, he's cute

"Okay, my pretties, it's getting kinda hot in here, so we're signing off," said Saff, fanning herself. "But remember—watch the SunnTech feed. Five Pacific. You do the conversion. Tell the whole fucking world."

Who the hell needed a press pass? Our purple shirts were like all-access badges to every nook and cranny in the con. By this late in the show, con volunteers were like that old familiar side table you're used to seeing in the corner of your living room. You're not sure how long it's been there because it's always been there—right there. In fact, it would be weird without it there. In the same way, every con-goer had become used to the purple wave of arms and legs making sure hallways were clear and rooms were set up for upcoming panel discussions. We were like the fucking Batman of tackily dressed menial labor.

"I'm seriously thinking of a unionization effort," muttered Saff. She, like the bulk of actual volunteers in Hall H, were handing out promotional flyers for upcoming SunnTech games to press people typing up reports on their laptops. "I mean, this is intolerable."

"Right," said Ryland, who was carrying a box full of promotional flyers meant to be distributed to the crowd. "Long will your tales of sacrifice be sung in the mead hall."

We were drafted into the volunteer corps as soon as we set foot into the room by Zeke, a jittery English dude who was all gangly elbows and knees. He was the designated head coordinator for this event. Not a minute would go by without him zipping back and forth across the room to make sure everything was going smoothly.

Zeke had cause to be anxious. In the world of major triple-A video games, this was a huge honking deal. To say that *Ancient Tablets* was "a phenomenon" didn't quite cut it. For many, these games encompassed whole lives lived in an alternate virtual universe, with husbands and wives, children and grandchildren, death and rebirth into a new adventure. Theoretically, you could log an unlimited amount of time in those games as whatever you wanted, be it a swashbuckling hero, conniving wizard, or the local bartender eking out a meager life by tips and wits. You could buy your own virtual house and keep. You didn't even have to pursue the main quest of the game if you didn't want to. In *Titan's Reach*, the third game in the series, I personally racked up a hundred and seventy-three hours taking advantage of an oversight in the in-game economy allowing me to produce copper gladiuses for 15 gp each and sell them for 30 gp each. That's right—I spent more than a week of my life committing virtual fraud on the poor inhabitants of Crag's Cove. Meanwhile a secret coup had caused the king to mysteriously abdicate his throne to his brother, a conniving villain and secret necromancer. Whatever. Someone else could stop him. Gimme my ducats.

It had been two years since *Titan's Reach* came out. The world was ready for another quest.

I was covering the west exit to the room, giving out flyers as games press walked through the doorways carting camera equipment, laptops, and other gear they needed to cover the event. This was going to be epic. There were going to be at least a dozen streams capturing this event. Millions of people all over the world would be watching.

Saff sidled up to me. "We have ten minutes before this shit begins. What's the plan?"

"Don't you have a plan?"

"Me?"

"I thought you had this part covered!"

"I did?"

Gaaaaah! She needed to come up with something quick! The best plan I could come up with was to wait until the lights went down and rush the stage. Of course, we'd never make it past the mooks. And by "mooks" I meant the swarm of burly dudes in black caps and bright yellow "SECURITY" jackets sporting Tasers on their belts—not exactly the *electrifying* way I wanted to end the night. They were already forming a wall at the front of the hall between the first row of seats and the stage area. Any effort to gang-rush the stage would end in a savage beating, no doubt.

"There's that door," she said. Yeah, I'd been eyeing the same door to the left of the stage. Even though it was locked (I'd seen Zeke use a key to get in from our side), he'd doubled up security by having a pair of purple shirts checking badges and radioing in the names of people trying to get past them. Pretty good setup. In my head, I imagined timing myself just right to slide in when Zeke rushed in or out, but of course, my mind-self had superhuman dexterity (at least a 21 with a +7 bonus to pick pockets, climb walls, and find/remove traps). There was no way I'd make it through without security or those volunteers stopping me cold.

"Sup, lady and gentleman." It was Ryland, freshly finished with handing out her stack of flyers. "Buzz is tight. My body is ready. What's the plan?"

"We don't have one," I said.

She looked at Saff. "Seriously?"

Next, Austin made his way to where we were all standing. He, too, had gotten rid of his stack and had come to hear out the next part in our grand scheme. If only we had one.

"I'm nervous," he said. "How's this going to play out?"

Silence. All eyes were on Saff.

"I don't do well under pressure!"

I noted the fabled doorway backstage to Ryland and Austin. They agreed. Getting beyond that door was the goal. What we needed to do was get through without being seen.

"A distraction," said Ryland. "Something that would make someone from the other side come out to investigate."

"It would have to be pretty big and loud," said Austin.

I shook my head. "Loud enough to be heard over the sound system? Got a spare elephant?"

"The sound system," Saff whispered. "We wouldn't have to be louder than the sound system if we were in control of it." That same sparkle, the confidence in her voice. We all turned to look at the very, very back of the conference hall. There, behind what was probably air-tight, bulletproof glass, was the sound booth, the nerve center for all the sound and lights. There were two people inside twisting knobs and throwing switches, getting ready for the show.

We had to get in there.

"Okay," said Saff. "Now I have a plan."

Saff huddled us together to go over logistics. As we listened, it was clear that we were going for broke. If this didn't work, we'd probably get in serious trouble. Like a lot of it. But if I'd learned anything about life in that week, it was this: you gotta take risks, no matter how scary, if you wanted to do something great. That didn't mean that you wouldn't pee in your pants while doing it, but you have to do it (and really, you should pack extra underwear, too). We went over the plan twice before the lights dimmed and epic music started to play.

It was go time. I took off my backpack and handed it to Ryland, who slid it onto her shoulders. That allowed me to be as light as possible. I had to be quick, after all.

But would I be quick enough? We were going to see.

17

THE SAFFRON REDEMPTION

When you think of the great schemes in all of pop culture, you can't help but think of Andy Dufresne in *The Shawshank Redemption*. Dude was cooped up for nineteen years for a crime he didn't commit, and he used all that time to grind away at the walls of his prison cell with only the sultry image of Rita Hayworth protecting his escape tunnel from discovery. For him, that promise of freedom was well worth slowly picking at those walls with a rock hammer for longer than I've been alive. All he needed was pressure, time, and a big goddamn poster.

We didn't have a poster. But we did have pressure and time. And by pressure, we weren't talking about natural geologic processes. No, we were talking about the soda-filled bladders of hapless teenage boys who volunteered to check for staff badges at the backstage door. Austin and I positioned ourselves close to where they were standing and did our best to loudly carry on about Niagara Falls, the 2004 tsunami that hit Thailand, monsoon seasons, and SeaWorld. It didn't take much for those Mountain Dew-chugging dudes to feel the, uh, waters swell.

"Hey!" one of them called out. "Hey, man. Could you spot us while we run to the bathroom?"

"Sure thing!" I said. "Anything for a fellow volunteer!"

Away they went, handing over their posts and, more importantly, their walkie-talkies to me and Austin. At the same time, Ryland was on point, maneuvering her tiny self through the crowded aisles of Hall H to snag a good position front and center. Placement was key. Her job was to wait there until just the right moment, and then unleash the full glory of the Chalice of Malice. In some ways, this was a simple task. But in other ways, it was a suicide mission—security would be on her in a second, and then who knew what would happen? Still, she insisted that she wanted it, that she was born for it. No time to argue.

The glue to this plan lay with Saff, who wouldn't have had it any other way. While we were off doing conventionally sneaky things, she was actually doing really sneaky things. Saff may come off as being flighty and effervescent, but the true Saffron Raj was a cold, calculating genius. Just when you thought her bag of tricks had run out, she surprised you with one more. In Saff's world, it was foolish to settle on one costume change when you could have two. So while everyone's attention was on the stage, with its signature theme being performed by a troupe of Tuvan throat singers while a montage of all the *Ancient Tablets* games played on the main screen, Saff stole off into a corner and did her thing. If anyone had bothered to look back, they would have seen Episode IV Princess Leia step into the shadows, only to have the jaw-dropping, libido-exploding top dog of sexy cosplays step out.

Saff's masterwork—Vampirella.

With verve, she strolled along the back wall of the hall until she stepped in front of the window to the A/V room. Needless to say, the poor saps inside had no chance. Saff tapped lightly on the glass and waited for the door to open. From there, things happened about the way you'd expect. I mean, Saff was able to convince a guy to trade a goddamn car for a date. How much more could she finagle wearing a costume that looked like it had been cut out of a Fruit Roll-Up? No fucking chance. Within a few minutes, the dudes were locked out of the room, probably sent on an errand to fetch the only coffee-esque drink she'd deign to put into her body: matcha tea spiked with almond milk (both must be certified organic) and a slice of shaved ginger twisted into a corkscrew. That left Saff with sole and unlimited control of Hall H's multimedia. To signal her sudden rise to audio/visual monarch of the room, she sent out a simple two-word text message to the rest of us:

MadAboutSaff

Get ready.

Then all hell broke loose. Harry Leeds had taken his first steps into front stage when the *Ancient Tablets* montage abruptly stopped. Replacing it was a fuzzy, half-obscured image that at first I didn't recognize. Then auto-focus did its thing, allowing me to recognize the location—it was Bryan's place, in the dining room where we were having dinner post-tournament.

Then find the son of a bitch who sold me out—the other half of the video game division, boomed Bryan's voice out the loudspeaker. *His uncle was a bigwig business guy—I think he even worked for SunnTech itself. I have no doubt they brokered a hush-hush deal behind all our backs.* As it turned out, Saff had been recording the whole exchange back at Bryan's. Something about having behind-the-scenes bonus material, she explained afterwards.

The *Harry Leeds?*

My best friend. That fucker sold out every single person who worked for Achilles by organizing that deal. And me? He stabbed me right in the gut. The entire audience was silent as it listened to every word Bryan was saying, from implicating Harry Leeds in the fall of Achilles to our impromptu revenge quest.

Everything was out there now. The fact that Harry Leeds was on stage looking like a total shitheel was one thing. The double whammy of the dozen news feeds going live onto the Internet was ten times worse. The Internet never forgives. It never forgets. And if you give it a reason to fuck with you, that fuckery will follow you to the end of time.

The walkie-talkies crackled to life. "What's happening?"

"Don't know, sir," Austin replied. "I think you better come out here, though."

A second later, Zeke came running out from backstage, through the door we just so happened to be standing next to. So as he ran out, Austin and I snuck in. At the same time, the rotating spotlights overhead started to go haywire until they focused on a single person in the front of the audience raising a golden chalice above her head.

Shit was going bananas. People were scrambling to figure out what to do. Radios were blazing with chatter:

"Someone's in the sound booth—"

"Will anyone tell me what's going on—"

"Get security down to Hall H—"

Goings-on were mad enough that no one paid any heed to two lowly volunteers making their way onto the stage. No one tried to stop us until we were already under the harsh glare of the stage lighting. The crowd looked like a single black blob, backlit by the bluish glow of cell-phone screens and HD cameras.

Bryan's speech continued: *Oh, I know what he is today— he's a great ambassador to the industry. An icon. But I also know who he really is. He's was fucking lucky to be in the right place at the right time. He's a rat who cares about no one but himself.*

"Cut the sound!" Leeds screamed into his mic. But we controlled the sound. Austin and I took main stage next to SunnTech's golden boy/mad prophet. Leeds took a good long look at us, and he knew—I could see it in how he stood on his heels, how his frown sunk into his face to cast off that roguish smirk he wore in interviews and photo-ops. He knew that we were the ones making this happen.

Think he cares about gamers? Nope. Only money and his ego.

300

The feed abruptly changed to Saff's face. Holy shit, she was streaming on our channel and simultaneously broadcasting out to every screen in the room.

"Um, hi. My name is Saffron. And this is my channel, Natural 11." She zoomed out, and boom, there were her boobs and her toned stomach and very little covering any of it. "While our erstwhile host continues to jabber on, let me tell you why you are all really here. See, back in the day, there was this video game company called Achilles. And Mr. Leeds—or as I like to call him, 'Jerkface'—sold out every single one of the people who worked there for his personal gain. He sold us out too. Because of him, the greatest contest in video game history never got its just due. If you really want to know what that's all about, you'll just have to like, comment, and subscribe to our channel." Then she blew a kiss into the camera just as the door to the sound booth crashed in.

Closer to us, security surrounded Ryland, who was holding onto the chalice like a baseball bat. Shit was degenerating quickly. I reached out to Austin to pull him back so we could get out of the light, but it was too late. A flood of angry security dudes descended upon us from behind. As we were dragged away, all I could focus on was the image of Harry Leeds's stunned expression.

The security dude dug his fingers into a bag of Sour Patch Kids and stuck the gummy mass into his lip like a wad of tobacco. The other one talked on his cell phone, staring straight at me. He recited my name, where I lived, what school I went to, and a general description.

Man, it was cold in there. They'd made me sit in a chair right in the center of this room in the convention hall's main office, right underneath a vent blasting frigid air. Was this an elaborate interrogation technique designed to get me to spill the beans on what we were doing there? It wasn't necessary. I'd already told them everything, confessed to everything bad I'd ever done, including that time in third grade when I considered looking at Polly Dallas's social studies quiz because I couldn't remember the capital of North Dakota (it's Bismarck, by the way).

"Where are my friends?" I asked Fun Dip.

Neither of the security guys gave enough of a shit to answer me. The one on the phone finished giving my info out to whoever was on the other end of the line. He hung up and approached me.

"We're moving you."

"To where?"

"You'll see."

Fun Dip stood me up and pushed me forward, the end of a baton on my lower back. I was escorted into a much bigger office, where Ryland, Austin, and Saff were waiting with security details of their own. None of them looked beat up, which was good—just about the only good thing I could squeeze out of this rotten, shriveled situation. A minute later, who would come walking in but Harry Leeds, his normally perfect hair disheveled, one side of his shirt collar sticking up, the other folded down.

In his hand, he was carrying my backpack—the same one security had taken from Ryland when they took her down.

"You all can leave now," he said to the security mooks. They did the one thing they did best and followed orders, Fun Dip glaring at me with his bottom lip bulging with sugar. Leeds closed the door quietly and then turned around to face us. "That was quite the shitshow."

Quite. Ryland, Saff, Austin, and I looked at each other. There were no signs of forceful interrogation at the hands of a heavy. But the effects of being sequestered in these offices, away from our phones, away from contacting anyone who could help us, was more than evident on our faces. Ryland, physically, looked the worst. Her hair was all wild, and her Jedi uniform had a rip down the side. She'd put up the most fight, after all, and none of the rest of us could get over to save her.

Austin and I were looking okay. Definitely stressed, but more or less fine. It was Saff, I think, who we were most worried about. If I was cold enough to be shivering, her blood had to literally be freezing. But that's what you get for wearing a costume with less material than your standard dinner napkin. Harry Leeds noticed this, took off his sport coat, and draped it around her shoulders. Normal Saff would have rebuffed the gesture with a snarky sendoff, but freezing Saff just needed to be warmer. She curled the coat around her.

"You," he said, with his gaze transfixed on Austin. Under these office lights, his superstar glow looked more like greasy blotches, like his stage makeup had melted slightly, revealing the true creature beneath. "Your father won the first *Forever Throne* tournament."

"How do you know that?" said Austin.

"Oh, there are cameras all over the place." Leeds nodded

to several black shiny globes jutting out of the ceiling. "I've watched all your interviews."

"You mean interrogations," said Saff.

He ignored that jab. "We have, of course, informed all of your parents. Except for yours—Austin, is it?"

"My father's dead. And my mom's not around."

"I'm sorry to hear that." Leeds took the opportunity to straighten his collar and re-fasten his cuff. He stood up, puffed his chest out. "You have no idea how much time that premiere took to plan, how much money and how many people it took to put on a good show."

Austin stood as tall and as straight as Leeds. "Sir, I don't care. I came here to learn more about my father. And I came here to make sure that the final tournament happens."

Leeds crossed his arms and shook his head. "Goddamn it, Bryan," he muttered. Back to us: "The damage has been done. The premiere is ruined, not to mention my name—"

"Tell us all about it, Captain Sleezebag," said Ryland.

Glare of death. "As I was saying, the show was ruined. But we may have a way out of this. You're going to have to cooperate. Are you willing to listen?"

"What do you want?" said Austin.

"To give you what you came for. A video game tournament? Sure. We can do that."

"Only, there's this one catch, right?" said Saff.

Leeds's famous smirk made its reappearance. "Miss," he said to Saff, "in the inside pocket of my jacket, there should be an envelope. I don't want to be untoward."

Saff felt around the jacket and pulled out Leeds's envelope. Inside it was a single piece of paper folded neatly into thirds. She read it, then flipped it over. "What is this?"

"A contract. More specifically, a waiver."

Austin eyed him suspiciously. "For what?"

"Bryan no doubt told you about our company's obligations. He wasn't lying about that. You—and LeRoy, is it?—being the winners of what could be construed as the first and second *Forever Throne* tournaments would be required to sign that agreement."

"What would we be agreeing with?" I asked.

"That the promised tournaments took place to your satisfaction, and that the third and final one—when it takes place—will relieve all responsibilities SunnTech bears on that front. In exchange, you get the publicity you want for your channel. We'd even let you keep the chalice, even though it technically is stolen property. The dollar amount on that crime would get someone in pretty big trouble if charges were pressed."

Shit. Instead of having him over a barrel, he had all four of us strung up by the neck waiting for the floor to drop. I could see why he was such a successful businessman. He saw all the angles, adjusting on the fly with precision and confidence. I wonder if he'd figured that this Achilles shit could come back to haunt him. Did he have contingency plans in case? That kind of pissed me off—even after getting BTFOed in front of millions and millions of viewers online, he was still trying to weasel a victory for his corporate masters.

I took the paper from Saff and read it over. The agreement wasn't complicated. We'd agree to stand behind SunnTech if anyone took them to court over the *Forever Throne* clauses in their Achilles agreement. In exchange, there would be a third and final tournament. Cut and dry, except for one loophole the size of Las Vegas. There was no stipulated time when the tournament would take place. For all we knew, Leeds could take our signatures and then wait twenty years. So I called him on it.

"This isn't going to work," I said. "There's no date that the tournament will be held."

"How about tomorrow?" Leeds shot back. "The hall is already set up for us, and I'm sure the con won't mind if we hold another high-profile event. It's yours if you want it."

Shit. The next day? It was everything that Bryan had begged us to do. I looked over at Austin to see what he thought.

"We agree," Austin said. "With one more condition. I want all the information you have on Nathan Squires."

"Done. Oh, and miss," Leeds said to Saff, "keep the coat."

With that, Austin and I signed our names on the page, come what may.

Coming out of the offices, we were greeted (read: overrun) by an army of press people jamming mics and cameras into our faces. *Flash, flash, flash,* followed by *Who are you, and how are you connected to Harry Leeds? Tell us more about Achilles Corporation. Are you taking legal steps against SunnTech?* The questions blended together into a wall of static. The four of us tightened ranks until we couldn't get any closer, and still random hands crowded into any tiny space they could.

Nevertheless, this mayhem was preferable to what lay on

the other side of the crowd: Mom and John standing alone, waiting for the sea of media to part. Saff noticed them, too. John looked tired—I mean more tired than his usual haggard yet jovial self. The travel combined with a string of junkets and countless fans asking for his autograph must have left him with bags under his eyes and a slump to his shoulders. Mom was Mom, which was to say pissed as hell with me. She refused to make eye contact with me. Every time the crowd jostled us closer to them, she averted her gaze. This was the tyranny of silence, the treatment reserved for when I'd committed the worst atrocities, like the time when I failed my physics midterm or the time she found a couple of scans from vintage *Playboy* magazines in my browser's temp folder while snooping around for just exactly that.

Slowly, I pressed through the crowd, warding away one ridiculous question after another until we broke free. Before either Mom or I could address our lingering questions and long-withheld answers, John swooped in and said, "We should get out of the open."

Following John, we rushed into one of the many secret green rooms sprinkled all over the convention center. These private lounges were set up for con guests to get away from the madness and relax with snacks and drinks continuously refreshed by our fellow purple shirts. He sat us around a free table, where we were finally able to all look at each other.

"I'm trying to stay calm," Mom began.

"Let me explain—"

"No explanations," she said. Up this close, I could make out her bloodshot eyes behind her wavy bangs. "You lied to your father and used me as an excuse. Then you lied to John when you said you were going home. And now? Are you going to lie to me again when you tell me why you're here?"

This was it—the moment I had been dreading even before we left Chicago. I wouldn't have agreed to go at all if I thought that we'd actually get caught. Groundings for weeks. Privileges revoked. No fun ever again. But now that it had unfolded, what else could I do but fight that dying fight? It's like when you're at the final boss of a game. All those items and power-ups that you'd been storing and saving up had to come out. Because this was it. My one last chance to make my stand.

"No," I said. "No more lies."

"Then why, Lee? After everything I've told you?"

I looked at my friends, who were all looking back at me. "Because I needed to do something for me," I said. "And for them."

"Hi," said Austin. "Please don't blame your son. He was only trying to help."

"Austin, right?" John asked. "We met before."

"Yes, sir. For what it's worth, I really am a big fan."

Mom shook her head, sneaking a couple of cold glances at Saff. "Were you put up to this?"

"I think, dear, that we should give the kids a break," said John, placing his hand on Mom's. She pulled it back, and he sighed. "After tomorrow, they can explain everything. But for now, they have to get ready."

"John!" Mom snapped.

"Mr. Leeds explained to us what they did and how they can make it better. As long as they appear tomorrow like they agreed to, no charges will be filed." Right. About that.

In a fit of desperation, I had blurted out John's name in the hopes that his celebrity status could get us out of our jam. Harry Leeds didn't seem to care that I'd mentioned John, but it turned out that perhaps wasn't the case.

Still, a personal call from El Numero Duderoso de Video Games wasn't enough for Mom. Crossing her arms, Mom stared past me and breathed through her nose. This was her at her most angry, past the shouting and the arguing and onto the silent treatment. I knew what she was thinking: *He's ruined everything for himself, for his future! What schools are going to take him when they can just fire up a video and see him embarrass himself in front of thousands of people? After how hard I've tried!*

I reached over and took Mom's hand, held her fingers tight in mine. She looked up at me, shocked. I'm not sure why, but I suspected that it was because I'd never done anything like that before. I wasn't the most touchy-feely. I got that from Dad. *Standoffishness*, Mom called it. *Aloof.* But it wasn't the time to dwell on me. She had to know the truth of things, the truth that I finally knew.

"I love you," I whispered. "I don't tell you that enough."

"Lee, why—"

"Dad told me everything." The second I said that, it was like her spell of beauty shattered. She looked uncharacteristically lost, unable to form a coherent thought. "I know why you've been pushing me so hard, what you lost because of me."

She started to cry. "Never! I never want you to think that! Why did he . . . ?" She hung her head and placed it against my chest. "He was so scared," she said. "But he stayed with me, anyway. I'll always love him for that."

"But you left."

"I love him," she said. "But I was never *in love* with him. I don't know if you understand."

I did. Fuck, did I ever.

"I've taken the liberty of flying Walter out here," John interrupted. "Your mother, too, Saffron."

"Was Dad mad when you talked to him?" I asked Mom.

"He seemed well."

Define *well*, I thought, right before my phone started to ring. In fact, all four of our phones—mine, Saff's, Austin's, and Ryland's—started jamming and jiving. We reached for them at the same time, but in a race to see who was fastest on the phone draw, it would be pretty dumb to bet against Saff. She tapped over to her text messages and read out loud to the table:

Unknown

Attention: We have set you up with accommodations at the Marquis Hotel across the street from the Moscone Center. It's close, so be sure to show up tomorrow by 11:00 AM. In fact, be early. H.L.

Sure. Like we'd miss it. A few days before, we'd just been some joker kids with a far-fetched scheme and a handful of names that had been lost in history. Now, we were only a few hours away from altering that history forever. Was I being a bit presumptuous? Well, sure. I mean, it was just a video game tournament. Then again, it was a video game tournament for an audience of potentially millions.

"Lee, your mother and I have to get to a press conference in a few minutes," said John. "But you—all of you—are welcome to come if you like. I'm going to make a pretty big announcement."

"A three-picture deal, right?" I said.

"How did you know?"

"Cassidy," I said. "When you get a chance, you should call her. She really needs you." For the first time ever, I felt comfortable with the idea of John being part of my family. Not because he was actually a pretty cool guy (I mean, that didn't hurt), but because his life wasn't nearly as perfect as I thought it was. He'd made some mistakes in the past, just like all the rest of the people around that table. Just like me.

He and Mom got up to go. But before she left, Mom took me aside.

"Maybe after this, we could have a night. You and me."

"That would be great," I told her. That was the truth.

"That did just happen, right? I mean, we did just rock the fucking shit, didn't we?" Ryland was in a good mood, jumping on the bed in her underwear, slam-dancing to the titanic riffs of heavy-metal-meets-rockabilly outfit Volbeat pouring out her phone. "Had a one-night stand with a chick from Denmark. Ah Frederikke, she loved this shit."

It was pretty obvious that Ryland was trying her best to lighten my mood. And maybe it was sort of working in the *I-can't-believe-how-far-you're-taking-this* way. I mean, there wasn't much reason why I should have been so dour. Because that shit did just happen. We just hammered Harry fucking Leeds in the proverbial nutsack and gained a buttload of notoriety as a result. I'd quit checking my phone when a new YouTube DM came in and eventually just notifications on mute. Judging from the sidelong glances we were getting from people in the lobby—and from the explosion of subs we were getting on the channel—that next day was going to be the most surreal of my life.

And yet, only two things were on my mind. One was Mom. I'd never seen her so uncomfortable before, like a knight without his trusty sword. The way she looked at me when I told her that I knew her secrets—it was like looking backward in time to that scared sixteen-year-old who'd taken pregnancy test after pregnancy test hoping that they were just all defective, someone who didn't have the future in the palm of her hand. That was the mother I wish I'd gotten to know a long time before. Maybe she'd been there all along, but I wasn't willing to let her have her say.

And then there was two: Saff and Austin were sharing the room next door. I'd hoped and dreamed that one day it would be me making her laugh like she was on the other side of that wall. Now it was just another fantasy for the pyre. Yet, despite me finally, really accepting this reality, my heart—that tiny piece that wasn't broken, that part right there that hadn't been battered yet because I'd managed to swing my elbows out and let out one last King Kong bellow to keep it from cracking—well, it went ahead and broke.

Dreams die hard, especially when they thrash around scratching and clawing for life.

Ryland leapt from her bed to mine in a swan-dive cannonball. Then she rolled over and grabbed the hotel info book on the nightstand. "Look at this. Twelve dollars for a bag of peanuts from the mini-bar! They must be amazing if they're that expensive."

"I'm not hungry."

"You're killing me, Smalls," she said. "We have a hot tub with jets, a fifty-inch TV with surround sound, and a ten-page room service menu that includes fries of both the regular and curly persuasions!"

"Sorry."

"My high is officially murdered." She mimed herself being strung up by an invisible noose. "I thought . . . we were . . . friends!"

There was a thump from next door, like a body had rolled off a bed and landed hard on the floor, followed by more laughing. What the sounds didn't directly state, my head filled in using the spare parts of my fantasies from the last four years.

"I know what you're going to say," I said. "Somewhere out there is a girl who wants to be with me, and there are plenty fish in the sea. Like little baby walruses."

"Fuck the walruses. Let's get shitfaced."

"Wha?"

"There's a bar downstairs, and you look like you need some booze."

I looked at Ryland. "We're not old enough, and last time I drank, it wasn't pretty."

She draped her arms around my neck. "A fake ID is a

girl's best friend, Double-J. And I'll be right there to make sure you stick to barely legal Shirley Temples. To start."

"I don't know."

"Of course you don't. That's why I'm here. C'mon. I'll text Clancy to meet us." Speaking of our nonresident resident Scotsman, on our way from the convention center to the hotel, we ran into Clancy fresh off a run down Market Street to the Embarcadero Fountain. He excitedly told us that he'd made around four hundred dollars that day alone from taking convention-goers into the city and down the waterfront. While he was sad that we wouldn't be staying with him an extra day, he was glad to bring the rest of our stuff back to the hotel.

Post pants, Ryland and I ventured out of the room and took the elevator down. She elbowed me playfully, mussed up my hair—anything to get me to smile. It worked. If anything, I was most grateful on this trip for meeting PoltergeistRalph in the flesh. She was just as broken as all the rest of us, just as damaged. But she was trying not to be. It was a good reminder that sinking into myself wasn't the only way to handle shit. You could face life with open eyes, with an open heart, and with a nice pair of brass knuckles. I let myself relax and checked our channel counts again.

Views were multiplying exponentially. People tuned in just to see who the hell this mysterious scantily clad beauty was, who these dudes on the stage being dragged away were. The history of Achilles Corp. The soul of what video games once were. That might sound hyperbolic, and it is. But seeing that sub count rise in real time, and the view counts spiral into five and six, then *seven* figures?

I was ready to believe just about anything at that point.

Ryland took my arm, and we walked out of the elevator together. Great timing, too. Clancy had just walked in the front door trailing Saff's bag and wearing Ryland's. He waved hi with a big smile on his face. But that wasn't what we were focusing on in that moment. It was the blue and red flash of police lights outside. No sirens were blaring, but the lights were constant and consistent—the car was parked and not moving.

"Hey, you know what's happening with the fuzz?" asked Clancy.

"No idea." Sure, though my instincts didn't like this development. "We should go back upstairs, I think."

Ryland insisted on going forward instead. "I wanna know what's up." We started our approach to the front desk to ask. At the same time two uniformed police officers—both lady cops—were en route to the same destination from the outside. They got there first.

"We're looking for Ryland Taggart," one cop said to the desk clerk.

We skidded to a halt. Ryland ducked her head and did an about face.

"Shit! Shit, shit! I bet calling the cops on me was better than sex for Eugene," she hissed.

"Let's get out of the open," I said.

The three of us walked briskly down a hallway from the lobby to Barnaby Chen's, the hotel's Pan-Asian fusion restaurant. The place was pretty packed with an odd mixture of industry hobnobbers positioned at the bar enjoying pricey drinks and superfan con-goers in Pikachu tees and cat-ear headbands crowding around pu-pu platters dripping with deep-fried goodness. We plowed into the masses waiting at the front for a table to open up. For the moment, we were safe.

"We can't just hide here all night," said Ryland.

"Then we just have to stay one step ahead."

"Why are they lookin' for ya?" asked Clancy, confused.

"We kind of stole a car on the way here," said Ryland. "I was gonna bring it back. Eventually."

"Why don't we sneak out the back and then hide out at my place?" Clancy suggested. "They'll never find you."

Ryland seemed to consider the possibility. "Please tell me you have a green card."

Clancy smiled. "I haven't played field hockey in years."

"Yeah, and I'm sure Carmelo, Arturo, and Juan are in the same boat as you."

"I won't let them take you away," I said.

Ryland closed her eyes and took a deep, deep breath. "This is my shit. I have to own it."

"No," I said. "No way."

"I'm doing this." She took a step toward the door into the lobby, but I grabbed her arm and pulled her back into the crowd.

"You can't. Please."

"Will you fucking listen to me for once!" she said, looking almost like she was going to punch me. "You have a chance to do something fucking spectacular. And I sure as fuck am not going to ruin it." Another pair of police officers came through the doors hunting for their quarry. Ryland was right. It was only a matter of time. "Now get out of here. I got a scene to make." She motioned toward the swinging door to the kitchen.

I knew she was right. But I hated it. It's said that we are

the heroes of our own stories. If that's true, I'd done a fucking amazing job of shirking that duty. Saff had to save me, Austin had to save me, Cassidy had to save me, and now Ryland had to save me. I was little more than dead weight (a lot of it), a damsel in distress without the cleavage.

Ryland stopped and turned around.

"Can I ask you guys one question, though? It's important."

"Sure. Anything." I kept my eyes trained on the cops surveying the scene.

"So," she began, "when you take a piss . . . and there's like shit stuck to the toilet bowl . . . do you ever make believe that your dick is a spaceship and the shitstains are enemy ships that you blast with your piss ray of death?"

"What? No!"

She nodded. "Okay. I've always wondered that. About guys." Clancy handed Ryland her backpack, and with that, she broke away from the crowd and headed directly for the officers. Clancy and I stayed behind and ducked into an alcove next to the kitchen out of sight, so we could only hear but not see the ensuing chaos.

"You looking for Ryland Taggart?" she screamed. "Well that's me!" Chirps and chatter from police walkie-talkies sounded out, along with the *tap-tap* of hard soles on premium marble tile. "But if you want me . . ." Ryland continued, dishing out her best Bonnie and Clyde, ". . . you'll have to catch me first, coppers!" What followed was a dizzying smash-up of sounds, from hotel staff yelling to luggage carts upturning their contents onto the floor. There were gasps from hotel guests and even the sound of a wheelchair *clatter-clanging* onto the ground, all to the epic score of Ryland screaming "Attica! Attica! Attica!" Then, as we listened, her voice became fainter and fainter as the police were taking her closer and closer to the hotel doors and farther and farther away from us.

Until she was gone.

"Boyo," said Clancy, shaking me out of a trance. "I'll find out where she is, okay?"

"Be careful."

"I'm pretty smart, you know," he said with a crooked smile. "I'll make sure she's good."

I could only nod while he ran out in hopes of catching the police car before it was too far to follow.

After dropping off our luggage back in my room, I wandered around the hotel in a fugue state somewhere between sleepwalking and drug-induced amnesia, like Ace Harding in *Déjà Vu* (great point-and-tap detective noir on the NES, BTW). Oh, I still knew that I was LeRoy Jupiter Jenkins and that through a quirk of fate, I'd found myself on the precipice of Internet fame (and more probably infamy). But was that accurate? Did I really know anything? Surely not some things, like what the hell I was supposed to do with myself. Ryland was gone, hauled off to jail, and Clancy had left to tail her. Mom and John were presumably being bombarded with questions about the brand spanking new Carmine Stockton cinematic universe (or CSCU as it has come to be known). Austin and Saff were *occupied*.

I was all alone.

Eventually, I found myself walking next to the indoor pool, which was—like every other part of the hotel—jam packed with people. I didn't know what I was there for, what exactly I was looking for until I found it. In an alcove next to the bathrooms was a bank of vending machines—your classic chip and candy deal, your pop machine, and something more enticing: a machine that spit out ice cream bars at two bucks a pop. Ah fat, my old friend. Do you know the Klingon proverb that tells us ice cream is a dish that is best served cold? The answer to that was *of course you do*. If it's not cold, then it would just be like a disgusting sticky soup, and no one likes that . . . I said to the ice cream vending machine.

Ho-kay. Best to make my purchase and move on. But which one? After scanning my choices, I saw that there were some real classics: Choco Tacos, patriotically colored Firecrackers, Blue Bunny Screamers, Orange Creamsicles, Drumsticks. Down at the very bottom was one kind of ice cream bar that I'd never seen before called Bubble O'Bill, shaped like the head of a ten-galloned cowboy, complete with handlebar moustache and a bullet hole in his hat. The pièce de résistance was the source of the name. In the center of his face, Bubble O'Bill had a big round nose made out of a green gumball.

The choice was made, the money was paid, and I was the proud owner of my very first Bubble O'Bill bar. I stepped back from the machine, letting the dude behind me have his turn. The cool touch of ice cream on my tongue made me feel so much better about the world. Sure, I knew that this was a temporary high—my sugar-loving endorphins kicking in and swearing at me for making them wait so long for the good stuff. It wasn't the best ice cream novelty I'd ever had, but something was better than nothing.

"That's just my luck, eh?" I heard someone say behind me. Turning around, I spotted a man in swim trunks with a towel draped around his neck. Immediately, I was struck by a sense of knowing him, though I couldn't quite place the face. He was an older gentleman with a swoop of auburn hair on his head, not unlike John's but with much more of the red intact. By his accent, I placed the man as English. And if I didn't know any better, I could have sworn that he was . . .

Oh my fuck, he was.

"You . . . you're . . ."

As soon as I started stammering, he placed his fingers right on my lips.

"I assure you, I'm not who you think I am." Bull fucking shit. This dude was only the biggest walking, talking, dancing, and singing Internet meme of all time. Bigger than fucking me or even my *World of Warcraft* namesake. Swap out his swim gear for comically oversized 1980s sunglasses, a black turtleneck, a trench coat, and too-slick-to-believe moves, and you fucking have the one and only—

"You're still thinking that I'm him, aren't you?" he said.

"C'mon, man. You're clearly—"

Fingers on the lips again. "Let's suppose that I am this person—which, I again assure you, I am absolutely *not*. One would imagine that a performer whose mystique is tied to him appearing when least expected would most likely not want his name announced to possibly tip off bystanders to his presence."

"So, you don't want me to say your name?"

"Except you weren't going to say *my* name, were you?"

"Um, then what is your name?"

"My name is George. George Washington."

"You clearly just made that up."

"I did not! My mum adored the great statesman."

"Who helped defeat the British."

"She was rubbish at history," he said, rubbing his head in frustration. "Look, I was just hoping that there was more Bubble O'Bill. It appears you bought the last one."

I glanced down at the ice cream machine. Sure enough, next to the button for Bubble O'Bill was the red light indicating that the supply had run out.

"Sorry," I said, holding up the bar with a big chunk bitten out of it.

"Damn," he muttered. "They're pretty rare in these parts, you know."

"Here," I said holding it out for him to take. "You take it. It won't help me. Not really."

"Nonsense. We can share."

Together, we walked over to a bench next to the indoor pool frothing with kids doing belly flops, sat down, and took turns taking bites out of Bubble O'Bill's strawberry-flavored face. My companion draped his towel over his head like a cowl. He'd made the excuse that it kept his head cool, but I think I knew what he really needed it for.

"I sense that you're troubled," he said, after taking a big chomp of ice cream. "Thoughts?"

"I'm tired of failing. At everything. Life."

"I'm sure it's not that bad. Everybody is good at something."

"Sure. Video games. But so what? Beating a fucking game

doesn't make you a smarter person, a nicer person, a better person. Your parents won't like you more. Girls won't like you more—that's for damn sure."

"Well," he began, "let's once again imagine that I have intimate knowledge of what it feels like to be the ass end of a good time. It would be reasonable to conjecture that such a person could live through such tribulations and come out okay."

"What if okay isn't enough? What if you can't overcome who you are, which is a fuck-up?"

He shook my shoulder. "If I was, indeed, a person whose trade relied on me performing in front of people who have real and likely unrealistic expectations, it would stand to reason that I'd sometimes suffer crises of confidence. Am I the man they want me to be? Will they feel that they got fairly compensated for the ticket price? In the end, you won't know. In the end, you don't have control over how others see you."

"I'm not asking for control—just a break, you know?"

"Ah, but a break from who? Are all these people beaming their thoughts into your brain, or are you telling yourself all these things? Who calls you a failure?"

"I guess it's me, mostly."

"Right. And do you know what I would do in the hypothetical situation that I was a world-renowned singer and musician suddenly plagued with doubts about my self-worth? I'd look into a mirror and tell my reflection that I wasn't ever going to give him up. And, by George, there wasn't any chance that I'd ever let him down. And let's not even mention running around or deserting him, because they're straight out."

"Did you just . . ."

"Yes. Yes I did. May I have the gumball?" Over the course of the conversation, we'd reduced the stalwart countenance of Mr. O-Bill to the late cowboy's nose resting on a sliver of ice cream. I nodded, and Mr. Washington greedily popped the gumball into his mouth.

"Sir?"

"Call me George."

"George, are you here for the convention?"

"Convention?"

"WrathOfCon. It's why there's a whole bunch of people running around in costumes."

"I don't know what you're talking about," he said, but the smile on his face told me otherwise. Our mutual connection reduced to a flimsy stick of wood, he got up and thanked me for sharing the last Bubble O'Bill. "I hope this has helped you a bit."

"It has," I said. "But I get the sense that it's up to me to figure this shit out."

"Indeed," he said. "No matter the circumstances, you are always the ultimate master of your own fate. Change your viewpoint, and your reality changes with it." He took a few steps backward, disappearing into a plume of steam that rose from the hot tub. "And remember, you didn't see me. You didn't see . . . George Washington."

I was in my room again, but not alone. George had left me with a bit of wisdom to keep me company. Before anyone else, I'd been letting *myself* down. I'd given up on things before they started. I deserted myself before ever giving shit a chance. I didn't like to take risks, to go for long-odds chances. Make sure I get the right power-ups at the right time, and I'll have enough to kill any enemies that storm the dungeon or swarm the space station. Find the one spot where the boss can't hit you with his fireballs, and I'll win every time. But there are no cheat codes in life. No warp zones. No invincibility potions or screen-clearing cluster bombs.

In video games, though, I'd take all of those I could get. I was sitting on the floor, my back against the bed, laying into my Achilles Mark II controller. My headphones were turned up high, immersing me into the game (and fully shielding me from noises that might leak through the painfully thin hotel walls). I was back at *Forever Throne I*, building up muscle memory to help me with the next day's challenges.

There was a loud knock on the door. My heart rate shot up, thinking that it might have been the police back for more after grilling Ryland for answers. I paused the game and momentarily thought about sneaking out the window. But seeing as that I was six stories off the ground, that didn't seem like a very good idea. I gritted my teeth and answered the door, keeping the chain hooked up in case I had to make a break and leap out the window anyway.

"Hey man." It was Austin. "You busy?"

"Just practicing," I said. "Where's Saff?"

"Out for a walk. She says her pores need it?"

"Oh yeah," I said. "She thinks you absorb fresh air through your skin, so she likes to go on walks to 'invite the nutrients in.' Please don't ask me more about it."

"You and Ryland just hanging around?"

I shut the door, unlatched the security chain, and invited him in. "Something happened," I said. "Something bad." I gave him the short, short version of what happened with Ryland, sparing the parts in which I cowered like a ninny.

"Shit," he said, copping a squat onto the bed in front of the TV. "Should we do something?"

I showed him the text she'd sent me earlier.

PoltergeistRalph

Hey, DJ. I'm spending the night in jail, and they're letting me have my one phone call in text form.

Remember my dad, the evil corporate lawyer? He did his black magic sweet-talking and sprung me out. Bad thing is that I fly to Seattle tomorrow morning to have an "intervention." Fuck if I know what that means.

BTW, Clancy came and checked in on me. What a perfect host! Remember, you got this, bro. After you kick Austin's ass (I like the guy, just like you better), you're gonna really need those diagrams. Just say the word, and I'll send.

"Diagrams?"

Thinking fast, I picked up the controller and offered it to him. "I'm on level fifty-four, and it's kind of a bitch."

Austin started up where I left off and was immediately assaulted by the newest challenge that level fifty-four had unlocked—the centipede warriors. At least that's what I called these long worm-like creatures who wound about the level trying to ram you into submission. They moved a lot like the centipedes from *Centipede*, the classic Atari arcade game, only it was worse since these things had shields they could hold up to deflect projectiles you shot at them.

Centipede warriors swarmed him and mowed him down again and again until he stumbled upon the solution—maneuver yourself perpendicular to how they're moving and pummel them then. They can't turn their shields sideways, so that was their weak spot.

"Shit, it took me ten minutes to figure that out!" he said, lamenting his slow uptake.

"Don't worry about it," I told him. "It took me twenty. And a lot of dying."

He smiled. "It's weird, you and me competing against each other tomorrow."

"How so?"

"I mean, the idea was probably to pit these two winners who'd never met against each other. Then you could play up the drama of a title match."

"Yeah, sometimes things don't end up like you imagine they'd be, so you take what you get."

"It feels more like a play," he said. "It's not like a real competition. You'll wipe the floor with me, we give Harry Leeds his PR boost, and everyone gets what they want."

"That sounds okay to you?"

"Sure," he said. "You and me—it's not like we're against each other. I did this whole thing to find out more about my father, and I will. It's a no-lose situation." Yet here he was practicing the game, getting into it enough that the muscles in his forearms were constantly tensed. "I never thanked you, you know. Not face to face, man to man."

"Thank me? For what?"

"For all of this."

I looked all around the room. "You can thank SunnTech."

"That's not what I mean. I mean this whole trip—you and Saff coming to my house."

"And then destroying it, remember?"

"It wasn't a home," he said. "More like a rest stop. You know, I probably would never have followed up with Achilles. I'd get on with getting on. I'd forget and just keep scrapping. That's how you survive—you don't think too long term. You learn not to want things, not to get attached."

"I need to learn that. All I do is want shit I can't have."

My headphones were still plugged into the TV, so game sounds couldn't fill in the silence that Austin and I shared. But that was okay. We were content to game in silence, save for the subtle clicking of the controller buttons and whirring of the air conditioner.

"Can I ask you a personal question?" Austin asked after a while.

"Okay." At this point, permission was a formality. We'd both been through enough shit together that it wouldn't matter what he asked.

"Back there, when you were talking to your mom, were you afraid of what she would say?"

Hmm. Well. "I guess it didn't matter how afraid I was. I had to say *something*."

"I know how you feel about Saff."

"Dude, it's okay—"

"Let me finish," he said. "No matter how jealous you might feel of me for being with her, I want you to know that I'd never felt more jealous of anyone when I saw you, your mother, and your stepfather with your real father on his way. All I'd ever wanted was to have that—even just to have my grandma back. A real family."

"Want some of mine? I got plenty to spare."

We both laughed at that one and kept playing the game.

18

I'M ALL OUT OF BUBBLE GUM

I woke up the next day to all the lights in the room being on. My arms felt like jelly and my legs felt like cinder blocks, and for a second, I thought that I might have dreamed that whole previous day. A look around the room sadly told me otherwise. The Mark II was hooked up to the TV via the BossBox and one of the dragon carts was plugged into the top. But Ryland's bed didn't show any sign of being slept in.

It had all happened. Everything.

Sitting up, I grabbed my phone to check in and see if Harry Leeds had sent any more information on what was going on today. I didn't expect the torrent of messages I found:

Dad

Hi Lee. It's late, and you're probably asleep. Anjeli and I have arrived in San Francisco. We'll talk tomorrow morning.

Mom

Meet us in the lobby of your hotel in the morning. 9 AM or so. We can have breakfast together. Love, Mom.

Cassidy

Hi, LeRoy. I talked to dad this morning. It was nice. I hope you're okay.

And then one more message from that morning—fifteen minutes before I woke up, as a matter of fact:

MadAboutSaff

Where are you? I told everyone to let you sleep. Don't tell me you chickened out! If you did, I'll kick your ass.

P.S. Sorry about Ryland. She was okay, I guess.

Shit. I rolled over right off the bed and onto the floor. Getting up, I dragged myself over to the bathroom and flicked the light switch, then leapt into the shower for a much-needed wash. I figured that everyone would gladly trade more waiting to not be subject to that combo of residual road grime, con funk, and anxiety stank that I reeked of. I got dressed in the only clean T-shirt and shorts I had left, gathered all my shit into my backpack, and walked to the door, stopping short when I reached the mirror.

By George . . .

No lie, I felt good. Like better than I'd felt in a good long time. I should have known that was a hint that the situation was about to go belly up. I opened the door to my room, stepped into the hallway, and rounded a corner straight into a wall—or what felt like a wall. Only, this wall had two gargantuan legs, arms like twin pythons, and a stench like the worst stogie you could imagine.

Oh shit was what I thought.

"Oh shit," was what I said, because standing right there was the absolute last person in the entire world I wanted to see: the battle-scarred, cauliflower-eared, raggedy-bearded monstrosity of a man who had plagued both my dreams and waking hours. And he was a little bit pissed.

The Sheriff hauled me up to my feet by the collar and held me against the wall with a forearm to my neck. Fishing out my room key from my back pocket, he dragged me back over to the door, unlocked it, and took me back inside, where he threw me onto the bed.

Gulp. This was it—an inglorious end to an inglorious kid by an inglorious hand. I felt my pockets for my phone, but even if I could have reached it before he snapped my neck, I wouldn't have been able to text out a message, wouldn't have been able to dial 911 fast enough before he punched a hole in my soul and executed a *Mortal Kombat*-style fatality.

"Funny meeting you here," he said, lighting up his cigar. I pointed at the no-smoking sign on the wall and then held my arms up to ward away an incoming flurry of blows that never came. "Not so brave when you don't have other people running interference for you."

He stepped closer to the bed, and that's when I executed my crazy ninja move of rolling away and onto the floor. I popped back up and ran the only way I could—farther into the room. I don't know what I was thinking. Actually, I know exactly what I was thinking: death by gravity surely beat out a slow, prolonged pummeling. Why did I never figure out how to work the window lock?

"My family is downstairs," I said. "They're expecting me."

"What a coincidence," he said. "Because I'm all about reuniting families too."

The Sheriff was right on top of me. His tobacco-stained grin smelled like death.

"Look, I know what you want, but you can't have it," I said, mustering up my last shreds of courage. "The game doesn't belong to you!"

"Heh. All this time, you thought I wanted that piece of shit? My job was to get the kid."

"You're supposed to kill Austin?"

"Kill? If I wanted to kill the twerp, I would have. Nah, I was supposed to bring him to my employer, who just so happens to live here in Frisco. If I'd known you were coming here, I'd have paid for your ride myself." Fuck me. The Sheriff was a hired thug for the real mastermind, cloaked in shadow, still unknown. But who could that have been?

"Why didn't you just tell him that when you knew who he was?" I asked, trying to stall my inevitable demise.

"I was scouting him out, trying to find the right time to give a few explanations. You know, how civilized people behave. Unlike some people who go off and steal other folks' stuff."

"What about someone who wrecks your stuff and acts like a complete psycho?"

The Sheriff grunted with amusement. From his pocket, he produced a cassette tape and tossed it at my chest. I caught it and held it up to the light. It was scratched up and partially melted in the corners, but I could still make out the name of the group on the side.

Grim Reaper.

"Eye for an eye, kid. That's how the world works."

This was my chance. I feigned a big sigh, and instead threw the cassette in his face and imagined myself like a cannonball fired straight ahead, aimed for the open doorway. If I could just make it past The Sheriff's giant mitt of a hand . . .

The dude dodged the tape, caught me in a bear hug, and threw me onto the bed. Fuck! This was it! He was going to bludgeon me to death with the telephone. Or whip out a sawed-off and blow my brains out. Or fold me like a pretzel and leave the mess for the maid to clean up.

Here Rests LeRoy Jenkins, Twisted Motherfucker, my epitaph would say.

"You got guts, kid," he said, standing over me. "No brains, but guts. I like that. That's why I want to make you an offer that you really shouldn't refuse. You deliver the Austin kid to me, and I'll split my finder's fee with you. Ninety-ten."

"That doesn't sound like a very good trade."

"You also get to walk normally for the rest of your life."

On paper, it was a pretty sweetheart deal. I could still win the *Forever Throne III* tournament and make extra cash by selling Austin out. On the other hand, what did paper ever do for me besides give me cuts on my fingertips and allow my teachers to give me bad grades? No. No way. Austin was my friend, and I wasn't going to give him up, wasn't going to let him down, and all the other things. *Thank you, George Washington, for this little piece of dignity before I get my face beaten in.*

Only, that didn't happen. Instead, The Sheriff let up and took a step back from the bed.

334

"I can see you need more time to think about it, so I'm going to give it to you."

"You're letting me go?"

"Don't say I'm not a nice guy." He tore a piece of stationery off the complimentary pad on the nightstand, wrote something down on it with the fancy hotel pen, and then let the paper fall onto my chest. He ashed his cigar, took a long drag off of it, and puffed out a huge plume like he was Smaug the Dragon. "We'll talk again soon." Then, without another word, he turned and walked out the door.

I raced downstairs to the restaurant where I was supposed to meet up with everyone else. My heart was pounding from my meeting with The Sheriff. What did he mean about *time to think about it*? Did he actually believe I'd sell out my friends for some crappy commission? And who was this mysterious employer he spoke of? Nothing in the Achilles story thus far pointed to anyone besides Harry Leeds in the Bay Area. Is that who he was talking about? No, couldn't have been. Leeds was blindsided by us the previous day. It wouldn't have made sense that he was the mastermind.

But then who?

Until I could figure this out, I decided to keep The Sheriff's presence to myself. He'd demonstrated that nothing Earthly could stop him from coming after us, so there was no need to introduce additional anxiety into the situation. I resolved that next time we met, I would be prepared with backup and a gameplan.

I entered the restaurant to see my family and friends sitting at a big round table enjoying breakfast. There were Mom and John, and across from them sat Dad and Anjeli. Dad looked good, maybe even *happy*. He'd trimmed his beard and gotten a haircut. And were those new glasses? Either that, or he'd decided that cleaning them might make a better public impression than leaving dust and grime on his lenses.

Saff and Austin were there too. Saff was dressed in an uncharacteristically reserved wardrobe: a plain long-sleeve T-shirt with black pants that were—dare I say—business casual? It turned out that when she'd heard that her Mom was on her way, Saff phoned and asked for a wardrobe infusion, only for Anjeli to bring pieces of her own wardrobe for Saff to wear (which she didn't look too thrilled about). She should have been thankful Anjeli didn't bring a nun habit for her to wear.

I took the empty seat next to Austin.

"Hey man," said Austin. There was something in his voice, a waver that I hadn't heard since that bomb-out of an encounter at Golden Gulch.

"You okay?"

"Sure. Nervous about today."

"Good morning, Lee," said Dad. I looked down at his breakfast, a big hungry-man skillet with eggs, potatoes, and sausage slathered in thick gravy. Nary a trace of a sandwich cookie in sight. "This is surely the strangest thing to happen to us in a long time."

"I'm glad they didn't get themselves killed," said Anjeli.

"Don't speak too soon," Mom quipped. "I fully intend to break new records in grounding."

She and Anjeli exchanged pleasant smiles, probably for the first time in a decade.

John handed me the menu. "Austin was just telling us about himself."

"There's not much to tell, sir," he said. "My father's deceased, and my mother is not in the picture. My grandmother raised me, but she died."

"My grandmother raised me too. She was my role model."

"Mine too."

I sat back in my chair and listened to the conversation go back and forth. As every person at that table opened up, it became apparent (at least to me) that we all came from family situations that were fucked up in some way. And hilariously enough, I kept coming back to the same realization: I came out ahead of all of them. I had two fathers. I had a mother who literally gave up on her own pursuits for a decade and a half in order to have me. I had friends who would literally jump into a jail cell for me.

Maybe it didn't suck so much to be LeRoy Jupiter Jenkins.

"So . . . I want to make an announcement," said Dad. "When you kids left, Anjeli and I . . . well, we had a lot to talk about. And we . . . well . . ."

"What Walter wants to say is that he and I . . ." She raised her arm to show that she and Dad had been holding each other's hands under the table.

"So you're dating?" asked Saff.

"I am too old to date," said Anjeli. "We're spending time together."

"I'm happy for you, Walter," Mom said. And I believed that she meant it. Because I was, too. I was past the point of trying to construct the world to suit me, mostly because it was a lost cause. No matter how much I rued fate, it had a way of tooling around with shit to get what should happen to happen. Like I said before, we're tasked with being heroes of our own stories. But this wasn't only my story—it was Mom's and Dad's. It was Saff's. It was Austin's and Ryland's and Bryan's and Ed's and Benny's and Clancy's. Even Harry Leeds had a part to play.

The waiter came around and, spotting a new arrival to the table, asked me, "What would you like?"

"I'm good for now," I said. Fuck breakfast. I was ready to game.

In one big group with us kids in the middle, we walked into Hall H strong and together. Overnight, the venue had undergone a transformation from an ordinary presentation hall into a concert stage, complete with a pit for audience members to stand in. Two more huge-screen televisions had been brought in and suspended from the ceiling for the benefit of anyone watching from the back of the room. Dozens of purple shirts were flitting from corner to corner as crowd control to funnel the dozens—no, hundreds—of people streaming in from all the entrances.

"Holy fucking shit," said Saff. "This is crazy!"

I was speechless, my head on a swivel.

As we walked into the room, it was like a spotlight was on us. Folks milling around in the back caught one look at us and ran up, hugged us, treated us like they'd known who we were. In fact, they kind of did. One of them slapped me five while six more dudes huddled around us to cheer us on. Fans leaned into the aisle to snap selfies with us. Turns out, while we were sleeping, our stunt had made the rounds, got featured on all the shows, lit up social media like a death star being run through by a star destroyer.

480,000 new channel subscribers in less than twenty-four hours. Not bad for a day's work.

"You're so beautiful," a little girl said to Saff.

"Oh my god, I know!"

"I want to be like you."

"Of course you do!"

"You're my favorite YouTuber."

"Because you have eyes and a brain!"

More than us, our parents looked positively dumbfounded, even John, who I'd have thought was used to the limelight. When we reached the gate surrounding the stage area, security made an opening and ushered Austin and me past their impenetrable wall. Catching my hand at the last second was Saff, wheeling me around.

"Jupes . . ."

"We did it," I said.

"Yeah, we really did," she said. "Now get up there and win the whole fucking thing."

"What about your boyfriend?"

"We're not talking about my boyfriend."

"Then what are we talking about?"

"My best friend," she said. "The one who deserves a fucking trophy for all the bullshit I've put him through— even though I was right about everything, and it was all worth it."

"I think you're insane," I said. "And I love you."

I smiled as I turned to go with security up onto the stage where Harry Leeds was waiting. He led me and Austin behind a curtain to wait while volunteers pushed past us, wheeling more large-screen TVs onto the stage.

"Do you have any idea how hard this is trending, guys?" Leeds, too, was in a much better mood than the previous day in the con office. "Stay put here, and just come out when I call you. Make sense? Now, if you'll excuse me, I need to finish preparing." Leeds went off back onto the other side of the curtain, leaving me and Austin in the middle of this buzzing about. Once Leeds was out of sight, Austin turned to me.

"Did something bug you about him?"

"You mean other than *everything*?"

"Yeah," he said. "Remember when he seemed really defensive yesterday? Like we'd spooked him off his game? Today, it's like he has us right where he wants us."

Leeds was a slimy guy, but he seemed the same amount of slimy that day as he did the day before. I froze with another thought. *What if Austin could detect the same thing in me?* I thought back to less than an hour before, when The Sheriff had me cornered, the deal he offered me. Not much of a deal when the use of my legs was involved, but still— through very little effort, I could have sold him out and saved me, Saff, and everyone else from his unstoppable machinations. That deal was technically still on the table.

"I have something to tell you," I began, not knowing where I was going to end.

"Wait. Me first," he said. "Having breakfast with your family. They really love you."

Orchestral music suddenly blared out the speakers in the exhibit hall. It sounded very *Lord of the Rings*, very stock fantasy film with dragons and knights and princesses. For the second time in a week, I was heading into a test of my gaming skills—only this time it wasn't in front of a handful of people. Millions were going to be watching me succeed or fail. True, in the back of my mind I knew that all I had to do was beat Austin, a fairly inexperienced gamer, but he'd proven that he wasn't someone to underestimate. I was relieved, though, to know that even if I lost, he'd get the prize. I mean, sure he'd gotten the girl. And his story was compelling enough for an '80s after-school special. But I was at peace with whatever happened. While we waited for our entrance cues, we watched Saff's livestream on our phones. She was totally in her element, going from fan to fan, making girls giggle and guys go ga-ga. And, of course, our usual crew was on board for the ride:

HorizontalJustin: First, bitches.

KackelDackel: Prost!

OraCleXX: this is insaaaaaaaaaaaaaaaane

FaztJak: I see you! I see you!

MaxMouse: ya fucking hipster

HorizontalJustin: whatever. we in with the win!

And one more:

PoltergeistRalph: Godspeed you black emperors!

"Good morning, ladies and gentlemen!" blared Harry Leeds's voice over the loudspeaker. "Today, we have an unbelievable treat. For the first time ever, thirty years after it was created, SunnTech will unveil a game long thought lost, until one of you found it. *Forever Throne III!*" On one of the monitors in the back, we watched as he unveiled a large poster depicting the blue knight from *Forever Throne I* jumping into a pit full of dog-faced warriors. And standing on the side of the pit was the sorceress from *Forever Throne II*. Father and daughter reunited in time?

"And now, we want to introduce our contestants!"

That was our cue. Austin and I walked out onto the stage from the back, the bright lights bearing down on us. There were now two huge monitors on stage, and in front of each was an Achilles Mark II console.

Harry Leeds swooped in and did his whole game-show-host bit: "Please introduce yourselves," he said, placing the mic first in front of Austin.

"Austin Squires."

And then me. I opened my mouth, and it went dry. Any anonymity I'd enjoyed before would be obliterated the moment I said my name. Because people liked saying my name. It was the butt of a joke that had once been *the* joke of online gaming. "I'm, um, LeRoy Jenkins."

The audience erupted with laughter and shouts echoing the *WoW* video. I heard my name called out a dozen times in the same style as I'd heard so many times before: "Leeeeeeeeerooooooooy Jeeeeenkiiiiiins!" And once it was let out, it multiplied like a gremlin dropped into a swimming pool. Cue dry ice. Cue flashing lights and sinister Christmas music.

"Don't listen to them," said Austin.

So I didn't. *Leeroy Jenkins* didn't define me. He was a figment of someone's imagination, a caricature of what a

WoW player was. I was real, and so was this. I wouldn't be defined by someone else's shitty meme. I stood tall and let the chants wash over me.

"Now not all of you are aware of what we're doing here," said Leeds. "So let me tell you. Once upon a time, I was a young man." Up on the screens appeared a grainy photo of Harry Leeds looking a bit leaner and much less gray, but it was clearly the same dude wearing bell bottoms and a shirt with a collar as wide as airplane wings. "Go ahead, laugh. But I thought I was pretty damn cool. Anyway, I worked at *this* place." The screen changed to a picture of the front doors of Achilles headquarters from back in the day, a full-size suit of black painted armor greeting visitors as they came in. "This was Achilles, a kitchen appliances company. Nothing too out of the ordinary. But in the back, as a secret to everyone, we were making magic. We were making video games."

The photos stopped, followed by old video tape footage showing offices and people, a warehouse full of toasters. The camera roved and panned across room after room, wandering around halls and cubbies, showing people from thirty years before. They were phantom images, celluloid ghosts trapped in time.

"What we're doing here," began a voice, "is creating a new kind of video game." The face that appeared was Bryan's, albeit thirty years younger. He didn't look older than sixteen, but he spoke with the same controlled fire that I'd seen a couple days before. "We're not trying to compete with Atari and Coleco and Mattel." The camera panned out, and there was Leeds taking Bryan by the shoulder in a friendly hug.

"Yeah," said the young Leeds. "We're going to beat them. All of them."

The lights let up. "We were a bit naïve," said the older version of Leeds. "But we did believe in what we were doing. As most of you know, 1983 was a hard year for video games. If it wasn't for SunnTech buying us out, we would have disappeared, and with it, our games."

I bristled at how he was framing the situation. Leeds had an active role in tanking the company, of selling it out for a buck. How fucking dare he? I started to step forward, but Austin grabbed my wrist and held me back, mouthing no. I took a breath and relaxed. We—and Bryan—would get our say eventually.

"Luckily, we did manage to finish our masterpiece—a three-game series called *Forever Throne*. Each game was made to be extremely difficult, but that was because each had a glorious prize awaiting the few who could find out its secrets. The Medallion of Time, the Chalice of Malice, and the Sword of Ultimate Truth." A montage of the three items flashed across all screens. "They were thought lost until yesterday, when Austin and LeRoy showed up here and surprised us all. Now, let us surprise them, shall we? You notice up here on stage we have two spots for two players. Except, that's not altogether true."

Stepping past Austin and me were purple-shirts wheeling out a third station on the far left side of the stage.

"So we've brought in a surprise guest to make it more interesting." A spotlight appeared at the very back of the hall, and from the PA, hardcore heavy metal erupted, much like a professional wrestling intro theme.

Emerging into the light was someone I didn't expect to

see, someone I definitely didn't want to see if I was interested in actually winning something: Miski "FilthKiller" Rhee, the most feared member of Team Dominatus, that year's world champion *Starcraft II* team. That made her a top gamer in Korea and literally one of the greatest gamers *on the planet*. She was renowned for her ability to somehow predict her opponents' moves, like she could read their minds. Saff believed that she was actually psychic, a product of late twentieth-century genetic engineering projects. You think you can set up a Zerg ambush behind enemy lines? Too bad that base you're attacking is a clever decoy, and she's already demolished your forces.

Like a grim reaper coming for our souls, FilthKiller marched up the center aisle of the hall and took her place on stage next to us. Of all of us, she was the smallest, but her steely expression told everyone in the room—and everyone watching on the Internet—that this was one gamer not to be fucked with. She'd crunch glass in her teeth and spray it in our eyes if it meant victory. She turned her head and glared at me up and down, then did the same to Austin.

Leeds motioned all three of us to take our seats at a station.

"Why do I feel like we've been set up?" asked Austin.

"Because we have."

We parted ways and took our spots. I sat down and picked up the controller sitting on top of the console. It felt fresh from the package, never been played. The fire buttons were stiff, as if they'd never been pushed before. And the joystick creaked and squeaked when I moved it from side to side. Jesus, they'd had this shit in storage all this time? No time to conjecture. The lights in the room lowered, and the crowd settled into silence.

"Allow me to recap the story," Leeds began. "In *Forever Throne I*, the player was Voltan, famed knight of the realm, who sought to end the tyranny of Isak the Death Enchanter. Voltan succeeded—at a price. He was seduced by the power of Isak's Forever Throne and became a new villain who continued to plague the land. In *Forever Throne II*, the player was Sorscha, Voltan's daughter and a great wizard who returned to Isak's fortress to free her father, only to find out the horrible truth. At the end of that game, the Forever Throne was shattered, sending Sorscha back in time. Now, father and daughter fight together to rid the land of evil for all time."

Game music rang through the hall. None of this recorded orchestra stuff that came along with CD technology. No, this was *bleeps* and *bloops* straight from the silicon chips. A green screen loaded and the platinum sword emblem of *Forever Throne III* slowly faded into view across the top of the screen. The game hadn't even started yet, and already my fingers were sweating.

Then we were off. The screen flickered, and I found myself in control of Sorscha the sorceress. All her powers of pulling and throwing blocks were present, as was the ability to fire stunning bolts of energy. I looked upward, where all three competitors' screens were being displayed. Austin's screen, front and center, revealed that he was controlling a different character—Voltan, the Azure Knight, which was pretty lucky for him. He'd had the most exposure playing *Forever Throne I*, so he'd had some practice with the knight's preferred weapon of war, the spinning ball and chain. Over on the left was FilthKiller's display. I was surprised to yet see a third character: a thin, wispy figure in a ghostly white cowl. With a tap of the fire button, she could shoot a fire arrow that burst into smaller ones on impacting an enemy. That weapon could mow down legions of foes with a single attack.

This was quite the curveball. Each of us had to figure out how to navigate the labyrinth's challenges using our character's strengths. That meant that we had to be quick on the uptake. Too many silly mistakes, and we'd be done for. But what was the exact challenge? Time trial between the three of us? Were we point scrounging or power-up gathering?

The action started fast and furious in some kind of dungeon labyrinth with no direction on what to do or where to go. All we knew was that we had to survive the rampaging baddies swarming us from all sides. Austin's character was pretty well equipped for this carnage, but my character was too slow, her powers too limited, in such close quarters. If an enemy managed to score a blow on me, a pretty hefty chunk of my life bar drained away. *Forever Throne II* was built for a slower pace, a more careful style of gameplay.

No time to feel sorry for myself. Rock-hurling beast men were pressing their relentless attack, and all I could do was dodge, let loose a couple of stun bolts, and race past. That only served to make them angry as they gave chase. Each time I encountered another enemy, I did the same stun-and-run gameplan, resulting in an ever increasing mob on my heels. Eventually, I traversed this seemingly endless corridor until I came to a brick wall. Crap! I was trapped!

Then I remembered Sorscha's other power—that she could pull these special bricks toward her and shoot them like big stone cannonballs. I started disassembling the wall and pelting my foes with the blocks. When I'd brained my last beast man, I sunk into my chair and glanced over to see where my competition was. Austin seemed to be doing pretty well. His time with Voltan had paid off handsomely. Throwing off spear-chucking goblins was no sweat with his weapon. I admit it—I was a little jealous of it. The range attacks with my character were handy, but in the wrong environment, I was toast. His dude could at least stand his ground and take some punishment.

Meanwhile, FilthKiller seemed to take to the controls like no big fucking sweat. I mean, she was used to keyboard, mouse, checking multiple screens and mini-maps. Here, she could give her full attention at raining fiery death upon her enemies. And she did. She was putting on a clinic on how to skillfully pull aggro to group the enemies and then decimate them with a perfectly aimed explosive shot.

I was still bothered by the fact that we hadn't been told what our ultimate objective was. Twenty minutes in, and all three of us had advanced a few levels, gotten treasures and points. But what was this all driving at? As I wondered about this question, I thought back to the tournament at Bryan's place. At least there, I had one directive—make it to the last level. Here? Bupkus. Except maybe not. *Forever Throne III* was Bryan's game too. There had to be some kind of riddle here we had to solve if any of us was going to win. *Think, LeRoy, think!* What did he say about the game? We tried to get any info about the third tournament out of him, but he sidestepped those blunt attempts. What about stuff about the console? Well, he'd harped on it being pretty advanced for its time, which this game definitely showed off. Transistors . . . pixels . . . and online multiplayer. Inspired by old modem games, Bryan had pushed Achilles to implement some kind of multi-console communication, just like the arrangement the original *Dandy Dungeon* had at MIT. He said that that before SunnTech scrapped everything, they'd managed to daisy-chain consoles together to create one massive game world. Multiple consoles connected together . . .

Holy shit, we were in the same game.

"Austin!" I called out. "Can you work your way right? I'm coming your way!"

"What are you talking about?"

"I think we're in the same game. At the same time."

"How? We're on different machines."

"Just trust me, okay?"

He nodded and started moving right. The bigger challenge would be dealing with FilthKiller. Even if somehow *Forever Throne III* had PvP enabled, I believed I could trust Austin enough not to bust me in the face before hearing me out. Miski, on the other hand, had no allegiance to me, so she had no reason at all to listen to what I had to say. Still, I had to try.

"Miski!" I called out. No response, but that didn't mean she wasn't listening. "I think we're in the same dungeon. I think we're meant to work together to solve a riddle." That had to be it. That was Bryan's M.O. If she heeded my calls, there was no indication. Fuck it.

I proceeded down another hallway and filled it with energy bolts to stun the baddies thundering toward me. I glanced over to Austin's screen, where he was surrounded by dark armored knights who pressed on with the attack. He pushed them away with his ball and chain, but they were pretty resilient to damage, so they were able to shrug it off and keep coming. Suddenly, a pair of crackling energy bolts sailed in from off screen and hit the knights in the back.

"That's me!" I yelled. "When they turn around and come after me, get them from behind. Their shields can't protect them, then."

"Got it!" he said. Once again, we were a team, only this time, I was pulling aggro, and he was cleaning up the mess. I felt a small measure of relief but still had a fair bit of doubt. I mean, he was still officially my opponent, and on the other side was the best gamer on the planet.

The crowd erupted into applause when they saw Austin's pixelated character on my screen, and vice versa. They'd realized that this was a multiplayer game, that we were all together in the same monster's lair. Austin and I proceeded north (toward the top of the screen) to explore a section of the dungeon that neither of us had seen up to this point. FilthKiller was content to stay by her lonesome, killing baddies and forging ahead on her own.

"What's the plan?" asked Austin.

"Keep moving forward."

In general, that was correct. But there had to be some kind of trick to all this, some additional sleight of hand that Bryan had planted deep into the game all those years ago. The revelation of these consoles creating a rudimentary MMO was a big deal historically, but for the task at hand, it was only a piece of the puzzle. What I didn't get was what we were supposed to do with that knowledge. Austin and I just continued to fight onward, delving deeper into the twisty labyrinth we'd been dropped in, killing bad guys along the way. Eventually, we arrived in a chamber with pixelated torches lining the walls. My instincts immediately made me pause. There wasn't an exit to the room, and in game language that meant a trap. Unfortunately, Austin didn't get the memo, because he kept moving until he reached the center. That's when three doors opened in the walls, and out of each of them came what looked like big cyclopses, their eyes blinking and then shooting red energy rays out in multiple directions.

Without thinking, I turned tail and started back toward the way we came in. Only, before I could make it, the fourth Cyclops reared its ugly head to block my way. Shit! I knew it was a trap! Fortunately, while I was flailing and getting the shit kicked out of me by these death rays, Austin had found out that he could bat the rays away with his ball and chain. If he timed things just right, he could protect himself. But that's all he could do. He was locked in place just trying to make sure he didn't die while I scrambled to get out of the way of the eyebeams.

All of a sudden, that fourth Cyclops exploded into a puff of smoke. Emerging behind him was the ghost wizard—it was FilthKiller! Her speed made it easy for her to dodge the beams and notch a few arrows toward the other cyclopses in the room. Better still, she'd given them yet another target to focus on, opening avenues on the right side of the screen for me to smash one Cyclops with a flurry of energy bolts.

That left one Cyclops, which made it easy for Austin to inch closer and closer, putting up shields when it fired an energy ray. Once he got close enough, he spammed his attack, and together with arrow and magic backup, he finished the last one off. As soon as the last Cyclops died, the screen went black. Then came the words:

Level 2

"We have to work together," I said. "We won't make it to the end if we don't."

"Together," said Miski. "For now."

Level 2 flooded the screens with green and blue. This seemed to be a courtyard or garden setting, and the enemies seemed to fill in that flavor. Carnivorous plants, giant insects, and what looked to be badgers throwing buzzsaws accosted us from all directions. Slowly, we made progress. I held my own fairly well, but Miski, with her speed and timing, was a fucking legend. Austin took to his tank role like a champ, marching into the fray and then using his ball and chain as a wall to give Miski and me cover. Our elite fighting unit pushed toward the right until we reached what looked like a portcullis into the castle proper.

Level 3

On this stage, more armored warriors rushed at us down narrow passageways. The confined space made it harder to maneuver, and we were left to power through the enemies' defenses instead of flanking them. My hands were getting tired from slamming on the fire button so much, but timing and precision were even more important than ever. Austin took point while Miski and I lobbed shots from behind his cover, allowing us to navigate the halls safely. When we were caught from behind, we turned and belted those enemies with max firepower. In this way, we conserved our life bars while making progress toward our nebulous goal.

Finally, we made it to the door at the end of the hall. Upon entering, the screen went black. My nerves, which had been firing constantly this entire time, had gone into hyperdrive. Everything shook. I couldn't tell how Miski was feeling on account of her hoodie, but on Austin's face, I could see the combo of fear and excitement. And to think— he hadn't had any exposure to the video game world before this week save for his distant memories of *Street Fighter II*.

The screen stayed black for another ten seconds. Then music, sinister and low, followed as the screen slowly lit up. On a dias at the head of the room was a golden throne, and upon it sat the form of a pixelated tyrant—Isak the Death Enchanter himself. For two, almost three games, fate had thwarted the forces of good against Isak's machinations. Finally he was within reach.

Above his head appeared the words of his final speech:

I did not believe you would make it this far, but you have. And I am proud. Geldor, my greatest pupil, you have shown your ambition.

Geldor—that must have been Miski's character.

You, sorceress, have shown great skill in magic. And your power, knight, has proven most formidable. The fates have shown me how countless times we fight, and countless times I die, only to come back to this moment. So instead of fighting, I offer you a choice. One of you can sit at my right hand as general of my armies. Prove to me who deserves this honor, and together, we will claim the world as our own!

At that, the whole screen opened up into an arena with cover zones and power-ups spread throughout. Before I could even get my head on straight, Miski charged to take cover, but not before loosing an arrow that hit me straight on and ate up a chunk of my life bar. Holy shit, we were suddenly in PvP mode! Bryan's final twist was as lethal as it was perfect. Austin looked shocked at what was unfolding. I took that chance to bolt him in the face.

"Every man for himself," I said, giving him a beat to realize and get to cover. I did the same. The screens, which for a while showed a unified field of battle, split into three as we claimed parts of the map as our domain. Miski feverishly gathered power-ups to make her bow a lethal cannon of destruction. Meanwhile, I tried to find a well-fortified cubbyhole with one entrance and exit. At some point, I figured that one or both of them would come after me, and when they did, I'd be able to spam my energy bolts until they died. The danger, of course, was that Austin's shields could probably deflect what I could dish out, and Miski's weapon probably outclassed mine. So I went out to gather some power ups when I could, but I mostly stayed close to home.

Austin wasn't used to any of this. He didn't know the concepts of gathering boosts, not getting domed, keeping out of LOS, and achieving a high KDR. He knew all that he'd been able to glean off a few hours of practice, and that was it. Sad to say, but this competition would come down to me versus Miski. My only chance was camping until she lost patience and came after me.

The downside of this strategy was that Miski only gained power as time went on. With every power-up, she gained more life, got faster, shot stronger. If I had any shot at winning, I couldn't wait very long. All of us felt this pressure, and that's what forced us to go out and rove for our once-allies-turned-adversaries. The screens above gave our electronic kumite an extra element. Since we were able to see each other's locations, ambush attempts always had a few seconds of warning. That made us super careful when positioning ourselves to strike.

That didn't stop Miski from taking initiative. Using an extra-far-shot power-up, she was able to take pot shots at me from across the screen. I took cover behind a fortunately placed rock. That, however, didn't prevent her from repositioning to take aim at Austin on the other side of the arena. He spammed his weapon to ward away shot after shot, but she was fast and persistent. That's when I struck, peeking out from my hiding spot and hurling stun bolts at her, forcing her to retreat.

I fled my temporary hiding spot to enact my overall plan to lure the others down to the lower right section of the map, where I'd scouted some great ambush areas that had the benefit of environmental protection. Rock outcroppings would prevent attacks from behind, hopefully buying me enough time to smash one of the others with a few well-placed shots. Alas, Miski was experienced enough not to take the bait. Austin, however, was not. He wandered down to where I'd been hanging around, thinking to take me off guard and hit me up close.

That's when he found himself inopportunely surrounded by rock pillars. Without a quick way to flee, he was unprepared for me to turn around and start nailing him with energy bolts as fast as I could dish them out. He started swinging his weapon to block the flurry, but I knew he wouldn't be able to leave up the shield forever. Keeping a reasonable distance away, I maneuvered around the alcove, keeping the pressure on in an effort to get around his defenses. He rotated in place, blocking my shots. But I had him. Eventually, he'd get tired—especially if he was too busy using his main offense to play defense.

I admit it. I got too cocky, thinking that I had one of my two adversaries finished off. I didn't imagine that there would be a surprise third one making his presence known right behind me. Appearing in a poof of 8-bit smoke was another character, dressed in a red and blue cape and holding a scepter that pulsed deep red with power. Isak himself had entered the fray, shooting a couple of fireballs straight at me. I moved out of the way, twisted around, and unleashed my own projectiles at him, but I was too slow. He vanished as quickly as he had appeared.

This allowed Austin to re-establish position dangerously close to me. If he got too close, he could spam his weapon and drive my health bar down to zero. Laying down suppressing fire to force him to put up shields again, I squeezed past him and out of the alcove. That was close.

I needed a breather, but Austin wasn't about to give up chase. Dude was persistent, but his character was also slow. I managed to get a good lead on him, pausing every so often to turn and pelt him with a few bolts to keep him back. In a vacuum, I would have been fine with getting away to fight another day. But Isak made random appearances to take shots at both of us, making me scramble to safety and making Austin go shields up.

To make matters even worse, while we were tangling with each other, Miski had all the time in the world to eat up enough power-ups to become a one-person wrecking crew. She picked the perfect time—when Austin and I were exhausted from our fight with each other and our skirmishes with Isak—to re-enter the fray. She came, arrows a-blazing, and hit me square on with two suped-up shots. I was down to half health. Austin and I both got the fuck out of there and retreated back out of her territory, taking cover behind the same rock face.

We were right next to each other. Right there. We could resume our fight, and one of us would win. But by the time the dust cleared, Miski would be right there to sweep up the mess. Austin and I both knew this was the case.

"We have one shot at this," I said.

"What do you mean?" He looked confused, and rightly so. This was a tournament. There wasn't supposed to be a *we*. There could be only one winner.

"If we don't team up, she's going to beat us."

He nodded. "What do we do?"

"You lead and make sure to keep up the defense." We inched back toward the left side of the arena, wary of both Miski and of Isak appearing out of nowhere, with Austin in the lead and me coming up from behind him. It felt somehow against the spirit of the game to team up one on two, but with her skills, it only served to even up the odds.

I glanced to the left to sneak a peek at her screen, but it was like she could read my mind. As soon as I took my eyes off my own screen, she made her move, leaving me and Austin scrambling to mount a defense. He put up shields, deflecting a couple of arrows, and I let loose a volley of energy bolts that narrowly missed her. She fired again, this time a three-way shot, and nicked me yet again.

"We have to get closer! We're dead at range!" I yelled at Austin, who responded by pressing forward and putting back up his shields every other second. Shit, that was a recipe for disaster. As soon as Miski got his timing down (which wouldn't take long), she'd be able to get a shot right in his face. To make matters even worse, Isak decided to raise his ugly mug once more in the one place he could wreak the most damage—behind our wall. We were pincered, and all I could do to avoid instant death was dodge projectiles coming from both directions.

We were fucked. Like seriously fucked. Miski pressed her advantage, snapping off a couple of shots while Austin was making his move, taking his health down to emergency levels. Something had to give. The way I saw it, we had a single option—if we rushed Isak, he was apt to vanish again, giving us the numbers advantage again until he popped back up.

"Cover my back," I shouted to Austin and slammed my joystick in the direction of Isak on track for a collision course. My hope was to close the distance faster than he could charge up another volley of his own fireballs. He held out his scepter, and it started charging up with power. I got close enough and started spamming my bolts in his direction. As predicted, he noped out of there.

Advantage back to us. For the moment.

"What now?" said Austin.

I didn't know what the right course of action was. All I knew was that if I didn't do anything, Austin and I were both sunk—if not by Miski, then by the computer-controlled Isak. Dammit! It couldn't come down to this—to one competitor winning because of faster reflexes and keener eye-hand coordination. At this point in the game, Bryan would have one more trick up his sleeve, one more wrinkle to make things interesting. But what was it?

And then I remembered *Forever Throne II*. What did we learn from the story? Isak's power came from the throne, the same seat that he'd left standing idle. Fuck me, that had to be it, and not only that—it was in my grasp. Austin was in between me and Miski, providing the perfect barrier. All I had to do was walk up and take it. Take the whole fucking thing. I'd win.

But that win wouldn't have been mine. This win belonged to Nathan Squires thirty years before, to a young boy whose life didn't turn out like he wanted, and whose son was desperately trying to piece that fractured past together. For me, sure—I could get some pub, add a trophy to my dresser to compete with my future stepsister. Or, I could put right what had gotten all fucked up. *Right the wrongs of the past*, as Bryan put it.

"Austin, I have a plan!" I shouted.

"You better spill it then!"

"When I start firing, you make for the throne."

"The what?"

"Where the wizard was sitting! You have to destroy it!"

"That doesn't make any sense!"

"Just trust me. I'll clear the way! Now go!"

At that, I started spamming stun bolts and tossing blocks

at Miski. She dodged out of the way long enough to give Austin time to break into a straight run for the throne. All I had to do was make sure she didn't score any more hits on him, as he was at the last sliver of his life bar. The problem was, me pouring on the juice made it almost impossible to maneuver out of the way if she got her bearings. My only hope was to keep her off kilter.

LeRoy, you are stupid as hell. She was Miski fucking Rhee, FilthKiller, top 5 gamer in the world. Ain't no YouTube kid gonna show her up. She did a dance with her ghost wizard, ducked behind a pillar, and waited for the perfect split second between bolts to duck out and fire a single explosive shot that hit true. My health bar drained to zero, and the now-familiar animation of an angel replaced my sprite.

I was the first one to die. On that day, I'd taken my rightful position of last place. I did what Benny said I had to do, what George Washington knew I was going to do, what The Sherriff expected me to do.

I lost.

However, in that same handful of seconds, Austin rushed up to the throne, only to be confronted by Isak charging up more fireballs. Austin was ready, though, and spun up his ball and chain in time to knock away Isak's fireballs and crush the wizard all in a single blow. The throne empty once more, Austin maneuvered Voltan right in line with it, and then he hammered the fire button. I grimaced as I watched this happening, because it was all based on a shadow of a hunch. If I was wrong, Austin was wasting his time, and Isak and Miski would seal the deal, making Miski the ultimate winner.

One, two, three swings from the knight's weapon was all

it took to shatter it into a million pixels. Then, a second later, all the screens went black. An image of Voltan standing atop the broken throne appeared on screen, and then with another flash, Isak's shocked face, his flesh purple and desiccated before he vanished from existence. His pupil, the ghost wizard, faded away as well.

Voltan, beaten and bloody, rushed to his daughter's side.

"You saved me," Voltan said, leaning over Sorscha.

She smiled as she closed her eyes.

Austin had won the tournament. And with it, redeemed Voltan. There were still so many questions I had—what would have happened if Miski's or my character had ascended onto the throne? Would we have had our own cut scene endings? Voltan's ending seemed so perfect—would we have won at all? Was the point that we should have stayed a team and stood strong against Isak? No one in the room could have answered those questions.

"Ladies and gentlemen!" announced Harry Leeds. "I give you the *Forever Throne* champion, better late than never—Austin Squires!" The crowd erupted into applause. I allowed myself to bask in it for a second, which was all it took for Saff to barrel her way to the front, leap on stage, and jump into Austin's arms. They locked lips, causing the front row to jeer and cheer.

The perfect storybook ending.

19

IT'S A RATIONAL TRANSACTION— ONE LIFE FOR BILLIONS

After the fervor had died down and the audience had ushered themselves out and onto other goings-on at WrathOfCon, I was backstage, sitting on a stack of boxes filled with promo brochures for the new *Ancient Tablets* game. The new installment was slated to be called *Ancient Tablets: The Jeornean Maelstrom*. If you're familiar any of the lore from the games, you'd know that the Jeornean Maelstrom is an actual location in the *Ancient Tablets* world. Located south of the tip of Valespire in the Sea of Barbs, the Jeornean Maelstrom was a kind of eternally raging storm, making what should have been a fairly easy trip between continents a wager between life and death. Legend had it that the storm was the result of an endless war waged by Horrag, the witch of the sea with her seven ghastly heads, and Lord Zagami, king of the mer-people and master of the famed Sapphire Trident. The tragic twist to the legend was that once they ruled together as king and queen of all the oceans. The game looked kick-ass. I said goodbye to a hundred-plus hours of my life in advance.

Out on the stage, members of the press were interviewing Austin because he was the big winner and Miski because she was such a star. I sat on the sidelines waiting for this whole thing, the *Forever Throne* saga, to come to its end. I knew I should have felt happy. Accomplished, even. We'd done a crazy fucking thing, survived all our bungles, and found ourselves on top.

Strangely, I didn't. All the action of that day had fried and then refried my nerves with extra breading. All I wanted to do was curl up and will the world away for just a few minutes of quiet. Ever since Austin won the prize and the competition ended, there was something not quite right. But I couldn't put my finger on exactly what.

"Hey," I heard from over my shoulder. I turned, and there was Miski—FilthKiller—looking down, her face still half-obscured by her hoodie. It took me a second to realize that Miski Rhee was actually talking to me, maybe even on purpose. "I hate interviews," she said, sitting down next to me. "Such a waste of time."

I didn't know what to say. I mean, I agreed, but it wasn't like anyone was lining up to know what I thought about anything. She was someone special, someone who'd done great things. People waited hours to get her autograph. In Korea, she was one of the main spokespersons for Coke. You know, like Michael Jordan and Selena Gomez and Jay-Z.

"Did you fly in from Korea just for this?"

"I live in San Pedro with my mother half the year. The other half I'm in Seoul with Dad."

"Sounds like a lot of travel."

"Yeah," she said. "But sometimes I just wish I could stay home." Funny. You always want what you don't have, right? "I wanted to ask how you knew about the throne."

"I didn't," I said, hoping I didn't sound too stupid. "It was a guess, a desperate one."

"But the right one. Why didn't you take it for yourself?"

I didn't answer.

She glanced back over to the stage. "You're friends—you and Austin and the pretty girl."

"Yeah."

"I've played with a lot of people. Good ones. They'd stab me in the back to get ahead of me on a leaderboard. That's why they're good players, but not friends."

I stayed quiet, not knowing what to say. If this was her way of making me feel better, maybe it was working. A little. For sure, talking to a prominent gaming icon was honor enough for me. So I went for it. Just like that.

"There's an expo in Chicago next April."

"C2E2?" she said. "I'll be there."

"Wanna hang out? I mean as friends."

"Okay," she said. "You're not very good at being a competitor." We shook on it, and then she got up to leave. Soon enough, reality flooded back in. I just asked FilthKiller Rhee to hang out at a gaming convention. And she said yes. This had to be an alternate dimension, a universe different from the one I'd woken up in that day fate delivered *Forever Throne* into my hands. But which universe were we in? Was it the normal universe where the Berenstain Bears were a family of charming old children's book characters? Or was it a bizarro nightmare dimension where the Berenstein Bears maintained the führer's abattoir in the basement of a Nazi moon fortress?

The curtains whipped around me, catching me completely off guard. I shrieked and fell backward onto my ass.

"Lee?" It was Mom and John coming in from stage left, followed by Anjeli and Dad.

"Hi," I said looking up from the floor.

"I'm sorry you lost," said Dad.

"Lost?" said John, bursting with energy. "It was incredible!"

I sat up. "Mom," I began, not really knowing how to complete the sentence. She didn't need me to. She knelt down and kissed me on my forehead like when I was little. Flooding back were time-swaddled memories of me coming home from school in tears because of kids teasing me. I'd open the door, and there would be Mom sitting at the kitchen table. She'd let me cry in her arms, and that would make it better.

I'd forgotten. Forgetting made it easier.

"Winnaz in the hiz-ouse!" yelled Saff as she came backstage. As soon as she spotted her Mom, she composed herself and restated the obvious: "This has been a pretty kickass day."

The gang was all here—all except one person.

"Where's Austin?" I asked Saff.

"Finishing up with Harry Leeds," she said, a drop of venom in her voice.

I got up and peered back through the curtain onto the stage. The once-bustling event hall had emptied out almost completely. Purple shirts coordinated by Zeke scrambled to make the changes needed for the next event. The press people who had been interviewing Austin were packing up their gear to get a leg up on other goings-on at the con, leaving only him and Leeds to chat quietly with each other. Leeds noticed me looking on and waved me back on stage.

"That was drama!" he exclaimed. "And you! We need to get you back for the premiere."

"Premiere? Of what?"

"The special edition remasters of *Forever Throne*! Enhanced graphics, soundtrack, steelbook—the whole thing." He shook our hands in turn. "I'll be in contact. You can be sure of that. Anyway, I really do have to get to a meeting—"

He was leaving? "What about the prize?" I asked.

"Of course," said Leeds. "You'll get copies of the new editions when they're out."

"No," I continued. "The sword."

"The sword." At those words, his smile faltered and his eyes lost a bit of that twinkle. His illusion factory out of order, Harry Leeds looked more his age, less like a showman and more like a tired old man. I guess you can only fool everyone so long as everything remains a game. But when it comes down to business—when it comes down to life—time drags you kicking and screaming and thrashing toward the end of the universe. "There is no sword."

"But it existed. Bryan said—"

"I don't care what Bryan said. We don't have it. We never did. Both the cup and sword disappeared in the move. At least now we know what happened to the cup. But the sword? It's gone. And if we did have it, I'd never have the permission to hand it over to you."

"Just like the deal that sold out Achilles?" I said. "All those people losing their jobs?"

"Is that what Bryan told you?" At that, Harry Leeds threw off any pretense of being in a good mood. It was clear that this whole affair had caused him an assload of stress and that he was just glad to be out on the other side of it. The last thing he wanted was a bunch of punks grilling him over shit he did thirty years before. "Who do you think I am?" spat Leeds. "I was a stupid kid when I worked for Achilles. Did I have power? No way. Alvin liked me, and that's how I was able to get him to sell to SunnTech. Because you know what? Achilles was dead. There was no chance of anyone there getting anything. The SunnTech deal saved over a hundred jobs, got people severance packages when most other companies would have just sent them packing! Bryan doesn't know what the hell he's saying."

"He said you used to be friends," I said.

"Used to be. That's the important part." He stared at us, at first not knowing what to say. "Sorry to disappoint you, but you have to see that you still made out here. You got your channel in front of millions of people. Do it right, and you can make a lot of money."

"But Achilles—"

"Is dead," he said. "Leave the ghosts of the past to die like they should have."

With one last handshake—a cold, stiff one—he turned and left.

"He told me that they didn't have any information on my

father," said Austin. "Apparently a lot of things got lost when the company moved to California."

Dammit, no! This was not how the story was going to end, with bitter, empty disappointment. That's when it clicked. I knew what the missing piece was, *who* it was.

Austin and I rejoined everyone else backstage. John, in what I'd come to learn was his typical John Stalvern way, invited us all out to a big lunch to celebrate. Normally, free food was like, well, free food to me (as in *yes, please*). But I only had one chance, so I had to take it.

"There's something I need to show Austin and Saff upstairs in our room."

"Okay," said Mom. "We'll meet you in the hotel lobby in fifteen minutes."

Once separated from the 'rents, I made double-time to the elevator. At that point, Saff and Austin had stopped trying to hide their PDA, which served my purpose well. They held hands and whispered inside jokes to each other. Meanwhile, I slid a folded piece of hotel stationery out of my pocket and carefully unfolded it away from view. I tapped out the number printed there into my phone and sent a single text:

(734) 397-0027

Meet me at my room.

The elevator ride to the tenth floor felt like it lasted an eternity. Was anyone else hot? Because I was hot. It was definitely hot in that vertically moving sauna box. Once the doors opened on our floor, we stepped out into the hallway. I looked around, paranoid that somehow Saff and Austin had my horrid plan all figured out. Maybe there was a way I could prep them for what was about to happen. I sped up to beat them around the corner, catching a small amount of relief to see an empty corridor where our rooms were.

"Jupes, are you okay?" said Saff, startling me.

"It's been a crazy day," I said, hoping that was enough.

"That's an understatement," said Austin. "I can't wait to take these shoes off and relax."

"Me too." Ugh. Lies. All lies. And the lying liar was me.

I turned to look behind us one more time. Still no one there. So I unlocked the door and pushed it open.

That's when Saff screamed.

Waiting for us inside our room was The Sheriff reclining on the bed. Spread out around him were bags of snacks he'd plundered from the mini-bar. Cheeses, meats, all manner of fancy mixed nuts, all opened and irreversibly charged to the room.

By instinct, Austin took Saff's hand and tried to bolt back out into the hallway. But I stood my ground and blocked their escape. That's when it hit them—the realization that I'd somehow known The Sheriff was there, that this was happening according to plan, hastily assembled as it was.

"Jupes, what's going on?" said Saff, but I was too heartbroken to answer.

"Business," The Sheriff called out. "Come in. Oh, and I'm not asking."

"We gave the game back to SunnTech," said Austin.

"I don't care about that shitty game," The Sheriff said. "The goods I want are right here."

Austin looked back. "What are you talking about?"

Moment of truth. "The Sheriff cornered me this morning," I explained. "He wants you, not the game."

"I'll call the cops," Saff threatened.

"Sure. And you'll tell them all about how you stole federal property, and not just the little blonde girl they took in. How your Scottish friend is currently an undocumented immigrant in this country. How you trespassed into the convention without tickets. I'm sure they'd be interested in all that."

Stone fucking cold. All three of us walked through the doorway, with me heading up the rear like a jail guard. Austin shuffled in with shoulders slumped. Saff tightened her hand around his and glared back at me with a look that could melt adamantium. The Sheriff stood and met Austin eye to eye. Then he took Austin's arm and yanked it hard to break Saff's grip.

"I'm in a bit of a hurry, so we should get going."

"Wait!" I said. "We're coming too."

The Sheriff mulled this demand over, scratching his thick, unkempt beard. "I see no problem with that. But you're paying for the cab."

All of us crammed into a taxi and zoomed across the city. The Sheriff, jammed into the front seat, gave directions to the terrified cabbie. And by *gave* I mean barked instructions brandishing a fist made of mangled finger joints and scarred-over knuckles. Saff, Austin, and I sat in the back all mushed together. But I might as well have been strapped to the hood for the amount of angry vibes I was getting off them. I wanted so bad to lay out why I'd done it, why I'd partnered up with The Sheriff, of all people.

We ended up blowing right through Clancy's neighborhood in the Tenderloin and then emerging back out into an even more ritzy part of town that featured tall condo buildings lining Lombard Street, a stretch of road known as the most crooked street in the world. This was a literal thing (Chicago probably had the most metaphorically crooked streets in the world, thanks to Al Capone). Green tresses hugged the sides of Lombard Street as it exaggeratedly zigged and zagged down a steep hill. I marveled at it, and at the cars that dared take on its merciless slopes.

"Stop here," The Sheriff ordered. The cabbie pulled over to the corner of the street at the bottom of the hill. The Sheriff turned to the back seat, stared us down, and then said, "Get out."

I paid the cabbie and got out with Saff and Austin. We followed The Sheriff upward to a blue-colored building. Goddamn was the hill steep.

He knocked on the front door and waited.

"I can't believe you did this, Jupes," whispered Saff.

"I'll explain everything. I promise." Well, I hoped that I could, anyway. I didn't want to tell her that I'd delivered us into the hands of The Sheriff on little more than a hunch. See, after Harry Leeds told us that SunnTech didn't have the sword, the last puzzle piece seemed to fall into place. This whole time, I'd been pondering what The Sheriff's true role in all of this was. I'd first come to believe that he was some kind of retrogame mercenary out for blood and money (mostly money, but incidental bloodshed didn't seem to bother him much). After talking with Bryan, I came to think that he'd been employed by SunnTech to retrieve their "property." But that didn't quite make sense, either. Why would they need Austin's copy of the game, and moreover, why did they care? They had *Ancient Tablets*. They had all the other game franchises that were making a butt-ton more money than long-forgotten *Forever Throne*.

When Harry Leeds said that he didn't have the sword, when he acted so surprised that someone other than him even remembered *Forever Throne* existed, that cemented one fact for me—whoever sent The Sheriff after Austin didn't do it for money (hiring The Sheriff undoubtedly wasn't cheap) and didn't do it to reclaim property (because it officially was SunnTech property). The Sheriff was sent for a personal reason, and there was one person left in this whole story that we still hadn't heard from.

Opening the door was a woman in her forties, Mexican or Dominican with dark skin and dark hair. All it took was one look at The Sheriff for her to turn and let us through. No words were exchanged, no pleasantries. We followed The Sherriff up the winding wooden staircase up to the second floor, where the house opened up into a living room area with the comfiest wraparound couch one could conceive. This place was decked out with antique lamps, vases, and ornamental pieces from countries like Japan, China, and India.

"Is the man in?" The Sheriff asked the woman.

"He is with señora."

"Go call him."

"Sí," she said, and disappeared out one of the doorways into the rest of the house. I motioned to sit down on said comfy couch, but The Sheriff stuck his arm in the way.

"Don't get too situated. We won't be here long."

I wasn't about to argue with him.

After a minute, shuffling footsteps could be heard on the hardwood, and coming into view was a thin older man with a scraggly moustache and thinning white hair. There were bags under his eyes like he'd just gotten up from a several-years-long nap. Wrapping his robe tight around him and tying the belt, he stepped forward, the expression on his face ranging first from confused to concerned to, strangely, relieved.

"Alvin Meadows," I said. The Sheriff swung his head quickly at me. I couldn't help but smile that I'd managed to pull one over on him. Albeit a really small thing.

"Job's complete," said The Sheriff, stepping forward.

"Yes, the money." He pointed to a small leather pouch next to the fireplace.

The Sheriff strode over and swiped it up with a single movement of his orangutan arm. He peered into the inside.

"I'd appreciate it if you took your leave now."

The Sheriff motioned toward us. "What about them?"

"They're my guests. I'll take care of them."

The Sheriff lifted the bag. "It's all there?"

"I trust you'll come back if it isn't."

"You know me pretty good, old man." The Sheriff wrapped the strap of the leather pouch around his hand, turned, and started toward the stairs back down. Stopping in front of me, he opened the pouch again, took out a short stack of bills, and tossed them at me. "Count five."

I did as I was told. I counted five crisp *thousand* dollar bills, slid them out of the sleeve, and gave the rest back.

"Like I promised. See ya, LeRoy." We all watched as this mysterious beast of a man who had crash-landed into our lives once again disappeared. To this day, every time I tell this story, The Sheriff is the one part where people stop me and say, "You're shitting me about that guy, right?" All I can say in response is, "I wish I was, man."

"Now then," said our host. "Are any of you hungry?"

Saff, Austin, and I looked at each other. I could only speak for myself—which I did. "What do you have?"

Mr. Meadows smiled, laugh creases spreading out from the corners of his eyes.

"Come with me."

We followed him through his house, which was quaint compared to a place like Bryan's. Still, it was located in like the richest part of San Francisco, and it was loaded with enough antiques to hold a personal roadshow. We followed our host down to the kitchen, where he sat us down at the table. He opened the freezer and took out a big plastic bag.

"Pizza bagels?" he said.

Even Saff was savvy enough not to pip at Mr. Meadows's hospitality. He pulled four frozen pizza bagels out of that bag and laid them down in a metal pan before shoving them into a toaster oven that creaked like a rusted robot after the apocalypse.

"My father's pride and joy," said Mr. Meadows. "You know, when we sold Achilles, it was RCA that bought us.

SunnTech wasn't even a division yet, let alone its own company. It was a single desk next to the copy machine, if I remember correctly. And the games we were making? They weren't worth a damn thing."

"But Bryan told us you sold the company and retired," I said. "They had to be worth something."

He smiled and tapped the toaster. Taking a closer look at the thing, I noticed the Achilles logo—the black knight. It was tarnished and scratched up, sure. But there it was. And right above it was a name etched on the cloudy glass door.

"Achilles Mark I," I said out loud.

"Sir . . ." Austin began.

"Please call me Alvin."

"Alvin, you sent The Sheriff after us?"

"The Sheriff?"

"Big guy who smells like motor oil and despair," said Saff.

"Oh, Mr. Little."

"Mr. Little?!"

He smiled again. "We don't have much choice about the names we're born with."

"He said that his job was to bring me here," said Austin.

Alvin nodded. "Truthfully, it was to bring your father."

"Did you know him?"

"In a way," said Alvin. "We exchanged letters for years. Sometimes only one a year. Sometimes several. He was a bright boy, but a troubled man."

Austin seemed to deflate at the mention of his father writing letters to Alvin. And why not? Of all the people in the world he would want to communicate with, he'd pick someone he may have met once when he was a kid rather than his family—his own son? Gingerly, I put my hand on his shoulder, expecting him to shrug it off. But he didn't. He just let it sit there.

"What kind of troubles?" asked Austin.

"Have you ever met someone who knew what kind of person they would turn out to be? Someone who seemed to have figured it out, or someone who seemed to have a perfect spot for them carved out by the universe?"

I glanced over to Saff. She was certainly one of those people. At least, she seemed to be. I think that's part of what made her so alluring. In a chaotic world full of batshit crazy, having someone so sure of where she was and who she was felt like a life preserver in the middle of a hurricane. All you knew was that you had to hold on for dear life.

"Your father was not one of those. And neither was I. He never felt 'right,' no matter what he tried to do. That's how he put it. He wanted to be somebody, like how he felt that day when he won the tournament. It was like he was trying to capture that feeling again, but never succeeded. He'd told me about getting jobs and losing them. Meeting people and then losing them. You know, he didn't have a family. He grew up in an orphanage."

"I don't know anything about him."

"And I didn't know anything about you. He never said anything about you or your mother."

Austin sat there for a time, looking at the same spot on the flower-patterned tablecloth. Even when the bell on the toaster oven rang and Alvin served us perfectly toasted pizza bagels, Austin didn't move. Saff placed her fingers on his hands, but he didn't respond.

"Do you still have the letters that Nathan sent?" I asked.

"Yes," said Alvin. "You can take them with you."

"He really never said anything?" said Austin.

"Now, my memory isn't what it used to be, but I don't believe so." Alvin got up from the table and ventured back into the living room. After making some sounds like he was rummaging through drawers, he came back holding a yellowing cardboard recipe box in his hands. "Here they are. I only started looking for him when he hadn't sent me something in more than a year."

Austin flipped open the top cover of the box, and inside was envelope after envelope, each with a folded slip of paper inside. Letters upon letters with postmarks dating as far back as the mid-1990s and as recently as the previous year.

"I can see this is hard—"

"I don't understand," said Austin, wiping his face with the back of his hand. "Why you?"

"I don't know," said Alvin. "Truthfully, I don't know how he found me. After leaving Deadwood, I tried my best to fall off the planet. I traveled constantly, and I would probably still be doing that had I not met my wife." He quickly changed topics. "I wish I could have reached your father before he died and helped him more. I wish he was honest with me about you."

"So what now?" I asked. "Now that Austin is here, is there some way you can help him?"

"I'd like to show you something." Alvin hopped up to his feet and bade us to follow him deeper still into his home. He led us through a pair of French doors into an office. His desk was messy with papers—writings and drawings—but the most interesting thing in the room stood in the far corner. It was a suit of armor, painted black—the Achilles logo come to life. "They let me take whatever I wanted from the building on that last day. So I made sure to take my favorite thing. I used to call it Spanky. Spanky the knight."

Spanky was definitely old and had rust spots in places, but it was still hella cool to see. The thing looked just like the logo, from the red feather plume on its helmet to the shield it held in its right hand. And on its left—hold on. Something was off. There was one significant difference between the Achilles logo and the full suit of armor in front of me. The logo's armor was fully black and unadorned. This in-the-steel suit, on the other hand, had a leather belt and scabbard strapped onto its waist. And in the scabbard . . .

"Holy fuck," I muttered. Saff gasped when she understood what I was looking at. Austin stepped forward, placed his hands on the leather-wrapped pommel sticking out of the scabbard, and pulled.

With that unmistakable *shing!* sound, he had unsheathed the pure silver blade of the sword, the rubies, sapphires, and emeralds inset into the hilt. It was as beautiful as it was valuable—a treasure priceless and without peer—the Sword of Ultimate Truth.

"Yesterday I got a call from someone I didn't expect to hear from—Harold Leeds. He told me that a bunch of kids had shown up mysteriously asking about *Forever Throne* and wanted to know if I had a hand in it. I wish I did."

"Alvin?" spoke a faint voice from behind us. Standing and holding the door was a woman in blue pajamas and a blue knit cap on her head. Extending from her nose was a transparent tube connected to an air tank she dragged behind her. "Rosita said you had guests."

"Yes, dear." To us: "This is my wife, Sarah."

We made our introductions. When I shook her hand, it

was like shaking a bundle of drinking straws that had been scrunched and unscrunched several times. The bones in her fingers felt as fragile as glass. If I squeezed too hard, they'd shatter and pierce my palms.

"Please," said Alvin, taking Sarah's arm. "Make yourself at home. I want to accompany Sarah back to her room." He and Sarah exited up another staircase, leaving me, Saff, and Austin alone together. Again.

"You knew!" Saff squealed, shoving my shoulder. "All this time! You're so in trouble."

"I wasn't sure! Hey!" But she wouldn't stop playfighting. In seconds, we were both laughing out of relief and a sense of triumph. That's when we turned to Austin, still holding the sword. He was staring at it like it was a radioactive rod, the ark of the covenant, and the Holy Grail all wrapped into one thing. In many ways, it was. It had symbolized so much on this journey. And yet, when looking at it for what it was—a hunk of metal and sparkly stones—it couldn't live up to what we'd built it up to be.

"It's yours, you know," said Alvin, who reappeared at the foot of the stairs. "From what I've been told, you earned it."

"I didn't," said Austin. "LeRoy did. He should take it."

"Well, someone has to. I don't plan on packing it up when Sarah and I move."

"Move from here?" said Saff. "It's none of my business, but this place is pretty nice."

"The weather's better for Sarah in New Mexico. We're relocating there in a couple of months. I want to make her as comfortable as possible."

"Is it bad?" asked Austin.

Alvin's eyes fell. "It feels like you spend your life chasing things. Dreams, money, love. And all the while, you don't realize that death is chasing you—not until it's too late. Even when you find all those things you're after, death never stops."

"I'm sorry."

"So am I. I've made a lot of mistakes in my life out of fear, out of inaction. It was my hope that finding Nathan would help me tip the scales back, convince whatever power is out there to throw one more dash of good luck my way. For Sarah. So I was saddened to hear of Nathan's passing, but when I heard about you, I had to meet you. Tell me, what are your plans from here?"

"To be honest, I don't have any idea," said Austin.

"Would you think about staying, then?" said Alvin. "We could use help packing, and afterward, I need someone to take care of this place."

"Me? But you don't even know me."

"We could get to know each other."

Austin looked at me and Saff to gauge what we were thinking. Saff put it best: "Say yes, you dummy!"

So he did.

20

THE CIRCLE IS NOW COMPLETE

I smell like overcooked hot dogs, thanks to the moist heat. Maybe this is a sign of the coming apocalypse. Global warming for sure, a long-term campaign to overload our planet's core by the Reptilians of Gamma Draconis. If Saff were here right now, that's what she would say.

I wonder how long Saff's roommate will last before she files a formal complaint. My money's on a week. Maybe a week and a half if the roommate is particularly strong. Not that I have any right to talk. Although I know my own soon-to-be roommate, I'm not sure how shit's gonna be. Maybe it'll be weird. Maybe we'll find out that we actually don't like each other for real.

We'll see.

This slushy is supposed to last me the entire time I'm here, but I hadn't factored in waiting. One can only look at water shooting out from a hole in the ground so many times before it looks like all the other times water shoots from holes in the ground. Old Faithful. You know, if you just did shit that was less expected of you once in a while, folks just might leave you alone.

I'd never thought I'd be at Yellowstone National Park again, given the shit we'd gotten into last time I was here. I almost thought they would have had my face on a poster at the entrance of the park—"Have you seen this boy?" stated in Robert Patrick's T-1000 voice. But no. I was able to drive in no problem, park in front of Old Faithful with no problem, and use my debit card at the snack bar no probs, with the cashier even making a snarky remark upon seeing my name on there.

"LeRoy Jenkins," he said. "That's your real name?"

"Yup." Grr.

"You play *World of Warcraft*?"

"Never heard of it."

He handed me my blue-raspberry slushy with a wide smile on his face. Ah, the first few sips of crushed-ice goodness are always the best. But now that I've been waiting here for twenty minutes, it's basically over-sweetened Kool-Aid. I sit on the scalding-hot bench, burning my legs and pretending that I'm awed by Old Faithful for the sixth time.

She's late. I send a quick text, but I don't get an answer. So I wait and I pop into a game ROM I loaded onto my phone—*Double Dragon 3*. You might be wondering what kind of new frontier of masochism I'd broken into, how deep my fetish for self-punishment had gotten. It's not about that (or all about that). It's more about getting so good at this hard-as-balls game (several levels, unfair bosses, and ONE FUCKING LIFE) that when I do my speedrun, I won't shit the bed.

Except *Double Dragon 3* is, as I said, hard-as-balls— mostly because of that *one life* thing. I've managed to get as far as the Japan level with my sanity intact. Only the end-level boss, Ranzou, is really pushing me toward the edge of madness. I swear to god, if I was sitting in front of my computer with a real controller, I'd have this cut-rate *Ninja Gaiden* wannabe figured out. The piss-poor controls on my phone aren't at all adequate to enact the pixel-perfect precision required by this hellbeast of a game.

Out of the corner of my eye, I see someone sit next to me—uncomfortably close. Glancing over, I see that it's a slender woman in a sleek black dress with a pink running stripe down the side of her body and a lacy bra poking out of the dress's low-cut chest. Long, curly auburn hair tumbles down her shoulders.

"*Buongiorno,*" she says, hiding her eyes behind a pair of sunglasses with smoky lenses. "*Ti scoperò fino a farti esplodere di piacere.*"

"No understando?"

She lowers her parasol to the ground, folds it up, and then hits me between the eyes with it.

"How are you ever going to get laid, Double-J?"

"Ryland?"

"Don't say my name so loud! I'm undercover." Yeah, undercover as a smoking-hot could-be Kardashian. The long hair, the tight dress, the ruby red lipstick. Her super-secret spy cred is god-tier right now. "I feel like a fucking clown in this getup. Skirts are of the devil. I mean, I shaved my legs." She grabs my hand and puts it on her thigh. Butter smooth.

"I would have had an easier time trailblazing the Amazon with a spoon."

"You're pulling it off," I tell her.

"Thanks to Saff's tutorial. *Trashy Chic-a-Go-Go.*"

"I know the one. Six hundred thousand views."

"I tell you what—this is the last time I wear a thong."

"Could have left that out."

"Right. TMI." She smiles. "It's good to see you."

"You, too." I'd spoken to Ryland a couple of times in the past year over Skype—it's almost a year to the day that I saw her carted off by cops. Fortunately, her lawyer Dad was able to pull a few strings and get her a community service sentence. Other than that, we hadn't really had a chance to process anything that's happened since San Francisco. A lot of shit has changed—not only for me, but for everyone involved in our scheme. From the look of it, the same goes for her. "I missed you."

"Sure you did, now that you're all famous and shit."

"Hardly. Internet famous isn't real fame."

"Famous enough."

On one hand, it's not like I'm an A-list movie star or a supreme athlete or supermodel. On the other hand, our channel has become a full-time job—one that pays me way more than what some seventeen-year-old could normally make in his room, excluding occupations involving illegal substances (although some of the shit I'd eaten for the stream should have been illegal).

"Where is your partner in crime, anyway?"

"About to start college at NYU. She's going into law."

"Seriously? Her boobs are already in contempt of court. What about you?"

What about me? Man, when I told Mom and Dad my plan after graduation, both of them had the same reaction—*absolutely not*. Mom, especially, had a fit. *No way are you skipping school*, she said. I had to explain that I wasn't skipping. I was just planning to wait until I really knew what I wanted to pursue. In the meantime, the channel was kind of booming, and with Saff easing off somewhat with school starting, it became up to me to either put it to rest for good or keep it going. I had been leaning toward hanging it up when I got a call from an old friend—Austin, wondering what I was up to. I told him what I was thinking, and he wouldn't have any of it. If Saff couldn't be the co-host, then he'd be, and he sweetened the pot by offering to convert part of his place into a studio space.

It was an easy decision to put off applications, buy a car (this one *not* a junker van off a dude who huffed paint in his spare time), and make the journey back out west to San Francisco.

"I'm meeting Austin at his place."

"I still can't believe that dude just gave him a house." But that's exactly what happened. When Alvin moved down South, he handed the keys to Austin with no strings attached, no timetable, no nothing. For all intents and purposes, Austin had just been given the most prime-time real estate in the country.

"I can believe anything at this point."

She stares off into space. Then: "On second thought, you're right. The world's a fucked-up place—in good and bad ways. It's been kind of a crazy summer for me."

"Oh really?"

"Yeah," she says. "I met someone."

"What's his name?"

"You're lucky I like you, you fucking asshole. *Her* name is Madeleine, and she's from France."

"Sounds like you're in love."

"Don't jinx it, Double-J. What about you?"

"Nah."

She shakes her head, smiling. "You lying sack of shit. You got with someone, didn't you?"

"I did not!"

"That's what liars say! I can tell."

How in the world does she always know? I mean, she's right. Over the past Christmas break, I accepted an invitation to come to Korea to visit Miski. How could I say no to a front-row seat at the World *Starcraft II* Championships? True to her word, in between stomping fools who thought they'd beat her RTS skill, she showed me around Seoul, we sang karaoke, and maybe we kissed a little. Maybe we kissed a lot.

"It didn't last," I say. "Long distance is hard."

"I know. France, remember?"

"Thanks for coming all this way to meet me."

"Definitely. You are coming down to visit UT at some point, right? Go fucking Longhorns?"

"Austin and I will both come."

"Good. Because otherwise people won't believe that I know you."

"It's not like I'm special or anything."

"Or anything. I'm done with you making excuses."

Okay, fine. I lean back on my arms and watch Old Faithful blow its top like it had done approximately an hour before. I'd read that it had done so more than a million times since they'd started keeping records of it. That's a fuck-ton of times that it could have messed up, could have totally fallen on its face in front of everyone, but didn't. It's funny—we're obsessed with being neat and tidy, narrow and focused, but here we all are, careening on this mudball through a universe with no promises of anything save shitting and dying. It's a harsh place out here, and all we have to shield us from the vast, meaningless void are other people frantically grasping for the same sense of significance.

Heavy shit.

"I have something for you," she says, holding up a plastic bag. I peer inside and pull out a strangely deformed aluminum can. There's no English written on it. Instead, there's a logo of a red wolf, and underneath a long, scary word made scarier by the presence of an umlaut.

"Surströmming," I sound out loud. "What is it?"

"Something for *Culinary Distress Theater*."

"I thought we were friends."

"We are," she says. "And do you know what friends do?"

"What?"

"Friends help friends draw dicks on all the Etch A Sketches in Grant General Store."

I laugh. "Time's up. Let's do this."

THE END

BACKGROUND AND ACKNOWLEDGEMENTS

This book sure has had a circuitous path to completion, one that spans more than a decade of writing, rewriting, giving up hope, gaining some hope, losing it again, borrowing hope from others, more writing, an exhaustive amount of rewriting, editing, and finally closing the deal. *Lords of Badassery* originated as a project started on the heels of my graduation from the New School's MFA program in fiction writing in 2006. I'd been fortunate to be part of David Levithan's amazing class on children's fiction—a course that opened this writer's eyes to the fun and wonder of young adult novels. As a writer, originally, of experimental short fiction, I found YA freeing in both subject matter and language, a strange departure from the formal rigors of my favorite authors, like Georges Perec and Italo Calvino.

At the behest of my classmates and of David himself, I tried my hand at YA. Of course, as a young person living hand to mouth in New York City, survival came first. I worked odd jobs trying to make ends meet—most notably as a bookseller for a company called Mobile Libris. If you frequented NYC author readings in the early- to mid-aughts, you may have noticed luggage-toting salespeople at the back of the bar or bookstore or coffee shop, timely selling copies of the author's book. That was me.

Of course, the only time I could write was on my commute to and from work. So I wrote my book in shaky longhand on every single subway line and through every borough in New York City. Then titled *Guessing and Keeping Still*, the book was about a film-obsessed kid who gets a mysterious entreaty in the mail from a long-lost friend to help bust him out of a psych ward. Mid-writing, I moved back home to Chicago to take up an offer for a more stable corporate job. Even though I suddenly had money, that type of desk job was never what I really wanted to do. So I kept writing. Ultimately, in late 2007, I finished the draft and, after a few people read it over and gave me feedback, I determined that I just didn't have the writing chops to pull off what I'd wanted to. The manuscript sat on my computer and was ported to various hard drives until 2011, when I saw the Angry Video Game Nerd's video on Atari's *Swordquest* games. I became enthralled by this real-life treasure quest and started to retool my story to fit the video game world. I decided to invent a fictional company to stand in for Atari in order to more adequately and respectfully tell the tale, since many of the programmers, artists, admins, and decision makers involved with *Swordquest* are still around and able to tell their own real-life stories (which I hope will happen soon). Unfortunately for me, just a month after James Rolfe's video, Ernest Cline's

Ready Player One came out, taking the same base *Swordquest* kernel and spinning it into a mega-bestseller.

Yay me. Nevertheless, I continued working on the new version of the novel, since mine and Cline's only shared a core motif. Mine was destined to be a contemporary YA novel, whereas his was a fantastical, pop culture–infused sci-fi romp. Since 2011, I'd been working on retooling this novel, having written its sequel in the interim between 2009 and 2011. I hope that this work has proven entertaining and informative in the same way the last decade of my life has been for me. At the beginning of this book's creation, I was an eager MFA graduate living in the most amazing, most infuriating city in the entire world. And now, as I pen this final section, I'm nearing forty (what used to be called "over the hill"), I'm married, and barely two weeks ago (as of this writing), I celebrated the birth of my daughter. The world, in some ways, is a much darker and more confusing place than it was when I was in my early twenties (in post-9/11 NYC, which is saying a lot). That's why I think stories can and should illuminate the way—or at least *a* way—to approach the world for each individual reader. I hope that this can be that light for someone out there.

My thanks will start with my fellow writers at the New School, especially Scott Larner, Meredith Franco Meyers, Sara Ross, Amanda Miller, Connor Coyne, Marco Rafalà, and Camellia Phillips, who have helped me maintain that writing dream. All of us have grown in so many ways since we were kids running around the city, and I couldn't be prouder of everything they've done and become. I also want to thank the members of David Levithan's class, especially Amalia Ellison, Lukas Klauss, Veronica Wong, and Morgan

Matson. Morgan, in particular, is always near to my heart as I write. Many, many long walks through picturesque Manhattan, many, many pretzel croissants at City Bakery, our shared love of France and cupcakes. I've loved following her successful career as a writer and hope to share some time with her again.

I also want to thank the weird ersatz family that I assembled at the now-defunct Chelsea Bally's in New York City, especially Ed Harris and Vlad Kowal. It's odd how strange bedfellows find each other, and in this case it was a young punk writer from the Midwest finding solace and companionship from a gym full of old, rugged New Yorkers and fabulously buff gay men.

James Rolfe's video was undoubtedly an inspiration for this iteration of the novel. However, there are many web content producers whose research proved key to presenting the unique and colorful history of the video game industry. First and foremost is *The Golden Age Arcade Historian* blog run by Keith Smith (allincolorforaquarter.blogspot.com). I don't believe there is a better source of information on the beginnings of the video game age available on the Internet. In the same vein, Tristan Donovan's book *Replay: The History of Video Games* is as comprehensive a guide to video games and their associated personalities as you will find. As well, the work of YouTube content producers such as John Lester (Gamester81); Shane Luis (Rerez); Norm Caruso (The Gaming Historian); Wood Hawker (BeatEmUps); AlphaOmegaSin; The Game Chasers (what's wrong with these guys?); Jason Pullara (LordKat); Joe Vargas (Angry Joe); Pat Contri (Pat the NES Punk); 8-Bit Eric; Matt Barton (MattChat); Metal Jesus; Lydia from Squid Gaming; Game

Sack; Guru Larry; PushingUpRoses; Noah Antwiler (The Spoony One); Kim Justice; and Johnny Millennium (Happy Console Gamer) were great inspirations for the online exploits of LeRoy and Saffron. Finally, I'd love to use this space to pay tribute to our Internet forefathers, those late 1990s-early 2000s bastions of geeky fandom that now exist as digital ruins for our descendants to mine for embarrassing nuggets of, well, embarrassment. Sites like Lance and Eskimo, Internet Explorer Is Evil, and Hamsterdance proved that people are funnier and weirder than we care to admit. And some of these are still around, so why not pay a visit to Jabootu's Bad Movie Dimension?

I'd like to give thanks to the staff of the American Library Association's Booklist Online, especially Brianna Shemroske, Ada Wolin, Daniel Kraus, Julia Smith, and Sarah Hunter, who, for some bizarre reason, allow me to be on their roster of book reviewers.

I would be remiss if I did not credit the valiant efforts of Keith Burrows, who eagerly became my first reader, and whose insights were spot on and true. I also could not have brought the book to fruition without the otherworldly editorial insights of Erin Liles. Her compassionate and thorough eye guided me through developmental edits and allowed the story to blossom. And to top it all off are the mega-proofreading chops of Jason Mortensen to polish the manuscript off to a mirror shine.

Wes Alexander, my travel companion through life and its craziness, provided a steadying voice through the late iterations of the novel, helping me construct a backbone and plotline out of the chaos in my head. Our long talks about character motivation and interplay were exactly what

I needed to reflect on as the novel sharpened into focus.

I could not have completed this book without the support of my wife, Kristin. I can't count how many times she's talked me off the ledge of writing frustration, of work frustration, and of life frustration. She's been someone strong I can lean on, and I hope that I've been that for her.

And finally, I need to give thanks to my daughter, Morrigan Lee. As I'm writing this, you're two weeks out of the womb. Barely. And in that time, I've begun to more fully understand—as I believe this book shows I've sort of understood—the trials and responsibilities of being a parent. That encompasses not only those mundane things like food, shelter, love, and care; it also includes being true to one's self and not using the duties of parenthood as an excuse to extinguish your own dreams. Like LeRoy's father did in this book, my own father penned an email to me in which he relayed those things he couldn't say to my face— how he'd wished that he'd been able to adventure when he was young and even when he was a young father, how he'd buried his own ambitions in exchange for the obligations of fatherhood. His regrets. I remember feeling such guilt over this, such loss. It's not something that I feel is right for a child to bear, whether consciously or in secret. I want, when you finally are able to tell me your dreams for yourself, to have more than an empty platitude to offer back. The last pushes of effort on this book were done up to the eve of your birth, and now that you're here, I hope that someday you read this and understand who I was before you were around, my hopes and dreams and ambitions. At the very end, this book was written for you.

About the Author

Reinhardt Suarez is a Chicago-born, Minneapolis-based writer, editor, and raconteur. He has an MFA in fiction writing from The New School in New York City. Among other things, he enjoys a good slice of deep dish (Lou Malnati's is manna from on high), a night of quality karaoke, and eking out thoroughly undeserved victories at Friday night *Magic: The Gathering* events. He lives with his wife, Kristin, their daughter, Morrigan, and their feline overlord, Karl.